Praise for the novels of J.T. Ellison

"Outstanding... Ellison is at the top of her game."
—*Publishers Weekly* (starred review) on *Tear Me Apart*

"A compelling story with a moving message."
—*Booklist* on *Tear Me Apart*

"Well-paced and creative... An inventive thriller with a horrifying reveal and a happy ending."
—*Kirkus Reviews* on *Tear Me Apart*

"Exceptional... Ellison's best work to date."
—*Publishers Weekly* (starred review) on *Lie to Me*

"Comparisons to *Gone Girl* due to the initial story structure are expected, but Ellison has crafted a much better story that will still echo long after the final page is turned."
—*Associated Press* on *Lie to Me*

"Immensely readable...lush."
—*Booklist* on *Lie to Me*

"Fans of Paula Hawkins, A.S.A. Harrison, Mary Kubica, and Karin Slaughter will want to add this to their reading list."
—*Library Journal* on *Lie to Me*

"The domestic noir subgenre focuses on the truly horrible things people sometimes do to those they love, and J.T. Ellison's latest, *Lie to Me*, is one of the best...an absolute must-read."
—*Mystery Scene Magazine*

"Wonderful... A one-more-chapter, don't-eat-dinner, stay-up-late sensation."
—Lee Child, #1 *New York Times* bestselling author, on *Lie to Me*

Also by *New York Times* bestselling author J.T. Ellison

Look for J.T. Ellison's next novel
available soon from MIRA Books.

Recycling programs
for this product may
not exist in your area.

ISBN-13: 978-0-7783-3077-6
ISBN-13: 978-0-7783-0918-5 (Library Hardcover Edition)

Good Girls Lie

J.T. ELLISON

GOOD

GIRLS

LIE

mira

For all the girls out there seeking to better themselves through education, I salute you!

Vita Abundantior.

And, as always, for Randy.

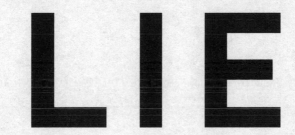

GOOD

GIRLS

LIE

"And now I'm going to tell you about a scorpion. This scorpion wanted to cross a river, so he asked the frog to carry him. 'No,' said the frog, 'no thank you. If I let you on my back, you may sting me and the sting of the scorpion is death.' 'Now, where,' asked the scorpion, 'is the logic in that? For scorpions always try to be logical. If I sting you, you will die. I will drown.' So the frog was convinced and allowed the scorpion on his back. But just in the middle of the river, he felt a terrible pain and realized that, after all, the scorpion had stung him. 'Logic!' cried the dying frog as he started under, bearing the scorpion down with him. 'There is no logic in this!' 'I know,' said the scorpion, 'but I can't help it—it's my character.'"

—**Orson Welles**, *Mr. Arkadin*

1

THE HANGING

The girl's body dangles from the tall iron gates guarding the school's entrance. A closer examination shows the ends of a red silk tie peeking out like a cardinal on a winter branch, forcing her neck into a brutal angle. She wears her graduation robe and multicolored stole as if knowing she'll never see the achievement. It rained overnight and the thin robe clings to her body, dew sparkling on the edges. The last tendrils of dawn's fog laze about her legs, which are five feet from the ground.

There is no breeze, no birds singing or squirrels industriously gathering for the long winter ahead, no cars passing along the street, only the cool, misty morning air and the gentle metallic creaking of the gates under the weight of the dead girl. She is suspended in midair, her back to the street, her face hidden behind a curtain of dirty, wet hair, dark from the rains.

Because of the damage to her face, it will take them some time to officially identify her. In the beginning, it isn't even clear she attends the school, despite wearing The Goode School robes.

But she does.

The fingerprints will prove it.

Of course, there are a few people who know exactly who is hanging from the school's gates. Know who, and know why.

But they will never tell.

As word spreads of the apparent suicide, The Goode School's all-female student body begin to gather, paying silent, terrified homage to their fallen compatriot. The gates are closed and locked—as they always are overnight—buttressed on either side by an ivy-covered, ten-foot-high, redbrick wall, but it tapers off into a knee-wall near the back entrance to the school parking lot, and so is escapable by foot. The girls of Goode silently filter out from the dorms, around the end of Old West Hall and Old East Hall to Front Street—the main street of Marchburg, the small Virginia town housing the elite prep school—and take up their positions in front of the gate in a wedge of crying, scared, worried young women who glance over shoulders looking for the one who is missing from their ranks. To reassure themselves this isn't their friend, their sister, their roommate.

Another girl joins them, but no one notices she comes from the opposite direction, from town. She was not behind the red-brick wall.

Whispers rise from the small crowd, nothing loud enough to be overheard but forming a single question.

Who is it? Who?

A solitary siren pierces the morning air, the sound bleeding upward from the bottom of the hill, a rising crescendo. Some-one has called the sheriff.

Goode perches like a gargoyle above the city's small down-town, huddles behind its ivy-covered brick wall. The campus is flanked by two blocks of restaurants, bars, and necessary shops. The school's buildings are tied together with trolleys—enclosed glass-and-wood bridges that make it easy for the girls to move from building to building in climate-controlled comfort. It is quiet, dignified, isolated. As are the girls who attend the school; serious, studious. Good. Goode girls are always good. They go on to great things.

The headmistress, or dean, as she prefers to call herself, Ford Julianne Westhaven, great-granddaughter several times removed from the founder of The Goode School, arrives in a flurry, her driver, Rumi, braking the family Bentley with a screech one hundred feet away from the gates. The crowd in the street blocks the car and, for a moment, the sight of the dangling girl. No one stops to think about why the dean might be off campus this early in the morning. Not yet, anyway.

Dean Westhaven rushes out of the back of the dove-gray car and runs to the crowd, her face white, lips pressed firmly together, eyes roving. It is a look all the girls at Goode recognize and shrink from.

The dean's irritability is legendary, outweighed only by her kindness. It is said she alone approves every application to the school, that she chooses the Goode girls by hand for their intelligence, their character. Her say is final. Absolute. But for all her goodness, her compassion, her kindness, Dean Westhaven has a temper.

She begins to gather the girls into groups, small knots of natural blondes and brunettes and redheads, no fantastical dye allowed. Some shiver in oversize school sweatshirts and running shorts, some are still in their pajamas. The dean is looking for the chick missing from her flock. She casts occasional glances over her shoulder at the grim scene behind her. She, too, is unsure of the identity of the body, or so it seems. Perhaps she simply doesn't want to acknowledge the truth.

The siren grows to an earsplitting shriek and dies midrange, a soprano newly castrated. The deputies from the sheriff's office have arrived, the sheriff hot on their heels. Within moments, they cordon off the gates, move the students back, away, away. One approaches the body, cataloging; another begins taking discreet photographs, a macabre paparazzi.

They speak to Dean Westhaven, who quietly, breathlessly, admits she hasn't approached the body and has no idea who it might be.

She is lying, though. She knows. Of course, she knows. It was inevitable.

The sheriff, six sturdy feet of muscle and sinew, approaches the gate and takes a few shots with his iPhone. He reaches for the foot of the dead girl and slowly, slowly turns her around.

The eerie morning silence is broken by the words, soft and gasping, murmurs moving sinuously through the crowd of girls, their feet shuffling in the morning chill, the fog's tendrils disappearing from around the posts.

They say her name, an unbroken chain of accusation and misery.

Ash.

Ash.

Ash.

2

THE LIES

There are truths, and there are lies, and then there is everything that really happened, which is where you and I will meet. My truth is your lie, and my lie is your truth, and there is a vast expanse between them.

Take, for example, Ash Carlisle.

Six feet tall, glowing skin, a sheaf of blond hair in a ponytail. She wears black jeans with rips in the knees and a loose green-and-white plaid button-down with white Adidas Stan Smiths; casual, efficient travel clothes. A waiter delivers a fresh cup of tea to her nest in the British Airways first-class lounge, and when she smiles her thanks, he nearly drops his tray—so pure and happy is that smile. The smile of an innocent.

Or not so innocent? You'll have to decide that for yourself. Soon.

She's perfected that smile, by the way. Practiced it. Stood in the dingy bathroom of the flat on Broad Street and watched herself in the mirror, lips pulling back from her teeth over and over and over and over again until it becomes natural, until her eyes sparkle and deep dimples appear in her cheeks. It is a full-toothed smile, her teeth straight and blindingly white, and when combined with the china-blue eyes and naturally streaked blond hair, it is devastating.

Isn't this what a sociopath does? Work on their camouflage? What better disguise is there than an open, thankful, gracious smile? It's an exceptionally dangerous tool, in the right hands.

And how does a young sociopath end up flying first class, you might ask? You'll be assuming her family comes from money, naturally, but let me assure you, this isn't the case. Not at all. Not really. Not anymore.

No, the dean of the school sent the ticket.

Why?

Because Ash Carlisle leads a charmed life, and somehow managed to hoodwink the dean into not only paying her way but paying for her studies this first term, as well. A full scholarship, based on her exemplary intellect, prodigy piano playing, and sudden, extraordinary need. Such a shame she lost her parents so unexpectedly.

Yes, Ash is smart. Smart and beautiful and talented, and capable of murder. Don't think for a moment she's not. Don't let her fool you.

Sipping the tea, she types and thinks, stops to chew on a nail, then reads it again. The essay she is obsessing over gained her access to the prestigious, elite school she is shipping off to. The challenges ahead—transferring to a new school, especially one as impossible to get into as The Goode School—frighten her, excite her, make her more determined than ever to get away from Oxford, from her past.

A new life. A new beginning. A new chapter for Ash.

But can you ever escape your past?

Ash sets down the tea, and I can tell she is worrying again

about fitting in. Marchburg, Virginia—population five hundred on a normal summer day, which expands to seven hundred once the students arrive for term—is a long way from Oxford, England. She worries about fitting in with the daughters of the DC elite—daughters of senators and congressmen and ambassadors and reporters and the just plain filthy rich. She can rely on her looks—she knows how pretty she is, isn't vain about it, exactly, but knows she's more than acceptable on the looks scale—and on her intelligence, her exceptional smarts. Some would say cunning, but I think this is a disservice to her. She's both book-smart and street-smart, the rarest of combinations. Despite her concerns, if she sticks to the story, she will fit in with no issues.

The only strike against her, of course, is me, but no one knows about me.

No one can ever know about me.

AUGUST

Marchburg, Virginia

3

THE SCHOOL

"It's hard to imagine a prettier place, isn't it?"

The driver, who has been trying to engage me in conversation for fifty miles now, isn't wrong. The farther west we drive into Virginia, the more beautiful the scenery becomes. Wineries, horse farms, stone walls, and charming cottages dot the landscape. The ridge of mountains ahead looks like an ancient dragon curled up and went to sleep and the trees grew over its skeleton. I can see each bump of its spine, the ribs curving gently in the air, moss growing over the sharp tips, and the roots of the trees sprouting from its heart inside.

It is a far cry from the noise and dirt of the DC airport, and even further from the world I've left behind. *Good riddance.*

"Mmm-hmm. Pretty."

The car turns south, moving along the Blue Ridge, down I-81, and the scenery is breathtaking. I glance at the map stowed in my purse, a detailed topographical imaging of the area surrounding Goode, which is situated near Wintergreen. Another hour to go, at least.

"Where'd you say you were from?"

I drag my attention back to the driver. He's decent looking, dark hair and skin tanned from a summer outdoors, hazel eyes. He'd said his name when he opened the door for me, Rudy or Ruly, something like that—I didn't pay attention, why should I? He's just the driver, a stranger I'm sharing a fleeting moment with. I'll never see him again after today. Don't get into the car with strangers, we're taught. Don't talk to strangers online. Stranger danger. Now, it's as much a part of life as breathing.

And who's to say I'm not the stranger to be worried about?

"I didn't. England."

"Thought so, from your accent. Ever met the Queen?"

Hardly. We don't exactly run in the same circles.

But I'm embarking on a new life. Perhaps it's time for a bit of embellishment.

"We go to the same church in the countryside. Have you ever heard of Sandringham? There's a beautiful little stone church there, with a graveyard that dates back to the 1300s. They— the Queen and her husband, I mean—spend much of their time in the country, especially now they've been handing over duties to the younger members of the royal family. We saw them only last week."

"I know exactly where you're talking about. That's the place they filmed part of *Game of Thrones*, didn't they?"

"The very one."

The best lies are based in fact. The stone church at Sandringham exists. It's called St. Mary Magdalene, and it's a bit more than a stone cottage, but I have no idea what it's really like. I've never been there. I've never met the Queen. I have exactly zero idea where *Game of Thrones* was filmed, but I assume it wasn't on the royal estate.

The driver has no knowledge of what I'm talking about but

doesn't want to seem stupid, so he is more than happy to pretend. He grins at me in the rearview, and I smile in turn. We're connected now, over this lie. We both know it. Accept it. These are the social niceties of a modern civilization.

I resume my outdoor viewing, pretending I didn't enjoy the tiny frisson of excitement I got from the dopamine rush of telling a lie.

Why did I do it? I swore to myself I wasn't going to lie anymore. All part of turning over a new leaf, as my mum would say.

And I have no business lying to this stranger, one who knows where I'll be for the next few years.

But it is so easy. And what will it harm? He's practically a child himself.

I've never understood my compulsive desire to lie. I've read so many articles I've become my own sociology experiment. Everyone lies. To themselves, to each other. It's a way to belong, to be included. To look important.

In the past, it was much, much easier to get away with these transactional lies. Purveyors of falsehoods were con men, flimflam artists. Now, everyone is a grifter. With the advent of social media, allowing the masses to peer in through the open windows and doors to your home, to your mind, your body, your soul, the only way to lie properly is to curate your life for the masses to behold, carefully, carefully. Stage. Filter. Design. My very existence is so much better than yours. Hurrah!

I have no accessible online accounts. I don't tweet or book or gram or snap or tok. I've never been interested in living out loud, and now, it's working in my favor. It's much, much too dangerous for me to have a past. I'm forward-looking, *marching* ahead. My life, my new life, waits for me on top of the mountain, in a town appropriately called Marchburg. The Goode School doesn't allow the students to have mobile phones. There's a solid chance I can get away without the accounts for the next few years. There's luck, already going my way.

In the modern age, with the ubiquitous connections available, not allowing personal mobile phones on campus is believed to be an archaic approach to education. I've seen the reviews, the message boards; the students hate it, hate leaving behind their screens. Even some of the mothers and fathers think this is a ridiculous rule, too, often sneaking one into the luggage for a midnight texting session with their little darlings.

We top another rise and finally, I can see the city of March-burg ahead. It looks like an Italian hill town, accessible only through winding switchbacks, a fortress behind a redbrick wall.

Lies have kept me safe, kept me protected, my whole life. But here, in this new place, in this new world, I don't need them anymore. I will be safe on the mountain. Protected.

"Starting over is always hard," Mum told me, "but you can do it. Go far, far away from here, daughter mine. Reinvent yourself."

This is exactly what I intend to do.

4

THE ARRIVAL

The drive up the hill makes me slightly queasy, all the switch-backs, the steep drop-offs, but soon enough we are on even ground again. The little town of Marchburg, its streets form-ing an X, surrounds the school which sits in the middle, at the crossroads. I ignore the stores and restaurants and their quaint, New World names, focusing on the behemoth ahead. A castle, for that is what it looks like, an overly large country house, like those of my homeland, spreading across the glossy green acreage like a stone gargoyle, but with red brick instead of gray stone.

The original building was damaged by fire in 1890, and the phoenix rebuilt in the traditional Jacobean style using the fa-mous Virginia bricks known as Chilhowie, the name stamped across the face. "Chilhowies have been found as far away as Paris, France," says the literature. A bell tower rises above the entrance, perfectly centered on the main building, which is five stories high. Similar Jacobean-style buildings wing each side of the main hall—their signs denote they're creatively named Old East and Old West—but these were added later, and aren't the same exact color as their mother. They are three stories each, with white wooden balconies that jut out from their top floors.

Taken in one shot, the school is monstrous in its austere beauty.

The massive black wrought iron gates to the school stand open in greeting for orientation day. Term starts tomorrow, Wednesday, so Monday and Tuesday are set aside for students to get settled in the dorms, buy their books, sign up for activities and sports teams, hand over their phones, and otherwise run amok on campus, reuniting with their friends and making new.

What must be freshmen stand in bewildered clumps under the oak trees bordering the wall. Parents stumble around with furniture and boxes in hand. It is a bright, sunny late-summer day, the sky so blue it is hard to look away.

When the town car slides to the curb in front of the huge redbrick building with Main Hall carved into the gray stone lintel above the door, all heads turn. Hiding in the back, I feel unaccountably shy, embarrassed to be the center of attention, even for a moment. But the driver pops out of the town car and comes round to the door, flinging it open as if I am the Queen herself. He practically bows.

"Here you are, miss. Your very own Sandringham, tucked into the Virginia mountains," Ruly, or Rudy, or whatever his name is, says, and I shiver. He knows more than he lets on. The school does look quite a bit like Sandringham. How very eerie. I must be more careful going forward.

With him standing there, holding the door, the smile turning quizzical, I have no choice but to get out, unfolding my long body from the back seat. I have a cramp in my thigh, but I smile winningly.

"Thank you for the ride."

When the students realize I'm just another one of them, they go back to their conversations. Ignored, I feel better. I'd truly like to stay anonymous, do my work, study hard, get into Harvard, and leave my wretched old life behind. Strangely, I've never felt so alone as I do at this moment, watching the joyful faces of my soon-to-be classmates as they run and shout and hug tearful parents goodbye.

My watch twitches with a reminder—I have a meeting with the dean of the school in fifteen minutes.

Ruly Rudy, who has wrestled my massive suitcase out of the car, is standing nearby with a hopeful grin on his face.

I hand him five precious dollars, heart in my throat at the thought of letting go any of my hoard. But it is expected. "Thank you again for the ride."

I shoulder my backpack and drag my suitcase up the stairs, entering Main Hall.

It is cool and dark inside, a welcome respite to the late-summer heat. Oddly empty, too, and quiet to the point of austerity. White columns, marble floors. There is a great sense of space, two massive staircases curving into the second-story balcony like a theater. On either side, unmanned tables are set up with engraved metal signs: A–E, F–K, L–P, Q–Z.

Why am I the only one here? Have I already done something wrong?

A middle-aged woman with gray hair in a chic bob, black glasses, and bright red lipstick that makes her look like an aging Parisian model, steps out of the office and hurries over, beckoning, and I make my way to the first table.

"Here's a new face! Welcome to Goode. I'm Dr. Asolo, English department. You've missed the masses, lucky girl—most have already registered. We were getting ready to break things down, just waiting on the stragglers." She looks over my shoulder. "Where are your parents?"

The lie comes easily, smoothly, without thought. "They dropped me."

Dr. Asolo's lips purse in disapproval but she puts a hand on the metal sign, tapping it with her thick gold wedding band. "We usually like to meet the new students' parents, but if they're already gone…"

"They are. So sorry."

"You didn't know," she says absently, waiting. Her hands are captivating, capable, nails short and buffed, with clear polish—another Goode regulation. No hair dyes. No colored polish. Au naturel. The ladies of Goode will not be fake.

Dr. Asolo clears her throat. "Name, dear?"

"Erm, Ash. Ash Carlisle. With a *C*."

"I am a professor of English, dear. Your accent isn't so heavy that I need subtitles." She chortles at her joke, and I smile, a blinding, perfect smile that nearly makes my cheeks crack. I've almost forgotten. Charming Ash.

"Very good. Carlisle, Carlisle…" Dr. Asolo roots through the box on the table, then pulls out a packet like she's retrieved Excalibur from the stone, triumphant. "Here we are! You're in Main, Room 214. Freshmen and sophomores are on level two, juniors on level three, and seniors on four, in the attics. You're class of 2023, so you're an Odd—staircase on the right only. If you take the wrong staircase, you won't graduate. And you're not allowed on the seniors' floor without an express invitation. Don't let them catch you trying to sneak in, either."

This is said with such alacrity I feel a stab of panic. "You mean, like, it's a rule? You watch everyone to make sure?"

"Oh, no, dear. It's *tradition*. You'll find we have a few here. Now, your roommate is already upstairs getting settled. I'm sure she's very anxious to meet you. You're from England, isn't that right? Well, Camille is from DC but she lived in England when she was younger, so you'll have lots in common."

A knot of girls enters the hall, creating a commotion. At their center is a tall, willowy blonde, ethereally pretty, with shrewd green eyes. The girls stop in front of the tables. I know I'm staring; I can't look away. Epochs of instinct tell me this is an important moment, an important person I need to impress. I'm nervous to be singled out so soon, so quickly, though. My

God, I haven't been here ten minutes and I'm already drawing attention. I smile. Wide. Molars showing.

The blond goddess stares back, a perfectly groomed eyebrow cocked. Her voice is sharp and low, demanding. "Class?"

"Um, '23. Sophomore." As if they can't do the math.

"Hmm. Be sure you take the *left* staircase, wouldn't want you not graduating, now would we?"

I glance over my shoulder at Dr. Asolo. Hadn't she said Odd classes were to take the right staircase? But the professor is busying herself with another student folder and doesn't look up.

The girl turns back to her crowd and says, sotto voce, "Did you know if your roommate dies, you get the room all to yourself for the rest of the year? I wonder how long this one will last."

The girls surrounding her titter, and a chill spreads down my spine, making me stand straighter. We are the same height, eye to eye, and there is something smoldering in the other girl's depths. Fire and hate and more, something wrong. I am the first to look away.

Dr. Asolo, who is paying attention after all, takes exception. Her pleasant tone is gone now. "That is quite enough from you, Miss Curtis. You are excused."

With another coy smile, the girl floats away, her hair drifting down her back in a perfect, shining blond curtain. The circle of girls around her giggle loudly as they follow. My eyes stay on the older girl until she is out of sight, through the doors.

Jesus. What was all that about? It's like she knew. It's like she looked right through my Cheshire smile and into my heart and twisted the tiny knife she found there, like a key in a lock.

This is a very bad idea.

I fight the urge to run, plant my feet, flexing my quadriceps so I am grounded, stable.

Dr. Asolo retakes her seat. "That was Becca Curtis. Senator Curtis's daughter. Becca's a senior and loves to spook the incoming girls. She's only playing with you. Ignore her."

"It wasn't very funny. Is she always so mean?"

"No, actually. She's quite a lovely girl. One of our best students. A true leader. Just a wee bit sadistic when it comes to newbies. You'll see. You're in sister classes, after all, and many of the school events are done with your sister class. Odds and Evens."

"I see."

"Kitchen rules are straightforward and posted on the door. The Rat—that's the little café over there, through the staircase in the back of the building—is open until 10:00 p.m. If for some reason you miss a meal, you can always grab a latte and a banana or a sandwich. I highly recommend the tuna melt. Library hours are in your packet, along with your class schedule and everything else you might need, including your keycard for the buildings and student ID. Don't lose them—there's a five-hundred-dollar fee to replace them. Can you manage that bag by yourself or do you need some help?"

"I can manage." I slide the packet into my backpack and redirect my suitcase, immediately wishing I'd agreed to help. The bag is so heavy, but it's all I have.

"Excellent. Welcome to Goode. You're going to love it here." Dr. Asolo starts away but I stop her.

"I'm sorry, Dr. Asolo, I'm supposed to meet with the dean. Can you point me toward her office?"

"Oh!" Dr. Asolo peers at me curiously. "The dean doesn't usually meet with students on their first day. And opening convocation is in an hour. Her office is just there, through the doors, down the hall." She points toward the right side of the building. "You can leave your bag with me if you like."

"Thank you. I'll bring it with me."

"Suit yourself. It's been a joy, Ash Carlisle." She smiles briskly and disappears back into the office, shutting the door behind her.

I take a huge, shuddery breath, blow it out, hard.

I've got this.

5

THE DEAN

Dr. Ford Julianne Westhaven watches from the attics as her girls arrive for term. She loves it up here. When she attended the school, she was desperate for a glimpse into the seniors' hall, for an invite to the forbidden level. As the ultimate legacy, she thought it was her right. But traditions are traditions, and the only time she'd been allowed, up until her own senior year, was blindfolded, being dragged up the wrong set of stairs during a secret society tap.

The room is cozy. The windows overlook the Blue Ridge Mountains on one side and down the mountain to the green valley on the other. If she could set up her permanent office here, she would. Instead, she uses it for escapes during the day when she doesn't have the time to flee to her cottage on the grounds.

She knows she has to go down and greet the classes, is excited, in her way, but turning herself from a months-long private life to a public one always takes a toll. She is at heart an introvert, has to force herself to smile and laugh and participate in her own world. Being continually thrust in front of the microphone as the mentor to two hundred impressionable young women is alternately terror-inducing and exhausting. She is expected to speak at every opening convocation, every graduation, and several times in between. She is their lodestone, their shining light, their leader.

Ford aspires to be a novelist, not headmistress to a band of brilliant young girls. Oh, she knew she would take over the school eventually, but hadn't planned to be doing this in her thirties. She assumed she'd step in once her mother was too infirm to handle the school, that she'd have a full, laudable writing career first.

But her mother screwed up everything, so instead, here Ford is, hiding in the attics, dreading the start of term as she has the past nine autumns. She can hear Jude's voice echoing through the chambers of her mind.

It is expected of you, Ford. It is your role in life to be the dean of this school, as I and your grandmother and hers were before you.

Ford doesn't like doing what is expected of her. And yet, she does it anyway.

A Westhaven has held the top position since the school opened, in the early 1800s, as an Episcopal-run home for wayward girls. Girls who needed to disappear. Girls who'd disgraced themselves and their families. Girls who would have otherwise ended up in bawdy houses, as prostitutes, or worse. Decidedly not Goode girls.

Ford's namesake was a nun who served the school when it opened in 1805. Sister Julianne was a radical who thought all women should be educated. She felt the poor, lost girls of Virginia who found their way to Marchburg needed to serve a purpose and started teaching them to read and write. Quietly, stealthily, she turned the ones who were capable of change into ladies. Some even managed to return to Virginia society, though most moved west and started over under new names. The illegitimate children were adopted out or put into service at the plantations in the area.

The school's mission changed in the late—nineteenth century, when Sister Julianne, then Mother Julianne, ancient and bent, stubborn still, was given a gift. One hundred thousand dollars from the father of her own illegitimate daughter, bestowed to them upon his death. With this absolute fortune, she bought the school outright, a legacy for her child.

All girls who entered the gates were good, in her mind, no matter the sin they'd committed. She, too, was capable of sin. She changed the name of the school to reflect this opinion and created a new mandate—the school would take in needy girls and turn them into governesses and schoolteachers. Her descendants would run it, using the Westhaven name. The name of her illicit lover.

Soon enough, The Goode School, as it was known, became a destination for young women who wanted to break free of societal norms. Goode gave the girls who landed there a chance at an extraordinary life, a contradiction to anything they'd been taught or thought before.

When Mother Julianne died, her wishes were followed to the letter. Her daughter—a woman with Julianne's own gray eyes and her father's name—took over the school.

And so it went, generation to generation, a matriarchal line who took it upon themselves to educate the daughters of the land. To teach them how to be self-sufficient women, teachers and influencers in their own right. Seven generations committed to carrying on the school, its mandate as an all-female powerhouse, and the Westhaven name, of course. It is their brand as much as the school's.

Each class has fifty girls, hand selected by Ford herself. Fifty brilliant, impressionable girls, all there to be molded into Ford's own image, all of whom go on to college. A full 90 percent go traditional Ivy. The remaining grads either attend specialized programs—Rhode Island, Julliard, Oxford, MIT—or the approved Southern schools that are understood to be their own Ivy system.

It is a laudable record. Goode accepts only the best, guarantees a serious return on investment. And in turn, expects blood, sweat, and tears. And future endowments. Elitism costs.

Ford successfully shot down an attempt last year to admit a male student. She led the fiery charge and won, though the board wasn't as adamant. More students meant more revenue.

But Ford made them understand the power of an all-female education, how admitting boys would affect the tenor of the day-to-day, would alter the very mission of the school. If girls can focus on their studies exclusively, she argued, without the distraction of having boys in the classroom, their grades are better, their confidence soars, and they are more effective in and out of school. Their eventual insertion into the real working world with this focus means higher paying jobs, more influential roles. Goode creates strong female leaders. Full stop.

They listened.

And unlike her mother, Ford has been blessed with a tenure free of heartbreak, free of scandal. Oh, there have been a few little things here and there, mostly girls caught with cell phones or cigarettes, marijuana in their vape pens. Beer. Shoplifting. Little transgressions, things that in the grand scheme of things don't matter. Non–life altering. Nothing like what Jude dealt with, thank God.

Goode is a success under Ford's stewardship.

She runs through her upcoming speech in her mind. She's given variations on the theme every year to kick off the term, been the recipient of several as a student herself under her grandmother's reign. Her words are echoes of her past, spoken in the voice of her ancestors.

The girls will beam, reveling in being the chosen ones. They will do anything to please her, as Ford and her classmates would have done anything to please their masters.

She notices the black town car pulling into the drive. Another congressional or ambassadorial child—those parents always too busy to see their darlings to the doors of Goode sent them in style. She is drawn, for some reason, to the shadowy figure inside.

From the car emerges a tall, thin blonde. It takes Ford a moment to place her, then she realizes she is seeing Ash Carr—no, it's Carlisle, she reminds herself, they're keeping her identity private, for now—in the flesh for the first time.

Poor dove. The trauma of the girl's past few months almost derailed the application process, and the subsequent lack of funds was a serious issue, but something about her spoke to Ford, especially in their interview. The girl has a certain spark, is appealing on many levels. Ford allowed her acceptance to stand and, with the blessing of the board, granted one of the school's rare private scholarships to bring her from England to Virginia.

Goode scholarships are based on need but can't be applied for. It's the school's way of carrying on the tradition from which it was born. A small nod to the past.

Ash is sworn to secrecy; so long as she keeps her mouth shut, no one will have to know. She will be treated as just another Goode girl, accepted because of privilege, brains, and whatever inestimable quality Ford has seen in the application and interviews.

Ford waits another moment, surveying the acreage, the students, the gentle slope of lawn and trees, the possibilities ahead for another year at Goode, then turns to go. She has a meeting with Carlisle in a few minutes. She has rehearsed what she will say, as she does with every interaction. So long as Ford has time to prepare, she is perfect.

Always.

6

THE MEETING

I knock on the thick, tall wooden door and am rewarded with a trilling "Come in!"

I step through into a lovely large space. Bookcases line three walls, floor-to-ceiling built-ins with crown molding, stocked so full it makes me itch to stand in front of them, run my fingers along their spines, ignore the dean entirely.

Along the fourth wall, flanked by tall casement windows, is a creamy red marble fireplace, wood stacked in the grate as if ready for the match despite the warm day. Two gray tweed sofas face one another in the center of the room, perched atop a thick wool Oriental rug in shades of green and cream. The big wooden desk looks like a French antique; the right side of the top is taken up by an old-fashioned typewriter, a crisp white page rolled onto its platen, the carriage slide half-mast as if the writer stepped away midreturn. I can see the faint image of words through the sheet.

Above the desk is a framed map of 1900s Virginia. A flag of the United States, stars out, housed in a triangular black frame, sits alone on a shelf in a place of honor.

The entire room is elegant, feminine, old-school, and inviting.

Dean Westhaven, too, is elegant, feminine, old-school, and inviting. Her dark hair is swept into a classic chignon; she is draped in a nubby Chanel suit, discreet black pumps with a two-inch heel on her slender, high-arched feet. She is not beautiful, her gray eyes with their large pupils too widely set and her nose a shade too thin to balance the sharp cheekbones, but she is striking, a presence. And watchful. So watchful. Like a gray-eyed hawk, measuring and peering.

Those disconcerting eyes hold unfathomable secrets and take my measure, and this unerring attention is intimidating. I am not used to being looked at so closely; I much prefer to hide in the shadows. Choosing to come to Goode means I won't be able to do so, this I know. I am going to be seen. As one of only two hundred in such a small space, with my height, my hair, my face, there is no way to hide. Not completely.

Despite this scrutiny, there is something about the dean that makes me want to know more about her, and this puts up my guard.

Careful. Don't go getting attached.

The dean gestures toward the two chairs in front of her desk. "Sit, sit. You must be exhausted after your journey."

I take a high-backed wing chair, one leg bent beneath me on the soft seat until I remember my manners and put both feet on the floor, and watch the woman who is to direct my life for the next three years bustle around her homey office.

Dean Westhaven finally taps a stack of paper together, sets them on the desk, and smiles tremulously. "I can't abide a mess. I was so sorry to hear of your father's death, Ash. And your mother..." The sigh is audible, loud and sad. The words sound practiced, as if the dean has said them a hundred times.

How many students' parents have died?

Creepy.

"It was all very sudden," I reply, wooden, eyes cast down. I have learned this is an appropriate response.

"Yes. Yes, of course, it was. Forgive me, I hadn't meant to bring it up, but I saw the inquest has been resolved… Would you care for tea?" The dean plunks a cup and saucer down in front of me, pours out from a lovely floral teapot. "Take some sugar. It will help with the jet lag."

I dutifully reach for the sugar and drop two brown cubes into my teacup. I use the small silver spoon to stir, three times clockwise, then set it on the edge of the saucer. The tea is surprisingly good, hot and fragrant, and I close my eyes as I swallow. When I finish this display, the dean is looking at me curiously.

"It's quite good. Oolong?"

"Yes. Not surprising that you have a palate for tea." The dean smiles amiably, and I respond in kind, not the heartbreaking grin, but a small one, lips together, teeth obscured. It makes my dimples stand out.

"I was very pleased when you decided to join us for term after all. I know you weren't excited about leaving so soon after…"

"It's for the best. Thank you for having me still. I needed to get away."

The dean is looking at me closer now. "You've lost weight since we spoke last. Granted, I've only seen you through Skype—it's hard to get the full measure of a girl through a screen."

"Yes, ma'am."

The dean sips her tea, I follow her lead. Long silences are her thing, apparently.

"It's understandable, considering. With some tender loving care, you'll be back to yourself in no time. The loss of a parent—Were you close to your father, Ash?"

"He worked a great deal."

"Ah." The dean says this as if she's heard it all before—the daughters of scions are often neglected by one parent or another. The pursuit of power dictates long hours.

"I do miss him. But we didn't see him much."

"I understand. And your mother. To lose her, too, so soon after… It's simply tragic."

"Yes." I shut my mouth resolutely, praying the dean will take the hint and stop the inquisition. The way she speaks, a human ellipsis, waiting for me to fill in the blanks, is unnerving.

She does, changing tack entirely. "During our interview, we talked about the Honor Code, how important it is to the school, to our heritage, to our students. Absolute trust, that is what we ask. Lying, cheating, or other violations of the Honor Code will not be tolerated. There is no warning system—you openly violate the code and you're out. Lesser infractions will be dealt with by Honor Court, which is run by our head girl. Do you remember the Honor Pledge?"

"Yes. It is protection for both myself and for the students around me." I clear my throat, state with perfect clarity the words I am expected to say. "'I will hold myself and my fellow students to the highest standards. I pledge absolute honesty in my work and my personal relationships. I will never take a shortcut to further my own goals. I will not lie, I will not cheat, I will not steal. I will turn myself in if I fail to live up to this obligation, and I will encourage those who break the code in any way to report themselves, as well. I believe in trust and kindness, and the integrity of this oath. On my honor.'"

This recitation makes my heart thunder in my chest. My hands shake a bit as I clutch the teacup, but the dean either doesn't notice or doesn't care.

"Excellent. It will be up to you how much of your past you wish to divulge, Ash. I don't see keeping your family's plight to yourself as a violation of the Honor Code. I think the name change is a good idea, and support your decision to keep this unfortunate situation apart from your studies. Likewise, your status as a scholarship student is not something we discuss. Most of the girls aren't even aware this program exists. Since your case is so circumstantial, it will behoove you not to mention it. Teenage girls aren't very understanding in general, not to mention unaware of the issues with arcane British inheritance laws."

Oh, the irony—don't ever lie, cheat, steal—but lies of omission are just fine.

The dean briskly continues, "Because of your exemplary insights into Plato in your admissions essay, we've loaded you heavily into the liberal arts track. You placed out of math, so there is still an open slot in your schedule. There are three classes offered during that time period—French, Latin, and computer sciences. The former are eventual requirements junior and senior year and I highly recommend—"

"Computers, please. Ma'am."

"Dean, not ma'am. And are you entirely sure? This isn't a class to enter into lightly, Ash. You won't be able to use the computers to email with friends back home or work on your social media feeds. This is a nuts-and-bolts education on programming, highly advanced and usually reserved for the young ladies who have shown an aptitude and plan to head into engineering and aerospace programs at leading technical schools, like MIT or Caltech. We don't normally allow sophomores in this class, but we have a new professor and he wishes to expand the program to include all class levels. I disagree, but times have changed, and Goode must change with them."

I feel such a sense of relief at this option, this one small thing I know I'll be comfortable with, I nearly cry. "Yes. I am absolutely sure. I like computers. Not the social media nonsense. I like how the systems work."

"I noticed you aren't active online, unlike many of your peers. I was happy to see it. Unless you have private accounts we aren't aware of?"

"Goodness, no. I find social media a waste of time. Not to

mention an invasion of privacy." She has no idea what an invasion it would be. I plan to keep it that way. All my accounts were deactivated before I got on the plane.

The dean smiles wryly. "Good. Computer science it is. If you do like this sort of thing, you'll enjoy your professor, Dr. Dominic Medea. He used to work in Silicon Valley. And as for piano, you'll be with Dr. Muriel Grassley. She is a Juilliard-trained pianist who has wonderful connections, so you'll be able to work with some of the best programs in the country. She'll be expecting you in the theater after convocation. I knew you'd want to get started right away."

"About piano, I—"

A small chime dings, sweet and gentle.

"We're out of time, I'm afraid. Take your bags to your room, and then change for convocation. I will see you in the chapel in thirty minutes. Welcome to Goode."

Dean Westhaven turns her attention to the stack of papers on the desk in front of her.

I am dismissed.

7

THE ROOMMATE

Relieved and vaguely excited by surviving my first important meeting at Goode, I replay the conversation as I make my way to the grand staircase.

I was so sorry to hear of your father's death...

My parents are a sore subject, too fresh, too indecipherable, so I push their faces out of my mind. I don't want to think about them, nor about him. Not now, not ever.

Pale. So pale. Waxy. Quiet. Hair parted on the wrong side. The red of his lips unnatural as if he's been kissed too hard and too long. Crying. A crush of people. The smells: chlorine and stale, piped, air-conditioned air overlaid with overly ripe white lilies, stamens pushing aggressively toward the ceiling, stinking of death...

Vomit dribbling from his mouth, eyes staring, blank and empty... The screams...

"Stop!" I glance over my shoulder to make sure no one has heard. I am blissfully alone.

Get it together. You will not think of this now. You will never think of this again.

Lies. I tell myself such pretty lies.

I bite my lip so hard it makes me tear up, but I am back in control. I square my shoulders and wheel the heavy bag to the staircase, careful to remember I am supposed to go up one side only or I'll never graduate.

Nonsense.

But I stop anyway at the base of the stairs. Is it left, or right? I think back to the conversation I had with Becca the bully. I've already assigned her the role. Becca said left so it's right. Definitely right.

At the top of the first flight, I have to lean against the banister on the landing and readjust my grip on the heavy suitcase. Everything I own is inside. I don't plan to return to Oxford, ever. But the weight of it is untenable. On the second floor, I push through a door and stop, breathing hard, arms aching, and pull the packet from my backpack.

Room 214.

This is no hotel, there are no arrows to point me in the correct direction. There is a small kitchen ahead, and a grouping of soft tan suede sofas, chock-full of girls.

Make a good impression, Ash.

"Which room are you looking for?" one calls.

"214," and the girls point to the left as one, a flock of helpful, smiling little birds.

I drag the bag down the hall. One of the wheels has shattered, no wonder it's so hard to move along the carpet. There is a piece of paper taped to the door at the end, 214 written in bold black Sharpie. Steeling myself, I open the door into…darkness. A heady, musty smell, overlaid with bleach. Across the room are two cobwebbed windows covered in smeary, dotted dirt. The floor is draped in tarps; neatly stacked ladders line the far wall, a row of paint cans in front of them. A fluorescent light swings from the ceiling. When I flip the switch, it comes to life with an ominous crackle.

What is this place? This isn't my room, it can't be. There's no bed, for starters. And it's so dank and dirty...

Peals of laughter.

It takes me a second to realize why they're laughing.

The assholes have sent me to the wrong room on purpose.

Oh, ha, bloody ha.

I look back up the hall and one small wren detaches herself from the flock and joins me. "Sorry. We like to have fun with new girls. You're Ashley? I'm Camille."

"My name isn't Ashley. It's Ash."

"Well, that makes no sense. Ash isn't short for Ashley?"

"No."

Camille's perfectly petite nose rises an inch, and one groomed eyebrow quirks.

Judgment made.

"Ash, then. Well, as I said, I'm Camille. We're here. *Across the hall.*" She gestures toward a pristine white door with 214 engraved on a rounded, champagne brass plaque bolted to the door. How could I have missed it?

Two corkboards are below the room number with our names on top: *Ash—Oxford, England* on the left, *Camille—Falls Church, Virginia* on the right. Both hold pushpins. Mine is empty, Camille's has photos of her travels—in a sari, on the back of an elephant, feeding a camel—and a few buttons with chirpy sayings on them.

"Don't be angry. The girls thought it would be funny if you believed the storage room was your suite."

"I didn't find it funny at all." An intimate staring contest ensues. Camille is the first to look away.

"Whatever. They're just goofing. You're the last one here. This is ours. The view is decent, but the room's nothing to write home about."

I follow Camille in and have to bite my lip again from exclaiming aloud. Gotta look cool, gotta look nonchalant. But… this is nothing like what I expected.

Oh. Oh, my.

The website showed rooms that were small, dingy, and dark, similar to the one across the hall, but this—this is practically sumptuous. Light gray walls, wainscoting, bright white crown molding along the ceiling. Spacious. Lovely.

The beds are bunked, one on top of the other, towering with fluffy pillows and warm down comforters. There is an overstuffed sofa, the windows have gray velvet hangings, two dark wood desks that look like priceless antiques sit side by side on the other end of the room.

This palace is mine. Mine, and Camille's.

It takes me a moment to focus back on my new roommate. Camille has been prattling on, ignorant to my awe.

"Are all the rooms like this?"

Camille pops a hip. "Ugh, yes. They redecorated last year and went with this neutral crap, and it's soooo boring. It's like living in a hotel. It used to be so cool, sort of dark and gothic, had its own personality, you know? Really old-school. More European flair. Granted, the building is super old, so it was probably time for an upgrade. I mean, nothing worked, the windows were stuck shut, and the bathroom pipes creaked and moaned. But this…it's, it's…"

"Monotonous."

"Yes, that's it, exactly. Monotonous. Monochromatically monotonous." She giggles at her alliteration as I move to the window. The view is pretty, the quad a green expanse stretching out in front of the building, lined with old oak trees and pathways. A large sundial stands in the center, circled by a stone bench.

Camille is still talking. "You're allowed one painting for above your desk, but we can't even put things on the walls outside of that. It is so 1984 here. Rules, rules, rules. Big Mother is always watching, too."

"Big Mother?"

"Dean Westhaven."

I bite back a laugh. The moniker fits.

"Anyway, I was saying, I never got your letter. I'm from DC. You're from England?"

"Yes. Oxford. It's northwest of London."

A full-blown eye roll. "I've been to Oxford. My father was ambassador to France for a time, and we traveled all over Europe. But you already know that from *my* letter."

"Yes. How nice for you."

"I took the top bunk and the left desk."

Camille promptly exits the room, I assume to insist on a different roommate. But she returns a few moments later with two more girls in tow.

"Ash, meet Vanessa Mitchell and Piper Brennan. Vanessa's mom works for State, her dad's off on some submarine somewhere for the Navy, and Piper's parents own like half of North Carolina. Ash is not short for Ashley, ladies."

Is she mocking me? Her smile seems genuine, but her tone is off.

I greet the two new girls, quietly assessing, being assessed. Vanessa is petite like Camille but athletic, with muscled calves like a runner or dancer, brown skin, and natural, riotously curly hair. Piper is almost my height, with red hair and freckles. Both seem friendly enough.

"You're from Oxford? Talk. I want to hear your accent. I love a good British accent." Vanessa is the imperious one. Piper only nods her agreement.

"Um, hullo? Care for a cuppa?"

The girls look at me impassively.

"Oh, stop torturing her," Camille says with mock severity. "It's rude. You'll hear her talk plenty. Vanessa and Piper are in the suite next door to us. We're going to convocation. Would you care to join us?"

I can think of nothing I'd like less, the jet lag is catching up to me and I'd like the bathroom and another cup of tea, but in the spirit of international relations, I agree and start toward the door. Camille clears her throat.

"Um, Ash? Aren't you going to change?"

I stop in the doorway, glance down at my outfit. I am wearing travel clothes, comfy ripped skinny jeans and an oversize plaid shirt.

"No, why?"

Only then do I realize the three girls are wearing dresses. And holding robes of some kind, cloaks, maybe, over their arms.

"We dress for convocation, always. Westhaven's orders. She likes us looking put together."

Oh, you idiot. Of course, they would. Whatever were you thinking?

"No one told me. I didn't pack any dresses. Just the white shirts for our uniform."

There is a momentary silence.

"No dresses?" Camille looks stricken, her head whipping between my ruined jeans and her own immaculate hose and skirt as if she can't believe she'll have to go out in public with her new miscreant roommate, but it is Piper who saves the day, crooking a finger.

"Come with me. I have something that will work for you. You'll never fit into any of Camille's things, she's a teensy little stick."

Camille tosses her head. "Rude. Shut up, Piper. We can't all be Amazons."

8

THE WARNING

The room next to ours looks exactly the same, like it's out of a sleek, modern hotel. The "something" Piper offers is a black satin sheath with a black lace overlay. Simple. Elegant. An Audrey Hepburn movie costume. She hands it over, the price tag still dangling from the collar. Rents can be paid with such a sum.

"You can keep it. I have another almost identical," Piper says.

I demur and hand it back. "Thanks. I'll take my chances with the dean."

Piper shrugs and hangs the dress back up in the wooden wardrobe. "Suit yourself. If you keep your robe tight, maybe she won't notice. It'll be in your wardrobe with your uniform skirts—standard issue, everyone gets them. The seniors' stoles are black with a white stripe, we lowly sophomores are blue. Freshmen are red—they stand out, trust me, I felt like I had a target on my back all last year—and juniors are dark green. Graduation stoles are different, multicolored based on your area of study, just like a college. I'm ready for the black-and-white stoles, they're so much easier to match. Our blue—" she pulls the stole out of her gown; it is a sickly pewter blue and doesn't work with her coloring at all "—is a pain, I look terrible in it. Though you can imagine how I clashed with the red last year. You will need to get some dressy clothes, though, we have a lot of formal events."

She closes the wardrobe and faces me, looking me up and down with cool, inscrutable blue eyes. She would look severe if it weren't for the freckles. They ruin the seriousness of her demeanor. She will always look like a girl, not a woman, even when she's fifty.

"You might as well stick to black. It goes with everything, looks good under the robes, and your coloring is perfect for it."

"Black. Right." The color of mourning. I've been in black a lot recently.

"I'll take you shopping if you want. There's a nice little boutique around the corner. Next to the laundry, which is part of the restaurant where we eat on the weekend, Jacob's Ladder. It has a pool table, too. It's not exactly couture, but they'll have a skirt or two that will work. What else do you need to know? Oh, stay away from the handyman. He's a creeper. And remember not to walk alone along the back path through Selden Arboretum if you take the shortcut." Her voice has taken on the warning edge I've already heard several times this afternoon.

"Not another 'I won't graduate' legend?"

"Oh, no. The arboretum is haunted."

"Haunted. A path? Ludicrous."

"Seriously. It cuts through the woods, and a girl was murdered there."

"How horrible. When?"

"Ten years ago. That's when Dean Westhaven—the current Dean Westhaven, I mean—took over from her mother. It's why she's so young. She was only twenty-five when it happened. The board sent Westhaven the elder packing over the bad PR. The student, Ellie Robertson, she was the heir to some massive New England fortune, I don't remember whose. Her dad has serious pull and, after the whole incident, got the dean removed."

"The incident? That's a mild word for a murder."

"The school's verbiage. They're always in publicity mode. Ellie had been complaining to anyone who would listen, the dean, school security, teachers, about a townie who was stalking her and the dean didn't do anything about it. One night, late, the guy followed her home from the laundry and killed her behind the dorms. Raped her, too. There are varying stories about the damage he did to her face, but supposedly, he carved out her eyes and took them home with him. They found them on his mantel. Really freaky shit."

An intense shiver goes down my spine. "I'll say."

"So seriously, you never walk the arboretum path alone. Even if it's not haunted, it's creepy and not safe. It's outside the walls." This last is said with such earnestness I simply nod.

"Outside the walls equals not safe alone. Got it."

"And stay out of the attics. They're totally haunted. Supposedly, one of the secret societies found several sets of infants' bones up there a few years ago, in between the ceiling and the wall. I don't know what they were doing there."

"The society?"

"The bones. They were probably the children of some of the girls who lived here, stillborns and the like. You'd think they'd bury them, the graveyard is actually pretty cool."

"Brilliant. Haunted attics with infant bones in the walls. This sounds like a stellar place."

"Well, Goode is old, and when you get old, you get weird. Oh, I almost forgot, be careful in the tunnels."

"The tunnels?"

"There was an Underground Railroad through here. You know what that is, right?"

"Vaguely. To do with slavery, yes?"

"We were a safe haven from the plantations down South to the free North. Pretty cool. The grounds are littered with tunnels and old cottages, but they're totally off-limits. They're dangerous, and most of them have collapsed in on themselves."

"Where would I find one?"

"I don't know, actually. I've only been told to stay away."

The deep, resonating peal of a very old bell shudders through the building, making me jump nearly out of my skin.

Piper intones, "For whom the bell tolls…. Don't worry, Ash. You'll get used to it. Even when the hauntings happen, the bells toll and chase away the ghosts. They don't like the noise."

She smiles, and I feel a spark of hope. She might be a friend, eventually.

"I can't imagine why not. It's unbelievably loud."

"It's really not to chase away ghosts. It's so we never try to use not hearing the bell as an excuse for being late."

"Right. Brilliant."

Camille sticks her head in the door. "Are you two coming? You heard the bells, we're going to be late. Ash, why haven't you changed yet? Hurry! I don't want JPs on my first day!"

"JPs?"

"Judicial points. It's like demerits. Get five and you're stuck in Saturday school. Hurry!"

Mum's voice rings in my head. *Pride goeth before the fall…*

"Hey, Piper? Thanks for the warning, and the offer of the dress. I would appreciate borrowing it. But just for today, until I get some of my own."

"Sure thing," Piper says, handing it over. I run back to the room, strip, and throw the dress over my head, careful to make sure the price tag is tucked into the collar. I fully intend to hand it back after dinner, though I should probably have it cleaned. The trainers I'm wearing will not do. I have a pair of black flats tucked away in my bag, shoved into the shafts of my beat-up

Dr. Martens. I dig through the bag; the boots are at the bottom. The second dong of the bell shakes the building, and by the third, I'm out in the hall, fully clothed, gowned, and shod, and we are racing down the stairs with the rest of the stragglers, out the back of Main Hall toward the chapel.

9

THE CONVOCATION

The chapel is, like most things at Goode, undernamed. It is more like a cathedral with its sandy stone exterior and stained glass windows, the roofline soaring a hundred feet into the air. The remains of two hundred young women push and shove their way into the chapel, chattering loudly, robes flowing behind them. One last toll of the bell, the ring dying into the early evening air, which still shimmers with heat, and we are all inside the nave and hurrying into our seats.

Inside it is a bit darker, but not much. The energy in the air is palpable, the noise deafening, not hushed and respectful. The rafters are so high the echoes reverberate. Voices call and shout, girls squeal with laughter. Trying to remember the class color schemes, I stick close to Camille, Piper, and Vanessa, grateful for their presence, especially when Becca Curtis notices me.

Becca and another senior are handing out some sort of pamphlet, and I try to duck toward the girl on her left so I won't have to come face-to-face with the bully again, but I'm jostled by the crowd right back to her. I keep my head down, avoiding eye contact, take the proffered paper, and start to move into the chapel, but the universe conspires against me. Becca rips the paper back, forcing me to a stop.

"So. You're our mad Brit."

Camille grabs my hand and tugs. "Leave her alone, Becca."

"Shut it, Shannon. Carlisle here can speak for herself."

I'd rather crawl into the nave's warm brown wainscoting and disappear, but Becca is staring at me, challenge in her eyes. "Well? What do you have to say for yourself?"

I know I can't let Becca bully me. I need to stand up to her. But I hate conflict, hate it. I say the words under my breath and Becca cocks her head.

"What? Speak up. I couldn't understand you. Surely you know how to speak."

The sneer undoes me.

"Yes, I do. I said, better a mad Brit than a daft cow."

"Ooo, snap," Camille says, eyes wide.

Becca's lips go thin, and her face turns red. Her voice is soft, deathly cool. "Aren't you clever, little Brit. We'll see how smug you feel later, shall we?" The threat in Becca's smile is unmistakable.

"Later?"

"Move along, little ones."

Becca resumes passing out fliers and Camille yanks on my arm.

"Come on. Hurry. Before she changes her mind."

We take our seats in the chapel, which is broken into class quadrants by layers similar to the dorm housing—freshmen in the front pews, then sophomores, juniors, and seniors at the back.

Camille's eyes are shining. "I can't believe you mouthed off to Becca Curtis."

"Whatever. She was hounding me earlier, when I was checking in. Told me to take the left staircase, the Evens' stairs, told me I'd get a single if my roommate died. I don't like bullies."

Vanessa shakes her head, lips pursed in concern. "That was a dangerous thing to do, Ash. Becca Curtis is powerful. Why did she single you out?"

"No idea. Her mum is a senator, I heard. Maybe she hates immigrants."

"No, I meant here, at Goode, she's powerful. Doesn't matter who her mother is, though it's hard to forget, sometimes. Camille told you my mom works at the State Department, right? She doesn't care for Senator Curtis. Anyway, Becca is head of the judicial board. She handles Honor Code violations, plus she's class president, and rumor has it she's head of Ivy Bound, too, but no one knows for sure, not unless you're tapped and get in, that is. And the odds of one of us getting tapped are slim. Not as sophomores."

"Ivy Bound? What is that?"

"It's a secret society. *The* secret society. Goode has quite a few, but Ivy Bound is the cream of the crop. It's the one everyone wants to be tapped for."

"If it's secret, how does everyone know about it? And what's *tapped* mean?"

"Shhh!" A sharp whisper behind us.

"Later," Vanessa says quietly. "Pay attention like a good little mad Brit." Her grin is infectious, and I relax, put my attention to the front of the chapel.

The professors have filed in and taken their seats. There is Dr. Asolo, who seems to be having a joke with the woman next to her, small, older, with a silvery bun knotted on top of her head. Most are unremarkable, outside of Asolo and one devilishly handsome man on the far left. He's younger than the rest, and I know this is Dr. Medea, the computer science professor. He alone sits at attention; the rest look alternately bored and tired. Moments later, when they sit up straight, all the girls rise. I leap to my feet with them as Dean Westhaven comes from the wings and steps behind the pulpit.

The dean waits until there is complete silence in the room before she begins to speak.

"Welcome to Goode, ladies. Welcome. I am Dean Westhaven, though you all know me already, either from our interactions here on campus or, if you're new to the school, through our entrance interviews."

A small, pale hand goes to the side of the dean's perfectly coiffed hair, patting and smoothing it into place. I watch the gesture with interest. She's nervous. Why?

"To matriculate from Goode is more than good fortune, it is to seize the future. The statistics don't lie—of the fifty graduates sitting before me today, the class of 2021, all of you will graduate, and all of you will go to college. Why? Because I, your dean, expect nothing less. Your fellow students expect nothing less. Your families expect nothing less. You will excel because that is what Goode girls do.

"You are here to learn. You will work harder than you have ever worked before. You will serve your classmates and this community.

"Never forget, it is a privilege to receive this education. It is your responsibility to step into the world with grace and dignity and an inquisitive brain. You are the leaders of tomorrow. Be a leader today. Show me, your fellow students, your professors how very special you all are. You have each been chosen to have a place behind the redbrick wall. When you leave these corridors, when you are no longer protected by our traditions and our campus life, you will always be safe in the world, because you bear the stamp of Goode on your soul.

"It is vital for you to understand how important a female-only education is to your future. You will be tried—it is our lot in life—and when faced with any sort of animosity or barrier because of your gender, you will have every tool imaginable at your behest. That is what Goode does for you. Yes, you will go to college. But it is more important to recognize the power you are being given. The power of the sisterhood.

"Look to your left. Look to your right. These young women are your future. The investment you make in yourself is an investment in them, as well. Together, we all rise. Together, we are strong. Always remember your sisters."

With a benevolent smile, the dean raises her hands and clasps them in front of her, palm to palm.

"Together," she says.

"Together," the room echoes as one, teachers and students linked together.

"Now, if you please, we will recite the Honor Code."

Two hundred girls draw a quick breath and speak as one, their voices filling the chapel to the rafters, repeating the words I said in the dean's office. This is our official claim, our pledge, our sacred word and bond. It is not unlike reciting a confession. The power of it rings through me. This is what it means to belong to something bigger than yourself.

"…On my honor."

Dean Westhaven touches one hand to her heart, then exits the pulpit, and the chapel resumes its role as school beehive, the girls buzzing with excitement. Convocation is over. Term has officially begun.

10

THE QUITTER

As instructed, I find my way from the chapel to Muriel Grassley's lair in the Adams Theater.

Grassley looks like she should be the subject of a modernist painting. Her face is square, her eyes almond, her lips overly lush—almost certainly the work of a needle, not God. Her brown hair is liberally dosed with gray as if she's walked through a cobweb. She wears flowing robes of turquoise and purple, silver rings stacked on her slim fingers. She is loud and brash, and I immediately like her.

Which is going to make the next hour of my life very hard.

The music lab is in the back of the Adams Theater, facing the mountains. Like many of Goode's buildings, glass is the predominant feature. The vista coupled with the sea of blue-green trees is striking. Happily, the piano faces into the room, instead of out. I'll never be able to focus if I face the windows.

"Ash? I'm Muriel. Come here, let me see you."

I dutifully cross the room to the woman in blue. I dig in my bag and extract a small gold box with a silver ribbon, which I set on top of the piano.

Those bee-stung lips part into a gigantic smile. "Welcome to Goode! I'm so excited to meet you. You brought me a gift?"

"I read that you love caramels but are allergic to tree nuts. There's a little shop in Oxford that is allergen-sensitive, none allowed on the premises. These are totally safe."

"What a darling you are! I will enjoy them tremendously, I'm sure." She links her arm through mine. "So, Ash. I've heard your tapes, you have quite an ear, such a way with the keys. Why have you never performed onstage before? From what I've heard, you're a shoo-in for Carnegie Hall!"

I smile—charming, dimples, with a touch of rueful thrown in for good measure. "My family frowned upon it. I've not played in a public venue, only privately."

"Do you wish to? I'm sure the dean told you about my connections. I could have you at the Kennedy Center in a few weeks." She slaps her hands together, back and forth, and the sound makes me jump. She is so vibrant, this woman, so loud.

"Oh, no, ma'am. I'd prefer not to."

"You don't want to perform?" This is said with such confusion I almost laugh. But I force my face into a downcast expression.

"Honestly, I've been considering giving up."

"Oh, no. A natural talent such as yours can't be squandered. The joy you'll bring to your listeners… It would be such a shame, Ash. I was so moved listening to your audition tapes. You're quite extraordinary."

Truth, then. "I haven't been feeling the music lately."

"Well, we'll fix that. Why don't we warm up with some chromatic scales, cadences, and arpeggios at all octaves, and then try a little Bach. I always find Bach so comforting."

Oh, yes. Bach makes me want to skip through a forest with

mice following my trail. Makes one wonder why I have no desire to play.

I sit on the bench and stretch, first my neck, then my back,
then my wrists. Muriel sets the metronome at sixty and I go
through a quick and easy series of scales, just to get the feel for
the keys. I grow serious. This is important.

I run through the second part of the traditional Hanon exer-
cises, do some chord work. My fingers are sluggish on the keys.
The strike is too soft for my liking, so I'm depressing the keys
harder than normal, banging out the notes.

After ten minutes of noise, I nod at Muriel, who places a Bach
fugue on the stand. I'm familiar with it, but I don't know it by
heart. I'll have to read the music and play.

I launch in, and almost immediately Muriel holds up a hand
to stop me.

"Slow down, Ash. You're pulling the notes. Make me feel it."

I continue to pound away. The next ten minutes are a study
in extreme frustration.

"Now you're pushing. And your texture is off."

"Stop chasing the note, Ash. Let it come to you."

"Feel the keys. Allow each to build on the last."

"Your placement, Ash, your wrists."

And finally, "Goodness, we *are* having an off day, aren't we?"

Yes, we are.

I slam down both hands, the discordant notes ringing through
the room. The acoustics are perfection, the sound lingers in the
air until I lift my fingers from the keys and my foot off the pedal.

Muriel's face is a mask of concern. Her star pupil hasn't made
an appearance.

"What's wrong, Ash?"

"I said I didn't want to play. I…can't. It's too soon."

"Now, now, don't give up so easily. You're sitting much too
stiffly and your fingers aren't flowing. If I were a betting woman,

I'd say you sound out of practice. Very out of practice. When did you play last?"

I don't have to lie on this one. "It's been a while."

"Why?"

"I told you. I've been considering giving up. It's not fun anymore."

"Is it not fun because it's gotten too hard? Or because you don't have anything to work toward? If your parents aren't allowing you to showcase your talent, I know I can speak to them, make them see how beneficial it would be—"

"My parents are dead."

"Excuse me?"

I stand too quickly and the bench scoots back with an echoey screech. My hand goes to my mouth and I squeeze my eyes shut. Finally, I catch my breath and open my eyes. Muriel is staring at this performance in shock.

"I'm sorry. This is too hard, yes, because every note reminds me of them. Every time my hands touch the keys, I see my mother. I don't want to play piano anymore."

"Does the dean know this? When? How? Oh, my dear, I am so very sorry."

I allow myself to be enclosed in a bosomy hug. Muriel is crying. I hang stiffly in her arms, a trickle of tears rolling down my neck. This isn't sanitary. Nor should I be comforting her. I begin to count. At thirty, I gently disengage. Muriel snatches a tissue from the depths of her dress and honks into it.

"Yes, the dean knows. I apologize for blurting it out, and for wasting your time today. I wanted to try, at least once, and see if it would work, but as you can tell, I'm too out of practice, and I simply don't enjoy playing anymore. I'm so sorry. I hate to be such a disappointment."

Muriel's eyes are still shining, her nose is red from weeping. It is a touching show of support. "My dear. Yes, of course, I understand. Though you will find me unconvinced of your true intentions. Some time off perhaps, a few weeks to get your bearings here at Goode, and you'll be itching to play again. A talent like yours isn't diminished overnight."

So you'd think. "But you'll allow me to speak to the dean about dropping the class? It's not you, I've been very excited to work with you, Dr. Grassley. It's me."

"Lord above, call me Muriel. Dr. Grassley makes me feel ancient. I will speak to the dean on your behalf. She is a stickler, you know. Doesn't like change. You leave it to me, I'll make sure she understands you need some time. And you will always have a place to practice with me, Ash. I know you've been through a horrible experience, but when a natural talent like yours comes along, I don't like to see it go to waste. Will you agree to meet with me again in a few weeks? Try again?"

I bestow my best benevolent smile. "You are too kind. Thank you for your grace."

Muriel pats my hand. "Off with you, now. You can come talk to me anytime, Ash."

I give the piano one last long glance as I leave the conservatory.

One less thing to worry about.

11

THE DINNER

According to the letter the school sent, perky Camille Shannon, from Falls Church, Virginia, is a Goode School legacy. Her father, currently the American ambassador to Turkey, has been in the foreign service his whole career; her mother is a lawyer. Her sister, who graduated Goode last year, along with Vanessa's older sister, was "former head girl and everything," which is why the two of them know more than the rest of the students about the secret societies and "won't breathe a word of it, no way, so don't bother asking details."

I think if they knew anything, they would spill because both girls are desperately trying to look important, but I don't care enough to be concerned. I'm comfortable never knowing what happens behind closed doors. This I've learned the hard way.

Camille relentlessly fills in the rest of her CV over dinner. Her ADHD and her Ritalin and her older sister's debutante ball and the beautiful drive down from northern Virginia and when do you think the first mixer with Woodberry Forest—that's the closest all-boys school, Ash—might be?

All of her conversation is rich with gossip and silliness. She inquires only once about my background and quickly takes the hint when I change the subject. For that alone, I am grateful, though it means we get to hear more about her, her, her.

"My parents divorced when I was eight and Emily was eleven, and our father won custody, so we traveled with him all over the world. I have some language skills and an impressive travel résumé, so I'm planning to study international relations at Brown. I have my eye on Georgetown Law so I can go into practice with my mother. I moved back home to DC to be nearer to her. She's so lovely, we've grown so close these past few months."

In case you're interested, I wasn't... Mummy remarried in the spring. Camille wants to play field hockey, almost ended up at Madeira, has a wicked crush on the son of the man her mother married, "but that's, like, incest, so it's a no go," and loves her chocolate Lab, Lucy. Full stop. Everything and anything of relevance to Camille Shannon laid bare on the white linen.

Will someone please come shoot me, relieve me of this boredom?

Jesus, she's still talking. I've tuned it out now. Chatter chatter chatter. She speaks so much neither Vanessa nor Piper are able to share much about their lives. Neither am I, but that is all good with me.

I try (and fail) to stay entirely focused. The dining hall is a pleasant surprise. Situated with floor-to-ceiling windows that look north into the mountains, each round table of eight is covered in fine linen. The cutlery is silver, the plates china. Waitresses—nicknamed waitrons—come to the table for our orders, as if we are in a fine restaurant. Several meal options take into account the various food allergies and preferences of the students. Hungry but nervous, I end up with a Cobb salad laced with cubed grilled chicken, like I'm eating at a country club.

"Well?"

I come back from my woolgathering to see all three faces staring at me curiously.

"I'm sorry. Zoned out for a moment. Jet lag. What were you saying?"

Camille tosses her head. "I said, which Ivy are you shooting for?"

"Oh. Harvard."

"Naturally," she drawls in a most annoyed voice, "but what's your *second* choice? Not everyone gets into Harvard, you know."

"I like my chances," I say lightly. My chances can be helped along at any time by a few clicks on a keyboard, but there's no reason to brag. Camille has that corner covered. But this is dangerous territory. *Back to you, roomie.* "Tell me about DC. I wasn't able to spend any time there."

Off she goes.

I have to admit, I didn't know what I was in for, agreeing to go to dinner with these three intimate strangers, but by the time the dessert plates are cleared, I know one thing for sure— I really need to watch myself. These are friends to be kept at a distance, especially the way Camille gossips. But the buffer they provide is vital, as is their intelligence on the strange world of Goode. If I'm totally friendless, a loner, I'll stand out even more.

Our plates have just been cleared when whispering starts on the other side of the dining hall, growing quickly, a tidal wave moving through the room.

I catch the name Grassley. The piano teacher.

"What is it?" I ask. "What's happened?"

A waitron stops by the table. "They've had to take Dr. Grassley to the hospital. Some sort of allergic reaction."

Oh, bloody fucking hell.

I dive into my bag and paw through, digging until I find the gold box with the silver bow. I flip it over and look at the ingredients label: *Manufactured in a facility that is allergen-free.*

Oh, my God. What a horrible, careless mistake. I gave her the wrong chocolates.

Jet lag, fear, whatever excuse I can come up with, I grabbed the wrong box from the depths of my bag.

I excuse myself and take off at a run, though I really don't know where to go outside of the dean.

Halfway to her office, I slow.

What is this going to look like? I gave the woman a dose of chocolates that made her sick. And I'm trying to get out of piano. Will they think...?

Stop. None of this matters. *You have to own up to this. The box will have both your fingerprints and the shop's address. Broad Street, Oxford, England. You can hardly play dumb. You're such a fucking idiot. Way to go, Ash. That's how to fly under the radar, for sure.*

I start running again, skid to a stop in front of the dean's office. Her assistant, Melanie, is there, and I don't even have to fake the tears that start when I ask to see the dean.

"What's wrong, dear?"

"I just heard about Dr. Grassley. Will she be all right?"

Dean Westhaven emerges from her inner sanctum, looking appropriately alarmed.

"Ash? What's wrong?"

"I heard about Dr. Grassley. Is she... Is she?" I collapse into sobs. God, this is too hard. I want to go home.

For the second time today, I am enfolded in a hug. It's the most mothering I've had in years. The dean strokes my hair, murmuring until I calm down.

"There, there. You're okay. Muriel will be fine. She had her EpiPen, she went to the hospital just in case. I'm sure she'll be back quite soon. It happens, Ash. Accidents happen."

EpiPen. She has an EpiPen. Maybe she's going to be okay after all.

"Did she say anything about our meeting today?" *Don't be so freaking suspicious, jerk.* I sniff, hard. "I'm sorry. I don't mean to fall apart like this. It's only I told her I didn't want to play piano anymore, and then she got sick—"

"Ash, this is not your responsibility. She's had an allergic reaction, but they caught it in time. She's going to be just fine. This happens at least once a term with Muriel, it's a hard allergy to manage. Now, what's this about the piano? It's part of your scholarship."

Careful now, careful.

"I haven't been honest with you, Dean Westhaven."

"Oh?"

"It's only… I hate it. I hate the piano. Yes, I know it's part of my scholarship but I want to give up. Every key stroke reminds me of my mother. I need more time."

Well, that part is true, at least.

The dean's face crumples in compassion. "Oh, my poor duck. I understand completely. Why don't we revisit this in a few days? See how you're feeling then."

I've bought myself some time. Excellent.

"Yes, Dean. I appreciate your understanding."

Her smile is genuine and warm. "Why don't you take yourself to bed now? You must be exhausted. I'll tell Muriel you've asked after her. And you can talk to her tomorrow. All right?"

I'd prefer never to speak to her again, but what choice do I have?

"Yes, Dean."

And I toddle off to bed like a good little girl.

That was much too close.

Walking up the Odd stairs, I run through the situation. I probably should have mentioned the candy, but if Muriel didn't sell me out, then perhaps I can slide through this one without some massive mea culpa.

God, I hope.

12

THE STOMP

Back upstairs, I am attacked by ravenous wolves desperate for gossip. I dutifully report my findings, brief and succinct, then scurry into our room. The sick bitches whisper disappointment in my wake; they would have been much more satisfied if Grassley had died instead of temporarily incapacitated.

I don't tell them my role. I'm hoping it never gets out, but I'm not too sure. Goode has no secrets. This will be an excellent test.

While Camille showers in preparation for bed, I rifle through her drawers. There is nothing exciting, nothing of consequence outside of a half-empty pint of vodka. The usual detritus of a teenage girl. Disappointing, but not surprising. I have no idea what I'm looking for, anyway. Clues, maybe, a guidebook for living in this new world.

By the time Camille returns, I've crawled into bed, stretched out on my side facing the wall, and am faking sleep, wondering if I've made a mistake coming here. I'm not ready to make friends. I'm not ready to answer questions. The energy it is going to take to keep people at a distance is massive. And what if I can't hack it? Not to mention the school aspect of all this? What if the classes are too hard?

I finally fall into a fretful sleep at midnight, restless and rumpled, and wake to the strange sense that something is amiss.

Singing. I can hear singing. Am I dreaming?

I sit up, rub my eyes. Stretch. No. Not dreaming.

But where is it coming from? Not my earbuds, though I've fallen asleep with them in. I pull them from my neck and toss them onto the night table. My laptop slips off the side of the bed, and I make a grab for it before it hits the floor.

Outside. The singing is coming from outside.

I go to the window. The night is black as pitch, deep as velvet. A glance at my watch shows it's 1:30 a.m. The singing is growing louder, coming closer. The hair rises on the back of my neck. This isn't a gentle, melodic song. This is coarse, meaningless; words shouted to a Sousa march beat.

Oh. This must be what the girls called a *stomp*.

Vanessa, when she could wedge a word in edgewise, explained the details over dinner. The secret societies are something like sororities at many Southern colleges, though you can't pledge or ask to join one. The sisters have to come to you, a process known as being *tapped*.

I already knew the secret societies at Goode are a very big deal; I'd read about them when I was investigating the school but hadn't paid much attention. I'm not much of a joiner, and seriously doubt I am the kind of person a secret society would want anyway. At dinner, Vanessa made them out to be almost mythical, as important to a Goode girl's résumé as a 4.0 GPA and an admission letter to Harvard. "The societies carry over into college, you know. It's the ultimate networking tool. Anyone can pledge a sorority. To be chosen, that's the true test."

The societies are secret for a reason. The members have been known to wreak havoc on the school from time to time. I'm not sure I understand how that works with the Honor Code, but I'm not worried. I'll never find out. I am not secret society material.

When I turn from the window, I realize my roommate isn't in her bed.

At the thought of Camille, I fall back into my bunk with a groan. The girl is just so…shallow. She's probably book-smart—how else would she have gotten into Goode?—but has already shown she has the common sense of a gnat.

I lie on the bed, stare at the slab of wood above me, rubbing my temples for comfort. Tomorrow is the first day of classes, I've almost killed a teacher, my roommate is a jerk, and I'm wicked tired. I took some melatonin to help me sleep—I read it was good for jet lag—but all it's done is give me a splitting headache.

The singing and stomping grow louder. Should I go to the door and look out to see what's happening? Tempting. But no. *Again, stay off the radar, Ash.*

They are on the hall now, which means everyone is being disturbed. Earlier, I wondered aloud about the split floors and why they aren't inverted, with freshman having to hike the three stories and seniors only one, but Camille made it very clear the attic rooms are incredible, with sloped ceilings and big windows with clear views of the Blue Ridge Mountains all around the campus. They are the most special. Sought after.

The seniors have their own staircase, too. I was warned three times today to never, ever, go anywhere near the seniors' curli-cue staircase. "Underclassmen who go up to the attics uninvited will never graduate," Vanessa said, eyes wide and serious.

I rolled my eyes at yet another ridiculous infraction rule to be obeyed. I am the least superstitious girl on the planet, but fine with me. Like I told my suitemates, I'm here at Goode to study my ass off and get into Harvard. If I excel and fit in, I will have an easy path to Boston.

It has been drummed into me all day—a diploma from Goode

guarantees you placement wherever you want to go. Women from The Goode School hold the highest positions in every industry, from politics to business, law to medicine. Some are published authors, some are tenured professors. There are research scientists and a cadre of CEOs. Goode is the foundation upon which all things are built.

The singing stops abruptly. The silence is deep, as can only be found isolated away in the mountains.

I begin to drift, then start awake to the sound of whispers. I strain but can't make out the words, only the gentle susurrus of girls' voices. A giggle.

Then, "Ash."

It's quiet, almost inaudible, but it is definitely my name. I sit up so quickly I smack my head on the bottom of Camille's bed.

"Ow. Bloody hell."

The whispers stop.

It must be Camille and Vanessa and Piper in the hall, talking about me. *The new girl poisoned the piano teacher. Watch out, she'll come for you next.*

I slide out of bed and make my way in the dark to the door. I fling it open, step into the hall.

It is empty.

I move next door and put my ear to the wood. The doors are thick, but I can hear the barest hint of gentle, wheezy girl snores. Either they're pretending to be asleep, or I'm hearing things.

You're exhausted. You've been on guard all day. You're jet-lagged and stressed, in a new environment, and you're being silly. Go back to bed.

A door is ajar at the end of the hall. There is a flickering light inside.

Just a glance. One quick little look.

"Ash?"

I jump, my heart taking off at a gallop, whirl around to see Camille, her face red, eyes puffy.

"What are you doing in the hall...?" *Standing in front of their*

71

door? she might as well add, though she trails off, watching me inquisitively.

"I thought I heard my name. Someone was outside the door whispering. Are you all right? You look like you've been crying."

Camille gives a big sniff and gestures toward our room. I let her go in first, stop at the door. Turn my head toward the open doorway only to see nothing but deep, velvety darkness where the light once shone.

Inside our dark room, Camille climbs into her bunk. She lies there, sniffing.

"What's wrong?" I finally ask.

"It's nothing. Go to sleep."

"If you want to talk—"

"I don't. Okay? I didn't feel well, and now I'm all right. Go to sleep. Big day tomorrow."

She falls asleep quickly, but I'm awake for good, it seems, so I pull my worn copy of *The Republic* from the bedside table and fasten a nightlight to the thin cover. If I can't sleep, I might as well study.

But my mind is wandering. The whispers, the crying, the light in the ajar door like an invitation. A decade-old murder. Secret societies. What purpose could they possibly serve? And what sort of secrets do they hold?

Worse, a galvanizing thought.

What have I gotten myself into?

13

THE INSOMNIAC

The dean can't sleep.

She's been tossing and turning for the past hour, running the day over in her head, looking for mistakes, issues, pitfalls. She has a staff meeting tomorrow with all the teachers to address any concerns that have arisen, and she's not looking forward to it. It's always the same, every year, teachers immediately singling out the students who need extra help, who are being disruptive, who are not fitting in, too sad, or too stupid, to cut it. All that negativity is such a downer. She's not had to intervene in any disciplinary actions so far, which is good—maybe she's worrying for nothing. Maybe tomorrow's meeting will be smooth sailing.

She has Ash Carlisle on her mind—not surprising, after her tearful breakdown over Muriel's unfortunate incident. If Ford's being honest with herself, though, she's been thinking about the girl for weeks, ever since the news of her parents' passing, so unexpected, so lurid. When Ash appeared in the doorway to Ford's office—thin, tall, haunted—Ford was torn between offering a hug and sending her back to England.

Something about Ash bothers her. She doesn't have the whole story of the girl's past, this much is clear. The shadows in her pretty blue eyes aren't something brought about by a loving, stable life. With her parents' deaths... Yes, that's all. The shadows are grief. Grief explains everything—the weight loss, the soft voice. How the girl seems to scurry. A broken heart. Shadows. So many shadows.

Ford hadn't noticed when she interviewed her. The computer's camera wasn't great; the room Ash had been in was dark and gloomy, lit only by the natural light from the window. They lived in an estate in Oxfordshire, Ash explained, on a vast expanse of land. Ford had looked up the house itself during the background check—harled stone, three stories, covered in ivy, elegant grounds. Quintessentially British. The parents were the right sort. Ash herself was the right sort. Some spots on the academic record, to be sure, but so often the children of these kinds of people lash out until they find themselves.

Discipline. Focus. Identity. That's what Ford offered here at Goode, in addition to being a ticket to ride.

The Ash she'd talked to was gregarious, insouciant, brilliant. Not mousy. Not hunched in on herself. Not stricken with fear at every question.

What's happened to her since her father's death, her mother's death? Has Ford made a mistake allowing her to come?

Considering the rumblings...

According to Erin Asolo, Becca and Ash had clashed. Becca had said something wildly inappropriate and was scolded. Erin explained the tiff at the first-night-of-term cocktail party, an annual tradition for the Goode faculty and staff. They all got tipsy and divvied up the chaperone schedule, from dorm duty to offsite dances with the local boys' schools.

Ash managed to secure the attention of Becca almost immediately, and who knows where this will lead. To be honest, Ash managed to secure Ford's attention, too. Perhaps she is that kind of girl, one so unforgettable obsessions are born.

Ford knows this is a situation worth watching. Time will tell. She also knows that sometimes, with teenagers, things sort themselves.

Becca can go either way—wonderful, loving friend or cold, heartless bitch. She's off-the-charts intelligent, absolutely. But there is a coldness in her, deep down in her core. Ford can easily imagine her as a little girl, that direct, unblinking gaze as she pulled the wings off a butterfly in her mother's garden.

This event is in the psychological profile on Becca Curtis. Her mother, Senator Ellen Curtis, mailed it to Ford two weeks ago. A disturbing report from a psychiatrist in McLean, Virginia, who stated her concerns for Becca's welfare in plain language.

Summary: Patient lacks empathy. Knows right from wrong, but isn't concerned with following rules. Lies about inconsequential things, evades my questions. Reckless behavior noted by mother— disobeying curfew, drinking, drugs. Patient shows contempt for her mother and authority figures in general, including myself. Possible borderline personality disorder, possible bipolar disorder, possible depressive disorder. Or possibly a teenager trying to get attention from an absent parent. Recommend therapy three days a week and a course of medication.

Along with the psychiatrist's findings, there was a typed letter. *Dear Dean Westhaven…* This was crossed out with a flourish and *Ford* written in blue-black ink, a heavy blot on the bottom of the *d*. Ford knows it was written with a fountain pen, which is meant to impress, and also knows the senator's aide typed the letter and shoved it in front of her boss's face to be signed and personalized. A DC special.

Dear ~~Dean Westhaven~~ Ford,
Becca has been having some issues. We had a clinical assessment
(attached) and she's been diagnosed with some sort of depression.
She will be returning to school with a prescription for Zoloft.
    I know you will keep an eye on her. She's been improving rap-
idly since the medication kicked in and seems quite excited to re-
turn to school. Please keep me abreast of her progress. You may
email me anytime at senator@ellen.curtis.senator.gov.
Yours,
Senator Ellen Curtis

Ford read this and thought, *Her public email address, too. My God,*
Ellen Curtis is a heartless bitch. No wonder Becca is acting out at home.
And the diagnosis could hardly be called *some sort of* depression.

But Ford dutifully updated the senator on her observations
with an email earlier this evening.

Senator,
Becca seems to have settled in just fine. Excited for her classes,
already showing true leadership for the student body. I will
keep a close eye on her. Good luck in the midterms.
Fondly,
Ford Julianne Westhaven
Dean, The Goode School

Titles. People do love their titles.

Ford doesn't see the same girl the doctor does, which is wor-
risome. Becca has never struck her as deliberately cruel, but
perhaps Ford only wants to see the best in her girls. And she understands the desire to get attention from an absent mother, even
if it's negative attention. Ford was—is still—known to disregard
her mother's advice in favor of making some colossal mistakes
of her own. Her mother made the worst one, and now Ford is

shackled to Goode, for better or for worse, forced to read something much too personal about one of her students. Penance.

Yes, Becca needs some extra attention this year. She will be graduating in the spring, already has an early acceptance to Harvard. She might start slacking off, and Ford can't let that happen. Perhaps Ford will offer a tutorial. Becca has shown a propensity for short stories. She'll challenge her to write a small collection, with Ford editing. With the right topics and guidance, perhaps she can even submit to magazines at the end of the semester.

That's Becca sorted.

So what else is bothering her?

Ford finally throws back the covers and goes to the kitchen. Makes a cup of tea, chamomile, and adds a few drops of CBD oil. She needs her rest.

She sits at her desk, sipping, allowing herself a few moments to worry. A good exercise, this. When her mind is cluttered, she indulges it for ten minutes. Then she puts it aside. She sets the timer and lets her thoughts tumble.

She is interrupted by the phone, an unrecognized number. She answers.

"Dean Westhaven? This is Dr. Aquinas, I'm at County General. I've been treating your Dr. Grassley."

"Oh, yes. Is she all right?"

"I'm so sorry to have to share this, Dean, but you are Dr. Grassley's primary emergency contact. She didn't respond well to the epinephrine—I see in her chart that she's had several incidents in the past year. Sometimes the body simply can't get out of reactive mode and the flare-ups are too much for the heart to handle. These long-term anaphylaxis cases are so difficult—"

"Excuse me, what are you saying, exactly?"

"I'm sorry, Dean. Dr. Grassley passed away an hour ago."

JUNE

Oxford, England

14

THE FIGHT

Gravel spits and an engine revs, then cuts off. The front door slams a second later, shaking the mullioned windows. My father screams my name from the foyer. I can hear him though I'm on the third story of the house. I wince. He knows. He knows I know.

"Ashlyn Elizabeth Carr! Where are you?"

I weigh my odds. If I stay here and he has to come up, will he be more furious or less? Time heals all wounds, though whoever penned this bon mot clearly didn't have a teenage daughter. Our wounds only get deeper, wider, nastier. They fester.

"Ashlyn! Come down here immediately."

I creep from my room to the hall. I can hear my mother now, emerging from the solarium where she keeps her office. She spends all day in there, arranging dinner parties and sojourns to the countryside, writing thank-you notes. She is useless. Meaningless. Living a pretend life in a pretend world. Since my brother died, she's done nothing but plan her stupid parties and nip on the sherry. *A tot in your tea, dear?*

"Damien? Whatever is the matter? Why are you out here screeching like a lunatic? I thought you were in London today."

"Is she here?"

"Ashlyn? She's in her room, most likely. Why, what has she done?"

There is a momentary scuffle.

"Damien, really. There's no need to manhandle me. It's beneath you," and my father's ironclad voice, "Step aside, Sylvia."

Footsteps now, running up the stairs, *thunking* hard against the gray wool runner. Father used to be thin, but years behind computers and rich meals in his clubs have robbed him of his runner's physique.

I scramble back to my room, slam the door, and try to turn the lock, but his hand grips the knob and the door swings open, jettisoning me across the room.

Damien Carr is suitably named. He has eyes like burning coals. Possessed. Driven. Evil. He looks to have the devil inside him now.

"What did you do?"

"I didn't do anything. I haven't a clue what you're speaking about."

"You've cost me the deputy exchequer position. They've pulled my name from the short list. Someone sent a salacious email from an anonymous account. I know it was you."

"It wasn't me, Father. I don't care enough about you to bother destroying you. It must have been one of your other enemies."

This brave speech costs me a molar. The pain of his fist blinds me; I see stars. When my ears stop ringing, I spit the tooth into my hand and sneer at him.

"You can hit me all you want, but I didn't do it."

"You're lying. You're a lying, thieving little cunt, aren't you? How did you do it, Ashlyn? How did you manage? I know it was you, don't bother denying it. The IP address was from that dingy café you skulk about, off Broad Street. Oh, you thought I didn't know where you spend your days? Who'd you open your legs for to get this done, eh, Ashlyn? I know you're not smart enough to have managed on your own."

"Damien!" My mother watches this scene with horror from my bedroom door. I can only imagine what it looks like. A play in which I am the writer, director, and producer.

Here's what I want to see.

Ashlyn: grinning maniacally, teeth rimed in red, holding a tooth in her hand. Her cheek and jaw are already swelling, she can feel her skin stretching out so it's shiny and tight. She knows what this looks like; she's been on the receiving end of her father's fist many times.

Damien: his face puce with fury, eyes bulging with hate, spittle in the corners of his mouth from his buffalo clumsy sprint up the stairs, desperately trying to restrain himself from attacking again and failing.

Now start the fight again, only this time, give the audience a second, a beat, to realize he's going to punch her before he does it.

The two of us face off as we have so often lately: my body bruised and battered, his sides heaving like a prized Thoroughbred flogged to the end of the race.

A beat. Yes, that's right. That's better.

My father hates me. Always has. All my parents see when they look at me is the irresponsible twat who let their beloved heir drown. It doesn't matter that I was barely more than a wee babe myself, I was supposed to be holding his hand. I looked away for a moment and when I looked back, he was facedown among the lily pads.

Ever since Johnny died... Well, there's no reason to pretend we ever were a happy, loving family, but the rift was complete when Johnny was four and I was six. Johnny, sainted, beloved Johnny, forever cast as the four-year-old cherub. The innocent facing the monster's maw. I sat with my hand on his tiny back and wondered if Monet would have liked to paint him there, his sturdy little legs disappearing into the muck, the green of the lily pads vibrant against the white of his shirt and the brown of his wet hair.

Then the screaming. So much screaming.

I prodded at him, yes. But I did not hold him under. I did not push him in. No matter what the witnesses said. They lied. They realized who my father was and wanted a piece of the action. As if Sir Damien Carr would reward them for their accusations.

I don't think my father cared for me much before the accident, though his animus after was legendary. He expected decorum at all times; I was a wild, rough-and-tumble girl child who liked to set fire to the curtains and tear apart the ancient silk and wool rugs with my rollerblades, and, because of the Queen's magnanimity, could inherit all of Damien's vast fortune. Not that I wanted it, who cares about money?

He started cheating on my mother well before their marriage bed grew cold and distant. I walked in on him once, with another woman in my mother's bed. They were giggling and laughing and happy. She was blond, ice blond, like my mother, even looked like her a bit. But she sounded so different. So light and loose.

These sounds were unfamiliar, they drew me, a moth to the flame. I wanted to see what had finally, finally, made my parents happy.

Silly me. Silly, dangerous me. He came to my room that evening. Explained my role in their complicity. *Tell your mother and I'll kill you*, he said, giving me his lopsided, gap-toothed smile. A smile to others, a threat to me.

And I, weak little mouse, thought, *Sure, Daddy. I'm happy to cover up for you.*

No, I didn't. I put his words in my growing databank of slights and hurts and nasty things, ready to be pulled out at a moment's notice, a sharpened razor to the wrist. To the throat.

Don't worry, Daddy. I know your secret now, and I'll keep it in my heart where no one can find it until the time is perfect, and then I will use it against you and laugh while you burn.

Our relationship worsens the older I get. I push my father's buttons, as my mother likes to say. She does it now, her lips pursed. Instead of kicking his sorry, cheating, lying, homicidal ass out of the house or offering to get me to a dentist or even have Cook bring up an ice pack, she takes his side.

"Ashlyn, don't push your father's buttons. Tell him what he wants to know."

"I. Didn't. Do. Anything. What do I have to gain seeing you humiliated further? It's embarrassing enough the whole world knows you're fucking that trollop. It reflects poorly on the family."

Ah, the time-honored tradition of daughter throwing her parents' words in their faces.

He roars and his hand swings again but I'm faster this time, braced and ready for the blow the moment the words leave my mouth. I duck, grab my bag with my right hand, and scoot out the door, leaving them both staring in shock.

I clatter down the stairs, one flight, two. I can hear him behind me, shouting. He's gaining. My boots are at the back door. I detour through the kitchens, past the shocked face of Dorsey, our family's cook for my whole tender life. She steps out to stop me but she's too late, and my father crashes into her. They go ass over teakettle into a heap on the flagstones, giving me the break I need.

"Ashlyn," my mother calls again, pleading this time, but I grab my boots and I'm out, doing a runner through the labyrinth and out the back garden. Thanks to Dorsey, I've escaped.

Again.

Half a mile down the lane, I scoot through the hedgerow into our fields. I smoke here by the stone fence. It abuts the graveyard, where I like to go after dark. I sit by Johnny's grave. His presence comforts me. He, unlike the rest of the family, forgave me ages ago.

I find a spot out of the wind and assess the damage with my hand. My face hurts, but my jaw isn't broken. I still have my tooth clutched in my left palm. I wonder if anyone can put it back in for me. No, too dangerous.

I have a water bottle in my bag, dregs from yesterday. I swish out my mouth, spill the last of it over the bloody stump of gory white, then press it firmly back into place. The pain makes me go wobbly in the knees, so I sit down hard on the ground. Shut my eyes and grit my teeth, praying the tooth will take root.

I need a cigarette. Or a bump.

I have to get out of this hell.

There have been rebellious daughters since the beginning of time. Most are like me, I assume, stuck in a house with people whose priorities put them last, who don't care a whit about them, except to see what price they can fetch, what ladder they can be used to help climb, which advantageous match can be made. Too rebellious, and they shipped you off to a nunnery (or school, nowadays) or pawned you off on the first idiot man who'd take you. And if you thought Daddy was bad, just wait until you understood what the rest of your life was going to look like, on your back or on your knees, being forced, getting pregnant, and good luck living through the birth of the first, not to mention the thirteenth.

Female rebellion is a time-honored tradition, yes, but it's usually more genteel now, death by a thousand cuts. Mine is coming to a head, soon, and I won't bother with a thousand cuts. Just one. Well placed. Well timed.

Finality, Damien, comes for you on the wings of chariots.

The last fight we had, Daddy swore to cut me off, and I told him to go ahead, I didn't need his money, his filthy blood money. Lord knows there's none on my mother's side; she married up, way up.

Without my inheritance, I suppose I'll have to get a job. I can get an ID card that states I'm eighteen, forge enough documents to establish a short-lived work history. Rent a flat. I've been saving money—it's one thing to have access to Daddy's accounts, those can be frozen at any moment by the solicitors. No, I'm smarter than that. I've been filtering money for the past few years. Granted, a lot of it went up my nose or down my gullet, but I have over forty thousand quid stashed away now.

I don't want to work, but I'll do what I have to if it means escaping. I just want to get away. Find some peace.

My God, do you blame me? My parents are the real monsters.

AUGUST

Marchburg, Virginia

15

THE MISTAKES

Bewildered. That is the only word for it. I move from class to class, borne along the flow of girls like a mountain stream down a hill, relentless.

I already feel behind and this is only the first day of classes. I've taken so many notes my fingers are raw and bruised, wrists sore from balancing on the sharp edge of my laptop.

My classmates are smart. Seriously smart.

And the teachers expect nothing less than intelligent discourse. Lectures are informal conclaves where topics are discussed, rhetorized, not taught. With the small classes, the teacher-to-student ratio less than ten per class, there is no opinion, no idea, left unturned. The teachers don't lecture, they posit a theory and open the floor to discussion. I am expected to be informed and have opinions. I am expected to participate. I feel nauseated at the mere thought of three days of this level of inquisition, much less three years. It will get worse as term goes on.

I am in trouble. Over my head. Already.

It is 2:00 p.m. and time for my computer science class. It is the second to last unit for the day. The lab, deep in the bowels of the science building, is quiet, illuminated by canned lights, the walls cherry and glass, arranged so the screens won't get a glare.

And the screens—four to a table, three rows—are all run off professional-grade Dells, black towers humming quietly to themselves, busy bees at work crunching data. Complete overkill for a high school class. But that's Goode. Overkill is their middle name.

The Silicon Valley professor, Dr. Dominic Medea, is as good-looking up close as he is from far away. More so. *Dashing* is the first word that comes to mind. A tall, dark, handsome Heathcliff, I can easily picture him striding across the moors, bellowing Catherine's name. I read his CV over lunch. He's worked at all of the major FANG companies, has developed more software than they can conceptualize. I'm lucky to be studying under him.

When I take a seat at the first table, he looks at me with an interested gaze, and like an idiot, I blush under the attention. I'm relieved when his eyes trail over my shoulder to the door. His face breaks into a wide, welcoming smile, and I glance, too. My heart sinks as Becca Curtis strides in.

The bully, stealing all the air from the room.

Dr. Medea claps his hands. "Wonderful, wonderful, now we're all present. Becca, you can take the terminal right here." He points at the seat next to me.

Oh, sweet Jesus. Not only am I sharing a class with my nemesis, I have to sit next to her, too? Why hadn't I just kept my fat gob shut? Then she wouldn't give a crap about me, and I could write my code in peace.

I fiddle with the strap of my backpack, determined to stay out of eye contact. Becca takes her seat, whispers, "Stupid Brit," under her breath.

So much for that. I clench my teeth and ignore her. The only chance I had with the girl is long gone. I've been in these schoolyard battles before. I thought, naively, obviously, I wouldn't face the same in America. That somehow, the girls of Goode would be different.

But human nature is what it is, and someone will always be there to prey on the weak.

The girl behind me whispers loud enough for me to hear, "What is *she* doing here? Isn't this an upper-class seminar?"

"All levels now, apparently," her tablemate says. "She'll never be able to keep up. I give her a week."

I turn and look over my shoulder. The girl's thick brunette ponytail skims the green stole around her shoulders and she smirks.

Ignore them. Ignore them.

Dr. Medea stands in the front of the room, smiling cluelessly at the vicious discourse happening among his ranks. "Welcome, welcome. I'm Dr. Medea, and today, we're going to do some kernel hacking. Sounds like fun, yes?"

And we're off. He assigns a basic Python sniffer script, a baby script, and by the muttering and groaning and lack of typing around me, I realize I am finally going to excel at something and my heart lifts. I am well ahead of the rest of the students, these advanced young ladies who are supposed to be moving on to MIT and Caltech, so much so that when Dr. Medea comes to check my code, he whistles softly through his teeth.

"You should have told me this was remedial work for you, Miss Carlisle. I daresay you could have taught today's class."

I am aware of every eye on me, including Becca Curtis, whose right eyebrow has shot to her hairline.

"Meet me in my office after class, if you would."

I nod meekly.

The bells toll at three and we're dismissed. Becca saunters past. "Maybe you're not so stupid, after all."

I can't read her tone so I ignore her and Dr. Medea waves me into his office. It is a simple room, brick walls, the desk clean of everything but a freestanding iMac, a small Moleskine notebook, and a black desk pad. His brown leather messenger bag, worn and frayed around the edges, sits at his feet like a loyal old dog.

"You have experience with computers," he says, and I nod. "Just how experienced are you?"

For once, I don't lie. "I can hold my own. It's easy for me. The rest of this…" I wave a hand, then freeze. God, what a stupid mistake. *Way to go, Ash, admitting to a teacher you're finding Goode anything less than a breeze.*

But Dr. Medea bestows a gloriously kind, benevolent smile that warms me to my toes. "Goode is a challenging curriculum, a challenging environment. You're going to do fine. New school, new country, it's bound to be a bit jarring. Cut yourself some slack. Now, tell me about that line of code you just wrote. What does it do?"

I know he understands exactly what the code will do. Why in the hell was I showing off? "It allows large packets of information to be transferred through small pipes. Specifically, encrypted pipes that would otherwise stay closed."

"And where did you learn it?"

"The newspaper."

"Come again?"

"An article in the *Daily Mail*—that's a paper back home. They did a story on Stuxnet last summer. They talked about how the Israelis pushed the virus into the Iranian nuclear systems. It looked interesting so I thought I'd try writing a compression code to enable the backdoor to close quicker as you leave. A footprint eraser, so to speak. Like an impression in sand just before the water covers it and it disappears completely."

Dr. Medea laughs. "So, you just thought you'd write some encrypted compression code in class to perfect your earlier version, did you? Best be careful, Miss Carlisle, or the NSA will come calling."

"I didn't do anything—"

"Not to arrest you. To hire you. It's an elegant bit of code. You are far more advanced than most of the girls here. I'm going to talk with Dean Westhaven about placing you out of this class and developing a one-on-one program for you. You clearly have talent, I'd like to nurture it."

"No, no, that's fine. I'm happy to stay in this class."

"You won't learn anything of use if you're already at this level, Ash. It's a waste of time. And talent, I must add."

"But—"

"Listen to me. I know what it's like to be the smartest person in the room. It makes you a target."

"I'm already a target," I grumble, then kick myself again. *Stop, for heaven's sake.* He's too easy to talk to.

"Oh, that won't last long. Trust me. I know this breed. You might be an oddity right now, but in a few weeks, you're going to be the toast of the town. Especially when they figure out you're smart. At Goode, the best currency you have is your brain. So, relax. And let me do a tutorial so we can enhance your skills. No sense holding you back."

"I— Thank you. That's very kind of you."

"Yes, well, we'll make sure you use your skills for good, not evil. I'll leave a note in your box as to when our first session will be. Good day, Miss Carlisle. Go enjoy the rest of this beautiful late summer before we're all stuck inside shivering."

I hurry from his office before he can change his mind. One-on-one instruction from the man who helped devise the modern end-to-end encryption protocols for private email services isn't a bad thing.

Except…to be singled out by a teacher, any teacher, goes against my ethos here at Goode.

But I couldn't help myself. I wanted to show off a little bit. It was the first time since I left England that I've felt at home. Fingers on the keys, tapping away, the lines of code spooling out from my mind. I've always been good with computers. A few books checked out from the library taught me the languages I needed, and then I played, developing my own code, writing programs to fulfill basic tasks.

Not that I've ever actually tried hacking. Well, not really. Okay, maybe a little, here and there.

16

THE DEATH

Outside, the sun is beating down, the air thick, almost sticky with humidity. I grab a bottle of water from my backpack and cross to the large oak tree in front of Old West. Despite the sunlight, the building stands in shade as if a cloud hangs above it. From this vantage point, I have a perfect view of the dorms and of my window. Oddly enough, as I watch, the curtains twitch. I glance at my watch. Camille shouldn't be in the room right now. She is supposed to be at choir practice. We compared schedules this morning, taping them to the inside of the closet doors so we could find one another if need be. At the time, I was touched by her concern—wanting me to fit in, to be happy, seemed paramount to Camille this morning.

Now it's obvious she just wanted to know when I wouldn't be in the room.

What is she doing? Going through my things?

Rage fills me, and I start to get up, to run to the room, to confront her. This will not stand.

The shadow moves again, the curtains fall back into place, and I catch a flash of dark, curly hair. Vanessa is in my room. Are they together? Has Camille skipped class? Or have I simply remembered the schedule wrong?

I'm torn now. Confront them, having made a mistake, and I look like a fool.

It's not like I have anything that will reveal all to them. I've been very careful.

Cool off. Take a breath. Wait and see what shakes out.

Good, bad, or indifferent, I have to make my way here, and to do that means not drawing notice to myself. And yet…here I am, doing the exact opposite. Showing off for the hot teacher was beyond stupid. I've managed to get myself singled out three times, from the dean, Dr. Medea, and Becca Curtis.

One of the three is going to be a big problem. I can feel it in my bones.

The bells ring, shuddering through my skin. It's biology now, with Dr. Hall, but as I walk past the dean's office, Westhaven comes out and stops me.

"Ash? May I have a word?"

She looks tired today, not the same elegant creature I encountered when I arrived.

I follow her into her sanctum. "How is Dr. Grassley? I meant to come by earlier and ask after her. Lost track of myself."

"Have a seat."

Uh-oh.

"Ash, I have some bad news. Dr. Grassley has passed away."

The words reverberate through me as intensely as the bells. "What?"

"The doctor at the hospital said she had an underlying issue, exacerbated by multiple incidents this year alone."

Holy shit. There's no way around this, my actions have just killed a woman.

I'm too upset to cry, just sit, frozen, listening to the dean's platitudes.

She's dead. Dead. A mistake. A simple, stupid mistake, and a talented, lovely life is crushed forever.

Do I have to admit what I've done?

I tune back in when I realize what the dean is asking. "Are you okay, Ash? I know this must be such a shock. I got the sense you and Muriel hit it off. You were so concerned about her…"

Tell her. Admit your sins, be absolved.

Tell her. Tell her!

She's watching me with that curious hawk-stare, and I chicken out.

"Yes. We did. She was very kind."

"There will be a memorial service soon. And we will start the search for a replacement right away. It may be more than a few weeks before we can find someone of Muriel's caliber to take over. It looks like your wish is granted. You may take this time away to decide what you want to do going forward."

I killed her I killed her I killed her.

But I only nod and say, "Thank you."

"Off to biology. I'll let Dr. Hall know you were with me. Stop by the ladies room and wash your face. And, Ash?"

"Yes, Dean?"

"Try not to worry yourself too much. This is a rough start to term, I know. But things will calm down. You're going to fit in here very well."

"Thank you, Dean."

If she only knew.

I scamper off as if I'm heading straight to biology, which is, thank heavens, in the building behind the theater. On my way, I stop by Grassley's office, my eyes peeled for a small gold box.

There. On her desk.

I snatch it, jam it in my bag, and take off. I will dispose of this later.

My God, not only have I killed a teacher, now I've stolen the evidence.

What the hell is next?

I have no answer to that.

17

THE SUMMONS

Dinner is crazed, as only the first few days of classes must be, but coupled with the news of a dead teacher, the hall is incredibly loud.

The students are either zombified or frantic. New friendships have blossomed; tablemates change freely as alliances are struck, cliques formed. The buzz is electric, the hive at work. In the middle sits the queen bee, Becca Curtis, serene as a country brook. Her very being commands attention, allegiance.

I watch quietly, eating another Cobb salad with grilled chicken, drinking ice-cold water. The box from Muriel's office sits in my bag, taunting me. I ignore it, watch the scene unfolding before me.

These very rich girls and their privileged lives are at once familiar and alien. They have a sense of intimacy with each other; they're more like sisters than friends. Traditionally isolated by my circumstances as an only child, I am both fascinated and jealous. They fit together so clearly. Will I always be on the outside, looking in?

If I keep killing people, yeah, probably.

Accident, accident, accident...

Camille pushes away her plate, those doll eyes shining. "Ash, I heard you had a private coaching session with Dr. Hot. Is it true?"

"Dr. Hot? Oh, you mean Dr. Medea? Yes, we talked after class. I would hardly call it a private coaching session. We're to do tutorials going forward."

Vanessa throws me a smug smile. "Better be careful. The dean won't like it if she hears about it."

"I think it might be hard for the faculty to avoid being alone with students if they're ever to counsel them."

"What did you need counseling about?" Vanessa snaps back.

"He liked the code I wrote and realized I had more experience than the rest of the class. That's all. Nothing exciting about it."

"Au contraire, mon frère. I heard you tested out entirely and he's going to be tutoring you privately. One-on-ones with Dr. Hot. Better make sure he keeps it in his pants, or you'll be in major trouble." Vanessa looks both triumphant and angry. I fear she has taken a dislike to me.

"Where do you hear all of these things?"

She shrugs, but Piper leans over with a conspiratorial grin.

"She's just jealous because she has the hots for Dr. Medea. I've heard he's really quite brilliant. If you're getting one-on-ones from him, I'd say you're either extremely talented or extremely lucky."

"Maybe both? I feel quite lucky."

"I'm sure you do, bitch," Vanessa says, voice laden with sarcasm.

No. We are not doing this anymore.

"Stop it. I am not a threat to you. I don't like it when you pretend to be all tough and cool. And what were you doing in my room earlier?"

"I wasn't in your room."

"I saw you. The bells had just rung. You were in the window looking out on the quad. I assumed you and Camille—"

"I wasn't in your room. Was I, Camille?"

Camille, who's gotten distracted watching a group of seniors playing some kind of seated game of Duck Duck Goose with their waitron, shakes her head. "Nope. I haven't been back to the room since I left this morning. You must have had the wrong window, Ash. They all look alike from the outside anyway."

I prefer not to mention I've counted them inside and out, in case I ever need to depart in a hurry, that I know exactly which one is ours because of the small trail of thick ivy that forks three times just below the sill, so I sit silently, chewing the inside of my lip. They're lying. I know they're lying. I know what I saw.

There is a gentle *thwack* by my elbow, and I draw my attention back to the table. A waitron has dropped a creamy envelope, which sits askew on my knife. My name is spelled out—black ink, elegant cursive, the letters drawn carefully and precisely. Camille, who's been picking at her food, snatches it up immediately.

"What's this?"

"An envelope. Give it back."

"'Please return my property' is the more polite way to phrase it, Ash. Gawd, don't be so touchy."

If I murder her in her sleep, will anyone blame me?

"Camille, please return my property."

"There, that wasn't so bad. We'll tame the savage in you yet." She giggles and tosses the envelope at me, winking at Vanessa.

"What's the note? Is it a love letter from Dr. Hot?" Vanessa asks.

I roll my eyes and crack the wax seal, thick and red as fresh blood, slide a finger under the edge of the envelope. The card inside is heavy stock. Three words are written on it in black ink, the same flourishing script as the envelope.

Fourth floor. 10:00 p.m.

"What is this?"

Camille takes it from me, and her eyes grow wide and wild. "My God, it's an invitation to the attics."

"An invitation to the attics. And you've been here two days. What the hell, Ash?" Vanessa's newest indignation puts me on alert.

"I have no idea what this is. I take it this is unusual?"

"You're a *sophomore*. No one gets to go to the attics without a written invitation, but no sophomores, ever."

"But I don't know any seniors."

As I say it, I feel eyes on me, coolly appraising, and turn to see Becca Curtis, four tables over, staring. The goddess has spoken. All hail the goddess.

I whirl back around. "Oh, God. You don't think it's from *her*, do you?"

"*Her*, meaning Becca?" Camille laughs, but the sound is joyless. "You did make an impression. Listen, Ash, don't worry. She probably just wants an apology. She'll embarrass you a few times, make you grovel, and it will all be over quickly."

"I won't go."

But even as I say it, the draw of being in the attics, seeing them, makes the words ring hollow in my ears. I don't want to draw attention to myself, yet being singled out by this girl makes my heart flutter in my chest and my mouth go dry. I want to be singled out. I want it very badly.

"Quite a day for our mad Brit," Vanessa says, and while it sounds like she's teasing, and she's smiling, I can't help but think she's genuinely furious at the unbidden attention.

18

THE WAITING

The hours drag between dinner and my appointment in the attics. I check my watch so often Camille leaves in disgust to study in the sewing circle—the nickname for the grouping of couches on the landing where the girls hang out, chatting and gossiping, sneaking tokes off vape pens in the bathroom, listening to music, and occasionally studying.

Alone, with another hour before my rendezvous, I do something I've promised not to do. Something the dean said yesterday has been niggling at me. I activate the VPN on my computer, override the school's meager parental block on the Wi-Fi, open a browser called Brave that doesn't track my actions (bravo, Brave!), then a private window, and type a name into the browser. The hits pile up, the most immediate a story from the *Guardian*. At the headline, my eyes go swimmy.

SIR DAMIEN CARR'S DEATH INVESTIGATION CLOSED
Banker Died of Drug Overdose, Inquest Confirms

London Wire
29 August, 2020
Chadwick Staff

The coroner's court today recorded a verdict of misadventure in the July death of Sir Damien Carr, Viscount Eldridge. Carr, a graduate of Eton who read law at Cambridge and subsequently became one of London's premier wealth managers, was found unresponsive in his home in Westminster this past 14 July.

Carr was known for his unrelenting desire to keep a discreet and low profile in the industry, and this moral rectitude was one of his hallmarks, making him one of the most sought-after wealth managers in London. He served on several boards and was thought to be in line to be named as under-treasurer for the chancellor of the exchequer. The position was filled by John Bamforth, Carr's former associate in the financial firm, only last week.

Family and friends, who saw him as a staunch teetotaler, were admittedly shocked by the news of the overdose. Carr's wife, Lady Sylvia Carr, suffered a breakdown after the incident and sadly took her own life. Their daughter—

"Ash? It's time. What are you reading so intently?"

I jump up so fast my laptop drops to the floor with a crash. I put a hand on my heart, *deep breaths, deep breaths. You are not in danger. You are not about to die.*

Vanessa stands in the door looking very young in her bathrobe and glasses, her riotous hair standing out like she's been pushing her hands through it.

Bloody fucking hell, why do they have to sneak up on me

all the time? Is there a class they teach at Goode frosh year in stealth? I could have used it.

"You scared me, Vanessa."

"Are you okay? You look like you've been crying."

It's the nicest tone Vanessa has ever used with me. I have been crying, I realize, tears are bubbling over the edges of my eyes and running unchecked down my face. I sniff and scrub them away.

"I'm fine. It's time?"

"Yes. You'll tell us everything, won't you?" Kind Vanessa is confusing. Vanessa whiplash, I'm starting to think of the girl's mood swings.

"I will." I open the laptop long enough to log out of everything and shut off the VPN, wondering briefly what the Honor Code would say about such a thing. Surely there is a difference between protecting my privacy and deceiving the school's IP filters. I plug it in and take the envelope with my name on it from the desk gingerly.

"Off I go."

"Go with God," Vanessa replies dryly.

In the hall, I can hear voices to my left, toward the stairs. Camille and Piper are standing there, whispering behind their hands. They stop when I approach, both smiling tremulously. It feels like I'm being led to the guillotine with friendly witnesses amassed to see me along the way, which is just stupid. I'm going to speak with my bully, get this situation dealt with once and for all. I will not spend term looking over my shoulder, waiting for Becca and her minions to make my life hell. I just won't. I've already been through enough this year. I refuse to be a victim any longer.

I give the girls an ironic smile, a brief salute, and step through the steel door into the stairwell. The first set of stairs is uneventful, but the second flight is blocked by two identically bored, sweatshirted, messy-bun-topped girls sitting on the last step. These are the twins I saw following Becca around that fated first day. Camille said their names are Amanda and Miranda and no one can tell them apart, even their mother, who is chief of staff to a corporate bigwig and isn't around enough to worry about it. In the murky darkness, I definitely can't see a characteristic or feature that allows me to distinguish between them.

One says, "Finally. Come here."

"Why?"

"Because we have to blindfold you, idiot," the other says. "You're not allowed to see the seniors' hall. It's bad luck."

I don't like the idea of being blindfolded at all, and my heartbeat kicks up a notch.

"We aren't going to hurt you," the first girl says. "You've been summoned. You have an invitation. And you don't want to keep Becca waiting. Come on."

I turn reluctantly and try not to bolt as the strip of cloth is tied around my head. It is black velvet, thick and close, and I can't see anything.

They lead me the rest of the way, soft hands, murmuring "step here," "watch out," "we're turning now."

One more set of short stairs and the air changes completely. Musty, evergreen, overlaid with the scent of bleach. A gentle coolness on my face; there is a window open, and the night air in the mountains already holds the hint of fall. My nose twitches, I smell marijuana, a scent as familiar to me as my strawberry shampoo. Someone is getting high in the attics. Naughty, naughty.

The hands leave my arms, and the door closes quietly behind me. I am alone.

19

THE COMMONS

But I'm not alone.

The voice comes from my right. "You can take it off now."

I rip off the blindfold, relieved.

The room is dark, but my eyes have adjusted. I'm in a large space, windowed along one wall, with a sloping ceiling. Sofas and chairs and oversize beanbags are scattered throughout. The windows are open, and the mountains are shadows outside, huge and ominous, their very presence pressing in on me.

A few lights shine in the distance; fireflies still dance among the trees. It is beautiful and terrible at once, and fear skitters through my body. I instinctively take a step backward. The open windows—it is a long fall to the ground.

"What is this place?" My voice is too quiet, my breath shallow. It is claustrophobic, this vast expanse before me closing in through the night.

Becca Curtis flicks a lighter and sets it to a candle, then steps out of the shadows with it in her hand.

"The Commons. It's a study room. It's quiet here. We're all very studious, you know."

In the candlelight, Becca's green eyes are a bit bloodshot. Has she been the one smoking? Surely pot isn't allowed here, even among the vaunted seniors.

"Thank you for coming," Becca says conversationally. "I wouldn't have blamed you for dismissing the summons out of hand."

"I had a choice? Then, by all means, I'll bid you goodnight."

Becca laughs. "Ash. Stay. We should talk."

"About what?"

"Do you think I'm stupid?"

"No. I've heard you're quite brilliant."

"Hmm. Do I look fat?"

"It's dark, but no. You don't."

"Then your insult was not only ill-advised but inaccurate and illogical."

"Excuse me?"

"Sit." Becca takes a chair, pats the sofa cushion nearest her. She sets the candle on the coffee table. I carefully lower myself, muscles clenched in case I need to flee. I don't like this place at all.

"If, Ash, by your own admission, I am neither fat nor dumb, then calling me a daft cow was a weak insult."

"I don't understand."

"Ash, Ash. You're a Goode girl now. Your insults must be precise. Cutting. Elegant. Intelligent. You're an intellectual girl, you can surely do better. Where did you learn computers?"

"In England. I like them. They're easy for me."

"Tell me about your life there. Tell me about your family."

"I have no family. I'm an orphan."

"A rich British orphan. How quaint. Let me guess, there's some mad aunt in the attic who left you her estate and money?"

"No. My parents were wealthy. They had accounts for me. There's a regent who handles the funds."

"A regent. My. Aren't you fancy. So very British."

Here we go.

"If you've brought me here to mock me or terrorize me, can we get on with it?"

It is a brave speech, but I'm not feeling very brave at the moment. The chill in the air is making me shiver, and I have the most awful sensation of someone watching me. The hair on the back of my neck is standing on end. I shift, sliding my head down into the couch cushion so I'm not so exposed.

"I have no intention of terrorizing you," Becca says. "I want you to do something for me."

Uh-oh. All hands on deck, this is going to be good.

"What?"

"I need you to hack into Dean Westhaven's email. She's been speaking with my mother and I want to know what's being said."

"Are you completely bonkers? No. Absolutely not. I'm sorry."

"No. You never apologize for something you didn't do wrong. You say 'excuse me.' Never 'I'm sorry.' If you spend your life apologizing, you'll never gain any confidence."

Becca takes down her ponytail and begins twisting her thick hair into a braid. Her tone is so casual I fear what else she's going to ask. Something's coming. Something's up.

"But in this case, I do apologize. I should have been more clear. I'll pay you, of course. I notice you've been borrowing your suitemate's dresses. You might appreciate being able to get some clothes of your own."

I borrowed Piper's dress once. My God, how closely is she watching me?

"You're raving mad. That's an Honor Code violation."

Becca laughs again. "Who are you going to tell? I'm the head of the judicial board. You're supposed to report code violations to me. And I'm giving you the instructions. You won't get caught, not if you're as good as you think you are."

"I am that good, and I still won't do it. You can tease and bully all you want, but I won't. If you push me, I'll inform the dean of your request. I doubt she'll be so amused. You're violating the code just by asking me to do this, aren't you?"

Dice, thrown. I keep my head high, staring Becca in her pretty, bloodshot, evergreen eyes. There is no way I'm going to play along with this girl. I have too much at stake to be tossed out of Goode because of someone else's mommy issues.

Becca smiles and does a slow clap. The transformation on her face is confusing. She seems almost…friendly now.

"Bravo. You've passed."

"What?"

"I was testing you. You passed. Now run along. I have work to do. That damn Python project will be the death of me. If I don't figure it out, maybe you can help me. Explain it to me, I mean. And feel free to have breakfast with me tomorrow. You might find my friends a little less backstabbing than yours."

She gestures toward the door, where the twins are waiting with the blindfold. They've heard the entire exchange.

"Get her safely downstairs. We don't want the bogeyman to get her. And then get back up here. We have a date."

"Is *he* driving?"

"Who else?"

Becca pulls her braided hair into a knot on the top of her head and blows out the candle, plunging us all into darkness. The audience is over.

I'm still standing there, staring, trying to figure out what in the world is happening, when the girls grab my arms and tie the blindfold tight around my head. The sudden loss of light and bearing makes my heart kick up again, but I'm prepared this time, don't panic. They can't hurt me. More, they don't want to hurt me.

And they don't. They walk me back down to my floor, take off the blindfold, and push me through the door. I stagger into my hall. The stairwell door closes.

The summons is over, and deep in my heart, a shift begins.

Becca Curtis was kind to me.

Maybe this place won't be so bad after all.

20

THE FEVER

I am alone on the hall. It's quiet, too quiet. The eleven o'clock bells haven't rung to signal curfew has started, not that it matters; normally the girls giggle and titter in their rooms until well past midnight. Now, though, the hall is silent. The lack of noise makes the hair stand up on my arms. I doubt I'll ever get used to the pervasive silence of this place. It must be the mountains, absorbing all the noise.

I cast a brief glance at the storage room across the hall as I slip into our room, trying not to wake Camille. I needn't have worried; she sits on the sofa, staring blankly out the window. She doesn't turn when I enter.

"Camille?"

"Mmm?"

"Are you all right? Camille?"

Camille's eyes are glassy, her face flushed. I instinctively put a hand on my roommate's forehead.

"Whoa. You are burning up. Come on, up you go. Let's get you to the infirmary."

"No!"

Camille jerks back, shrinking into the cushions. She's holding a heating pad to her stomach, disguised under a throw pillow.

"Camille, you're sick. You need to go see the nurse. I don't want to catch whatever you have."

"You won't," she mutters. "It's that time."

"Your period gives you a fever? Come now, you need to be seen."

"Sometimes it does. I just want to sleep." She manages to focus on me. "How was your audience with the queen?"

"Changing the subject won't deter me. You need to be seen."

"If the fever hasn't broken by morning, I'll go, I swear."

"Fine." I take a seat next to her. "She wanted to elucidate my manner of insults. She felt I was being illogical by calling her a daft cow as she's neither stupid nor fat."

Camille laughs softly, wincing at the effort.

"Then she invited me to breakfast."

"With the seniors? Whoa."

"Yes. Now that I've been properly chastised, if you won't see reason, I'm going to bed. Can I get you anything? Hemlock?"

"You are so strange. Maybe just some Tylenol? It's in my bag."

Camille's purse hangs from the back of her desk chair, easy to find. I start to dig in, but Camille says, "Wait. Just, hand me my purse, would you?"

I hand it over, and her clear, reusable water bottle with the school crest labeled on the side, half-full.

"Thanks." She digs in her bag, pulls out the white-and-red bottle, swallows down the pills. "Listen, Ash. I know this place is weird. Just stick it out. It gets better. The first couple of weeks in a new school are always difficult. Goode is exceptional. You're going to fit in fine."

I collapse onto my bed with my worn copy of *The Republic*.

"I admit to wondering if I should have been focusing on Machiavelli instead of Plato."

"Stop making me laugh, Ash. It hurts." Camille giggles and snaps off the light.

The darkness bleeds around us, sweet and velvet, and I think back to the strange sense I'd had in the Commons as if someone were watching me. I've been chalking it up to being surrounded by 199 other girls and the teachers, maids, groundskeepers onsite, all of us shoved into the tiniest fishbowl imaginable, but now I wonder if there's something more. This school is old for America; these buildings stretch back hundreds of years. The area is isolated; the mountains whisper secrets on the breeze. Places have memories, especially when there's been bloodshed. A walk along any battlefield will confirm that.

My mother would love it here. Would have done, that is.

My parents are dead.

A small voice from the ceiling pulls me away from the sharp pain that floods my chest at the thought of my mother's soft, lined face, worn and gray and riddled with worms. The notes from Grassley's Bach fugue rise in my mind.

"What's her room like?" Camille's question chases away the scene in the parlor, Father on his back. Mother, gray and lifeless.

"Becca's? Don't know. They took me to a big room that overlooked the mountains."

"The Commons?"

"Yes."

Camille's disembodied head appears over the side of the top bunk. "Holy cow, Ash."

"What?"

"The Commons is where you go if you get tapped."

"I thought you didn't know about any of that?"

"I know a few little things. I mean, my sister..."

Humblebrag, humblebrag. Camille is just so good at it.

"It's supposed to be a really weird spot."

"I'll admit, it was a bit odd. In the dark, it feels like the room is suspended in midair over the mountains. I would like to see it during the daytime."

"Maybe you wouldn't. There's a closed-off stairwell from it—now this is part of school lore, I've never seen it—but it's called the red staircase because a girl committed suicide there after her boyfriend was killed in a car accident. He was coming to see her and never made it. She hung herself from the banister, but she also cut her wrists, so the blood dripped down the staircase. She was in there over a break, but no one knew about it because the school thought she'd gone home. When they finally looked and found her, the blood had soaked in so deeply they had to paint the stairs red to cover it up. Supposedly, one of the secret societies makes you spend a night locked in the stairwell."

"And I thought I left all the crazy ghost stories back in Oxford."

"Piper told me she warned you about the arboretum, too."

"Oh, she did. It seems Goode has had its fair share of student deaths over the years."

"There are a ton of legends here, some true and researchable, like the girl in the arboretum, some harder to verify. But I think that's true of any boarding school, don't you? There are prerequisites—the school must have a dark past, be haunted, suffer a terrible tragedy—I mean, you've read all the books, I'm sure."

"I have," I say lightly. "Perhaps we can make it through the next three years sans scandal or tragedy, yes?"

"God, I hope so. I don't like ghosts."

I'm almost asleep when I hear Camille crying quietly. Should I acknowledge this? It feels private, but with her fever... Maybe she's more ill than she's letting on.

"Are you well, Camille? Should I call someone?"

A big sniff. "I'm okay. Thanks for checking on me, Ash. Just missing home."

"Is your fever down?"

"I'm okay," she repeats. "Go to sleep."

Soon after, the bed shifts and Camille slides off the top quiet as a stalking cat. She is out the door a heartbeat later.

I let her go. *Don't get attached. You'll only get hurt.*

But when she hasn't returned thirty minutes later, I am compelled to seek her out. My feet are chilled as I walk the abandoned, darkened hall toward the bathrooms. Privacy isn't important here; though there is a handicap toilet on each hall, each wing has its own bathroom, complete with showers and toilet stalls. Like a prison. Everything on display. Do you know how hard that is for teenagers? Torture, first degree.

I hit pay dirt. Camille is inside—I can smell her Philosophy perfume that reminds me of the marshmallow cream I had as a child. She is sobbing so quietly I can barely hear her.

I speak low so as not to startle her. "Camille?"

But it is Vanessa who steps from the stall. "She's fine. Go back to bed."

"She's sick. I think you should take her to the nurse."

"Mind your own business, Brit. I've got this under control." A low moan escapes the stall. "Go. Now."

Against my better judgment, I do.

Camille doesn't return to the room that night.

21

THE AFFAIR

Ford's inability to fall asleep has always been an issue. Though she dutifully climbs into bed at 10:00 p.m. every night, sleep mask on to help her melatonin levels rise, she often lies there, listening to her own breath, until she finally gives up and goes to her desk.

Tonight's nagging worry, the conversation she had with Muriel Grassley about Ash Carlisle before her untimely demise.

"She hasn't been playing, certainly. Said her parents' death has traumatized her. You should have told us, Ford. She shouldn't be held to such a standard, trying to hide the fact that her parents are so recently deceased."

"I will take your opinion under advisement, Muriel. She's planning to quit entirely?"

"Yes. Says her heart isn't in it. Honestly, Ford, I can't say I disagree. She certainly isn't the same player we heard on the tapes. Such a

shame to let such an astounding, God-given talent go to waste, but we can't force art. She's just a child. A hurting child."

"Oh, my. That is distressing news. We certainly don't want to force her. She seems to have shown an aptitude for computers, of all things."

"Really? Well, if she's giving up the piano, it isn't a bad substitution. Still a creative field, in many ways. I do hate to see her lose this much practice time, though. You know how hard it is to get yourself back to tip-top shape."

"Yes. Why don't we revisit the subject in a few weeks? Give her a chance to settle in. Thank you for letting me know, Muriel."

Ash is a concert-level player. Could be, that is. If she isn't interested in playing anymore, Ford isn't going to force her. And now that they've lost Muriel—what a shame. What a damn shame. The two would have made magic together.

She's left the window open to help circulate some air; even the night is warm still. The cottages have air-conditioning, but she prefers to leave it off, instead listening to the night sounds from the forest—the wail of a solitary mockingbird, the chirps of crickets, the rustling of nocturnal creatures coming out for their dinner.

If she can't sleep, she might as well try to write.

She rolls a piece of paper into the typewriter, runs through a few lines, stares up at the school. Lights flicker in the Commons, and she smiles. What are her girls up to tonight? Earlier, there was noise coming from the grounds. One of the secret societies, no doubt, titillated by roaming the grounds after dark.

The secret societies at Goode are a centuries-old tradition. Ford knows of at least ten, though some are secret enough they've stayed off even her radar. The school has been pressured to disband them over the years, and there have been quiet lawsuits now and again due to hazing gone wrong.

Ford is realistic enough to know Goode can ban the societies and they'll continue on regardless. Cliques form in large groups, this is simply a fact of life. Belonging is good for teenagers. Finding like-minded individuals, girls with whom they can feel at home, will strengthen them, ready them for the world. She has always resisted the idea that all the girls are equal. This is why Goode is so successful. All girls are not created equal. All girls do not fit a preconceived notion, a standardized cut-out. Some are good at math, some are good at English. Some can ride, some can run. Her job is to nurture their strengths and help them find ways to mediate their weaknesses. To make them strong, not delicate creatures easily crushed by the world.

She knows this method works. Not only did she graduate with honors, she'd been in a couple of the societies when she was a student, too. Whenever a parent freaks out, Ford has the right words: "Trust me when I say it's all in good fun. No one is getting hurt. They are doing nothing wrong outside of breaking curfew now and again. And it's good for them to find their allies in this world."

With one exception. Everyone knows Ivy Bound can get too intense. Every year, they skirt the edges of what's allowable, and Ford has had to have a word with their leaders before. But not recently.

She wonders who's taken over Ivy Bound this year. If pushed to guess, Becca Curtis would be the most likely candidate.

Becca, again.

Ford makes a mental note to have a private word with the girl in the morning. Ford has been accused of being too lenient in the past, but this is her school. Her duty. The girls are, on the whole, incredibly well behaved. She's found that giving responsibility and expecting maturity works. Ford's hands-on approach nips problems in the bud.

She doesn't want to make the same mistakes her mother did. The school can't survive another scandal like that.

She sits back in the chair, the sexy line of dialogue she was about to commit to paper retreating. Perhaps writing isn't the solution to her insomnia. Perhaps she needs a different release.

It's been a few days; she's feeling the pleasant pull of abstinence coupled with desire. She checks the clock, it's just past eleven. Not too late for a caller. Maybe he'll stop by, unbidden, maybe he won't. Their affair is casual, mutually beneficial, and totally, completely against the rules. That's what makes it so fun.

She shoots off a text and immediately receives a smiley face with a wagging tongue and the number ten in response. She likes the fact that he responds so quickly when she beckons. He's happy to be of service, asks nothing of her in return. He's not been burned by a woman before, his heart is still open, free. Undamaged.

She texts back—Careful of the stomp—gets a thumbs-up.

It wouldn't do for one of the girls to spy him entering her cabin in the dark.

She abandons the typewriter, opens her Clairefontaine notebook, runs a finger down the lines, the indentations made by her pen. She knows what the words say, doesn't bother reading them, comforts herself in the knowledge of their existence. Words are going to get her out of here one day.

The novel she's working on is good. Better than good, it might even be great. If she can bring herself to finish. And once she's finished, if she can bring herself to submit. She's such a private person, she's afraid of what might happen. To have her words, her story, in the hands of a stranger. To draw out a laugh, to bring a tear to their eye, to make them smile and feel fulfilled—this is her calling. Goode is her job, but her destiny lies ahead.

Who will take over as dean, though, Ford? A Westhaven has always run the school, it's tradition. You wouldn't shirk your responsibility to the family, to the school, to our ancestors.

Go away, Mother. You had your chance, and you fucked it up. My school now, my decisions.

Ford will take a pen name, this she's already decided. Her name is awkward at best: Ford Julianne Westhaven is a mouthful, too long for a cover treatment. F.J. West is her current favorite. Ford is her grandfather's name, both Julianne and Westhaven vestiges of the school's founding. She doesn't know her real father, only remembers the cheerful, kind Santa Claus who raised her while her mother worked and worked, keeping Goode in check.

Cliff Morley died quietly in his sleep when Ford was sixteen. She misses him still.

All she wants is to move forward, to make a life for herself, a name for herself. But Goode has drawn her back into the muck of her mother's disastrous life choices. She is mired in the past.

Then again, this angst makes good writing fodder.

Ash Carlisle is reinventing herself. Perhaps that's why Ford can't get the girl off her mind. A phoenix from the ashes, Ash is, exactly what Ford wants for herself.

Is she really jealous of a sixteen-year-old orphan? Is this the emotion she's been carrying around, this mild obsession with the girl?

"Don't be stupid, Ford." She slaps closed the notebook. Her date is arriving soon.

In the kitchen, she fixes two drinks, an old-fashioned with her new favorite recipe: Basil Hayden's whiskey, four dashes of orange bitters, a splash of simple syrup infused with cloves, a bourbon-smoked cherry for each glass, plus a lovely round ball of ice that she'll add when he arrives. Symbolism is everything in a cocktail.

There is a soft knock at the door. Ford loosens the tie on her robe, pinches her cheeks and bites on her lower lip to make it swell, drops the ice in the glass, and answers the door with his drink in her hand.

"Welcome."

He slinks in the door. Before the latch is set, he has her up against the wall. He is taller than she is by a few inches now, arms powerful and smooth, lips against her neck.

"I missed you," is all he says. He is already hard and has her legs around his waist and is inside her before she has a chance to blink.

No words needed, no foreplay, no candles and roses. Just raw, hot desire, satisfied. They both take and take and take. They rarely give.

The whiskey sloshes out of the glasses as he strokes her, in and in and in again, until the release builds like a wave, a scream, and he is right there with her, ready to go.

"Come for me," he says, and she does.

There is no cuddling. They sit at the table, refreshed drinks in their hands.

She asks about his day. Tells him she's worried about a student.

He tells her she always feels this way the first week of school, not to be nervous.

He finishes his drink, tossing it back, gives her a long, searching kiss, then leaves, whistling, his whiskey-tinged breath lingering on her lips as the door shuts behind him.

Ford puts the glasses in the sink, shuts off the lights. Washes up in the bathroom, then climbs into bed. She can smell him on her still, and it turns her on.

She is finally tired enough to sleep.

If anyone knew, she would be in so much trouble.

22

THE CROWNING

Breakfast is surreal. I'm sleep deprived, and everyone seems to be on max volume. I push my scrambled eggs around while Piper and Vanessa interrogate me about the summons, but I give them nothing of worth. I want to keep this to myself; besides, Camille can be counted upon to share the little bits I told her last night when she's feeling better. So far, she's ignoring all of us, looks utterly miserable, sniffing every once in a while.

They soon grow bored of my one-word answers and begin haranguing on about the creepy handyman they saw standing in the woods, watching the soccer team warm up. I tune them out. Their little melodrama isn't my problem.

No, what I woke worried about was Becca's strange request. I didn't lie to her; I can hack the dean's email. Was the request really a test? Or was it something more? It smells like a setup. Am I being tested on my loyalty to the school? To the Honor Code? I feel damned either way—report Becca and lose her trust forever, don't report the request and break the Honor Code. A conundrum.

As if she knows I'm thinking about her, Becca calls my name and waves me over to her table. Vanessa's eyes grow wide, and Piper looks suitably impressed. Only Camille doesn't seem over-awed. Honestly, I'm relieved to cross the room, until I realize all eyes are on me. Bugger.

"Join us," Becca commands, and I scramble to comply, taking the seat next to her. The table is comprised of the same tittering group of girls who surrounded Becca our first day. All are dressed in their school robes, black-and-white stoles around their necks.

"This little bird is a quiet one. But we'll get her to open up. Won't we?"

The girls chirp their assent, and then the barrage begins, the questions coming so rapid-fire I can't keep up, and in some ways, I'm happy to just smile and blush and laugh a little, demurring, bowing under the influx.

"So, Ash. Your family in England, who are they?"

"How do you get your hair so full?"

"Who are better, Hampden Sydney boys or W&L?"

"Those boots are divine. Where did you get them?"

"Why can't we find you on social media? Are you, like, a Quaker or something?"

"Which Ivy are you shooting for?"

This from Becca, and I answer "Harvard" to knowing nods.

"Excellent. Goode girls have a great legacy at Harvard. I received my early acceptance last month. Everyone else is waiting, but the letters will be coming any day now. Almost everyone at Goode gets snapped up on early admission. It's a tradition, so we can focus on our studies instead of worrying about writing applications essays. One of the many perks of Goode."

"It's a lovely place," I volunteer. "So old. I almost feel like I'm home. Of course, Oxford is very old, too."

"She speaks," Becca crows, delighted. "Tell us your favorite spot in Oxford. I've not been, Mother's leashed me to her side and I haven't been able to travel at all these past two summers. Though I will be applying for a Rhodes scholarship, so I need to know all the hot spots in town."

"Assuming you get it," Twin One says, and Twin Two sniggers.

"As if there is any question," Becca responds smoothly. "I'm Becca Curtis. They'll hand me a Rhodes without blinking. Now, Ash. What are your favorite hangouts? And are the boys adorable?"

Ah. I finally understand. Silly rabbit. The allure isn't me, it's what I know. Who I know. The styles, the places, the people. This I can handle. I know Oxford inside and out. Still, the crushing intensity of Becca and her minions is overwhelming. I haltingly begin to list the spots I know are the coolest hangouts and am saved by Camille, of all people. She stands nearby, clearing her throat as if afraid to approach, with Vanessa and Piper on either side.

"We're going to be late for English, Ash. The bells. Aren't you coming?"

The bells start tolling a moment later.

"I'll be along."

"Really, you shouldn't be late."

"You're fine, Ash," Becca says. "I'll explain to Dr. Asolo why you're tardy."

I tense, not sure if I should run off with Camille or stay put until dismissed by the seniors, and the seniors are silent, watching this tiny drama unfold until Camille shakes her head in disgust and walks away.

"Don't worry about her," Becca says, smirking. "She's just jealous you're sitting with us now. Her sister was hot shit last year before she graduated. Camille is a head girl wannabe."

I roll into English five minutes late thanks to Becca's insistence I stay behind. Dr. Asolo's lips purse and she says, "See me after class, Ash." Camille's victorious smile makes me flush and drop into my seat, head down.

After ninety minutes discussing feminist literature and social inequality in the 1800s, Asolo gives me a serious talking-to. One more tardy and I get JPs. I try to explain Becca was holding court, but Asolo is having nothing of it.

"Personal responsibility is the backbone of Goode, Ash. Never blame others for your own decisions."

Ouch.

Once I'm fully chastised and allowed to leave, I find Camille standing in the hall, her ever-present soldiers Vanessa and Piper at arms.

"You need to be careful with Becca, Ash. She's using you."

"I know how to take care of myself."

"Not with her, you don't. She's not as great as everyone says. I know some things. My sister told me—"

"Give me a break, Camille. I have to get to the lab."

I swear, she stamps her tiny little foot. The Converse high-tops she's wearing cushion the noise. "You know, Ash, at some point, you're going to have to choose. The seniors will graduate, and you'll be left with nothing if you don't forge some real relationships with your own class."

I am bloody tired of being scolded by this girl.

"You assume I want a real relationship with you, Camille. Just because we're roommates doesn't mean we're friends. Stop telling me what to do, how to think, and we'll be just fine."

"You're going to regret this. Mark my words."

She takes off through the glass-fronted trolley toward Old East, Piper and Vanessa in her wake—eerily similar to Becca and the twins, I realize—and I go the opposite direction, toward the computer lab, shaking my head at the childish argument.

My whole life, people have tried to get me to take sides. I'm tired of it.

Becca is at our table in the computer lab, waiting for me with a smile.

She's using you.

Probably so. Everyone in my life has been using me one way or another. What is one more? At least this one has power.

I know some things.

This is murkier ground. The innuendo in Camille's tone is clear. There is something more to Becca than meets the eye.

Part of me wants to scoff. The other, the wolf brain inside me, the survivor, knows I should find out what my new friend is capable of.

23

THE REJECTION

After Medea's tutorial, I spend the rest of the day avoiding both Becca and my suitemates, attending classes, scribbling notes, trying not to be called upon. Trying to disappear. To stay off the seniors' and the sophomores' radars.

I end up decamping to the library, ostensibly trying to catch up on my work. Dramas aside, I am already behind and I'm only just beginning to get a feel for the rhythms of Goode. The library is like a sanctuary. A safe place. It is cozy, wood-paneled with inlaid parquet wood floors. It seems to be one of the few places on campus that hasn't been renovated, though it is modern, well stocked, with a history section that doesn't quite rival the Bodleian but is impressive nonetheless. Private cubicles have a soft armchair in addition to the dark wood desks, scratched and worn, the relics of an earlier age, before Goode shed its past like a snake's skin and became the shining monument on the hill to all-girls education.

The many books stashed within its walls are friends in a way none of the girls on my hall will ever be.

I spend the evening in a private cubicle, working, until Ms. Morton, the librarian, comes to kick me out. Now I have no choice but to face Camille. Détente is necessary.

I wind my way back to Main, walking quickly through the trolleys. They unnerve me, for some reason, these glass tunnels suspended in midair. It is deeply dark outside in a way Oxford never was. On my floor, I creep to the small kitchen, fill my water bottle, then slink down the hall. It is relatively quiet; everyone is in their rooms. Some music plays behind closed doors, unidentifiable pop screeching, but I am alone. All the better. Perhaps this will be my routine—classes, a snack, the library. If I can make it through the term with as little engagement as possible with my suitemates, all the better.

I stop in front of our room. The door to the storeroom across from us is cracked open slightly. Why?

I hesitate, then cross and lean in, listening. For what, I don't know. Voices? Breathing? Vanessa and Camille, plotting as they've been each night?

This is silly. I reach for the knob to pull the door closed, but as I do, the scent hits me. Home. It smells like…home. Like freshly brewed tea and damp wool and my mother's signature perfume, the scent I used to bathe myself in when I was little, when my mother would be careless enough to leave the bottle on the dressing table, finely cut purple glass with an old-fashioned ball pump made of velvet. Gardenia and civet. Lush. Unmistakably female.

It is so intense, this memory, so immediate, I slam my fist into the door and it swings open with a creak. I enter the room, eyes searching. It is dark, cold, and empty.

"Mum?"

But there is nothing.

This is ridiculous. The room is no different than the first time I saw it, full of old paint cans and drapes, hardwood flooring and ladders stacked against the walls. Boxes and crates, covered in paint-dappled sheets. A storage room. A leftover.

But the scent lingers.

I shake my head, trying to get it out of my nose. Whatever am I doing? My mother is dead. And I don't believe in ghosts.

Camille isn't in the room again. Whatever. I grab my bathroom gear, hurry down the hall, wash my face, brush my teeth, braid my hair, and am back in less than five minutes.

I am unsettled. I can't fall asleep. And when I finally drift off, I dream of death. The slack jaw. The harsh scent. The blankness in my mother's eyes.

The blood.

I wake to the sound of weeping. It takes me a few minutes to realize the room is still empty, and it is my own pillow drenched in tears.

Camille misses breakfast, but when I go back to the room to switch books between computer and English, she is there, sitting at her desk, twisting a curl in her fingers, staring out the window. Pale, washed-out in the sunlight. Black circles under her eyes, the heating pad clutched to her stomach.

"Are you okay?"

"I'm perfectly fine."

Lies, lies, lies. Why not? After last night's little trip down memory lane, I'm feeling...vulnerable.

"I was worried when you didn't come back."

"I slept in Vanessa's room. I didn't want to wake you."

"You want to tell me what's really going on?"

Her eyes fill with tears but she shakes her head. "It's all good. I told you, my time of the month is rough."

I'm surprised to find myself feeling sorry for her. "If you ever want to talk—"

"I. Don't. So. Stop. Asking."

"Sod off then." I grab my books and leave. Screw her. I'm not here to make friends. I'm here to get the Goode stamp of approval. This is all that matters. The petty bullshit of my suite-mates isn't important.

Or so I think.

JUNE

Oxford, England

24

THE PROPOSAL

They are sitting together at one end of the dining room table when I drag in, high, drunk, dirty. I've come through planning to sneak up the back stairs to my room. This is a place I don't expect them to assemble, in either position or companionship. I don't know how they've managed it, how they knew I was coming home, how they timed it. Surely, they haven't been here waiting for two days—no, someone from the village reported that I was heading their way.

They look ridiculous, eclipsed by the grandness of the room, awkward, the two of them snugged together like this.

Mind, our dining room table might be a bit different than yours; it seats forty comfortably, forty-six in a pinch. The room is massive, echoing when empty, but the acoustics are perfect for a house party. The dark oak wainscoted walls are covered in priceless oils of hunting scenes. From forest to table, the Carr family philosophy.

It strikes me as funny, this. I, too, come from forest to table now.

Damien Carr has a reputation—likes to keep to himself, holds his own counsel, does everything with stiff-upper-lip discretion, which is why his clients love him. Why the Queen knighted the sick fuck "for service to the British banking system."

My mother, on the other hand, good old Sylvia, newly monied and married to an icon, loves to show it off. She takes full advantage of the Carr treasures to hold lavish feasts for important and interesting people.

This space used to be the site of so much fun. I'd watch the festivities from the anteroom, getting in Dorsey's way as she sent up the courses. Laughter, the clinking of china and goblets, the room growing more uproarious as the cellar was raided again and again.

He went along with it for a while. Then he put a stop to the parties. My mother cried and whimpered and begged, but Damien is like granite, implacable when he makes up his mind.

I've drifted. My parents are staring at me. My mother wears a semblance of a smile—the opening salvo. I laugh. I might be a little too high.

"Ashlyn, please sit down."

I've been sleeping rough for two nights, bunking on the floor of a friend's flat in the village. A rat has gnawed the edge of my messenger bag. I don't move. The Molly, whilst making me warm and fuzzy, has my feet planted.

My father gives it a try.

"Ashlyn, I shouldn't have lost my temper. I apologize." This is said stiffly, and I know he doesn't mean it. There's a reason he's seeking détente. Why?

I stay standing but sway a bit, toward the closest chair. Finally, I collapse into it. My legs are tired. I am so, so tired.

"Your mother and I have discussed this at length, and we believe it's time for you to go away to school. There's a lovely all-girls spot in America. It's called The Goode School. It's for children of the elite."

"I won't go." The words are out before I have a thought. I have no desire to go away to school. I barely go here anymore, why in the world would I agree to go to America and be locked away inside with a bevy of squealing quims?

"You don't have a choice. You are going. It's been settled with the school already. You must do a formal interview with the headmistress. We can set up a Skype call, she's agreed to it since you don't live close enough for an in-person visit in time."

I shake my head and he holds up a hand.

"You aren't happy here. I understand how hard your life has been—" *oh, the sarcasm, Daddy, so appropriate just now* "—being the daughter of two parents who love you very much and only want what's best for you."

Mum launches her gambit. "You've left us no choice, Ashlyn. The drinking, the drugs, the running away, it will stop now. You will go to America, which gets you far, far away from us, which is all you really want, as you've told us so many times. You'll be among peers, girls who are just as intelligent as you. You won't be bored by the provincial school districts anymore. It's like a college, really, you choose your path of instruction. This is for the best."

I have zero intention of following this course but I need all the information I can get.

"And when is this blessed occurrence taking place?"

"You leave in August. Term begins earlier there."

August. It is June now. I'll have to work fast. There's only one way for me to truly be free.

I have two months to plan how they die.

"Time passes, and little by little everything that we have spoken in falsehood becomes true."

—Marcel Proust

OCTOBER

Marchburg, Virginia

25

THE RISE

It doesn't take long to realize Becca's attention has given me the greatest gift—the cachet of approval from a senior. Why have I, a lowly transfer sophomore, of no real provenance, been singled out?

It is an instant anointment.

I employ the one tool in my arsenal—silence. It only adds to the mystique.

Who knew? I thought lies had power until I saw what silence could do.

Within days, Britishisms are popping up on our hall. Girls are nipping to the loo, sitting down for a cuppa, buggering off. Loosely styled fluffy ponytails appear. Boxes arrive in the mail room, and soon half the girls are wearing Dr. Martens boots with their chapel dresses. The infirmary runs out of Band-Aids for tender ankles, and the dean threatens to tighten the dress code; though shoes have never been on the list of required conformity like our white button-down shirts and green plaid skirts, seeing her school transform so quickly is disconcerting.

Despite my efforts to fly under the radar, and the reticence of my suitemates—no, let's call it what it is, I've been openly cast aside—I am becoming a popular student. I regularly field invitations to join in—meals, game nights, gossip sessions in the sewing circle, walks on the grounds. The girls of Goode want to get to know me, but I am enjoying being unknowable. I hang out in the library, night after night, busting my tail to keep up. It's safer that way.

The rumors abound, I hear them whispered as I walk by—I'm the daughter of rock stars on tour, or a Scandinavian princess, or the child of a famous actor, or even, maybe, the illegitimate child of the president. (This last is met with laughter, but still, who knows?) I could be anyone, from anywhere, and without the proven tracking system recording every move of the rest of my peers, duck face smiles and puppy dog nose shots taken from yachts and beaches and ski slopes, anything could be true.

They are children—sophisticated children, yes, but children nonetheless. The magic of possibility is still their favorite pastime, and since many regularly brush up against fame and fortune, live these privileged lives themselves when not stuck under the nursery rules of Dean Westhaven, anything goes.

That I look at my feet and shake my head whenever the subject of my family arises only feeds the flames. Let's be honest. I have no idea how to handle all of this attention. Ironically, my natural aloofness makes me seem unattainable, which means the girls want me more.

The days spin on. It is October now. Rain covers the campus, cold and drizzly, and when I'm not dodging rumors and false offers of friendship, I almost feel comfortable, like I'm home.

It's hard to believe I've been here a matter of weeks. I'm feeling less like a cornered animal and more like a student. Even though some of the girls still whisper behind their hands when

I walk by, thanks to Camille and her minions, it's more often the freshmen, now, who are agog by anyone in the upper classes.

I haven't yet been left behind in my schoolwork, and naturally, I'm excelling in my computer tutorials. I'm working harder than I've ever worked before to keep up with the rest.

Goode's teachers are strict and professional, and they seem to approve of me with an enthusiasm I have rarely, if ever, seen from authority figures. They encourage and push, enlighten and calmly correct. The dean, too, has been unfailingly kind, always stopping to ask after me or to bestow a compliment. "I hear the paper you wrote for Dr. Asolo was wonderful" or "Dr. Medea tells me you're coming along quite nicely in your tutorials. Keep up the good work." Every once in a while, "Have you thought more about your piano lessons?" At that, I always shake my head.

I see Westhaven sometimes, in the windows of the attics, staring out at the quad with something akin to longing. She seems to spend more time up there than in her office, which is strange, but everything about this place is strange. Strange, and oddly wonderful. The dean is so young to be in control of this school. Only thirty-five. Thirty-five and in charge for ten years. No wonder the school feels so current, so innovative. She is a startling figure to watch, with her elegance and shyness.

She reminds me of someone. Myself, perhaps.

Though the curriculum and mores are forward-thinking, Goode itself is mired in the past. Like home, I can feel the history emanating from the walls, but since almost every building has been renovated, at first glance, it's all crisp and clean. The basic architecture hampers adding windows or opening walls, but everything that can be is painted in the simple dove gray of our dorm room. The white wainscotings and moldings are kept polished, the parquet and marble floors are buffed daily until they shine. Everything reflects light, from above, from below.

The school is elegantly outfitted, no expense spared. Expensive and old, and for some reason, the two don't go together.

When I walk the corridors, it's so easy to imagine the way the school used to look—the wood floors battered and gouged, the dark corners of the rooms cobwebby, the drapes worn thin and shiny with the passage of time. As if there is a veil to be lifted. Maybe it's because I come from a city with exceptionally old buildings, but everything about Goode's shiny surface belies its true nature. There are echoes here, of the past. The heart of the school, written into the remodeled walls.

And the grounds are glorious. Especially now, in the fall, the combination of deciduous and evergreens gives the ground a multicolored show. The heat has broken, so whenever I have a free moment, I am outdoors, wandering. There are plenty of hiding places scattered throughout the campus.

The Selden Arboretum is a personal favorite. Despite Piper's dire warnings, I find it a quiet, restful space. There is a spot I favor above all, a small clearing, a tiny fairy meadow, where I like to read and smoke the occasional cigarette from the pack I have stashed in my closet. Such a move is risky, but I'm not afraid. Goode respects my need for privacy, for some reason. That could be Becca's doing, but I try not to think about it. Becca is fine. She's been very nice, very solicitous.

There have been a few more stomps, and the entire school is getting ready to celebrate Odds and Evens weekend, a tradition that dates back to the origins of the school. Some of the sillier girls like to tell stories of the ghosts and legends, but for the most part, I have tuned them out. My world at home was full of these tales, they don't frighten or titillate me at all. But I'm excited to do my part for the celebration—the sophomores are the sister class to the seniors and are expected to decorate the campus. Becca told me that last year, they made hundreds of water balloons and put them everywhere, and the seniors got soaked every time they opened a door or stepped through an archway. The idea of Becca being drenched makes me laugh; I wonder what sort of prank the sophomores will cook up.

Camille: there is still silent weeping in the night, but I leave it alone. If and when Camille wants to talk, she will. Lord knows she talks about everything else. We have set rules in the room—study hours and talking hours. And when it's talking time, Camille rarely ceases, waxing on about nothing, leaving me to find quiet elsewhere. I half think she does it so I'll vacate our room.

Piper: when she can be separated from her pack, she has proven to be an enjoyable companion. Camille and Vanessa are thick as thieves, and while Piper is their third, there are times when she steps out of their coterie and hangs out with me. She is quiet and wily, smart as a whip, and disinclined toward meaningless gossip, preferring to wait until she has something truly earth-shattering to talk about. She likes to share clothes and shoes, and I often find her draped over our couch, waiting for me to come back from class so we can go to the shops in town.

Vanessa: we will never be friends. There is something in the way she looks at me, head cocked to the side, assessing with those dark, intense eyes. Always assessing. At meals, or when I'm in the library studying, taking walks along the paths that meander through campus, at our yoga sessions and study halls, every time I look up, Vanessa is watching. It's creepy, the attention she pays to my every move, yes. But I ignore her. Which seems to piss her off even more.

There have been no more strange scents or cracked-open doors. Those things, I believe, were in my head.

It's been a successful few weeks. All is nominal. I'm fitting in well enough, I've kept the lying to a minimum. We've had a lovely memorial service for Muriel Grassley in the chapel, and the matter of her untimely demise has been put to rest. I've managed to put my complicity in her death aside. Muriel should have read the label. She shouldn't have relied on my word alone. Don't get me wrong, I do feel bad, but I don't see myself as responsible.

A bullet dodged.

So why, eating my perfectly scrambled eggs with the seniors, as I've been doing every morning since the first summons, listening to their nonsense, staring out at the mist-blurred trees, do I have the worst sense it's all about to come off the rails?

26

THE OUTING

The babble of two hundred teenage girls is normally a proper distraction, but breakfast today is a muted affair. There was a stomp last night, waking everyone at midnight. Because of the rain, fog wisps around the boxwoods and everyone is stuck inside. Three days of gray skies now, and the girls of Goode miss the sun, which makes them grouchy. The entire room feels off. Tense. Watchful.

I have been banished back to my table for Odds and Evens preparations. It's strange, I don't feel as if I belong here anymore. With the sophomores, I mean. I am Becca's mascot, the puppy at her heels. I'm no dummy, I know how this game is played. Her protection is power personified, and I have been taking full advantage.

But today, she's sent me down.

Camille and the others don't have the gumption to deny me a seat at their table, not while Becca watches.

I settle in. No one speaks.

We are finishing our orange juice when a *thwack* sounds by my left elbow. Our waitron's back is already turned as she moves away, the delivery made.

I glance down to see the same creamy envelope and steady, artistic hand I was presented with the day of my summons. My heart does a backflip. I reach for it, but quickly realize this time, the envelope bears Camille's name.

Camille's.

"It's for you."

Camille's china-blue eyes shine. Hands shaking, she examines the envelope from all angles, cracks open the wax seal, and draws out the note.

Fourth floor. 10:00 p.m.

The same instructions I received. Camille looks up, pupils dilated in pleasure. A small smile plays on her lips. I can practically read her mind.

It is so good to be singled out. This could make me at Goode, like Ash's audience did for her.

Vanessa, face twisted in anger, snatches the note away.

"Who did you two blow to get in Becca Curtis's good graces?"

And...we're back to normal. I shoot down my orange juice and gather my things.

"Shut up, Vanessa. You're just jealous."

"You and I are going to have words soon, Ash. Or should I say, Ashlyn?"

One extra syllable and I feel the blood drain from my head. "My name is Ash. I told you before."

"Oh? Funny. I thought your name was Ashlyn Carr. Daughter of Sylvia and Damien Carr. The late Lady Sylvia and Sir Damien Carr. Or am I mistaken?"

Vanessa's smile is feral. I fight to keep my breathing steady.

"Wherever did you hear that?"

"Ooh, it's true, isn't it?" Piper says. "Does the dean know you're using a fake name?"

Camille is shaking her head, both hands up. "Stop, you guys. Stop right now. We agreed..."

Everyone is staring at me. All the students in the vicinity have frozen, forks halfway to mouths. They are all listening. They all know. Camille's words—*we agreed*—how long have they suspected the truth? Why did they go searching for information?

You should have told them something, given them something. But I didn't want to lie about this, not with the Honor Code front and center like a matador's cape.

"Report yourself, or we'll do it for you," Vanessa says. She has clearly been planning to drop this bomb at the perfect moment. Now that she has the upper hand, I'm hardly surprised to see her turn the screw.

Panic floods my system, my vision blurs. Adrenaline or tears, I don't know which, but I'm going to fall apart in a moment if I don't do something. I can't stand here in the dining room denying my parentage, that *would* be a lie, and if they know the truth, lying about it *will* get me into trouble.

How did they find out?

What else do they know?

I think back to Becca's request for me to hack the dean's email... Did she find someone else to do it for her? Was Becca looking for information on me, not herself? Oh, bollocks. Great big bloody bollocks.

I bolt. There's nothing else for me to do. My bag slams against my hip as I run, the sharp edge of my laptop digging into the soft flesh of my thigh with every step. I don't care about the pain, I just want to get away. It's too much. I don't want to do this anymore. Balancing my old life and new is just too hard.

I *knew* something felt wrong.

The dining room is on the west edge of campus and leads to

the arboretum. This is the refuge I seek now. My precious little fairy glen. I'll hide here, maybe until dark, maybe forever. The trees, rattling in the breeze as their leaves begin to fade, still provide a great deal of cover. Shelter.

The arboretum is dark and cool. Quiet. The rain has stopped. I find a mostly dry patch of grass and moss under the spreading branches of my favorite hemlock. Whip the strap of my bag over my head and sink to the damp ground, wiping away the tears from my cheeks.

I have been so exposed the past few weeks, like a raw nerve ending on a sore tooth, being prodded and looked at and whispered about. Whatever was I thinking coming here? I want to go home. Back to the rolling hills of Oxfordshire.

Sadly, this isn't possible. I have no home, not anymore. No parents. No life back in England. I'm stuck here. I am officially under the dean's wing, her responsibility.

I pause my crying jag.

I could go to Westhaven. But what will the dean say? What will she do? "The girls found out the truth, so sorry, Ash, we've done our best to keep your past hidden, chin up, we'll get you through this."

Like that will help.

I have an overwhelming urge for a cigarette. There are three left in the pack I smuggled in, hidden inside the toe of my flats. It would mean going back to the dorm, though, and I'm not ready to face them, not until I get myself back together. Figure out how to handle this mess.

"Fuck!"

"Language," comes a quiet voice, and Becca Curtis steps around the trunk of the tree.

27

THE SENIOR

Ash looks so fragile, so alone. To have your private world laid bare in front of your friends—Becca knows how hard this is. Ash is clearly a rookie when it comes to having her dirty laundry aired; Becca lives with it every day. Not only under the scrutiny of her mother, last summer, Becca became a Twitter meme for one of her stupid antics. A crazy night in Georgetown that got totally out of hand was turned into a great, arty, black-and-white short film called *Vomitous Key Bridgius*. It was posted on Snapchat and TikTok, where it was amusing for the short amount of time it existed, but instead of disappearing into the ether like everyone else's snaps, someone captured it, posted it to Twitter, and suddenly, it was everywhere. Even the *Washington Post* did a story, the perils of teen drinking, blah, blah. She was mortified, and her mother… Well, suffice it to say the senator wasn't well pleased. Becca had been grounded for weeks.

Becca wants to give Ash a hug but knows she'll be rebuffed.

Instead, she sits, digs two cigarettes out of a pack, and offers one to Ash.

After a moment, Ash accepts, and the small spark of light in her eyes emboldens Becca. She's dealing with a rebel after all. She knew it. Could sense it in her bones. Ash has been swanning about for weeks now, head high, looking neither right nor left, ignoring the whispers and the innuendos, but at heart, she wants to run free. Becca feels the same way.

She lights both their cigarettes, then takes a long drag off hers and blows the smoke in a smooth stream toward the branch above. The nicotine is calming.

"Bad day?"

"The worst," Ash replies.

"I'm very sorry about your father. And your mother. It's horrible, what happened."

Ash stares at the ground, takes a puff. "How long have you known?"

"Since the first week of term."

"God," Ash says, voice breathy, accent stark on the one-syllable word, staring up at the tree branches to blink back sudden tears. "And everyone else?"

"It's been trickling through the ranks the past week or so. Your buddy Vanessa has been waiting to spring it on you."

"Brilliant. She's never liked me. We don't get on."

"They actually brought it to me last week as an Honor Code violation and I shut them down. Told them it wasn't their business, and it certainly wasn't a violation. I explained you have a right to privacy, especially in a situation such as this."

"Bollocks." But there's no heat in the exclamation, just resignation. A girl beaten, her gorgeous shell cracked open to reveal the soft, vulnerable innards. Becca resists the urge to run her hand down Ash's golden ponytail.

They smoke in silence for a few minutes, until the cigarettes are down to the filters. Becca scrapes hers in the moss to kill the cherry, does the same with Ash's, then carves out a small hole and buries the butts in the dirt.

"Why *are* you trying to hide it?" Becca finally asks. "I mean, it's not like it's your fault. No one is going to blame you for their bad choices."

"Why are you being nice to me?" Ash replies instead of answering. Her voice is a little wild, like she's about to become hysterical.

"You intrigue me," Becca says, then kicks herself. "That sounded weird. You're not like everyone else here. You're different. You try to hide your intelligence by being meek in your classes. You just listen and absorb everything around you. You don't want people to know who you are. You don't want to show off who you are. There's a humility to you, and considering the wealth and station you come from, it's surprising."

"I'm just a stupid sophomore with dead parents."

There are tears now, and Becca doesn't try to comfort, lets her cry it out. She has the sense if she tries to touch Ash, she'll go up in smoke or run screaming from the forest. Ash is shy, gentle. Sweet natured, behind the boots and the hair and the insouciant attitude. Becca has been observing the girl for weeks now, watching how she always lets the other girls go first, how she is content to let others take credit for her work. In the cutthroat world of Goode, this is unusual. They are taught to be assertive and confident, to debate and push and scheme. Cooperation is important, yes, but strength and individuality are rewarded. Ash's strength is quiet. But even granite can crack under the right sort of pressure.

"I get down myself sometimes," Becca confides. "The pressure of being a senator's daughter... The expectations are off the charts. I don't even like politics. But every summer, I'm interning on the Hill or going to ambassadorial camp, and every break I have to work in my mother's office, talking to constituents. It's mind-numbingly awful."

"What would you rather do?" The words are soft, spoken from behind a curtain of hair where Ash's omnipresent ponytail has fallen in front of her face.

"Anything. I hate DC. I hate the noise, the people, the self-righteousness. They're all so fucking smug. They pretend they run the world, but it's all nonsense. I'd like..."

"What?" Ash is looking at her now, her nose red as a cherry, eyes swollen.

"I'd like to move somewhere in the wilderness. Design an eco-friendly farm, live off the grid. It sounds stupid when I say it out loud, but I watched this show once, where they built a cabin in the wilds of Alaska. It seemed perfect."

"It sounds nice. I understand the desire to get away."

"I could reinvent myself if I didn't have my mother breathing down my neck. Oh, so sorry, Ash. That was insensitive of me."

"Don't worry about it."

But the dialogue is over. Becca is genuinely stricken to see Ash has retreated into that quiet, self-contained shell again.

"Do you want another?" Becca hands Ash a second smoke, lights it. Watches her inhale and blow, hard, like she can dispel all the negativity through the haze. She coughs lightly, hand over her mouth, polite. So proper.

"What do you want with Camille tonight?"

"I don't. That wasn't my summons."

"You don't like her, do you?"

"Camille? She's...not terribly bright. A lot like her sister. Emily was head girl last year, and was very full of herself."

"I think she's okay." The defense is half-hearted at best.

"No, you don't. You can't stand her, or her little dogs, either. I see how you recoil when they come near you. They are never going to be your mates."

At the terrible British accent, Ash laughs, and Becca's heart does a tiny dance.

"We haven't had any real issues, she's been decent to me. For the most part."

"So you think. Has she been openly mean?"

"Just at the beginning of term. She was sick and wouldn't let me help. Went to Vanessa. The two of them… Anyway, it doesn't matter." Ash takes a thoughtful drag. "But Camille wanted to take me to Honor Court about this? Allow me to remove the knife from between my ribs. Oh, yes, I can't reach it, it's in my back. Could you help?"

Becca spits out a laugh, and Ash smiles shyly. Clever boots, this girl.

"Speaking of, I did want to raise this issue with you. It's not an Honor Code violation per se, but you really should make an appointment and tell the dean that word is out. She'll appreciate the heads-up. We don't want her put in any awkward situations."

"Okay. I will. We thought it best to try to keep my family drama off the radar. I should have changed my first name, too, but I was worried… It was stupid, trying to pretend everything was okay. I suppose it was inevitable someone would find out about…their deaths. I never thought so many people would care, truth be told. I mean, I didn't. Not about my father, at least."

"You weren't close?"

"No, not at all."

There is a sharpness in her tone that stings Becca's heart.

"I'm sorry." Becca reaches out a hand and tucks a few strands of loose hair behind the younger girl's ear. "So sorry," she says quietly.

Ash freezes, shoulders suddenly tight, then unfolds herself from the ground like a young crane, dropping the last of the cigarette and grinding it out with the toe of her boot.

"Listen, Becca, you've been really kind today, I appreciate it. But I need to be alone now. Thanks."

Ash takes off into the arboretum, and Becca watches her go, the long, lean body so perfect, only interrupted by the wet bottom of her gown, the damp darkness cutting her in half. She shouldn't be alone in the forest, but it's daytime, she's heading toward town and Becca thinks Ash will run from her if she tries to stop her.

She's glad they had a chance to chat. She's been waffling about what to do tonight, but no longer.

Decision made, she pops a piece of gum in her mouth, sprays some perfume a foot away and walks through the cloud to help dissipate the smoke scent she knows will cling to her clothes otherwise.

There is much to do. Much to do.

She whistles as she walks back to the school.

28

THE HATE

Look at them. Sitting so sweetly in the moss.

They fit together so well.

They could be sisters.

They could be lovers. They probably are. She's probably been fucking this girl and there's nothing I can do to stop it.

Stupid girl.

This can't go on, not anymore.

She can't get close to anyone, or everything will be destroyed. And I'm not ready for things to go south yet.

29

THE FLIRTATION

I haven't been alone in town before. I shouldn't be cutting, there's a computer tutorial this morning, and Dr. Medea will be hacked off when he realizes I stood him up. But I don't want to go back. Not now. I can't face them, leering and curious. And Becca made me feel weird. Touching me like that, she was almost tender. Like a real friend. A close friend.

And we are not friends. Not by a long shot. No, I expect Becca just wants to be nosy and find out more so she can use it against me somehow.

It's cold and damp, the wind picking up as I walk down the street. There's no question I'm skipping class; even though I've bundled my gown into my bag, I'm wearing my Goode School uniform. And I don't fit in. Even now, with the uniform screaming *I am one of you*, I am apart, solitary.

I wander from storefront to storefront—the hairdresser, the dress shop, the laundry, the pub—until the rain starts again.

The coffee shop where the girls like to hang out on the weekend while they do their laundry, The Java Hut, is three doors down from where I stand. I hurry in, shaking out my ponytail.

The air is redolent of coffee beans. It is such an American smell. I'm used to the must of old buildings packed with books and antiques and carpets that have seen too many wars to count, and the wafting scent of scones overlaid with tea, but not coffee. Wet wool and cold stone and spilled lager and blood, the scents of my people.

The coffee shop is empty. It's like no one in town exists except for when the girls come to spend their money in the shops. It's creepy, Marchburg, creepy and strange. The buildings feel shallow against the two-lane roads, like in a Western movie, just fronts with no rooms inside, the streets almost empty as if the residents know a shoot-out is about to take place. Or rabid dogs are going to come screaming around the corner, or hordes of spiders will start carousing down the storefront walls.

My imagination is in overdrive today. A shiver passes through me and I debate just heading back to school, taking my lumps. As I told Becca, it was bound to happen, the girls finding out about my parents, no way I was going to be able to keep it quiet forever. Still, I'm overcome with disappointment. All I've done is try to keep people away so they won't find out about my life in England. Now even that's crumbling at my feet. I've failed in the one stupid thing I'm supposed to be managing perfectly—keeping my past to myself.

And Becca… Why is she being so nice? What does she really want? There might be a true overture of friendship there, but I'm only a sophomore. Becca is the shining light of the school. I'm nothing, or trying to be. We don't make sense as friends, not in the least.

I feel eyes on me, whirl around, and almost leap out of my skin.

My driver—the one who brought me to Marchburg from the airport—is standing by the counter of the coffee shop, smiling.

"Hey," he says.

My heart is cantering away from the sudden adrenaline rush. I put a hand to my chest. Is he following me? "Jesus, you scared me. What are you doing here?"

"What am *I* doing here? I work here. What are *you* doing here? Shouldn't you be in class?"

"I thought you were a driver."

"I thought you were a student."

"I needed a break."

"Fair enough. The Westhavens own most of the businesses in town, and I work for the family. Which means I'm whatever they need me to be. Today, I'm a delivery boy and barista. Would you like a coffee? Macchiato? Flat white? Or tea? You're from England, surely you'd prefer tea. All your meetings with the Queen and all." As he speaks, he moves around the counter, turning expectantly. "Tea, yes?"

I have the overwhelming urge to burst into tears again. This day is confusing, to say the least, and he's just called me out on my earlier lie. "Yes. Tea. Thank you. How come I've never seen you on campus?"

"Because you scurry around with your head down, your bag clutched to your chest like you're carrying diamonds inside. If you ever looked up, really looked up, you'd have seen me. I mean, I've seen you."

There is something in the way he says it that makes a tiny thrill run through me. I've been noticed by this man.

Then another thought, and my face flushes. "Wait. Have you been watching me?"

"You're very watchable, Ash Carlisle."

He grins, lopsided, and I realize he is very, very cute. A small thrum starts in my chest. I wasn't wrong, he is flirting. He moves around the small service area, grabbing the sachet of tea, pouring out the water, adding two biscuits to the saucer, with economy and grace, like a panther.

"Here you go, Ash. On the house. Want some sugar? You look like you could use it."

"No, thank you."

I accept the cup and the biscuits and sit at the table farthest from the door.

"Are you enjoying school?"

He's wearing a name tag that says Rumi. Rumi, that's right. Not Ruly or Rudy. I like Rumi much better. I smile—charming Ash, flirty Ash—and he joins me at the table.

"School is lovely. It's only…"

"Word's out about your folks, I presume?"

"How do you know that?"

He leans back, balancing the chair on two legs, arms behind his head, flexing the ropy muscles, the biceps defined. His shirt has ridden up and a line of dark hair disappears into his jeans. It seems so intimate, this, and I know I'm blushing. He's so casual about his sexuality. The images come alarmingly fast—white sheets, dark hair, the twisting of legs. A flutter in my groin.

"Don't be so prickly, princess. I was in the dining hall this morning, doing a delivery. I overheard. You caused quite the stir, running out like that."

I push the tea away with a heavy sigh. "This is ridiculous. Why does everyone care so much about who I am and where I come from? It's not like their parents aren't rich or important. Some of them are dead, too."

"You really are self-centered, aren't you?"

"Excuse me?"

"Poor little me, everyone's so fascinated by me."

I don't know whether to laugh or slap him. I settle for frowning and taking a sip of my tea. It's lousy, truly terrible, but I don't tell him.

"Feeling like you're in a fishbowl, princess?"

"Stop calling me that. I'm not a princess."

"Tell that to the man who has to work for a living."

"I have nothing. Nothing. As soon as I'm out, I'll be working, too."

"You have the school. The dean. Your friends. Your family's money. Don't talk to me about having nothing until you understand what it means."

Twice in one day, attacked. Forget this.

"You think listening to the rumors gives you some insight? You don't know me. Thanks for the tea."

30

THE REVELATION

I take off toward the coffee shop door, but Rumi leaps to his feet, imploring. "Wait, Ash. I'm sorry. I didn't mean to be a dick."

"Yes, you did. You wanted me to feel sorry for you because you have to work around all these little rich girls. We all make our choices, Rumi. You've made yours. And I've made mine."

"Stop. Really. Sit down. It's pouring. I'll drive you back."

"Oh, my God, no. I'll get in much more trouble if I do that."

"You're worried about getting in trouble?"

I pause. Am I, really? "No. It's not like they'll do anything awful to me. JPs. Saturday school. I'll probably end up folding laundry or sorting the costumes in the theater."

"Then stick around. Drink your tea."

"It's terrible," I blurt, slapping a hand over my mouth.

Rumi laughs. "What did I do wrong?"

"You scalded it. And the teabag is old."

"An espresso, then? I opened a new bag of beans an hour ago."

He makes two, sets the tiny cups on the table, one for me, one for him. I take the sugar this time, drop it in, stir. Rumi waits patiently until I take a sip and nod approvingly before touching his own cup. His fingers are long, the nails clipped short, and I want to touch them. I want them to touch me.

I don't understand myself. I'm furious with him, but I also want to see what it would feel like if he put his arms around me. He narrows perfectly from shoulder to waist. We'd fit well together.

Get a grip, Ash.

"Talk to me. I'm a good listener," he says, sitting again.

What do I have to lose? "The coroner's court found my father's death a 'misadventure.' That's the official story."

"Makes it sounds like he was a pirate on the high seas. What's the unofficial story?"

"A pirate. Oh, yes. He was. Until he took a handful of pills. When my mother found him dead in the dining room, she freaked out and shot herself."

"Damn."

"I found them."

"Double damn."

"We'd had a fight earlier in the day. We fought all the time, he and I. He…" I gesture to my cheek and Rumi's lips thin as he grasps what I'm saying.

"Bastard."

I shrug. "You can understand why I don't want everyone at school talking about it. It's bad enough they're dead, and in such a splashy way. But these girls, they live for the details. They'll be after me nonstop. And I can't stop seeing it. Reliving it. They were so… And my mum, too…"

Shit, now I'm crying again. Twice in one hour, on two different shoulders. Am I so starved for compassion? Or have I kept everyone at arm's length for so long I don't know how to properly connect with people anymore?

Rumi hands over a napkin.

I gather myself, wipe my eyes. "Sorry."

"Don't be. You've been through a lot. But you have to give the girls here a chance. They all come from some sort of dysfunction. Privileged people are all kinds of fucked up, and they fuck up their kids. Honestly, if you'd just been up-front about it, they wouldn't be watching you like hawks. Why'd you change your name?"

"I wanted to forget. I wanted to run away and forget everything. It was stupid, I know. But the dean agreed it was for the best. We thought it would give me time and space to heal."

"Well, Ash, your time is up. You're not going to be able to run away anymore. They know, and it's best to fess up and get on with things."

I drain the cup. There are sugar crystals creating sweet espresso mud at the bottom. I resist the urge to lick them. He's giving me good advice.

I turn the spotlight on him, instead. "Why are you here? In Marchburg, I mean?"

"I'm a Russian mole. I've had plastic surgery and am hiding out on top of this mountain."

"Stop. I'm serious."

"You really don't know?"

"No."

"You're probably the only one." His voice sounds inexplicably sad. He rubs a hand over his dark curls. "You've heard about the murder in Selden Arboretum, haven't you? Ten years ago?"

"I was warned never to go there alone. It's haunted."

Rumi spits a mirthless laugh. "Haunted. Right. It was my father who committed the crime."

Now it's my turn to be taken aback. "You mean, he murdered that girl?"

"He did. I was just a little kid at the time, only ten." His dark eyes grow distant, sad. "My mother split when I was a baby, and my dad, he wasn't ever totally right in the head after. The night…the night it happened, the police came to the house, broke down the door, found him in the living room with—"

Flustered, he slams the rest of his espresso. I recall what Piper said. …*he carved out her eyes and took them home with him. They found them on his mantel. Really freaky shit.*

Holy mother.

"Anyway, he went to jail, and I went to the state. Foster care sucked, so I emancipated when I was sixteen and came back to Marchburg. Dean Westhaven hired me on the spot, set me up in one of the little cabins on the edge of the forest. She's always been cool. Some of the parents balked when they found out, but she said it was her duty to the school and to the town, that I was as much a victim of my father as Ellie Robertson had been that night. She's a good lady, the dean."

"Wow."

"You sound downright American, Ash."

"'Wow' is a universal exclamation, Rumi."

"I guess so. My point is, we aren't so different, you and I. We both had horrible fathers, and we're both trying to escape our pasts." He glances at the clock. "You should let me drive you back now."

I peer at the clock, too. It's nearly ten. If I hurry, I can make the second half of the tutorial.

"No, that's all right. Thank you for talking to me, Rumi. I feel better."

"Anytime, princess."

This time, the nickname doesn't infuriate me.

He lingers for a moment, looking at me until the heat flushes my face and I have to break eye contact. It's so daring, this look. Like he wants to kiss me. I want him to. Even as I'm looking away, I'm leaning closer. But he laughs, and I snap back into reality. *Don't be an idiot, Ash.*

"Listen, I can trust you, right?" he asks.

"Of course."

"Good girl. If you ever need anything..."

I'm your friend, yada, yada, yada. "Thanks."

"No, I mean anything..."

"Right. Brilliant."

"Ash. Stop being dense. I'm talking about rides off campus. The girls use me as their own personal Uber. Here's my number in case you ever need to get out of here. Plus, you know, I can get other things. I'm your resource. I can help you establish yourself at the school. You could be very popular if you wanted to help me."

Drugs, he means. Apparently it is the day for propositions. "Oh. Right. I understand. Thanks, but I think I'm okay."

"You just shout if you need anything."

He hands over a slip of paper with ten numbers on it. I glance at it, memorizing them, then fold it away.

He takes our cups and disappears into the back of the shop.

The bell on the door tinkles merrily as I leave. The town is still weirdly deserted. I take the arboretum path back to school at a jog. Running away from my past, running toward my future?

Who the hell knows what I'm doing anymore.

But as I cross from the shelter of the trees onto school grounds, I can't help but think about a young girl, body splayed out on the forest floor, her eyes missing from her head.

And Rumi's own dark eyes, that spark of light in them as he told me the story.

The glimmer of tears?

Or something else?

PAST

Oxford, England

31

THE FUNERAL

I met her the day of Johnny's funeral. I shouldn't say met, I should say saw. Observed. Was made aware of.

We flew back from France the day after he died. Damien wanted to keep things quiet, had fixed it with the Giverny authorities. Sylvia was drugged up on Valium and went where directed without resistance, like a balloon half-filled with helium, listless and fading.

It was incredibly freaky to know his little body was in the hold of the plane, housed in a temporary wooden casket. I asked to go down and sit with him but it was a commercial jet and they wouldn't allow it. I screamed. I railed. I did all the things a good sister should.

Damien spanked me, told me to stop acting like a child, quit throwing a tantrum, so I subsided. A flight attendant brought me a cranberry juice and a magazine, *L'Officiel*. I could barely read it but I could look at the pictures, glorious, beautiful French women who seemed to live without care or proper sustenance, smoldering eyes looking vaguely into the cameras.

I wanted to be one of them. Very badly. Even at six, I was aware my life as I knew it was over, and a new one had begun.

We flew west, the flight short, and a hearse met us on the tarmac. I stood there in my little peacoat and waved as they pushed Johnny's wood-encased body into the back of the long car. Damien saw me and slapped down my hand. Sylvia moaned. She was especially good at moaning.

We buried Johnny in the family graveyard, half a mile into the lands from the estate proper. Foxhunts used to start at the cemetery gates before they were outlawed. It was grouse season; far-off shotgun cracks bled through the thin air. Each one made me jump.

The priest intoned. His words meant nothing to me. Johnny was dead. My little brother, gone. I didn't miss him, not yet. I drifted, searching the crowd for friendly faces: Cook, or the jolly man who came when we had parties and brought me sweets.

I spotted a strange girl. Her hair was blond, like mine, though long down her back, unlike mine, which was chopped in a ruthless bob at my chin. I suppose my mother didn't want the bother of putting it up in a braid anymore; she'd cut it right after we came home, with scissors from her sewing kit. I was not used to the feeling of cold air on my neck.

The girl was standing behind the skirt of a woman who wore big sunglasses and wept into a handkerchief; not a sweet, lacy one like my mother's, but a coarse one, like you'd buy in the shops. The girl looked terribly interested in the proceedings, but as I watched, she glanced up at the sky at a flock of geese flying overhead in a perfect V. She smiled at them, innocent and kind, and I wanted to be her friend.

When the priest was done, the body was put into the ground, gears grinding on the lowering device. The funeral was over.

Mother stood by the grave moaning, Father alongside her,

grim-faced and stoic. The girl and her mother approached my parents. There was a brief exchange, then they left. My mother watched their retreat, and I was surprised at the anger on her face. I'd never seen her look at anyone but me that way.

There was a party at our house afterward. I assumed I would see her there, but the woman and her girl never showed.

Several months later, we bumped into them in the village near our house. We never went there, Mother liked the shops in north Oxfordshire better than the ones in downtown Oxford, but there was something she needed that couldn't be found elsewhere, so we bundled off to Broad Street. I had been very good since the funeral, and Mother was in a fine mood. She secured her package and took me to the tea shop for a cocoa.

This generosity was the first of its kind since Johnny died, and I was careful with my cup so as not to spill and ruin my outfit, not to give her a reason to hate me more.

The woman from the funeral was there. I recognized her hair, piled up on her head. Without her sunglasses, she looked tired, gray, lined. She was older than Mother. It took me a moment to realize she worked at the tea shop. When Mother saw her, she threw a few quid on the table and hurried me away. I hadn't finished my cocoa, so I cried and wailed, and the day was ruined.

The girl stood by the doors as Mother dragged me away by the arm. I knew she would be my friend. At least now I knew where to find her. Maybe Cook would take me with her to the shops and I could speak to her.

I loved her, though I didn't even know her. Isn't that strange?

It didn't feel strange at the time. She was a silent compatriot, a kind eye. I imagined all the things we would do together: ride horses; play in the mill pond; trek across the estate by the stone fences; watch the strange, quiet falconer who came to the land every once in a while to let her bird hunt, her hawk's jesses jangling in the chilled air.

It was this fantasy that kept me going into my teens until I met her for real. She was shy. She was quiet. She was studious.

She was everything I was not, and I thought, more than once, she was the daughter my mother should have had, a changeling child—me with the fairies, punished for my deeds—and this sweet, biddable girl who was worthy of their love in my place. She was my friend before we ever spoke, and once we did, we were inseparable. Our lives intertwined; where one of us left off, the other began, our very own Möbius strip. I wanted to be her. I would do anything for her. I would give anything for her.

Until I had no choice. I had to kill her. It was the only way.

OCTOBER

Marchburg, Virginia

32

THE RULES

Ford is in the attics, practicing her usual "rah-rah Goode is all-girls for a reason" spiel for tomorrow's board meeting, when she sees a flash out of the corner of her eye. She goes to the window. It takes her a moment to realize what she's seen—Ash Carlisle emerging from the arboretum at a sprint.

Ford glances at her watch and frowns. What is her young charge up to? Skipping class, obviously, but why?

Ford gathers her iPad with her speech and heads down to her office. Melanie is seated at her desk with a cup of coffee in one hand and the *Marchburg Free Press* in the other. She smiles wide at her boss's entry.

"Dean? You're back early. All set for tomorrow?"

"As ready as I'll ever be, I guess. Pull Ash Carlisle's schedule for me, would you?"

"Ha—busted."

"What?"

"Ash. Busted. She missed her tutorial with Dr. Medea this morning. He came in to check on her a bit ago, see if she was sick. I asked around and it seems there was an issue this morning at breakfast. Ash had a fight with one of the girls and ran off."

"Why didn't you come get me?"

"Because you needed to practice your presentation. And Dr. Medea just phoned to say Ash showed up after all. Late, but she's there now. That man is handsome, Dean. Looks good in the morning, you know what I mean? Scruffy. And the way he wears those jeans—"

"Melanie!"

"What? He's a hottie. Seemed rather disappointed you weren't here, too. I think he likes you."

Ford rolls her eyes. "When you're finished trying to set me up with my staff, would you mind getting Ash in here? She and I need to have a chat. Don't interrupt her tutorial, she can come when she's finished."

Ford fixes herself a cup of coffee and powers through some email while she waits. Soon enough, Ash Carlisle is standing in the doorway.

Ford's sensitive nose can smell cigarettes.

She gestures to the chair in front of her desk. Ash slumps in the chair, her head hung low.

"Look at me," Ford says.

Ash meets her eyes.

"Want to tell me what's wrong?"

"Nothing's wrong, Dean."

"Oh? Then how about you tell me why you skipped class and went for a stroll in the arboretum instead of seeing Dr. Medea for your tutorial?"

Her face crumples. The story comes out in jagged waves. "They know. They know who my father is. How my parents died. They know I'm using a false name. I didn't tell anybody, I swear it. But they found out. Vanessa found out. And she outed me in front of everyone. I was upset. I ran. Becca—"

She cuts herself off and Ford gently encourages her.

"Becca what?"

"She just, came and talked to me. Told me not to worry about it. She was...kind."

"Good. Becca Curtis is a leader in this school and a good ally for you."

"I don't want allies. I don't want to be here. I want to go home. And I don't have a home to go to. I miss... I miss my mother." Her voice breaks and Ford can see she's fighting back the sobs.

Ford moves around the desk so they can sit face-to-face.

"Oh, Ash. Poor little duck. The world is asking too much of you. No teenage girl should have to go through losing her parents the way you did. I understand how hard this is, I truly do. But your teachers have reported you're doing well in your studies. I notice a number of the girls copying your style. You have friends here. You've been fitting in."

"It's not exactly the same, Dean. No offense, but I'd trade it all to get my mum back."

"I'm sure you would. I certainly don't blame you. I'm sure you're missing your piano training. The structure you must have had at home. I'm interviewing a new teacher tomorrow. Perhaps you'd like to meet her, as well?"

"No. I am finished with piano. It was something my parents wanted, not me."

"Talent isn't something to squander, Ash."

"I'm not squandering it. I'm just more interested in computers now."

Ford senses the anger rising but Ash shocks her when she continues.

"I saw it happen, you know. Have you ever seen anyone die? Watched as the light disappears from their eyes?" Ash's voice has taken on an eerie quality, and Ford feels goose bumps run across her flesh. "I couldn't look away from that spark dimming, growing distant until it was gone entirely. I dream about it every night, my mother's face as the life drained away, her eyes going blank."

"We need to talk about getting you some counseling, Ash." Ford's voice is soft, comforting. She needs to take better care of her young charge. She should have known this would be too much. She's been pushing her too hard.

But the tears stop abruptly. Ash sits up ramrod straight, wipes a hand over her face.

"No, we don't."

"You've suffered a trauma. It's incumbent upon me to get you some help so you aren't scarred by this forever. You can learn some coping mechanisms so you don't relive the moment over and over. It sounds to me like you have PTSD—"

"I said no. I won't do it. I'm fine. I was frustrated by Vanessa's attack this morning, caught off guard, but I am fine. I can handle this."

The note of steel in her voice is alarming, but more so the absence of all feelings. She's turned off her emotions quicker than flipping a light switch.

They sit in silence while Ford assesses her young student. She can't force her. But she can keep a closer eye on her.

"All right. No counseling."

"Thank you."

"That said, as difficult a moment as this is for you, Ash, I can't have you disrupting the school. Cutting will not be tolerated. You've got five points now. Instead of Saturday school, I want you here, in my office, every day at 4:00 p.m. for after-school detention. Do you understand?"

"I understand, Dean Westhaven." The soft voice is back.

"And hand over the cigarettes. And don't even think of lying to me, Ash, I can smell them on you."

"I don't have any more, Dean. That was my last one."

She meets Ford's eyes again, this time defiant. Ford doesn't know what to make of these personality swings, from soft, pliant girl child to steely, cold woman. She did not pick up on this young woman's darkness when she interviewed her. She knows now this was a mistake. Ash Carlisle bears watching.

"Four tomorrow, Ash. Bring your homework."

"Yes, ma'am."

Ignoring Ford's wince, Ash lopes from the room.

33

THE HACKER

Since I've been disciplined, the girls of Goode accept me back to the school with grace, almost as if the spat in the dining room this morning never happened. I walk the halls expecting the whispers and stares, but it's as if the whole school came to an agreement that they're going to leave me alone, and after my meltdown with the dean, I'm relieved to move through the rest of the day unmolested.

I didn't enjoy the disappointment in Dr. Medea's eyes at my late arrival this morning. He didn't scold or hand out JPs, as I expected, but that look was enough to make me vow never to be late for him again. And my programming sucks.

I want to get him back to that smooth, smiling, generous soul he was the first few weeks of school. I have to keep him on my good side.

In English, I receive a B on my Mary Shelley essay, with extensive notes on how to revise. I skip lunch, grab a smoothie from the Rat—no way I am going to face the wolves so soon—but talk myself into going to dinner, head up, eyes focused ahead.

When I sit at the sophomores' table, Vanessa stands and moves. Piper, after an apologetic glance, follows. Oddly, Camille stays, nattering on about her upcoming meeting in the attics, a cardinal seen flying into the open chapel doors, and a letter from home written by her stepbrother.

Battle lines drawn. I ignore Vanessa, roll my eyes at Piper, indulge Camille's soliloquy, eat my Cobb salad, then, back on the hall, purposefully sit in Vanessa's usual spot in the sewing circle for an hour, chatting with a couple of girls from my English class, bitching about my two weeks of detention. They are enamored. Better, though, is the look on Vanessa's face when she realizes I've captured her spot. She takes one look at me in the middle of the circle and her eyes burn with hatred. She huffs and disappears down the hall. Utterly priceless.

I mustn't allow myself to be cowed. If I show any more weakness like I did this morning, I'll be fighting them off the rest of term. No, staying calm and in their faces is the best way to handle things.

After study hours, I retreat to my room to draft the outline for an essay on the theories of Plato's Cave seen in Ayn Rand's *Anthem.* Satisfied with the bones, I settle in to indulge my inner naughty by writing some astounding code for Dr. Medea. I park myself at my desk with my usual setup—earbuds for some slamming music, a Diet Coke from the kitchen. A notebook in case the structure of what I'm developing doesn't show itself—all of my code have shapes in my mind. It's why I'm good at this, Medea told me. Some coders see in numbers or colors; my talent is shapes. Double helixes, braids, hearts, lately. A lot of hearts. The shape of the code helps me find the nuance of what I'm hacking. He says this is rare. It makes me feel special.

Technically, I shouldn't be writing hacks, but Medea seems to enjoy my white hat work so much, and I like showing off for him. It's like he understands me in a way most of the other teachers don't. After my screwup today, I want him firmly back in my foxhole.

I'm halfway through a complicated keystroke analysis when I realize there is movement behind me. I ignore it, turn up the music, but it persists.

Camille, clearly nervous, is walking in circles like a caged lion, waiting until her appointed time to go upstairs. She is making silly little humming noises and scraping her hand on the top of the sofa. I don't know how I can sense this through July Talk's intense lyrics, but I can.

I pull out my earbuds. "Will you stop?"

Camille shakes her head. "What if...?"

"What if what?"

"I don't know. Ignore me."

"Impossible. You're doing laps around the couch. It's a bit distracting."

"I'm just so nervous." She goes to her dresser and I see the flash of clear glass, hear the clink as the little bottle of vodka she keeps stashed in her top drawer disappears back into her socks. Camille plops down with an alcohol-tinged sigh. "That's better. Are you okay? You cut classes, you're going to be in trouble."

Oh, lovely. We're going to bond.

"Already am. Detention with the dean for two weeks to work off my JPs. I thought you'd heard?"

"I've been distracted today. Where did you go?"

"Town. The coffee shop. Do you know Rumi?"

She blanches. "Oh, my God, Ash. You can't talk to him. He's...he's dangerous."

"I heard. He told me about his father."

Camille's pale face goes even whiter. "He just told you? What did he say?"

"The truth, I reckon. He said it was hard on him. And if he

was dangerous, the dean wouldn't have him on staff here. He seems a decent bloke, for all I could tell."

"There are rumors about him. He likes to watch us, the girls, I mean. He stands on the path to the arboretum and watches the teams practice. He's some sort of pedophile. You really should stay away. He's not your type."

"There are rumors about everyone. Me included. And I seriously doubt he's a pedophile. He's just lonely. And how do you know what my type is?"

A small chime and Camille leaps to her feet, her face splitting into an incandescent grin, the specter of Rumi already forgotten.

"Finally, finally, it's time. Wish me luck."

I say, "Cheers," and mean it sincerely. I have no idea what the seniors want with Camille, can only assume it's about me. They want information and think my roommate is the best source. Why they don't have the balls to ask me directly or go to Becca, who knows. Sometimes the logic here is beyond me.

When the door slams and I'm finally alone, I sag against the chair. Why did Camille warn me off Rumi? He seems totally fine. Nice, even.

Okay, I'll admit, I've been thinking about my chat with him all day. How difficult it must be for him, to be the object of derision and scorn from the town where he grew up, to be looked down upon because of the choices of his parent. I understand more than he knows.

With all this chaos raging in my mind, I find it almost impossible to concentrate on my elegant little code. I'll work on it tomorrow. I might as well get ready for bed, snuggle under the covers and read. Dr. Asolo assigned Virginia Woolf's *A Room of One's Own* this afternoon and I'm actually looking forward to reading it. I understand the desire to have something private, a place where you can be yourself without guile. I don't know where that will ever be for me, not anymore.

I brush my teeth and get into my pajamas. Glance at the clock.

It's nearly eleven. Time for lights out. Camille has been gone for a while, longer than I was.

I read, get lost in the words, the rhythm. My eyes are starting to droop when the pounding begins, fists slamming against my door with such force the small painting above Camille's desk crashes to the floor.

34

THE TAP

The door flies open. Screaming, shouting, hands all over me. I am screaming now, too, completely freaking out. My mind is blank except for a single thought—*Get away! Get away!*

I struggle mightily, but there are too many of them. They get me by the arms and legs and push a rag into my mouth, then throw a bag of some sort over my head. It smells like pine cones and it muffles my screams. My ears feel like they're going to burst with the pressure of these internal yells.

They wrestle me out of the bed and out the door. I don't know how many adversaries there are, just feel so many hands yanking and pulling. Someone giggles and this infuriates me. They drop me twice, my back smacking into the stair tread, but as quickly as they lose their grip they have me again, wrapping arms around my waist, and they haul me up, up, up.

I am crying now, but my whimpers are drowned out by the rag, the hood, the shouts. A door swings open and I feel a cool breeze, then I'm tossed handily into the air and land with a thud on the floor. The door slams closed, and the screaming stops.

My hip hurts.

I am alone.

It is so quiet.

The bag is gone from my head. I had my eyes squeezed shut so tightly I didn't realize they'd removed it. I spit out the rag, heave in deep breaths.

Fucking Vanessa and Camille. Becca said the note at breakfast wasn't her summons. This was a setup. They just wanted me alone so they could fuck with me. Who did they recruit to help?

I will burn them down.

I get up, on all fours first, then stumbling to my feet. I don't recognize the room, don't know where I am. Where the cool air is coming from. But it's so cold my teeth begin chattering. I'm barefoot, arms uncovered; the short pajamas do nothing to keep me warm.

The door has a light on under it, weak and yellow. I can hear the whispering growing louder as I near. I try the door. The knob turns but something is blocking it.

"Bugger it all. Bitches!"

I walk left, fingers trailing against the wall to keep my bearing. My eyes are adjusting now, but even so, I bump into a table. I realize there's a glass on the table, filled with a small amount of clear liquid. A hand-lettered sign leans against it. I have to squint to read it in the darkness.

DRINK ME!

Oh, sure. Like I'm falling for that. It's probably drain cleaner or rat poison.

I pick up the glass and smell the contents. The sharp tang of alcohol makes my sinuses burn. Oh. It's vodka.

Why would Vanessa and Camille kidnap me, lock me in, and tell me to drink a shot of vodka? Is this an Odds and Evens thing?

I dip in a finger and taste, yes, it's just vodka. I toss it back.

Fuck them. Fuck them and this stupid school and this stupid night.

I don't fall to the floor in a sputtering mess and die, so I feel my way through the darkness to the other side of the room. The night is black as pitch and there are curtains on the windows, gossamer white billowing in the breeze. The windows are open, that's why it's so damn cold in here. And there is another door.

I put my ear to it. I can hear something. Echoes of voices.

I turn the knob slowly, and the voices halt.

Someone is in the stairwell. They've heard me.

Logic: it's Vanessa and Camille, waiting to jump out and scare me. They must have recruited several others to help pull this off.

But something about this room makes me feel like there is something much, much worse behind the door.

Reckless fury forces my hand. I whip open the door, only to see a dim light illuminating a set of winding stairs. Red stairs.

This must be the infamous red staircase.

I try not to focus on the horror story behind the reason the stairs are painted red, but my mind's eye supplies all the necessary pieces—the rope around the girl's neck, the blood dripping from her arms, her black hair streaming to her waist, the white gown stained gray with age. It's like she's hung here for centuries. The image is so vivid, if I reach out a hand, I can touch the body.

The air squeezes tight around me, and suddenly as it appeared, the apparition is gone. The stairwell is empty.

A door slams, a breeze passes, and the air changes. I am not alone.

Becca Curtis is standing behind me. That is, I think it's Becca, but something is wrong with her face. It's like she's dead, a skeleton, her eyes black holes in pale, pale skin, stretched tight across her skull. She is wearing all black; a hood covers her yellow hair, which makes that deadly pale face stand out in stark relief in the darkness.

She appears so suddenly I jump, stumbling down two stairs before I catch myself on the railing. My God, I could have broken my neck.

I reach out a hand to see if Becca is real, but my arm feels heavy. I can barely lift it.

Not just vodka. There was something else in the drink.

Becca is a statue before me. Her mouth moves, lips twisting in a command that sounds like we're underwater.

"Walk, Swallow."

"Swallow?"

"Walk. Down. The stairs. Now."

I wind my way down the stairs carefully, holding on to the railing for support, Becca following. We go on and on, circling down, down, down. My head is growing fuzzier by the minute.

Finally, we hit another door.

"Open it, Swallow," Becca says. There is no denying the authority in her tone. I comply. My hands look big against the wood. Clown hands. Carny hands. I giggle, this is freaking hilarious.

The door opens to a dirt hallway, and the smell of ancient things assails me. Suddenly, things don't seem so funny. My mouth is dry, so dry. I need to sit down. I lean against the wall, start to slide down but Becca hoists me up.

"Walk."

Becca lets go of my arm and prods me in the back. I walk, feet bare in the dirt. I can feel every pebble, every grain. Cold. There are dead things here, rotting things. Cobwebs spring from the ceiling, brushing against my hair and forehead. I gasp and swipe at them, but Becca just says, "Hurry, for God's sake," and I keep going, fighting the urge to sprint, walking on and on for what feels like forever. It is dark, and I'm cold, and the walls are vibrating.

The ground starts to slope upward, and the air gets better. I can see light now, *light at the end of the tunnel*, which strikes me as hysterical, and I start giggling again, softly. This is no longer scary, it is glorious and fun.

"Ready yourself," Becca mutters, and the door swings open.

35

THE SWALLOW

Becca pushes me into a room full of confusion. I see half-dressed girls and girls in robes with hoods. What the hell?

"Took you long enough. Did little Alice not want to drink up her cuppa?" I turn my head blindly but a female voice screams, "Don't you dare look at me!" She is definitely not Vanessa.

What is going on?

I look at my feet, dirty from the stroll through the tunnel. They pulse at me, friendly and kind. I like my feet. They have a good shape, high arched, toes long and elegant. But vulnerable, too. They get banged up so easily. I remember breaking my little toe last year, stumbling into a table. It hurt like hell. Took forever to heal. I couldn't wear boots for months.

"Sorry, toe," I whisper.

"Line up, you stupid twat. And stop talking to yourself like a madwoman." The screamer pushes me into the row of girls. I lose my balance, knock the one standing next to me with an elbow, and the whole line topples like dominoes. Hushed laughter fills the room, and I have to bite my lip to keep from laughing, too. If there are other people here, I'm not going to die.

I want to look and see who else is lined up, but I'm wrenched back to my feet.

"Stay," Becca says, and I plant myself. I am a tree. I have roots. That's why my feet are covered in dirt, I need to root down. *Root to the earth, daughter. Feel its energy flow through your body.*

I can hear these ghostly words but they don't make sense, not entirely.

"I think you gave them too much. None of them can keep their heads up."

"I didn't. They're just sleepy. It took me forever to get the last Swallow to cooperate."

"Are you sure, Becca?"

"Yes. Let's get started. Swallows!"

I look up. I know my name. I am the vessel for the dead. I bring death and destruction in my wake. The souls of my people are inside of me.

"When I say 'Swallows', you say 'yes, Mistress.' Swallows!"

"Yes, Mistress," comes the cry in unison.

"See?" Becca says to the screamer. "They're fine. Listen to me, little darlings. You are about to embark on the most difficult week of your life. Not all of you will make it. And if you don't make it, you will never amount to anything. You will be a laughingstock. You will be shunned. You will be cast out. Do you understand?"

Voices, stronger now, shout, "Yes, Mistress!"

"Yes," I add, a beat too late.

"Look at your sisters. Look to your flock. You will carry each other when you are tired. You will work together. You will grow together. Who you were before no longer matters. Who your parents are no longer matters. We are your family now. Do you understand?"

She bellows, and we scream back at her, "Yes, Mistress!"

"Good. Strip." The Swallows look around vaguely, then slowly, clothes start coming off. It's hard to imagine things could be colder, but they are. Naked now, I am covered in gooseflesh. I cross an arm over my breasts. The other is meant to shield me, but I can't get it into the shape of a fig leaf, so it dangles near my pelvis. Another giggle, this one from deep inside. Naked, in front of a group of strangers. This is the worst anxiety dream ever.

Becca says to the girl standing next to her, the one I'm having trouble focusing on—wait, it's one of the twins—"Do you have it?"

"It's in the bag."

"Swallow!" Becca is screaming in my face now. She shoves me toward a trash bag sitting in the corner. *We're in a cabin*, my feeble mind grasps at last. *We're out of the school. We're naked in a cabin. What the hell?*

"Pass it out. Down the line. Each Swallow needs a handful."

"Yes, Mistress." I pick up the bag. It smells of earth. I shuffle along, ignoring the variety in the body parts on display, trying to memorize the faces I see instead, as hands dip into the bag and draw out some sort of fall leaves. I recognize Jordan Swanson, the brunette junior in my computer class. Jordan is grinning, happy. All the faces in the line are happy in a sense, though some look scared, too.

It hits me, and I stagger a little under the knowledge of what's happening.

This isn't a joke. This isn't a revenge play.

This is a tap.

I am being tapped for a secret society.

And Becca is the Mistress. That can only mean...

"Rub yourselves, Swallows. That's right, rub the pretty leaves all over your sweet little bodies. Keep it away from your face, you fool, just arms, legs, and stomachs."

I comply. The scent of the leaves is slightly spicy, and I like the feeling of it on my skin. Soft, fingertips caressing, the veins in the orange leaves so pretty, so pretty...

"Now put the leaves back in the bag."

We do.

"Wash your hands."

I smell bleach, feel the rough clammy washcloth against my skin. This is like a game I played as a child—Simon Says. Simon says hold your nose. Simon says touch your toes. Touch your nose—nope, Simon didn't say it, you're out.

I was always good at this game.

"Drop them in this."

Another bag makes its way down the line. I divest myself of the stinky washcloth.

"Good little Swallows. Now, drink this."

The bottle makes its way down the line. When it gets to me, I take a mouthful. More vodka. I am so thirsty. I want water, or tea, not vodka. My head is swimming, and my stomach feels funny. I am drunk now, but more. Drunk and high on something. The room throbs with energy; my eyes can't focus. I stare at Becca, my Mistress, with one eye closed, then the other. It's better with one eye. Easier to focus.

A chant now, building: "Drink, drink, drink, drink."

The twins, a bottle to their lips, gulping and grinning. They pass it to Becca, who takes a long swallow, then another. Her teeth flash white in the gloom.

Swallow. Swallows. I snicker. I must have said it aloud, the whole line of us starts laughing.

And then there's screaming again, orders, chaos. Girls are pulled out of line, interrogated, bossed, forced to their knees when they get an answer wrong.

"What is my name? What is my name, you worthless piece of shit?"

"Get my shoes, not those, the red boots. Are you a total idiot?"

"Name every single headmistress since the beginning of Goode. God, you are so stupid."

"We thought you were better than this. We thought you had heart."

One of them is fighting back. Not smart. "How would you know what I am?"

"What, you think Westhaven picks the students? That is our job. We chose you. You're such a fucking disappointment."

"Why did you lie about your parents, Swallow? Why?"

This is directed at me, I realize.

"I... I..."

The girl who is yelling at me isn't unfamiliar, but I can't place her. "Quit stuttering. You need to learn how to speak properly. Stupid Brit. What is my name?"

"Erm..."

"How dare you not know who I am? She's out, Mistress. This one's too stupid to be Ivy Bound. They all are."

Girls are crawling on the floor, crying, getting snot in their hair. One is throwing up in a corner trashcan, two furious seniors standing over her. "Ewwww, what did you eat tonight, Swallow?"

I hear the reply through the girl's tears. "Raw cookie dough, Mistress."

"I'm not your Mistress, she's your Mistress."

A slap across my face, hard. "Focus, you idiot. I said, what is my name?" The tone is edged with such fury I crumple to my knees. I strain trying to come up with the girl's name, but my mind is mushy. It's the drugs, whatever they are, making it impossible to think. *Think, Ash. Think!*

"Oooh, look. One's starting."

"Shelley!" I shout, triumphant. "Your name is Shelley."

"Finally. Get in line, Swallow!" Shelley commands.

I do, accidentally rubbing up against the arm of the girl next to me. Oh, it feels good to touch like this. I do it again. It's like scratching an itch, warm and good deep inside. I look at my arm. It is red, streaked with white where I've been running my fingers along the skin.

"God, no, don't touch your face, dumb ass."

Becca is sitting on a long oak table, calmly smoking a cigarette, and I want a hit so badly.

"They're starting to scratch, you better do it now," Shelley says.

"Yeah, we better. Eyes front, Swallows."

It's been days, weeks, since they started yelling at us. Suddenly it's quiet. I feel myself swaying. God, my arm itches.

"Listen to me. I am your Mistress. I now run your lives. Anything I tell you to do, you do. Anything you need, you come to me. You are each assigned a Falconer, who will train you in our ways. Whatever your Falconer tells you to do, you do it. You will be at the Falconer's beck and call. Any hesitation to fulfill a request, and you will be cut. Tell anyone what you're doing, and you will be cut. Tell anyone, student or teacher, *anything* about this night, and you will be cut.

"You have been tapped. You are all Swallows of Ivy Bound now. Do me proud."

She smiles benevolently at us, the line of itchy girls in front of her, meeting each one's eyes as she goes down the line. Thirteen Swallows to be made into women. She has her job cut out for her this year.

The girl next to me starts to scratch.

"And for God's sake, keep your stupid hands away from your eyes."

36

THE IVY

We are taken back to the school through the tunnel, one by one, one Swallow to one Falconer, until Becca and I are the last ones in the cabin. I'm sobering up, I think, but my head feels like cotton wool. My arm itches, but I don't dare scratch. Becca hasn't given her permission.

Becca says touch your nose. Becca says touch your toes.

"Swallow. Can you hear me?"

Becca holds out the last of the cigarette. I take a deep, grateful drag.

"I am your Mistress, but I am also your Falconer."

"Why me?" is all I can ask.

"You will understand why if you make it through, little Ash. I hope I wasn't wrong about you. Now, let's get you back to bed."

I don't know what to say. "Thank you," I whisper, and Becca laughs.

"Trust me when I say you won't be thanking me tomorrow. Come on."

We follow the last of the girls through the tunnel and back into the school. As we go through the door to the red staircase, I catch a glimpse of the hanging girl again. The hallucination feels so real.

My words are slow and deliberate. "What did you give us?"

"Mostly just vodka. A touch of Molly. Just enough to make you happy and lovey. And Benadryl," Becca replies absently. "Damn, where is that key?"

"Molly. Ecstasy. That's why I feel so good. But Benadryl? Why?"

"You'll understand in the morning. Ah, here it is." She locks the door to the red staircase, pockets the key.

"Dean Westhaven knows about the cigarettes."

"What?"

"She questioned me today. Smelled it on me. I told her they were mine."

Becca's eyes are huge in the darkness. "You covered for me?"

"Yes."

"You lied for me?"

I feel the warmth of Becca's voice, approving, caressing my body. "Yes."

"Thank you. Now, off to bed with you, but wash up first. Do *not* touch your face, or your cooch, and make it a good, hot, soapy shower. Remember, don't tell a soul."

She pushes me out the door, down the stairs to the sophomore hall.

"Be waiting at the door to the seniors' hall at 7:00 a.m. Don't be late, Swallow. You won't like the punishment for tardiness."

And then the warm, sweet Becca is gone, back to her world in the attics, and I am alone, standing naked in the stairwell. My arms itch.

Ivy Bound.

The variegated leaves. Three to a stem. Itching.

Oh, bollocks!

I burst through the door and sprint to the hall's handicap bath.

I push the button with my elbow and dart inside. The sudden burst of light—the overhead is on a motion sensor—makes me wince, but not as badly as when I see myself in the mirror.

I am streaked in red.

They've made us rub ourselves with poison ivy.

"Those sadistic bitches." I start the shower and jump in to wash. It's not going to help, the leaves were crushed into my skin, the juice is already making blisters form.

Benadryl. To help counteract the itching.

Devious, and smart.

The hall is empty and quiet as I head back to the room. Out of habit, I look at the door across the hall. It is closed. But that means nothing. I try the knob, surprised to find it locked.

We don't have locks on our doors. It's part of the Honor Code.

I look closer at the knob. There are scratches in the fresh paint and a keyhole.

Someone must have reported that the door wouldn't stay closed and one of the janitors changed the knob. The lock was certainly for safety's sake—all that paint and raw wood, nails, all things that could hurt an unwitting student.

So why does it feel like someone is standing on the other side of the door, holding their breath?

Okay, now I really am wigging out. I move quickly toward my door. As I turn the knob, a voice bleeds into the night, and I can swear I hear my name being called. It is far away, though, and I shake my head and enter the room. I'm being paranoid. I'm still half-drunk and high, and have spooked myself. The drunken image of the dead girl in the stairwell, the red stairs, the murdered girl in the arboretum, the very heart of this school is its great ghost stories. But they're stories. That's all.

The room is still a mess, and Camille isn't back. She must have decided to bunk with another girl, or maybe she's been tapped for a secret society, too. No, probably not. They say sophomores never get tapped.

But I have been.

I'm special.

I open my wardrobe door and smile in the wavy mirror. I am Ivy Bound. Becca Curtis is my secret friend. There is a handsome boy in town who flirts with me, and the dean thinks I'm a weak little sobby snatch.

I have played this all perfectly.

On my mussed-up bed is a small brown lunch bag sitting atop a T-shirt with a picture of a small bird on the front. I put it on with a smile, then open the bag to find a whole kit—cortisone cream, calamine lotion, cotton wool, Benadryl, packets of Aveeno oatmeal tub soak. Nail clippers. And a note:

Go to the nurse, and you're cut. Sweet dreams, Swallow.

They are serious about their torture, but at least they've given me the remedy. Despite years tromping through field and forest, I've never had a case of poison ivy. *How bad can it possibly be?*

I cut my nails almost to the quick, take some of the Benadryl, spread cortisone cream on my arms, stomach, and thighs, then climb into bed. Set my alarm for 6:00 a.m. I'm not going to get much sleep, but I don't care. I don't care about anything.

I've been tapped.

I belong.

I am quite literally wearing the fruit of my labors on my body.

The spark of pride, of excitement, almost drowns out the incessant itching of my arm, and the creepy, crawly feeling of my name being called out, carried on the mountain breeze.

Almost.

I run the evening through my mind, over and over, the screaming, the instructions, who was there. Some girls I didn't recognize, some I did. No matter, we'll be marked tomorrow. All I need is to find the most miserable-looking faces and I'll know my flock mates.

"I am a Swallow. I am Ivy Bound." I whisper the words over and over until I fall asleep.

37

THE TRAGEDY

Rumi comes to Ford tonight without texting first, ravenous. He doesn't say anything, just smiles that come-hither grin, slams the door behind him, and takes her in his arms, kissing her deeply.

"Good day?" she asks when they come up for air, but he whispers "No talking," grabs her hand, and leads her to the bedroom, where he flips her on her stomach and takes her from behind.

While he makes sure she's fully satisfied, tonight is clearly about him. When he finishes, shuddering against her back, he simply pulls up his jeans, gives her another long, soulful kiss, and starts for the door.

"Wait. Don't you want a cocktail?"

He grins and shakes his head. "I only wanted you. Good-night, Ford."

He saunters off into the night. Ford closes the door behind him with an exaggerated sigh of pleasure.

Good grief. He certainly knows how to push her buttons and

leave her wanting more. Where did he learn all his tricks? For someone so young—it has to be online porn. She doesn't think he's sleeping with anyone else, but what does she know? She's never asked, and he's never offered.

Besides, dating is reimagined now. With Tinder and Grindr and swiping, sex is free, built to resist commitment and responsibility, often completely disengaged from the act of love. It plays well for her purposes, it's not like she wants a true relationship with him, for heaven's sake, but she feels sorry for the girls of Goode as they make their way out into the world. They won't know any other way. They will let strangers into their bodies and call it freedom.

Ford has had a few serious boyfriends and a few romping partners. She knows the difference between lust and love. She's resisted marriage, fearing that inexorable slide into the status quo. She was not built for two point three kids and a dog, a house in the suburbs, a nanny for her children. She prefers the writer's isolation, the romantic aloneness that will allow her observational access. One needn't experience things firsthand to be a writer, one must only be a keen observer of setting and human nature.

She pours herself another whiskey—it might help her sleep, and she needs her rest to face the alumni association meeting tomorrow. The usual agenda was amended this afternoon to include a fund-raising update. She hopes to hear that a new endowment has been made.

Despite Rumi's ministrations, she's still upset about her meeting with Ash. She needs to get it off her mind and move on.

Something about the girl makes her uncomfortable.

She sits down at her desk, reads the few pages she's written since term started. She hasn't been working enough. At what point is she going to have to consider a sabbatical to finish the book?

Her phone begins to vibrate. She gives the screen a dirty look, then sighs heavily, pressing the speaker.

"Hello, Mother."

"Ford, darling! How are you? Not in bed, I hope?"

"Why would I be in bed? It's past eleven on a school night."

"Sarcasm has never become you, Ford."

"Sorry. What's the matter?"

"Nothing's the matter, darling. I'm in town and I thought we could have lunch."

Ford sets her whiskey down with a thump. "You're in Marchburg? Why?"

"Do I need a reason? I wanted to see you."

"Are you staying at the house?"

"Where else would I stay? It's my house."

Perhaps that explains Rumi's sudden appearance. The house sits on the edge of town quite near his cabin. He must have seen the lights. He could have warned her, though.

"I thought it would be fun to come for Odds and Evens weekend. I haven't been here for an event in a long time. I miss it."

"Really? That might not be the best idea, Mom."

"Of course, it's a good idea. I am a Westhaven, and I am still an alumnus of this institution, if you recall. It's always been open to any alumnus who wishes to join in. Unless you've changed the rules?"

"No. We'd be delighted to have you."

"Excellent. Now, there's a little something I've been wanting to discuss with you. I'm sure you saw the new agenda item for the meeting tomorrow? A vast sum has been left to the endowment by Pearl George, class of '42, who just passed away. But there's a stipulation."

"How vast a sum are we talking about?"

"One hundred and eighty million."

"Holy cow. Seriously? That will push us over the billion-dollar mark. We'll be at Exeter's level. And how do you know about this?"

"Oh, you know how these things go. Little birds. I thought you'd want to know."

"It's fabulous news. What's the stipulation?"

Jude sighs heavily. "The money is contingent on the school going coed."

"You have to be kidding. An alum from that era wants a coed school?"

"Her husband inherited her estate, and he's attached this condition."

"Absolutely not. I will not bend on this matter. I will not allow Goode to go coed. It's a shame, but we've turned down more before."

She can hear the *tick, tick, tick* that signals her mother is flicking her nails against the table. "Here's the thing, Ford. The alumni association wants the money. They want to surpass Exeter and Andover, you know that's been on the ten-year plan."

"The plan is to have an all-girls school at the top of the private school endowment list."

"The *goal*, though, is to be first on the list. Goode could not only match but overtake Exeter with this bump."

"No way, no how, Mother. I can't believe they've sent you as their emissary on this. You, of all people, who drilled into me and anyone else who would listen the vital nature of an all-girls environment. You know we'll lose more than we gain if we go coed. We'd lose every endowment that specified all-girls."

"Actually, no, we won't. There are ways to keep the system intact and still go coed. We've been—"

"'We'? Who the hell is 'we'?"

"Now, Ford, there's no reason to get upset. The South needs a win. We must overtake the East Coast schools. This is our chance. The alumni—"

"You aren't a part of the school anymore, Mother. And trust me, the board will not allow it. I'm shocked you're even entertaining the thought."

Jude sighs again. "The alumni association disagrees. Unlike the board, they haven't cast me aside."

The recrimination is clear.

"I just didn't want you to be caught off guard, darling."

"Thanks for the heads-up. I should go, I'll need to prepare some numbers."

"Do that. You'll see how this can work. One more thing. I saw one of your girls in town today. She was talking to *that boy*. I trust you were informed?"

Oh, Mama, if you only knew. And fuck you, Rumi. You really could have given me a heads-up.

He'd met up with Ash? Neither of them had bothered to mention this.

"She's already been disciplined. It won't happen again."

"If you don't keep control of them, Ford, they will continue to walk all over you. I've told you time and again you're much too loose with these girls."

"No one is walking all over me. I handled it."

"I see you still have *that boy* on staff. You would do well to get rid of him, Ford. No good will come of your charity."

"Mother, this entire school was founded on charity for those who are in trouble. Rumi certainly counts. He wasn't responsible for his father's actions. He was only ten, for heaven's sake. Why you've chosen him to blame when it was your negligence that got the girl killed astounds me. If you'd told the sheriff that Reynolds was harassing—"

Her mother's voice is colder than ice. "How dare you? You listen to me, little girl. I most certainly did tell the sheriff. He chose not to do anything, which is why that idiot lost his job. Just like you took mine."

Ford's heard this all before. "It's late. Do we have to do this now?"

"You started it, Ford. I suppose I'll just go back to New York. You don't want or need me. You've made that abundantly clear."

"Wait, Mom," but the call has ended, the phone is back to the home screen.

Since when does her mother speak for the alumni? There's something bigger going on here.

Ford starts to dial Jude back, then changes her mind. She sends a text instead.

You could have warned me.

The reply comes almost immediately.

I gave you the strength to deal with her.

Strangely, she recognizes the truth in his statement. She'd gone into the call relaxed instead of tense and furious, her usual approach to her mother—and Jude to her. The bad blood between them is never going to be resolved. At least this argument has ended in passive-aggressive nonsense. No harm, no foul. What ridiculousness, to think of taking the money and going coed. It goes against everything Goode is.

Still, next time...a little heads-up would be nice. Also heard you met one of my girls today?

Three dots greet her. She waits. And waits. Then the screen clears, and there's nothing. She shoots the rest of the whiskey.

"Thanks for nothing, Rumi."

It takes ages to fall asleep, but she finally drifts off, only to be jerked awake by a scream, loud and piercing, over before her heart beats again.

The concussion carries, sounding for all the world like a cantaloupe dropped from a height. *Whump*. It is a sickening noise, and Ford, not knowing exactly what she's heard but fearing the worst, is out the door and sprinting toward Main Hall before the glass she is holding crashes to the flagstone tiles.

38

THE STORIES

She fell.
She jumped.
She was thrown.
Boo. Hoo.
She was a bitch.

39

THE BODY

The body is small, broken. The nearest lamppost shows this, but nothing more, not the face, not the identity, not the cause of the fall.

Blood. So much blood.

Ford is shouting, she can hear herself, shocked at how together she sounds even when the voices inside her are wailing, gnashing, *this isn't happening, this isn't happening*, but aloud, she's giving instructions.

"Call 911, immediately!"

She realizes she's screaming to the ether, to the air. No one is here but the dead girl and her headmistress. Ford looks up at the bell tower, assessing the drop. A hundred feet, more.

Wait.

A shadow, is that a shadow, lurking at the edge of the precipice? It is gone as quickly as she thinks she's seen it, and she turns her attention to the girl at her feet. Feels for a pulse. There is nothing.

Her phone. She has her phone. She dials, hands shaking. There is blood on the screen.

"911, what is your emergency?"

"This is Dean Westhaven at The Goode School. One of the girls has fallen, we need an ambulance."

"Can you tell me the nature of the fall?"

Ford looks up again at the darkness above.

"From the bell tower. She fell from the bell tower."

It doesn't take long for the crowd to form. Girls are hanging out of the windows, rushing down the stairs, squealing in the dark.

Dr. Viridian, the chemistry teacher, hurries out of Old East Hall pulling a robe around her bony shoulders. She's been at the school for decades, taught Ford herself.

"Dean? What's happened? Oh, my God, who is that?"

"I don't know yet. I don't want to roll her. Keep the girls away."

"Someone needs to open the gate." This from Dr. Medea, who is on duty in Old West. He is kneeling next to the girl now.

"Yes. Don't touch her, Dominic. I think… I think I saw someone up in the bell tower. There may be evidence."

Ford calls Security. Erik Peters, the head guard, answers. "I'm on my rounds, Dean. What's the matter?"

"Open the gates."

"It's late, I'm—"

"Open them! Right now." The wail of the siren brings cold comfort to her.

"Is that a siren?" Erik asks.

"Erik. Open the gates. Meet the ambulance and guide them to the back of Main."

"Holy shit. Okay, I'm doing it right now."

Medea and Viridian are whispering to each other, and she sees them start corralling the girls, pushing them back, instructing them to return to their rooms.

Ford tries to shield the body from the prying eyes of the students and teachers who are figuring out what's happened, arms wide like a falcon over her prey. Small screams and yells break the night air.

Asolo appears, blinking sleep from her eyes. She rushes to Ford's side, peers down at the lump at her feet.

"What's happened? What's happened? Oh, my God, is that Camille Shannon?"

Ford realizes, yes, it is Camille. Sweet little Camille, sophomore. Ash Carlisle's roommate.

"Fuck!"

"Ford, I don't think that sort of language—"

"Go help Dominic and Phyllis. Get all the girls inside, immediately. We need to clear this area. Do a head count. I want everyone accounted for." Asolo nods and turns, but Ford catches her elbow. "And find Ash Carlisle. Now."

Asolo is wiping away tears. She casts a last glance at the crumpled form on the ground. "I will."

Two fire trucks pull into the grounds, their massive gears grinding. A moment later, an ambulance blows past Peters's golf cart, and the scene is suddenly packed with people.

Ford is moved to the side as the first responders work on the girl. Queries and statements begin.

"Did you see her fall?"

"Did you touch anything?"

"I can't get a BP here…"

The sheriff arrives, two deputies on his trail. Ford sees a woman in jeans and a leather jacket, short blond hair and piercing dark eyes, looking like she rolled out of bed, with them.

Who is this? The sheriff's latest floozy?

The EMTs cease their ministrations. A yellow sheet is placed over the body of Camille Shannon, and Ford realizes she's going to have to make a very difficult phone call.

This can't be happening, and yet it is.

Ford's phone rings. It's Asolo.

"Ash is in her room. She was asleep, sound asleep. Smells like she's been drinking, she's a little giggly, too. I heard some goings-on earlier, I think there was a tap tonight."

"Ivy Bound?"

"If I had to guess, yes. It's the right time in the term."

"Oh, just what we need. How many of our students were out of bed tonight? Damn it all," Ford exclaims. "Sober her up. Fast. The sheriff is going to want to talk to her and we can hardly afford to have them questioning her if she's drunk."

"I wonder if Camille was a part of the tap and it went wrong?"

"Don't even say it. Get Becca Curtis, too. I don't know if she's running Ivy Bound, but it stands to reason she'd inherit the title. She's my bet. Get both of them to my attic office and keep them there until I arrive. Do you understand?"

"Yes, Dean. I'm on it." The phone goes dead. Out of the corner of her eye, Ford sees Rumi, standing nearly behind a tree. The look on his face is one of horror, the blue-and-white flashing of the sheriff's light bar washing him out. He looks like a ghost. A wraith. And then she blinks, and he is gone, disappearing back into the woods.

She feels disloyal even thinking it.

Where was he when Camille fell?

40

THE PIECES

"Dean Westhaven?"

Sheriff Anthony Wood is waving to her. Ford drags her eyes away from the blank spot where her young lover stood, straightens.

"Sheriff." She can barely speak the word.

"Do you know what happened?"

"I don't. I was in my cabin working when I heard the scream. By the time I got here, she was gone."

"Have you been drinking, Dean?"

"Are there laws against it?"

"I suppose you know we're going to have to have a chat."

"We should, yes. My office? Right now? I need to wash my hands."

Camille's blood is on her hands, her phone. God knows where else. She can't wait to get away from the body. She needs to get her shit together, stall the sheriff long enough to get Ash sober—Becca, too, probably.

The woman in plainclothes joins them, glances at the sheet-covered body dispassionately. "Who's the deceased?"

Ford deliberately ignores her. "Sheriff, let's go inside."

"Dean, this is Kate Wood. My niece. She's here visiting."

"Oh. I thought—"

"I'm with Charlottesville PD. Homicide."

"How are you enjoying Marchburg?" Ford sounds inane, and hiccups back a tiny sob. "I'm sorry. This is all so terrible. To lose a student like this... Truly, Sheriff, may we?" She points to the back door of Main Hall, and he nods, following her up the back steps.

"I'll be there in a minute," his niece says. Those dark eyes are cool, shrewd, and Ford squirms a bit under her attention. They're probably the same age, but Ford has the distinct feeling she is being judged and found lacking. She draws herself up to her full five feet six, squares her shoulders. Their footsteps echo on the tiles.

Her office is quiet, and she gestures for the sheriff to enter. "Have a seat. I'll be right in. I just need to wash."

Her bathroom is attached to the office, and she shuts the door with a shaking hand, starts running the water immediately.

Holy shit. Holy shit. What is she going to do? How in the world did Camille end up in the bell tower, how did she fall, and who, or what, had Ford seen up there?

The water is too hot but she doesn't care, she needs the blood off. She scrubs and scrubs and scrubs until her hands are raw.

Finally, knuckles stinging, she makes her way to her desk. The sheriff is on his phone but puts it away the moment he sees her approach.

"They're going to take her to Charlottesville for autopsy. You say she's a sophomore?"

"Autopsy? Is that entirely necessary? We'll need to get the parents' permission, and we haven't even told them she's dead. Oh, my God. This is a nightmare."

"It's necessary. We have to find out what happened, and we don't have the capabilities here, you know that. We always send our bodies to Charlottesville. Now, this sophomore, Camille Shannon. Who's her daddy?"

Ford bristles—though this is the truth of things, all the girls here are "someone's" daughter.

"Her father is the US ambassador to Turkey. Her mother is a lawyer in DC. They're divorced but it's amicable. Her mother remarried recently."

"Oh, great. Had to be a politico."

"Tony, really. I have to call her parents. Her mother first, she's custodial, but the father, too."

"We usually like to have local police do the notification. Where is the mom exactly?"

"Northern Virginia. Falls Church."

"I have a friend in Fairfax County. I can give him a ring. They'll have a chaplain on call who can go to the house."

"I really think she should hear it from me. I am responsible. Camille is my—"

Tony puts his hands on her desk, leans toward her. "Listen, Ford. There's protocol. Let us follow it."

"She's my student, and I want to be the one to tell her mother I've failed her."

"You're being noble, and I appreciate that. But it's really something best left to the professionals. Once they've broken the news, they'll let us know and we'll get you on the phone with her. All right?"

Ford nods, rubs her temples. "I don't know what happened, Tony. I heard a scream and heard her hit the ground… I rushed out of my cottage, found her lying on the concrete. She was dead before I got here."

"Oh, yeah, she went splat all right."

Ford feels her face flush, and the sheriff stammers out an apology.

"Sorry, Ford. That was inappropriate. Was she having problems? Fighting with anyone?"

"Not that I know of."

"If you weren't aware of anything, we should probably check with the nurse, too. See if she confided in her that she was feeling suicidal."

"You think she jumped?"

"You think she was pushed?"

Ford settles deeper into her chair. "I hadn't thought it through, to be honest. I haven't gotten past the pool of blood. And the noise when she landed... Tony, she's just a child."

Her phone rings. A quick glance showed the very last number she could possibly want to see at the moment. She clicks Decline, feels the phone shimmy a moment later to let her know she's received a message. *Yes, Mother. I'll get back to you.*

A knock sounds and Ford looks up to see Tony's niece standing in the door.

"Come in."

"We're just discussing whether she jumped or was pushed," the sheriff says.

"She could have fallen, too," Kate says. "It doesn't always have to be diabolical, you know, Uncle Tony." To Ford, "Do you have any idea what she was doing up there? Your security says it's always locked."

"I don't know. Erik's right, the bell tower is always locked. It's too old to let people roam around up there, we're very careful to keep it off-limits. The bells are controlled from the outer office here. It's all computerized. There's no reason for anyone to be up there."

The sheriff looks from Ford to his niece and sighs.

"We better go on up, just to see."

41

THE PLAN

I walk from window to window trying to see what's happening. Dr. Asolo has gone to fetch Becca. She won't tell me why I've been pulled out of bed and marched to the attics but considering they're bringing Becca, I have to assume we've been busted for the goings on in the cabin. The tap, come back to bite me already.

I shouldn't be surprised by this, but I am. I've had the sense that the school is proud of the secret societies. Not openly encouraging them, but doing nothing to stop them. Stomps happen regularly, and tonight's tap hadn't exactly been quiet. So why are we getting in trouble now?

The only real rule that's inviolable is not lying and cheating. The rest of it—Goode certainly has a *girls will be girls* mentality. I'm familiar with the sentiment. It exists back home, too. The rules just don't apply to certain kinds of people. The right kind of people, as my mother would say. If you have money, privilege, you can get away with most anything.

I am woozy from the alcohol, the Benadryl, the Ecstasy, sheer tiredness. Still feeling relatively cuddly toward Becca, though, even though I know I'm going to hate her when the already itchy rash comes up full force.

Why am I here? If we're in trouble, shouldn't we be in Dean Westhaven's office?

I am so confused.

Finally, I drop into a tufted leather club chair and look around. What is this place? It looks like an office, there's a desk with a typewriter and a stack of pages facedown, two chairs facing it—the one I'm in and its mirror mate—a thick, green-and-cream Oriental rug set at an angle. Fresh-cut flowers in a small square glass vase, lush, full-petaled pink roses, sit on the corner of the desk. English roses. Like from home, in the spring, when the gardens of Oxford burst to life. Bookshelves from floor to ceiling, but only two shelves are filled.

Spartan, but elegant, comfortable accommodations. Who works up here, in isolation from the rest of the students?

The dean, dummy. When you see her in the window, this is where she is.

A commotion in the hall and the door flies open. Becca stumbles through, eyes bleary, arguing, and Dr. Asolo follows behind.

"So, I was out of bed after hours, who cares?" She notices me, and her face changes. Gone is the compassionate friend, and in her place, the Mistress. A banshee, a furious, evil-tempered death-presaging spirit who will eat me alive. "Why is *she* here?"

She thinks I've outed them. She thinks I've told.

I duck down into my chair, legs drawn up to protect myself. "I—"

"Did you tell? You stupid girl, I will end you—"

"Stop it!" Dr. Asolo pushes Becca into the chair next to me. She lands with an *oof.* "Listen to me. A girl has died."

"Fuuuuck," Becca drawls, clearly assuming this is related to the tap, but I sit up, suddenly clearheaded.

"It's Camille, isn't it?"

"It is, unfortunately. She fell off the bell tower."

The shock goes through me and I close my eyes, send up a silent prayer for my hateful roommate.

"You're shitting me," Becca says.

"Young lady, your mouth is going to get you in trouble. Knock it off."

"Why are we here?" I ask. "And no, Becca, I didn't say a word to anyone."

Asolo's shoulders drop, the stress and tiredness showing plainly on her pretty features. "Because the dean requested it. She knows about the tap tonight—no, don't deny it, why else do you two stink of alcohol? I suppose she was concerned that Camille was a part of the tap. Becca?"

Becca is still slouching in her chair but answers immediately, and honestly. "No, ma'am. She wasn't. We don't normally tap sophomores—Ash is an exception."

"Ash?"

"Camille wasn't there. I swear it."

Asolo waits a beat. Both of us say, "On my honor," and she blows out a breath.

"Okay. You two stay here. Don't leave until either the dean or I come to get you."

She bustles out the door, leaving us staring after her.

"What the hell is going on?" Becca asks, curling deeper in the chair. "How did Camille get up to the bell tower? It's always locked. I should know, we've tried to get up there enough times. Westhaven keeps the key under lock and key. Ha!"

I feel sick. Camille, dead? It doesn't feel possible. She was so excited, so happy, and a few hours later, broken at the base of Main like a doll thrown from a height.

"I'm sorry I accused you, Swallow. That was wrong of me."

"Becca, what you said to me the first day, about a roommate dying..."

"I was just trying to rattle you, Swallow. I had no idea she'd be dumb enough to go through with it."

"She had an invitation to the attics tonight. Remember?"

"Yes. I remember. Like I told you this morning, it wasn't me. I don't know who sent the summons. We aren't the only society who tapped tonight. Though no one sends a summons to do a tap. We try to keep who we bring in quiet. Didn't you see her tonight?"

"She was in the room after dinner, yes. The last time I saw her was when she left at ten for the summons. She was so excited."

I run a hand over my arm.

Becca is looking at me curiously. "Does it itch badly?"

"Yes. You're a right cunt, you know that? The Benadryl is only sort of working."

"It will be worse tomorrow," Becca predicts, going to the window. "There's a lot of activity out there."

"I know. I couldn't see anything, just the lights off the fire truck."

"She must have gone off the back of Main, or else we'd see everything below. Was she bummed about something?"

"No. She was happy, excited. I mean, sometimes she cries at night, but—"

"Cries about what?"

"I don't know."

"You didn't think to ask?"

"I asked. She told me she was fine. I can't exactly force it out of her."

Heavy steps pass by us, and then above. It feels like the ceiling will collapse under them. I move out of the way, just in case.

"They're up there looking," Becca whispers.

"Looking for what?"

"I don't know. A note? I can't believe Asolo locked us up here."

"She's trying to protect you."

"Asolo?"

"The dean. She's trying to protect you. The police are on campus, and we were all drinking tonight. I hardly think they'd take it well, finding out the senator's daughter was behind it, especially with an ambassador's daughter dead. Not good press for the school and the dean."

"I suppose you're right. But you know nothing about this, do you, Swallow?"

"What do you mean?"

"I mean, I don't think it's me they're trying to protect. You're her roommate. You're the first one they're going to want to talk to."

"Bugger." I drop back in the chair, blow into my cupped palm. Though I've brushed my teeth, my breath smells like vodka.

"Yes, little Swallow. Bugger." Becca looms over me. "You can't say anything about what happened tonight. Not a word. You say anything and you're out. Do you understand?"

"Becca, I—"

"I am your Mistress. I command you to keep your big fat mouth shut."

"I can't lie. They'll kick me out."

"You breathe a word about what happened during the tap and I will make you wish you had never come here. Am I clear?" Becca again looks like an avenging angel, fury written across her face, her mouth tight, her eyes dark.

"I'm clear, Mistress. What am I supposed to tell them?"

"I don't care. But not a word about Ivy Bound, or we'll all be screwed."

"Oh, so you're happy for me to lie, but not you? What sort of bullshit is that?"

"It's a test, Swallow. One you don't want to fail."

I can hear them moving around upstairs. Soon they will come for me.

I am in an untenable position. Again.

Oh, Camille. What have you done?

42

THE DISCOVERY

Ford watches the sheriff and his homicide niece swing flashlights around in the gloom, combing the bell tower for clues. She is ignoring her phone; her mother clearly knows something has happened and is calling incessantly. The odds of her showing up in town unannounced on this night of all nights… It begs the question, why? And the sheriff just happens to have his homicide detective niece visiting? Before the paranoia sets in, she turns her attention to the conversation playing out in front of her.

"Got something here," Tony says.

Ford sees the lights playing on a scrap of fabric. It is caught in a splinter of wood at the corner of the cupola's edifice. It's hard to tell exactly what color it is, pale, though. She thinks back to the scene below.

"Camille was wearing a gray Goode sweatshirt and black yoga leggings. I didn't notice any tears in her clothes. Is that gray?"

Tony shakes his head.

"White. Thin. Cotton, like a T-shirt or undershirt. A scarf, maybe. I'm going to get my evidence techs up here. Collect it, take it to the lab, get some fingerprints. Too early to make any guesses as to what happened, whether she jumped or someone gave her a push. But if this isn't hers... Gotta get all our ducks in a row first."

Ford doesn't want to make any unsubstantiated claims, but she also doesn't want to make the same mistakes her mother made.

"Tony, I'm not 100 percent sure, but I thought I saw a shadow up here. When I found Camille."

His tone is sharp. "You think or you know?"

"It was dark. I looked up and saw...movement. An outline. Maybe I was seeing things. I can't be certain."

He examines the door with his Maglite. "It's a sturdy lock, not broken. No scratch marks, doesn't look like it was jimmied. Someone unlocked it."

"That's hard to believe. We've always been very careful about the keys, went to a keycard system a few years back for extra safety."

"Who has access to the keys?"

"I have a master set to the school, obviously. I keep them in my safe. Security has the second set, which are kept in their offices. It's attended twenty-four-seven. Impossible for one of the girls to sneak in and get a set."

"But this is still an old-fashioned keyed lock, not one of your keycard accessible ones. We should double-check, just in case. Still have those secret societies?"

"Yes, some exist. They're not openly sanctioned anymore, though. I keep a close eye on our girls, unlike some of my predecessors."

"Secret societies?" Kate asks. She has appeared silently after circumnavigating the tiny platform.

"Social organizations outside the school's normal activities. Little clubs that get together and raise spirits on campus."

"Raise a ruckus is more like it."

"Now, Tony, that's not fair. It's all in the spirit of things."

"But why are they secret?" Kate asks.

"It's a misnomer, really. They're just little off-the-books clubs. Like sororities, in some ways, but girls can't pledge. They govern their own membership. Choose their own members. It's a long-held tradition here, and at many of our peer schools. There have been secret societies at Goode for over a century. Which is why they still exist, though we're not as accepting of them as we once were. We see them now as more of a mentorship opportunity for our older girls."

Kate scoffs. "Mentorship? It sounds like a great way for some popular kids to exclude some of their classmates."

"You can't force children to be all-inclusive, Detective. The world doesn't work that way, and teenage girls don't, either."

"It should. The world would be a better place. Can any of them get up here?"

"No. There are only two sets of keys. Mine and Security's. Both kept in safes."

Tony chews his lip. "Where's that boy been lately?"

Fury rises up in her. "Don't you dare, Tony."

"What boy?" Kate asks. She's climbed up and is leaning out over the edge of the cupola now, her flashlight making long yellow swaths of light down the front of the building. She's so far out it's making Ford nervous. One tiny bump and over the edge she'd go. It's easy to see how Camille went screaming to her death.

Tony seems to read Ford's mind. He reaches out and grabs his niece's jacket. "Careful there, Kate. This cupola is old. Don't put too much pressure on the balustrade."

Kate shuts off the flashlight and jumps back down. "She would have to climb up to get over this edge. Or be forcibly lifted. We need to talk to the girls, see if they heard anything. Talking, or a scuffle. There are rooms below this, correct?

Maybe one of the girls will be able to shed some light on a time line, at least. What boy are you talking about?"

"Rumi Reynolds. Son of Rick Reynolds."

"The one who murdered the coed?"

"The very one. Ford here hired young Rumi to be a jack-of-all-trades."

"Come on, Tony. He isn't involved in this. Don't get lazy and start pointing fingers. It's not fair to him. He is not responsible for his father's actions."

"Ford Westhaven, the patron saint of lost causes. Something like that warps a child, Ford. What he saw…"

"What did he see?" Kate asks.

"According to him, he saw everything."

"The murder?"

"Yup. He even testified. The state's star witness was the murderer's ten-year-old son."

"I remember that now. Hmm."

They turn in unison to look out over the dark campus, and Ford loses her temper.

"Stop talking like I'm not standing right here. What do you mean, 'hmm'? He didn't do this. I know Rumi, quite well. He wouldn't hurt a fly. That's why he's working here, for me, for Goode. Someone had to give him a chance at a normal life, and that was me. He's dedicated to this school. It's completely unfair to leap to the conclusion that he's responsible before we even search Camille's room for a note, a diary, something to give us her state of mind. It was dark. I don't know what I saw. I would never have mentioned it if I thought you'd go tilting at windmills and jumping to spurious conclusions."

Tony and Kate share a brief look, then he shrugs. "No one's making judgments, Ford. I was just asking. Let's go look at the girl's room, talk to her roommate. There might be a clearer answer downstairs."

Ford lets them go ahead of her, then locks the cupola door.

Her hands are shaking, she can smell her own acrid scent, and under it, the musky notes of man. She needs to be very, very careful. They can't find out about the affair, it could ruin her. Rumi is of age, but still. She knows it looks bad. But she will not let Rumi get railroaded into an accusation, either.

Tearful girls are gathered in the sewing circle when the three arrive on the sophomores' floor. Ford calls out, "Man on the floor," loudly and there are a few squeals, the sound of running feet, then she nods to Tony. "Okay, follow me. They're roomed in 214."

The lights are ablaze in Camille and Ash's room. The room looks like it's seen a struggle. A painting is on the floor by one of the desks. Pillows are askew, blankets dragging on the floor, the lower bunk's mattress off center. There's something pink on the sheets, not dark enough to be blood. It takes Ford a moment to realize it's calamine lotion.

Ford recalls her own tap, looks briefly to the desk under a framed photograph of Oxford's doors. This must be Ash's desk and yes, there's a small brown sandwich bag sitting near the edge. Ford knows what it contains.

Damn it. Ivy Bound is explicitly prohibited from using poison ivy on the Swallows. The ruling was made three years ago when a Swallow's mother threatened to sue the school because her daughter touched her eye with a poison-ivy-tainted hand and it swelled shut, necessitating a trip to the emergency room.

Oh, Becca Curtis, you are in so much trouble.

Ford herself suffered the indignity, as did many of the Swallows who followed her, but the school has cracked down on hazing, majorly cracked down, and things like this are not supposed to be going on.

She can't disappear the bag, she's going to have to let that play itself out. But she can help distract attention.

Tony and Kate are rifling through the desks and drawers now, of both girls. Ford puts up a hand. "Hold on. You can't go through Ash Carlisle's things. Only Camille's. There are privacy concerns."

Kate stops and looks at Ford, incredulous. "You're joking. They're teenagers. Students. And one of them is dead."

"There's still an expectation of privacy. Obviously, Camille has none, not anymore, but Ash does. Please keep your search limited to Camille's things. Perhaps we should wait for your evidence team to do this?"

"I know how to toss a room, Ford," Tony says without missing a beat. He opens the top dresser drawer, digs his hands in deep. "What have we here?"

He draws out an almost empty pint of Stolichnaya. Ford feels a sting of fury—*damn that girl*—followed by a teensy little prayer heavenward—*sorry, Camille, but for heaven's sake, vodka in your socks?*

Tony keeps moving, though, tossing the rest of the dresser. "Where's the roommate? I wanna talk to her."

"I had her isolated. This is going to be a terrible shock to her, and she's already suffered a great deal of loss. Her parents died recently, and to have this happen so soon after their deaths will certainly affect her tremendously."

Again, that sly glance between uncle and niece. Ford wants to scream but keeps her temper in check.

"Just give us a few here, okay, Ford?" And to his niece, "Nothing's leaping out at me. You?" He eases himself down on his knees to look under the dresser.

Kate is holding a notebook with a floral cover, leafing through. "Other than someone's clearly been through this room already? She writes very pretty poems. Quite a few about death."

Ford isn't surprised. English is Camille's best subject.

Kate flips a few more pages. "She didn't care for her roommate, that's for sure."

"Ash? I didn't know they weren't getting along," Ford says.

"Not getting along is an understatement. Looks like there was some serious bullying going on. 'She made fun of me again today. She was sitting with the other bitches and looking over her shoulder at me with that stupid smug stare. Later, she told me how I would never get into Ivy Bound. Bitch.' Lots more in that vein. 'She was queen of the sewing circle again tonight. It's like I don't even exist anymore.'"

"May I see that?" Ford asks.

Kate hands it over, and Ford glances through, flipping pages, seeing phrases that shock her:

Stupid accent, dumb cunt, out of the room late again, should report her, she's Becca's bitch now. Bet the two of them are fucking. How else would she get on Becca's good side so fast? I hate her. I hate them both.

She closes the cover gently. The vitriol is surprising, she's always seen Camille as a gentle soul. Not this roiling mass of emotion, spilling hate into her diary.

Tony is on his back now, squirming on the floor, reaching under the dresser. "Thought I saw something…yep…hold on… just about got it… What's this?"

He drags his arm back and is holding a white bag with a green sticker on the front. It looks like it's come from the pharmacy in Marchburg, Ford has a few herself.

He opens the bag and out fall two pill bottles. They don't have the Marchburg Pharmacy label. He reads the label aloud.

"Cytotec. Place two pills in each cheek and let dissolve fully. What is this?"

Ford snatches it away. "Let me see that."

Camille's name is on the bottle, along with instructions to take the pills forty-eight hours after returning home. Ford is unfamiliar with the drug name, but Kate isn't.

"It's a chemical abortifacient," Kate says. "Dean Westhaven, were you aware that Camille recently had an abortion?"

43

THE INTERROGATION

The door to the attic office creaks open, and I raise my head blearily. I've fallen asleep in the chair; my neck is stiff. Becca is asleep opposite me, one leg pulled up, cheek resting on her knee. I'm filled with a rush of tenderness seeing her like this, so vulnerable, lips slightly open, face relaxed. She looks so young, so pretty. I belong to her now. I am her Swallow. She's chosen me.

As if she knows she's being watched, Becca's eyes open and she looks at me like she's happy to see me, and my stomach does a flip.

"Ladies?" Dean Westhaven's voice is soft, regretful. She's sorry to wake us. "Thank you for waiting for us here. I assume Dr. Asolo told you we lost a student tonight. Ash, I'm so sorry to tell you this, but your roommate, Camille, has died. This is Sheriff Wood, and Detective Wood, his niece, from Charlottesville. They're going to ask you some questions. Becca, if you'd please stay? I know you've been mentoring Ash and it would be helpful to have your support."

Becca smiles. "Absolutely, Dean. I'm happy to help."

They're being so kind. It strikes me, as I so desperately wished only weeks ago, I have found a new life, new friends. A new support system, one based on healthy boundaries and mutual respect. Yes, my roommate is dead, yes, I've been tortured tonight, but look at what I've gained. Look at Becca, eyes shining. Look at the dean, smiling encouragingly. Pity and love. These are confusing emotions for me, but I'll take them.

But the other two, the strange man and the young, crow-eyed woman, looking at me with matching dark, unfathomable eyes, make me nervous. The juxtaposition of the two emotions is too much. Tears prick my eyes. I blink hard against them, but one wells up and runs down my cheek.

"Oh, my poor duck." Dean Westhaven pats my hand. "We'll get you through this. Just answer a few questions and we'll get you back to bed. Tomorrow is a new day."

Becca places her hand on my other arm, which throbs. "You've got this."

Buoyed on both sides, I nod to the strangers, and the interrogation begins.

The sheriff kicks us off with a platitude so insincere I wonder how many times he's said it over the years: "I'm very sorry for your loss, young lady."

"Erm, thank you."

"You were close to your roommate?"

"Not particularly. I mean, we were friends, but she was closer with our suitemates. They've known her longer."

"You're British," the female detective says.

"Yes. Is that a problem?"

"No, of course not. I'm only surprised. I didn't realize."

"I'm from Oxford."

The sheriff tries again. "You and Camille weren't getting along?"

"I didn't say that. We got along fine. She was closer with our suitemates, that's all."

"If she were upset, she wouldn't confide in you?"

"No, sir. Probably not. Definitely not, actually. She cries herself to sleep every night, and when I ask what's wrong she blows me off."

The sheriff and the detective exchange a glance.

"Has she been sick recently?"

"Like, a cold? No. She had some…female problems. When term started." I mumble this last bit and look at the ground, mortified.

"Ah. So, she did confide in you about the abortion. When—"

"What?" My head whips up. "What are you talking about?"

Becca squeezes my arm tightly.

Dean Westhaven snaps to. "Oh, dear. I think we should stop it right here, Tony."

Tony is the sheriff, I surmise. "Camille had an abortion? I mean, it makes sense, she was hurting and feverish and said it was her time of the month."

The sheriff ignores the dean, just crosses his arms. "When was this?"

"The first week of classes. She left the room and I found her crying in the bathroom, with Vanessa. They told me to get out, so I did."

"Vanessa is one of their suitemates," Westhaven supplies.

"Do you know who her boyfriend is?"

"No. She has a crush on her stepbrother. Had."

"Remind me not to tell you my secrets," Becca says softly, chiding, but I shake her off.

"It was hardly a secret. Camille told everyone at dinner, several times. I'm not betraying a confidence. I wouldn't do that."

"When did you see Camille last?"

"Around ten. She received a summons to the attics."

Becca squeezes my arm again and this time, I do stop. Becca addresses the adults.

"Sometimes, when we take an interest in a student from our

sister class, we invite them to join us in the Commons, a study room, to get to know them better. As the dean will tell you, mentorship is encouraged at Goode. I did so with Ash early in term. But we don't know who gave the summons for Camille. It came in the usual method, left anonymously for the waitrons to deliver."

"Is that how you choose who to invite to your secret societies?" the sheriff asks.

Becca shoots a glance at Westhaven. "Mentorship is different. I can't comment on the societies, naturally. That's a question for the dean."

Spoken like a true politician. After what I've seen tonight, I realize Becca holds multitudes of secrets.

The sheriff seems satisfied, but the detective isn't buying it. "And you, Ash? How did you find Becca's *mentoring*? What sorts of things did she mentor you on?"

The slight emphasis on the word contains any number of meanings, and I don't like where this is heading. "I'm sorry, but this has nothing to do with Camille. I feel simply terrible that she's dead, but you're going to get to know her much better through Vanessa and Piper. We weren't close."

"You recently lost your parents, did you not?"

"Tony," Westhaven warns.

I push away the panic. "It's okay, Dean. Yes, sir. I did."

"How terrible for you. I am so sorry. Why are you so far away from home? Who's paying your tuition?"

"Dean Westhaven was kind enough to allow me to come here despite my personal tragedy. As for the rest, I don't think that's any of your business. And it has nothing to do with why my roommate committed suicide."

"You think she killed herself?"

"Didn't she?"

Silence fills the room, and a chill moves down my spine. What is going on here?

Becca says, "Wait, you think someone killed her?"

"We don't know anything yet. Dean, can we speak with Ca-mille's other friends?"

"Certainly. Ash, do you feel comfortable going back to your room?"

"Unfortunately, Dean, we need to spend some time in the deceased's room, have our evidence techs go over it," Sheriff Wood says, and the implication is clear. They don't believe me. They are going to take apart the room, my life. My heart begins to thunder in my chest. I run through the items in my closet and drawers that could get me in trouble. The cigarettes. The bag with the calamine. The note. Oh, God, the note.

I cast a panicked glance at Becca, who draws me close.

"She can stay with me tonight, Dean. I'll make her a bed on my sofa."

"Oh, thank you, Becca. That's a great help. I'll see you two in the morning. No wandering now, straight to bed with you both. Becca, I trust you can get the remainder of the seniors to their rooms, as well?"

The dean practically throws us out the door. I follow Becca. I'm almost to the hallway when the female detective says, "Hey. Hold on."

I stop. "What?"

"Your shirt. Come here."

I have seen this cold, calculating look in a law enforcement officer's eye once before. When the police sat me down for a chat about my mother's death.

"Were you aware...?"

"Are you sure...?"

"Why didn't you...?"

"Come with us..."

The detective spins me away and I can feel a hand on the hem of my pajama shirt. Lifting it.

I fight the urge to bolt, though I've done nothing wrong. Are they going to arrest me? Handcuff me? Is this all over already?

"What is it?"

The dean's voice sounds weird, strangled, hushed. "Ash. How did you tear your shirt?"

44

THE PREDICAMENT

I try to look over my shoulder. "What do you mean? It's torn?"

"There's a piece missing from your shirt."

The tone of the room has changed. I face the police and the dean, all three of whom are leaning toward me.

"I wasn't aware there was a rip in my shirt."

"Where, exactly, have you been tonight?" This from the detective, who has gone on alert, enhancing her resemblance to a raptor. Becca squeezes my hand even tighter.

"You two an item?" the detective suddenly asks.

"What?" My face starts to burn, and I jerk my hand away, but Becca has a death grip on me.

Dean Westhaven clears her throat. "That is a totally inappropriate question. I don't see the relevance—"

Becca interrupts, "Why would you say that?"

The detective gestures toward us. "It's nothing important.

You're holding hands. I was only wondering if you're in a relationship."

"I'm comforting her. You're accusing her of murder."

I yank my hand from Becca's, heart taking off at a gallop. "I
didn't murder anyone."

The sheriff has both hands up. "Whoa, whoa. We aren't accusing anyone of anything right now. We're just trying to figure out
what happened to your roommate, Ash. Please answer the question. What is the nature of your relationship with Miss Curtis?"

"We're not an item."

"All right. Where were you tonight? Can you account for
your whereabouts this evening?"

"I—"

"She *was* with me." Becca's voice is strong and clear.

Eyebrows rise all around.

"Not like that. We had a secret society meeting tonight. Ash
was tapped. She was with me from a little after 10:00 p.m. until
now. So, you see, she couldn't have hurt Camille."

Becca blows out her breath as if she's been holding it and
grabs my hand again. Squeezes hard. I get the message. *Do not
contradict me.*

"Well, that's very helpful," the sheriff says. "But, Ash, I'm
afraid we're going to have to talk to you alone."

The dean nods. "Wait outside, Becca dear. And see if you can
ferret out who sent the summons, will you?"

With one last squeeze so hard my bones crush and tears start,
Becca leaves.

"Why don't you take a seat, Ash. I need to speak with the
sheriff."

The dean takes the sheriff by the arm and escorts him out into
the hall. The detective follows, casting a last curious glance at me.

Oh, God. I am royally fucked.

"Tony, what is this? You can't possibly think one of my students had anything to do with Camille's death, especially Ash.

She is so reticent she couldn't hurt a fly, much less a person. There's no way she had something to do with this."

"She's wearing a shirt with a tear in it, made of what looks like similar fabric to what we saw up in the bell tower. And need I mention it's her roommate who died? I most certainly am not ruling it out. We need to find out if she was up there. And why. And what happened."

"Then I'm afraid, as her guardian, I will have to call our lawyers. Alan Markert is in Lynchburg, he can be here in an hour, maybe less. My God, Tony, I can't have you treating a student like a murder suspect."

"But what if she is a murderer, Ford? Have you thought about that?"

She bites back a sharp reply. "Detective Wood, could you give us a moment, please?"

Kate nods and steps away. When she's out of earshot, Ford whirls back to face Tony, whispering furiously.

"This is about us. You're trying to punish me. I get it. I'm sorry you're hurt, Tony. But we don't work. Not anymore. Don't you dare take your frustrations with me out on my girls."

Tony's lips press together in a thin line. "Ford, for an intelligent woman, you can be so colossally stupid sometimes. This situation has nothing to do with us because there is no *us*. There never will be. You made your position clear. I'm never going to leave this place, and you're going to get out the first chance you get. I understand completely. But don't think that just because I fucked you a few times it impairs my ability to do my job. If you want to call a lawyer, do it. I'll call for a deputy to take Ash Carlisle to the office and do this formally. And I'll give her a Breathalyzer, too."

"You wouldn't dare. You have no cause."

He laughs, low and mean. "You think I can't smell the alcohol on all y'all's breaths? I most certainly do have cause, they're underage. You aren't, but I've seen you bleary-eyed enough to recognize you've had a few yourself. Do you think the parents would be happy about that? One of their kids dies while you're partying?"

"I was not. My God, Tony. You can be so cruel. And you wonder why I broke it off."

He takes a huge breath, blows it out. "If you'd like to stop being dramatic, you can let me have a civilized chat with the kid, outside of the influence of her girlfriend. Or a lawyer. There could be a simple explanation. It was pretty clear the older girl—Becca?—was controlling what Ash had to say. She was gripping Ash's hand so tight it was turning white. Let me do my job, and I won't interfere with yours."

Ford is deeply stung by his words, by the truth she hears in them, though she isn't going to let him know it.

"Fine. I will have to be there. You don't talk to her alone. She's been through a horrible trauma and she's barely holding herself together."

"What trauma, Ford? Exactly."

"Over the summer, her father, Sir Damien Carr, committed suicide. When her mother discovered him, she shot herself. Ash found the two of them while her mother was still alive, barely. She died in her arms. It's been terribly hard for her, as you can imagine. Now this…"

A hard, pitiless edge flashes in the sheriff's eyes. He has cop eyes. Dead eyes. Ford shivers internally—this is why she and Tony can't be together. There is something cold at his core. He has a mean streak. It felt dangerously fun in the beginning, but she quickly realized he can't turn it off. It's his coping mechanism for all the horrors he's seen, or so he says. She knows exactly what he's thinking—Ash has been connected to three deaths in two months.

Four, really, there's been another death, but Muriel Grassley doesn't count. Ash had nothing to do with that accident.

Still, maybe she should call Alan. Or even her mother.

At the very thought of Jude phoning her relentlessly tonight from her command post at the house, the kitchen table scattered, no doubt, with crystal glasses and empty bottles, Ford's spine stiffens. No. She can handle Tony.

"I will shut this down the moment I feel it's becoming too much for her to handle. She has nothing to do with this, Tony."

"Understood. And I'm sorry to hear about her folks. That's tough. I'll be delicate. Kate?" he calls, and his niece hurries to his side. "Let's talk to her."

Tony's holster smacks against the doorframe as they go back into the room. The gun is big, wicked. Ford hates to see it in her school. It makes everything that happened tonight feel so irreversible.

Inside, Ash looks fragile and broken. She is slumped in the chair, tears running freely down her cheeks. When she sees them enter, she sits up and wipes her arm across her face.

Tony perches one butt cheek on the desk, and Ford grits her teeth to stop from snapping, *That's an antique, you moron,* at him.

"Ash, I know this is hard. I also know your friend was trying to keep you from talking to me. Now that we're alone, what would you like to tell me about this evening? You were tapped for a secret society?"

"I can't talk about it."

"Ash, I give you permission to discuss everything that happened tonight with the sheriff. Nothing said here will leave this room." Ford smooths a hand over Ash's arm. Within seconds, Ash is rubbing the spot. The poison ivy... *Lord, don't tell them about the poison ivy, he'll have all our heads.*

"There's nothing to say."

Thatta girl. Ford says aloud, "You can give us details about the night without divulging the secrets of the society."

"All right. They came to my room, yelled at me for a while, then we went to another room, they yelled awhile longer, then they sent us back to bed. Nothing that had anything to do with

Camille. Camille was gone before they came. She had a summons to the attics. I don't know from whom."

"Did you see anyone other than the girls from the tap while you were out of bed?"

"No. No one. We were… It was in a private place, and I'll be honest, I have no idea where it was. Somewhere on campus, though."

Ford interjects, "There are a number of abandoned outbuildings, old staff cottages. The societies like to sneak into them and have their meetings. It's not sanctioned, per se, but we do keep them in repair so no one gets hurt."

"All right. Ash, your shirt is torn. Did that happen during the tap?"

"No, sir. When I got back to the room, I took a shower and put on fresh clothes."

"This isn't what you wore for the tap?"

"No. I was…dirty. The room we were in was quite dusty."

"Are the clothes you wore to the tap still in your room?"

"Yes, sir."

"Your friend said she was with you all night. Was she also in the shower with you?"

Ash blushes to the roots of her hair. "No, sir. She'd gone up to bed."

"So, she wasn't with you every moment of the night."

"We were together all night. Just not for the ten minutes it took me to shower and change. Dr. Asolo came for me moments after I went to bed. And to answer your question again, no, she is not my girlfriend. Becca has been mentoring me. She's been very kind."

"Mentoring, how?"

"Today is a good example. I hadn't shared my history with any of my mates, and it came out over breakfast. I was upset and ran away, into the forest. Becca came to make sure I was okay, to assure me this is a passing moment. To give me perspective. There's nothing going on between us, not like you think."

"All right. Fair enough. Tell me about your relationship with your roommate again."

"We don't get on wonderfully, but it's fine. It was fine."

"And you didn't know anything about the abortion? She didn't mention a thing?"

"No. But she wouldn't have confided in me."

"Well, Tony? Satisfied?"

"We're going to have to take your shirt with us for analysis, Ash."

"No!"

All three adults look surprised.

"It was a gift. It means a lot to me. I need to keep it."

The sheriff stands. "Unfortunately, you can't. We will follow you to your room where you can change in privacy, and then you can meet up with your friend. Just so you aren't surprised, we may want to talk again. Get some sleep. Tomorrow will be a long day."

"Like that will happen," Ash mutters.

45

THE BETRAYAL

I am loath to give up the shirt. It feels like if I do, I'm severing my new and tenuous ties to Ivy Bound in some way. I hardly have a choice, though, the two police are standing outside my door and the dean is watching me expectantly.

I turn my back to hide the rash I know is blooming on my body. I strip off the shirt, scramble into another, and hand it over. What else am I going to do? If I fight this, it will look bad. I just need them to go away and leave me alone.

The dean gives me a watery smile, holding the T-shirt like it's a dead ferret. "It will all be okay, Ash. I promise. I'll send Becca to escort you upstairs. Try to get some sleep. I'll talk to you in the morning."

She pauses, as if she wants to say something more, then shakes her head and leaves.

Jesus, Camille. What the hell did you do? And what the hell have you done to me?

I move to the window, look out onto the darkened quad. It's almost three in the morning. Where is Camille now? In the back of an ambulance? In a drawer at the morgue? Still lying, broken and bloodied, on the concrete?

Stupid girl. Stupid, stupid girl.

"That's no way to talk to your Mistress."

Becca darkens my doorstep, and I bite back a scream of surprise. I didn't realize I said it aloud, and I am so damn tired of everyone sneaking up on me.

Becca's reflection in the window: the popped hip, the pouty smile, the ruffled, messy bun make her look so innocent. She is heartbreakingly beautiful and devastatingly cruel, and I am torn between loving her and hating her. I can't help but feel that somehow, because I came to Becca's notice, that Becca saw me and was compelled to tease me that first day, I have led us all to this precipice. A twisted kind of fate.

"I meant Camille."

"I know. Come with me, Swallow."

I'm reluctant to leave the sanctity of my room, but again, what choice do I have? Rush after the dean and the cops trying to explain myself? I want as much distance between me and the authority figures as humanly possible.

Becca marches to the stairwell without a backward glance. I'm both touched and angry that I'm expected to follow without question. I suppose this is what being a Swallow means. Obey your Mistress no matter what.

A little voice in the back of my mind says, *Even if you end up in jail?*

Stop. I've done nothing wrong.

Haven't you?

Dr. Grassley's pouty-lipped face floats in front of my eyes.

Not my fault, not my fault.

I shut the door on Muriel's death and go back to Camille.

I doubt most taps end in a student's death. But Camille wasn't with us.

Who was she with?

It takes me a moment to realize Becca has led me upstairs and I'm walking freely down the seniors' hall.

The attics. The coveted attics. And not shunted off into some strange, creepy room, this is the real deal.

Becca is moving quickly, but there are plenty of doors open—the whole school is awake and distraught. I see flashes from inside—colors, crying, insolent stares. A few exclamations of protest, but muffled. I'm with Becca Curtis. I'm protected. I'm golden.

Becca leads me to the end of the hall, a room by the stairs. "You may enter," she says, like I'm a vampire she's inviting in for dinner.

At first glance, Becca's room feels shockingly plain. One desk. The sofa is wider, deeper, and covered in dark blue velvet. There are two damask armchairs. Dormers, both with a window seat and fluffy pillows. Lofted ceilings with timber beams. A huge mahogany wardrobe. Bookshelves. There is a second room, too, the bedroom itself, and she has a private bath.

It's like a well-appointed Parisian garret, only not as small.

And it's original to the school. It has not been renovated into obscurity like the bottom three floors.

This, *this* is what Goode should look like.

"Holy shit."

"Yes, it's nice, isn't it? The former dean's space. It's always saved for head girl. I like it. My mother did the decorating. This style is one of the few things my mother and I agree upon. She has impeccable taste."

"Yes." What else am I going to say? My roommate just died but I think your mum has an excellent feel for drapery?

"Sit."

I collapse into a chair. It is wide and soft and I want to curl into a ball and go to sleep, preferably for days.

Becca closes the door and folds herself into the far edge of the sofa. Her knees are dirty. Like she's been kneeling in ashes.

"I have to say, you're well shot of that roommate. She was only going to hold you back. But what a fucking mess. What did you tell them?"

"Nothing of note. That I was bodily taken from my room to someplace I can't identify, yelled at, then brought back. I didn't tell them anything else about the tap."

"Did you give them the shirt?"

"I didn't have a choice. Becca, what—"

"Did you tell them we were together the whole time?"

"Yes. Mostly."

"What do you mean, mostly?"

"I had to tell them I took a shower. And you weren't in it with me."

Becca looks stricken for a second, then anger crosses her angelic face.

"I gave you an ironclad alibi, and you tossed it away? How stupid are you?"

"First off, I don't need an alibi. I didn't do anything. Second, I couldn't lie. They knew I'd showered, my hair and towel were wet, and they took apart the room. They asked if you were with me. Would you rather me lie and say we were showering together after hours?"

"You could have said it was Camille's towel."

I start to stand up. "I'm sorry. I don't think I understand how this game is played. Don't lie unless you need to? I signed the pledge, just like you did. I can't get kicked out for lying about something so inconsequential."

"But you'd let me? My God, Ash, you contradicted what I told the dean. I said I was with you all night. All you had to do was say the same. Then we'd both be covered. Instead, now there's a time gap, and it looks like I was trying to cover something up."

"Were you?"

The words are out of my mouth before I can think. Becca's anger turns to rage, billowing across her face, and I move so quickly I knock over the chair. I've only seen that look from one other person, and it scares me to the bone. I know what follows, and brace myself.

Becca, though, doesn't move. The color slowly drains from her face. I'm backed against the wall, waiting for the punches to come, to land, but Becca is frozen on the couch.

A breath. Another.

Slowly, I detach myself, flexing my hands. My shortened, clipped but unfiled nails have bitten into the thin skin of my palms; blood wells. "I didn't mean that. I'm sorry. I was thoughtless."

Becca speaks softly, a thin veneer of sadness over her words. "You thought I was going to hit you. That I could hurt you. After everything I've done, to help you adjust, to help you fit in, to cover for you, to pave your way, to be your friend, you thought I was going to *attack* you?"

How many ways will I screw this up?

"I'm sorry," I say again, my voice small, meek. I never used to apologize like this. I never used to be so weak.

"You don't know much about friendship, do you, Ash?"

"This is a strange kind of friendship, Becca. You're mean to me, alternately ignore me, then are nice and kind, lie for me, interrogate me, scream at me. I don't get you."

I sag into the chair again, put my face in my hands. The springs on the sofa squeak, then I feel Becca's arms go around me. I wait, unmoving, not leaning toward her, not accepting the hug.

After a moment, Becca peels my hands from my face, searching for the tears she's sure are there. Though I'm not crying, I don't meet her eyes. I am surprised when I feel her breath on my face.

The kiss is soft. Gentle. Sweet.

Then the pressure increases. A hand goes into my hair, pulling my ponytail back gently so my mouth is forced to tip open. Becca's tongue is warm, shockingly so, and I feel a rush move through me, longing, desire, and suddenly, I'm gasping for breath.

I'm confused by the emotions I'm feeling. Do I want this? This girl-woman who tortures me with sweet kisses and cruel words? Yes, I do. No, I don't.

Becca is emboldened by me not pulling away. The kiss deepens. Her long, slim hand slides under my shirt, grazing my ribs, moving up until she's softly cupping my left breast. She flicks her thumb across my nipple. Another surge courses through me, one so unexpected and strange that I stiffen and swat away her hand.

Becca laughs into my mouth and draws me closer, tucking my body into hers. The hug is almost as intimate as the kiss. Becca rests her face against my chest.

"Sorry, little bird. No reason to rush. We have all year to get to know each other. It's going to be so much easier now that we both have singles. At least you were wearing my gift tonight. You looked pretty in my shirt. Did you like it? I'm sorry they took it away."

"No. I mean, I'm—"

Becca jerks away. "You're what?"

My mind is a whirling mess. I can't form the proper words. Because I can't let anyone get too close. It's too dangerous. I'm too dangerous. *You gave me the shirt? The shirt that the police took into evidence? The shirt with the tear in it?*

My danger trigger is on fire. I have to get out of here. Now.

"I'm not sure I want to do this, Becca. I don't know. I've had a very long night. I need some sleep."

The words linger between us for a moment. They can't be taken back. And I know I've made a terrible mistake.

"Becca—"

Becca holds up a hand. She is brisk, businesslike. Her face

betrays no more emotion. She's become the Mistress again. Re-treated behind her perfect veneer. There is no more softness, no more vulnerability. She is hard, implacable, like diamonds. The switch is fast and unnerving.

"I understand. Forgive me for being so forward. I see how you watch me. Everywhere I go, you're just offstage, watching. I thought you were interested. I thought you wanted to be with me. But if you don't, that's fine. Completely fine. There is a set of stairs to the sophomores' hall right outside my door. Go to bed, Swallow. Report at 7:00 a.m."

I'm frozen to the spot. I have wounded her. The one person who's been accepting of me, kind, even if her attentions have been slightly twisted. She brought me into the fold and I've rejected the offerings.

"Go," she says.

Miserable and oddly relieved, I comply without another word. Out the door, into the stairwell, down, down, down. Every tread, her name rings in my head.

Becca. Becca. Becca.

Flashes of her face, the kiss, the way she stood up for me with the cop. The shirt, soft and worn, with the bird on it. A gift. *You looked pretty in my shirt.*

Becca more than likes me. That's why she has been so nice. These past few weeks have been a seduction.

Flattering. Interesting.

But there is something else Becca said that makes me stop cold, my hand on the knob.

It's going to be so much easier now that we both have singles.

It's like she planned this from the very beginning.

46

THE ABSOLUTION

The night is no longer so dark when I get back onto the hall. I shouldn't be surprised to see Vanessa and Piper waiting for me, but I am. Vanessa's lovely face is wrecked from crying, her nose and eyes swollen and red. Piper looks upset but in control. When they see me emerge from the stairwell, the two of them move, uninvited, to my side.

There is crime scene tape across my door, but no cops stand guard. I rip it down and enter. They follow me in, close the door behind them.

"Where have you been? We...we were worried." Vanessa's voice breaks, and I have to fight the urge to say, *Stop putting me on*.

"You weren't worried about me."

"Yes, we were," Piper says. "Vanessa?"

Vanessa is wringing her hands. "Ash, I need to apologize. I've handled everything so terribly. If I had any idea how today would end up, I wouldn't have been so mean to you. I wouldn't have gone along with Camille. Your parents… I'm sorry. For everything. I was a total bitch."

"Ditto," Piper says.

"If you're trying to get me to talk, I don't know what happened," I say, collapsing on the sofa. "Being nice now won't change anything. She'll still be dead, and I'll still not know anything about why. And what do you mean, gone along with Camille?"

Piper blurts the truth. "She's been spying on you for weeks now. She watched you input your computer password, memorized it, and used it to get into your system. She found the article about your father."

Now they have my full attention. "What? Camille? She's been in my computer?"

"She's been in everything. After she saw the report, her father did a background check. That's how she found out your real name."

I close my eyes, trying to rein in the panic. *You underestimate people, you always have. It's your biggest weakness, assuming people don't lie as well as you.* And then, *This is fine. Everything is backstopped. You are fine, if they knew anything, you wouldn't be having this conversation.*

"Everyone knows," Vanessa says. "About how your parents died. About your brother, too. Camille made sure."

Johnny. Oh, my God. Stay fucking calm.

"Everyone?"

"Yes. Becca, too. I know you think she's your special friend, but she's been aware of this from day one."

"You're lying," I say, trying hard to look bored. "Whatever."

Vanessa raises a brow. "I'm not."

"You are. Becca would have bounced Camille out on her ear for Honor Code violations. I know we are all guilty of bending the rules, but breaking into my computer is beyond the pale."

Piper shrugs. "Everyone has a price, Ash. And everyone can be

compromised. A lot of things at this school go through Becca."
She pinches her thumb and forefinger together, mimicking puffing on a joint.

I'm not entirely surprised to hear Becca is bringing drugs into
the school. Tonight, she gave me Ecstasy and vodka, and this
morning, the cigarettes. I've smelled pot on several occasions.
Rumi must be supplying her.

Camille hadn't been kidding when she said Becca was using
me. "Great. Just fucking great."

"The police have asked to speak with us. Do you know why?"
Vanessa asks.

"I'd think that's blatantly obvious."

Vanessa shakes her head.

"Camille's abortion, for one. I assume they think you know
who got her pregnant. I certainly don't, though they asked me
enough."

The two exchange worried glances.

"You do know who she was sleeping with, don't you? You
have to tell them. Maybe it will help them figure out what happened. Why she jumped. I didn't realize she was suicidal. I know
we weren't close, but I think I'd see that, at least."

"They think she jumped?"

"Don't you?"

"Well, sure," Vanessa says. "But you're right, she didn't really
seem *that* depressed or anything. We did think… I mean, only
for a second, we know you wouldn't have, but—"

"Me? You think *I* hurt Camille? You're insane, Vanessa"

"Like I said, it was only for a fraction of a second. Camille's
been making you out to be pretty awful. Everyone was saying
that you might have found out and confronted her."

"Everyone? Well, you can tell *everyone* to relax. I wasn't anywhere near Camille tonight."

"You were both gone…and the room looked like a big fight
had happened. We heard yelling," Piper says, haltingly.

Camille had gone to her summons, I'd been kidnapped for the tap. Naturally, they'd think we were off together since we were gone at the same time.

"Do you know who gave the summons?"

Vanessa shakes her head. "No one does. At least, no one will admit it. I'm sure they'll ask our waitron, but it's not like she'll know. Summons are usually dropped off in the middle of the night. That's how it stays anonymous. Do you think she got tapped? I heard there was a tap tonight."

"I seriously doubt she was tapped."

Awe dawns on their faces. "You were, though. You got tapped. Oh, my God. Congratulations, Ash. That's a really big deal." Vanessa's tone chills a bit. She shifts, and her hands tighten into little fists.

"No comment."

"Wait until everyone finds out." Piper's eyes are shining. For half a moment, I think she is actually happy for me. She has no idea what I've been through tonight, nor what I fear is to come.

"There's nothing to find out."

"Right. Our lips are sealed, aren't they, Pipes?" Vanessa's feral grin tells me the whole school will know by morning. "Oh, how did you find out about it? Camille's abortion, I mean."

"I didn't. The cops asked. They knew, but I don't know how. Probably her journal. I knew you were up to something that night, but I'm not a busybody."

"Point taken." Vanessa plops onto the sofa next to me, Piper sits on the floor. They're settling in. What the hell is this?

"So, who was the father?" I ask.

"If we tell you, you can't tell. I mean it, Ash. It has to stay between us."

I sigh. "Then don't tell me. I can't say the police won't talk to me again, and I won't lie to them. But if you know anything, you should go to Dean Westhaven and tell her. Give her some peace. She's having a terrible night."

Another worried glance bounces between them. What do they know?

"We can't. No way."

"Then I can't help you, and I don't want to know."

The silence bleeds around us. In the distance, I can hear people outside attending to the remnants of Camille's nosedive. A hose, spraying water full force.

"Is it true you found your parents dead? Was it awful?" Piper finally asks.

"Yes, I did. And yes, it was awful. If you're here to be ghoulish, I have nothing more for you. Please, go to bed. Leave me alone."

They look stricken but stand. "I really am sorry, Ash," Vanessa says. "We promise to make it up to you." Vanessa looks like she's going to reach in for a hug but I am done with these girls and their constant mood swings.

I reach for the blanket on the back of the sofa. "Turn off the light as you go, won't you?"

They do, silent as the grave.

I have my laptop open the second the door closes. Check everything public Camille might have gotten into. I see her footprints easily now that I know what to look for—times I wasn't in my room or online. The penetration is relatively benign. Most of what I find are Google searches for the name Ashlyn Carr and Oxford, England.

I normally resist falling prey to the egotistical urge to Google my life but out of morbid curiosity, I click on the links. It will help to know what has been discovered.

The obituaries pop up immediately. My throat tightens. There are hits on profiles of Damien, and on the third page, a reference to Johnny. Damien Carr's Lost Son.

I don't read it. I already know what it says. Know the photo is from the funeral.

The black clothes, somber and mothball scented, lifted from

trunks in attics. The thick black veil on Mother's fascinator, the grim look in Father's eyes.

The small girl, blond, blue-eyed, looking utterly terrorized. Burying her brother, her companion, her bosom friend.

Johnny's death isn't a secret that will be problematic to explain.

I breathe a little easier. Camille didn't make it past my fire walls into the private settings.

Regardless, I enter this forbidden space now and, with only a moment's hesitation, wipe everything from the computer.

I can't run the risk of someone else finding my secrets.

I lie quietly in the gray predawn light, praying for sleep. I itch. I am heartsick. The night has been too intense, too strange, too scary. Too many swings between high and low. A dog barks. A girl cries. The wind blows, rustling the leaves on the ivy outside my window. I am back on the edge of the lake, the lily pads so green and white, the sky so blue. Everything is sharper in memory, not dulled.

I want peace.

I want oblivion.

It is not forthcoming.

47

THE MOTHERS

Ford is beyond relieved when Tony and his niece release her from their attentions. It is almost five in the morning now. Camille's body is being transported to Charlottesville, the diary has been taken into evidence along with Ash's torn shirt, and Ford has been given permission to call Camille's mother.

Deirdre Shannon is clearly in shock when she answers the phone. She is not crying; her voice sounds frozen, robotic, almost. She's probably been given something to calm her. Though she sounds anything but calm as she starts the rapid-fire questioning.

"Dean? What happened? They told me they think Camille committed suicide. Is that right? Was she upset? I haven't heard from her in a few days but she seemed fine when I talked to her last. She's had such a hard semester with the terrible flu bug she's been suffering from. Just tell me what you know."

The flu? That's what she'd told her mother. Oh, boy.

"Deirdre, she was pregnant, and had an abortion. Were you aware?"

By the gasp, it's clear she isn't. "Oh, Ford. No."

"It seems she had a chemical abortion. Pills. Virginia law dictates a family member over eighteen give consent, there's no way she could get them without a prescription, an ultrasound. She had to have been to a doctor or clinic. If you weren't involved—"

"I didn't know. It had to be her sister, then. Wait until I get my hands on Emily." The threat hangs in the air, shimmering. Emily Shannon was head girl last year. Head of Ivy Bound. Smart, responsible. A solid Goode citizen. It's not a stretch to think Camille would go to her if she were in trouble.

"I'm trying to be delicate here, but do you have any idea who the father might be?"

A breath. A pause. Finally, Deirdre says, "Yes and no. She was seeing someone this summer, I do know that, but she refused to tell me who. Said it was a boy she'd met at school. I asked how serious they were, whether she was planning to have sex with him. She told me she'd decided against it, but I'm no dummy, I know what we were like at her age. Lest you think me totally oblivious and irresponsible, I did take her to the OB-GYN, put her on birth control. The pill. Just in case. It appears I was too late. Or she didn't take them."

"Ah. A boy she met at school—so it could be someone from one of the all-boys schools around here. Woodberry Forest is the closest, and the one Goode has the most events with."

"Possibly. She's mentioned having fun at the dances. It was someone she was seeing at home, though, I get the sense. But, Ford, do you think she was upset over having an abortion? I would think she'd be relieved. I know that sounds callous, but she's sixteen, for heaven's sake. It would have ruined her life." A beat. "Was sixteen."

And then she breaks, the tears and the wails and the moans,

and Ford hangs on to the phone and takes it all in. She owes it to Deirdre and to Camille. She owes it to them all.

She has failed. She has failed. She has failed.

When Deirdre gathers herself, Ford tells her the rest. "We are investigating the entire situation, how she came to be on the bell tower, which is always locked, what might have driven her there. Why she didn't reach out for help. The sheriff is running the investigation, but I'm looking into things here. I know we want to keep this private if possible."

"What about her roommate? That British girl? Camille said she'd been thinking about asking to move to a different room. I know they didn't get along."

"I wasn't aware they were having issues. Normally the girls are quite open with me about their personal problems. But the police did find Camille's journal, and she said some very unkind things about Ash. I suppose it stands to reason— Oh, Deirdre, I am so sorry. I just don't have any good answers for you right now. But we will continue talking. Let me know what Emily says. Anything she can share will help. We can at least get an idea of who Camille was seeing and find out if something happened with the relationship that made her want to hurt herself."

"I do know she hadn't seen him in a while. I asked, and she told me they'd broken up. I got the sense it was a quick thing, nothing terribly special. Honestly, she could have come to me, I would have helped her. She's my daughter, I love her."

"I know you do, Deirdre. I am so sorry."

"Ford, I want you to look closely at her roommate. This Ash girl. I— Well, to be honest, when Camille said she was rooming with a girl from out of the country, I was a bit concerned. I told Howard, and he had a dossier drawn up. It had some very disturbing details. You know about the brother, yes? The suspicions about how he died? And her parents—"

"You did a background check on one of my students? Deirdre, you know we handle these things in-house. I found nothing to give me pause. Yes, I am aware of the circumstances that bring Ash to us and trust me, she is a gentle, pliable girl. Devastated by the loss of Camille, too."

"Yes, well, girls do lie, Ford, you know they do. And in light of the situation, now aren't you glad we did a more thorough search? News of the parents' deaths was very upsetting to Camille. Not to mention the younger brother. She didn't understand why her roommate wouldn't tell her. And she has been using a false name. That girl has lost a lot of people. Now my daughter is dead, too."

Deirdre's voice is getting louder, stronger, more intense with every sentence. Ford is horrified by the implication that she is somehow neglectful, responsible for Camille's death, simply by bringing Ashlyn Carr to Goode.

"Deirdre, really. This isn't a path worth following. Ash and I discussed the name change at length and decided it was for the best. She didn't want her parents' deaths defining her here at Goode. Didn't want to be openly rehashing it over and over. I can't blame her. Truly, her desire for privacy is understandable. And I don't think Ash's personal situation has any bearing on Camille's suicide. The circumstances of an unwanted pregnancy alone shed a great deal of light on Camille's state of mind, not to mention breaking up with the boy who got her pregnant. It's a fraught situation."

Ford can hear whispers in the background, someone talking to Deirdre. Coaching her? Are they on speakerphone? Who's been listening to her trying to comfort this grieving mother? What has she said that can be used against her, against the school?

"I know my daughter, Ford. I know her well. If she was depressed enough to consider suicide, she would have reached out to me. I feel it in my heart." Deirdre clears her throat, and the broken mother is gone, replaced by the steely prosecutor. "And because of this, we will be recommending an independent investigation."

Ford tries to continue sounding conciliatory. "That is certainly your right, Deirdre, but believe me, we're looking into this. The sheriff has taken Camille's body to Charlottesville for autopsy, and—"

"Yes, we heard. Howard is on a flight home from Turkey now. He feels it should be looked at by someone closer to the family. He will be in touch with the sheriff to have Camille brought here, to DC, where we can keep an eye on things. I don't want to be going through an intermediary. You understand."

We don't want your local idiots to fuck it up, Ford hears clearly, though the line is silent.

"And of course, if there is a wrongful death suit, we need to be sure everything has been handled properly."

"Did you just threaten to sue me?"

"You are in charge there, Ford. I'm not saying it's a sure thing, but don't be surprised to be served. We thought you'd turned a corner with Goode, revamped all that your mother tore down. I suppose we were too quick to judgment."

Christ, she's cold as ice.

"That is your prerogative. But, Deirdre, I can assure you, Ash had nothing to do with this. She's a grieving sixteen-year-old who has been keeping her hurts to herself. I was up with her most of the night. She's terribly traumatized by Camille's death, as are we all. I know she'll want to attend the funeral. You can meet her yourself, and you'll see. She's just a young girl in a lot of pain."

"And I am a middle-aged woman in a lot of pain. My daughter is dead. *I'm* the one who's suffered the loss here, not some girl who's only known my daughter for a few weeks. No. She is not invited. There will be no students whom we don't approve. Camille's friends Piper and Vanessa may come, but no one else. Not even you, Dean."

Hurt, dismayed, frustrated, Ford realizes it's time to end the call. "I think you're in shock, Deirdre. We'll talk again soon. I am so sorry for your loss. For our loss."

"Thank you, Ford. I appreciate the sentiment. I'll be in touch."

The line goes dead, leaving Ford to wonder what, exactly, just happened.

A condolence call that ended up with a lawsuit threat. Intimations against Ash.

Who is this girl she's brought into her school?

And on cue, a knock on Ford's door. Jude Westhaven, draped in cashmere and pearls, perfectly power-bobbed and highlighted, stands in her doorway.

"Well. Isn't this quite a mess?" she says.

"Mother. What are you doing here?"

Her mother's face is unreadable, but her words are not. "My goodness, darling, I'm here to comfort you. I am so, so sorry. There is nothing worse than losing a student. I came because I know how you feel. I came because I'd like to offer my help getting things back on track. I came because I thought you might need me. And perhaps, you'd let me help."

Ford lets the words wash over her like a benediction.

"It wasn't my fault, Mom." And then she collapses into tears, and her mother's arms are around her.

48

THE BITTERSWEET

Glee. It's such a funny word.

So many meanings. The thesaurus is full of synonyms, all implying something beyond happiness. *Delight. Joviality. Mirth. Merriment.*

A song written for men in three or more parts. That's highly misogynistic, don't you think? Let's give it a fix, shall we?

A song written for women in three or more parts.

There. That's better. And it's more appropriate. We are at an all-girls school, aren't we?

Perhaps this story should have been called *glee*.

Then again, there's nothing about lying in these synonyms. Or is there? How much happiness really exists in a person? We're capable of great emotional swings, yes, but they shuttle between two normatives: happy and sad. It is only when we wish to impress or impart that the sliding scale of nouns goes into overdrive.

If we're trying to rouse someone with our vocabulary, we can find hundreds of words to use in place of these base terms. For example, I would hardly write an essay and say *I am happy* to be accepted to The Goode School. No, no, no. My essay would be littered with extremes: *ecstatic* to be accepted, *thrilled* to be joining you, *elated* to make the move to America.

You, reading my words, would smile, pleased with yourself (*happy*? Yes, of course, there's another, but the more sedate *pleased* is so genteel) at how *enthusiastic* I seem to be.

You would write back, a pretty little letter, more personal this time, about how genuinely *delighted* you are to have me joining you.

So *sweet*.

Yes, *glee* is a very funny word. A funny word indeed.

Though you really should start looking at the synonyms for *sad*. You have no idea what's coming. None of you do.

"The past beats inside me like a second heart."

—John Banville, *The Sea*

49

THE COP

Kate Wood takes 29 North to Manassas, one hand on the steering wheel, singing an earworm by Billie Eilish that got into her head back at Goode, "You Should See Me in a Crown." She heard the song coming from one of the dorm rooms and can't seem to shake it. She finally looked up the video and had to turn it off almost immediately. Spiders. Ugh. She doesn't like spiders.

The Goode School gives her the willies just like spiders do, sitting atop the hill like an ancient, cherry-round orb weaver in a desiccated web, waiting. Oh, sure, it's been renovated, updated, but paint and shellac can't scrub away ghosts. Just walking through the campus is like nails on a chalkboard. She has no idea how Uncle Tony can stand living there.

Something about Camille Shannon's death feels hinky to her. Tony thinks it's a clear case of suicide, the diary was the clincher for him, but Kate isn't so sure. Something about the roommate is off. Something deeper than British reserve and the aloofness of a teenager. Something in her eyes... A darkness, like she's hiding something.

Granted, Kate is a cop. To her, the whole world is hiding something. But this girl's empty eyes have been haunting her.

And how she's been roped into this case... Stupid. She's supposed to be at home, minding her *p*'s and *q*'s, waiting for the ruling on her suspension. Just the thought of the situation makes her blood pressure spike. She was executing an arrest warrant, a nasty drug dealer turned murderer named Gary Banner. Should have been standard fare, but the idiot had seen her and bolted, hid out in a barn, and when she tracked him down, he started shooting. She responded in kind, killing him.

Cut-and-dried case.

But said scumbag happened to be the beloved, railroaded, not responsible for his actions, must have been provoked—was that warrant properly drafted?—nephew of a state senator.

They took her badge and gun. Have had them for two weeks and counting.

Kate is in the right, she knows this. The department knows this. The media knows this. The city of Charlottesville knows this. But she's still on suspension pending a lengthy examination of the case by the new Police Civilian Review Board. And she has her doubts she's going to get a fair shake.

She took off for Marchburg to visit her mother's twin brother, her favorite uncle, both for comfort and, if she's being honest with herself, to lay the groundwork for making a jump to the sheriff's office staff in case she gets run out of Charlottesville on a rail.

Nepotism, but this is hardly an issue. Tony would never hold her back. And Kate's not going to give up her career because of a civilian oversight committee. She's just not.

Tony is laconic and acerbic and loves that they have so much in common, the two misfits who stepped outside of the Wood family tradition of producing country doctors to be cops, instead.

They talk regularly, and she wishes she could see him more, but she's been ridiculously busy since she made detective, and he's running the entire county under his office.

The visit has been good for them both. They've had some beers, told some war stories—crime scenes discovered, bodies in strange places, crazy methods of death—the kind of dark humor people outside of law enforcement find wildly offensive, but to her and him, it's life. You laugh, or you cry. It's the way of things.

He hasn't pushed her. He's been a sane sounding board. He's assured her all will be well. And now, she's stumbled into a case.

Not your case, Kate.

She drags her attention back to Goode. Nothing about the broken body of the teenager adds up. And the family slaps them all in the face by insisting on the body being posted up in DC? It's rather pointless, Virginia's OCME is an exemplary system of medical examiners all tied together under one umbrella, supporting one another throughout the state. But Tony had agreed without a fuss. The death is a sensitive one.

Another sensitive case.

So, Kate finds herself driving north toward the autopsy, singing a creepy-ass song by a wildly successful teenager with a clear talent for tapping into the emotional issues of her peers.

Kate isn't here to close the case, it's not hers, it's Tony's, and she's on suspension. She offered to go because if she's on-site, she can hear the results right away and can share them with Tony. And make sure they're all getting the same story, are all on the same page.

It's not like she has anything better to do. And she likes to drive. It helps her think.

Ash Carlisle—Ashlyn Elizabeth Carr, her real name. Five feet eleven inches, 130 pounds, blue on blond. Pretty. Intelligent. Cultured. Rich as sin. Parents dead. Roommate dead. Hiding something. Kate is sure of it.

The tear in the girl's shirt notwithstanding, her eyes had been glassy like she was on something, and her breath smelled overwhelmingly of Altoids. Deduction based on Kate's own teenage foibles: the kid had been drinking, and so had her girlfriend, the all-star senior. Funny, they look something alike, are of a similar height and build, but the senior is tougher, you can see it in the aggressive way she defended her younger compatriot.

Secret societies. What a ridiculous thing to allow in a high school. Granted, Goode is not your normal high school, nor your normal boarding school. The girls are treated as if they are much older, almost as if they are in college instead of high school. Self-reliance, independence, agency. All vital aspects for any young woman in the world. But how young is too young for such responsibility? Why can't kids be kids anymore?

Break it down, Kate.

Okay. A bunch of rich girls, smart, capable, rich girls, with access to drugs and alcohol, hold a secret society meeting and haze one of their own until she feels compelled to throw herself off a bell tower.

Boom goes the dynamite. Occam's razor. It's the first rule of investigation—the most obvious answer is your first path.

That the girl was bullied and killed herself is not an intuitive leap by any means. Rich, smart, determined, or otherwise, they're dealing with teenage girls. Kate remembers her own time in high school. Granted, she went to good old Orange County (go Hornets!), down in the trenches with the farmers' kids, but there was still money—horse farms and wineries—and those kids were always the ringleaders when there was hell to be delivered.

A whole school of them, all girls, to boot?

Camille Shannon might have been bullied into suicide, or felt left out and depressed. Add in the abortion, possibly an indifferent or ex-boyfriend, and there was a recipe for disaster.

Tony mentioned the mother is threatening a wrongful death lawsuit, and she probably has a case. Bad publicity is never good but isn't insurmountable. Goode is self-endowed and run by an old Virginia family with very deep pockets, but still, bad press on top of the murder a decade ago could at least affect them. Affect enrollment. Future endowments.

She takes the exit off Highway 29 into Manassas, her mind touching again on Becca Curtis. She's also curious about the senator's daughter. She's in this up to her delicate, pearl-studded ears. Put that girl in a crown and she fits the bill perfectly—a regal leader. The chosen one.

Add in this Ash Carlisle... Kate can't shake the feeling the two of them know something. But what?

Not your case, Kate, she reminds herself for the twentieth time. *You're doing Tony a favor, relaying the autopsy report to make sure he's getting all the facts right away, that's all.*

But when she pulls into the parking lot of the Manassas District OCME office, she impulsively sends a quick email to a friend she knows who can take a glance into the overseas aspect of this. It's a short email.

What's the deal with Sir Damien Carr's death?

She's surprised when her phone rings immediately, the number on the screen the +44 UK prefix.

"Hello?"

"Kate Wood, what in the dickens are you doing emailing me at midnight?"

"What are you doing looking at your email at midnight, Oliver?"

"Notifications from VIPs."

"Ah, I'm a VIP, am I?"

"Always. What's the sudden interest in British politics?"

"He's a politician?"

"Carr? No. A wealth manager for the upper crust. Knighted for his contributions to the security of the banking system a

271

while back. But he's very dead. Took his own life back in the summer. The inquest's just been closed. They found nothing suspicious. He'd been having an affair, his wife found out, he was humiliated. It's that stiff upper lip thing, gets us every time."

"The wife is dead, too, yes?"

"Yes. Found him, then shot herself. Word on the street? She wasn't stable to start with. After the affair, things were tenuous. But that's hearsay."

"And their daughter..."

"Teenager, if I recall. No idea what happened to her, she hasn't been in the press. The family kept her out of things. Carr was a private man. The scandal clearly cost him."

"The daughter is here in Virginia, going to a very expensive, private all-girls school."

"Ah. Makes sense. Get her away from the chaos, find normality, all that."

"Her roommate just died. We think it was suicide."

"Really? At an all-girls boarding school? How deliciously gothic."

Kate laughs. "You are a sick man."

"I take it you're on the case, Sherlock?"

She hasn't shared her status with him, isn't about to now. "No, no, not at all. The school is in my uncle's territory. I was visiting. Bad timing."

"What do you need to know, love?"

"I'm not sure. Something about the daughter feels strange to me. A lot of people have died around her recently. Seems odd for a sixteen-year-old. I'm grasping at straws, probably."

"Maybe, maybe not. You always have had sound instincts. You figured me out rather quickly if I recall."

Oliver is a closet queen, perfectly happy to lead a quiet, not-out life with his also closeted, quiet, not-out roommate, Eric. They're desperately in love but won't admit it. Not her problem, but she picked up on it when she met them the first time, at a cocktail party in DC, an international forensics conference they all attended.

It's a shame, too. They could be very happy together.

Oliver is also a proud member of the Metropolitan Police's Forensic Services division. She's used him as a sounding board in the past; he has a keen insight into murder.

She hears a keyboard tapping. "I'm sending you the files I have on the Carrs. I can look deeper—"

"It's okay, Oliver. I'm being gossipy, as well as morbidly curious. Must be hard for a kid to lose both parents like that. And then her roommate… It's just curious, that's all."

"Hmm. I'd say. Well, I'll send along what I have for giggles, and if you need anything else, you let me know."

"Wonderful. Love to Eric. Sleep well."

"Your lips to God's ears," he says, blowing her a kiss.

A moment later her email dings. The file he's sent is big enough she'll need to wait until she gets to her laptop to open it.

She gets out of the car and heads into the OCME. Might as well stay focused here. She can read all about British intrigue later.

50

THE SPEECH

Ford stands in her spot at the head of the chapel, looking at the sea of dazed, exhausted faces assembling before her as the girls of Goode file into the pews. She hasn't slept, knows she looks disarrayed. Nothing matters more than tending to her girls.

This was her mother's first commandment—a unity speech. Fill in the girls on the situation. Assure them they are safe, well looked after, cared for.

The logic is sound, so Ford called for an immediate convocation. The bells rang, word passed quickly, like a fire drill, and they came flooding in, wordless and crying, or laughing, some of them, nasty things.

She isn't used to seeing the girls mixed together, all classes merged, most not wearing their robes or properly uniformed, instead scared and exhausted and sad, doe eyes from almost all of them, waiting for her to share the horrible truth and then to fix things.

She has to do this, if only to quell the rumors.

"Ladies," she commands, and the room hushes.

"I'm sure you've all heard that we lost a student last night. I want to address what we know, and what we don't. First, the student was Camille Shannon, a sophomore. We believe, sadly, that she took her own life. A journal found in her room talks about death, and suicide, as a way out of a situation she found herself in. This is very private, and I will not be discussing it with you per her family's request.

"What I'm here to say is, I failed Camille. And in turn, I've failed you, her friends, her fellow students. I wasn't made aware of this situation. I didn't know Camille was hurting. It is not an excuse, though I can't begin to know what might have been if we were aware of her suffering. Rather than look back, we will move forward. I see this tragic moment in our tenure together as an opportunity.

"Our Honor Code exists for many reasons. Paramount is honesty and forthrightness in all facets of our lives, yes. But it is also meant to be a safety net. I'm not sure why no one came forward to let us know about the undercurrents that have been circulating the past few weeks. The health and welfare of your own selves is just as important as the health and welfare of your friends. Being honest and trustworthy is more than telling the truth. It is also reaching out a hand when a friend needs it. When someone is struggling. It might feel like you're betraying a confidence, but believe me, when the option is to tell one of us you're concerned about a compatriot's state of mind or lose your friend forever, you must always err on the side of caution."

Ford looks at Ash now, sitting meekly by Becca's side. "You are not to blame, not in the least, but we encourage you to share with your teachers, share with your student leadership, share with me. Anything and everything. In the spirit of this, we will accept anonymous insights this week. And you may feel free to leave concerns with me as well as with your head girl, Becca Curtis."

There are murmurs at this. The Honor Code model is sacrosanct; Goode has always insisted that the accuser and the accused meet face-to-face. Anonymity is discouraged. But no more. Ford will not have this happen again. Too much is going on behind her back.

"Yesterday morning Camille received a summons. None of the seniors we've spoken with know who sent the request for her to go to the Commons. If any one of you has knowledge of this, please, I urge you, come forward. We need to determine what might have sent Camille over the..."

Gasps echo through the chapel, and Ford kicks herself. She was about to say *edge*, a Freudian slip unintended and ill-advised. She's had no sleep, she is stressed and upset. *It's okay*, she tells herself, *everyone makes mistakes. Get through this.*

"Classes are canceled today, and counselors will be on campus to talk with you. I encourage you to be open with them. To lose a friend is a terrible thing, and you are right to be sad and confused, even if you weren't close to Camille. We are all affected by this damaged young woman's terrible choice. Suicide is a difficult topic, sometimes even a taboo topic, but here at Goode, where we strive to shine a light on all things, we will not be handling this any differently. All doors are open. All discussions are welcome and encouraged.

"Some of you may be contacted by the sheriff's office to answer questions about Camille's past few weeks. I encourage you to comply with all requests, and I will be available to sit in on any conversations you might be uncomfortable having alone."

Whispers surge through the chapel. When the speculation dies down, she continues.

"Some of you will want to attend the funeral. Her family has requested the funeral be family only, but any student wishing to attend may petition me and I will pass along your names. A memorial service will be held for Camille here, in the chapel, at a later date."

Ford feels a tear start in her eye and takes a deep breath, willing it away. She will not break down in front of them. They need to see her strong, today of all days.

"Remember your classmate, Camille. Remember a kind, sweet girl, with a bright future ahead. Reverend Morton will lead us in a blessing now."

She steps aside and the chaplain takes the pulpit. Reverend Morton—ancient, white haired, well loved—speaks a few words on comfort and the impermanence of life, then leads them in a nondenominational prayer for peace. This is a secular campus, after all.

Ford has a list the length of her arm to deal with today—most generated by her mother. The action items include drafting press releases, calls to alumni, donors, parents, and at lunchtime, an emergency board meeting. Not to mention the sheriff will be back to harangue her, she's sure of it.

No one wants her to make the same mistakes Jude Westhaven did when the murder occurred a decade ago. Goode needs to keep its sparkling reputation intact. To that end, Jude has both informed the alumni association the meeting for today is canceled and arranged for a phone call with a crisis management team out of DC, lawyers who advise people thrust into the spotlight, usually presidential and judicial nominees. Untried candidates for political office. Newly named CEOs.

They're not supposed to have to talk to young headmistresses about how to make sure their schools don't fall apart.

Chin up. If she handles all this right, Goode can weather the storm. The loss of a student—any student—is a tragedy, yes. But she will pull them through this. She refuses to let the school look bad.

Finding the missing key to the bell tower is paramount. When Ford walked the sheriff down to retrieve it, it wasn't in her safe.

Embarrassing. She looks negligent for that alone. Worse, she has no idea how long it's been gone. It could be a day, it could be ten years. She hasn't been in the bell tower, ever. She can't remember the last time she looked in the safe for the key. The ones in the security office are intact, so there's no question— the key used to open the bell tower and allow Camille out into the darkened sky was Ford's. She is responsible.

Solve the mystery of the missing key, first and foremost. A wrongful death lawsuit will hinge on this.

But if she can prove who got young Camille pregnant, she will be ten steps ahead. She has a sense that the pregnancy is the tie that binds all of this together.

Convocation is breaking up now. Ford takes note of where the players are in this little drama.

Ash is following Becca out the great wooden doors, rubbing her stomach and looking at the ground. They are heading toward the arboretum.

Camille's BFFs, Vanessa and Piper, are moving toward the dining hall with the rest of the girls.

Let them eat. Fortify their tiny bodies. She's going to do the same. A shower. Some toast. Strong coffee. Then she'll summon them, start the interviews, try to get some answers.

51

THE TURN

Jude is waiting for Ford in her cabin. She's impeccably turned out this morning in a cloud-gray cashmere twinset and dark wash designer skinny jeans, black mules with a white block heel. She's made a fresh pot of coffee; the cabin is suffused with the aromatic scent. It smells of home. Safety. Comfort.

All things Ford doesn't feel anymore when looking at Jude.

"How did it go?"

"It was fine. Hard. They're all so broken up. After breakfast, I'm going to talk to Camille's suitemates. See if they can shed some light on her actions. Then I have the board meeting."

"Excellent. I've drafted a press release for you, and the crisis management team from Owens & Tudor will be here soon. Get some caffeine in you, and I've made some biscuits, they're in the oven. You need fortification. And a nap."

"You made biscuits? Who are you and what did you do with my mother?"

Jude laughs. "All right, I sent up to the kitchens for them. But I also had them bring that honey butter you love so much. Eat. We have a long day ahead."

"We? You can't attend these meetings, you know. You're no longer the headmistress."

With a breezy wave of her hand, Jude smiles. "I'm still your mother, and I'm allowed to see to the well-being of my daughter. And our family started this school. I have every right to be here with you.

"Don't worry. I won't get in the way. I just want to be sure you have all the tools necessary to deal with this. Should the investigation show something more devious happened, you want to have all your ducks in a row, show you've done everything by the book. Suicide is a terrible situation at a school. It can engender others. Create clusters. We don't want that to happen."

This is true. Ford can fight this, or she can lean in, allow herself to be coddled, if only for a moment. It's not like the board can have her removed for letting herself be mothered a bit. Jude's words feel prophetic, though Ford knows it's only a reaction to the mistakes Jude made a decade earlier, trying to cover up her knowledge of the stalking that led to the murder.

Suicide. Murder.

That tiny scrap of fabric, though. Ash's torn shirt. Ash and Becca were out of bed. Becca hadn't told the whole truth, she wasn't with Ash the entire time. There was a ten- to fifteen-minute window...

Don't even think it. That's not what happened, and you know it. You read Camille's diary. She was suicidal. Upset. There isn't anything more to this than a disturbed young girl who felt overwhelmed by a choice she shouldn't have had to make. Combine it with being away from her support structure, and all the ingredients for a mental breakdown were present.

Jude is watching her. "Are you okay, darling?"

"Yes. I appreciate it, Mom. Thank you for looking out for me. Let's have some breakfast."

"Good girl," Jude says, smoothing back her hair, making Ford feel like she's nine. "You'll want a shower and some makeup before you charge into the day, too. You look all washed-out. My poor girl. You've been working too hard."

There is a soft knocking on Ford's front door, then it swings open and a male voice calls, "Ford?"

Ford freezes. Her mother looks at her quizzically and calls, "We're in the kitchen."

There is a pause, then footsteps. Rumi appears, looking as surprised as Jude.

"What are you doing here? You shouldn't be in the headmistress's cottage. You're a handyman." There is such vitriol in her tone, Ford flinches.

"Mom, stop. Rumi is always welcome here. What can I do for you?"

He's wearing a blue baseball cap with the stylized-G Goode logo. He takes it off and squeezes it in his hands, folding the bill practically in half. "I—I wanted to say how sorry I am about Camille Shannon. And see if there's anything I can do."

"You can leave and never darken our door again," Jude snaps.

"Mother, that is enough. Rumi? Why don't we step outside?"

She opens the French doors that lead to the small garden behind the cottage. In the summer, it is lovely, and such a different space than the imposing "family house" on the outskirts of Marchburg her mother renovated twenty years ago.

She'd done so assuming Ford would live there in the summers during high school and college, that they would be a family. But Ford hadn't wanted to live under her mother's roof once her stepdad died, even though Jude spent most of her time in New York or DC. Ford prefers her cottage. Her privacy.

Rumi pulls the baseball cap over his black curls. "I see your mom still hates my guts."

Ford blows out a breath. "Have you heard anything useful?" Her tone is cutting, she's being short without meaning to.

Rumi straightens. "Don't take this out on me, Ford. I only

came to see if you were okay. No, I haven't heard anything. I don't know anything. I had nothing to do with this. Isn't that what you want to hear?"

"Rumi, no. Please. I haven't slept and have barely eaten. I'm only trying to find out what happened. My key is missing, to the bell tower."

"I don't have it, if that's what you're asking. Why don't I text you later? Get out of your hair." His voice is quietly furious, and she can't blame him. He's come to comfort her, offer aid, perhaps even love, and her mother ruined everything, as usual.

Ford looks over her shoulder. Jude is standing by the French door, glaring at them.

"That's probably for the best. I appreciate you checking on me. And no, I didn't think you had the key. I was just telling you what's happening. But if you overhear anything, let me know, okay?"

His eyes are hooded when he strides off into the grounds. She can see by the set of his shoulders she's wounded him. Maybe their fling isn't as casual as she thinks.

Back inside, she holds up a peremptory hand to her mother. "I know what you're going to say. Trust me, he's a good kid. Devoted to the school, despite the way you've treated him."

"I don't need to remind you his father is the reason we're in this mess."

"His father has nothing to do with this."

"You're headmistress now, aren't you, Ford? That's enough of a mess for me."

You will never be a proper headmistress to this school.

"Now, there's the mother I know and love. Thank you for the insult. You can go now. I'll handle things from here."

"Ford, I didn't mean—"

"Yes, you did. And I'm sick and tired of your attitude. You fucked up, Mother. You tried to cover up your knowledge of the situation and it got a girl murdered. This is totally different, and I'm handling it. It's time for you to leave. Don't bother me again."

52

THE SLIGHT

I'm gritty-eyed with lack of sleep and bone tired. Because of the emergency convocation, I wasn't at Becca's door at seven as instructed. But I sat with Becca in the chapel, watching her hands. She needs to file her nails, they are ragged and broken after last night's excesses in the cabin.

When the convocation ends, I calmly follow Becca to the arboretum. A cigarette is offered and accepted with a nod. There are no words. There is no touching. I honestly don't know what to say. I don't know what she wants. And I'm too tired to explain myself, to smooth her ruffled feathers.

Becca, too, looks exhausted. Halfway through the smoke, she says, "This is going to be a massive clusterfuck, you know."

I'm not sure if she's speaking rhetorically, but I wade in. "Camille's suicide? Yes, it's quite a mess."

"No, stupid. Having cops on campus. They're going to be looking at everything. I'm supposed to meet someone tonight. I'll have to reschedule."

I'm surprised to feel a random spark of jealousy. "Someone like who?"

"Just someone. I'll have to warn him off."

"Oh, you mean Rumi? I know he's providing you with—"

Becca turns on me, eyes blazing. "Shut. Your. Fucking. Mouth. How stupid are you?"

"I'm sorry."

"Yes, you are sorry. God, Ash. You're going to get us all kicked out if you don't start acting smarter. I really thought you were different. You're supposed to be a genius rebel. I thought I could trust you."

"You can, Becca. I'm no rat."

"You're not much of anything as far as I can tell. And in case you have it in that pretty little head to say something about last night, if you say anything to anyone, I will bury you. Am I clear?"

Becca takes one last huge drag from her cigarette and drops the butt on the ground. She walks off, leaving it smoldering.

Mic drop.

I squat down and put it out, scraping it through the earth. My fingers come back sticky with Becca's lip gloss. I run my finger over my lower lip, smearing the remnants on my mouth. It tastes like cherry and old cigarettes.

I take a last drag of my ciggy, put it out, and bury the butts. I can at least help cover our tracks.

Becca is almost out of the arboretum now. The leaves are starting to fall, and there's a clearing toward the school where I can see people coming into and out of the forest. I can catch up to her if I get a move on.

I start after her but pull up when another girl steps out of the woods. I can't see who it is, but Becca talks to her for a moment, hands her something. I hurry forward but by the time I catch up, Becca is alone again.

"Who was that?"

Becca ignores me, strides out of the forest and up the path to the dining hall. I catch her by the door.

"Becca—"

"Just shut up, okay. Keep your mouth shut and we will all be fine."

Becca storms into the building, and I trail behind, uncomfortable being ignored. At the table, I start to pull out my chair, but Becca puts a hand on my arm.

"What are you doing?"

"Having breakfast, like normal. Though I don't know if I can eat."

Becca tosses her head like the Thoroughbred she is. She is a different person now. Cold. Aloof. Mildly aggravated and disgusted, like I'm a hair that's landed on her fork.

She waves a derisive hand in dismissal.

"Fly away, little Swallow. You missed your appointment this morning, so you don't get to sit with us anymore. Go play with your own friends. You aren't welcome here."

I feel my jaw begin to fall, snap my teeth together so hard they click. Becca has already taken her seat and is immediately flanked by the twins, one of whom pushes me rudely as she scoots by for the coveted chair to Becca's left.

Tears threaten, but I blink them back and head to my old table with Vanessa and Piper and the rest of the sophomores. As I approach, they start shooting me looks. It's clear they've been talking about me. They saw Becca's little power play. They have closed ranks. I am no longer one of them.

The seat where Camille normally holds court looks so empty, so out of place. Because so many have crowded the table today, it is the only open spot. I stop behind it. "May I?"

After an interminable moment, Vanessa nods and I sit, fiddling with a piece of my ponytail. My arm feels like it's on fire, and I force myself not to scratch. The will it takes not to claw my skin to shreds is Herculean.

"Are you okay?" Piper asks.

"Yes. It was a long night."

Laughter, loud and harsh, filters over from Becca's table.

"Becca pissed at you?"

"She thought it would be better for me to sit with you today. A show of solidarity because of Camille." The lie flows from my lips as easily as my breath.

Breakfast is served. I push the eggs around my plate, unable to eat. The girls are talking about Camille, primarily, but there are a few who seem nonplussed and are planning their attack, how they'll usurp the juniors when they try out for the fall play, Sophocles's *Antigone*. It is only in the past decade that the school dropped the requirement to have the play done in its original Greek.

I hear a name that makes my radar prick up. Rumi. Who's talking about Rumi?

It is the table next to me. Girls who live on the other side of the sophomores' hall.

They are whispering in a staccato shorthand; I only catch every other word.

"Do you…think… I mean, he did it?"

"Who else could… Someone… Rumi stole the keys."

"Come on, guys. You're… It's stupid… Like Camille would fuck a townie."

"Well, the dean—"

Raucous laughter drowns out the rest of the conversation. The seniors, amusing themselves.

"How inappropriate," Vanessa sniffs. "It's like they're happy about it. Oh, someone died, how sad, at least we get out of classes. Fucking bitches."

While I agree, I tune out Vanessa's complaints. I can't help but cast glances toward Becca as the laughter continues. I try to catch Jordan's eye, two tables over, but she is engaged in some sort of conversation with her roommate and doesn't look up. A few other faces from that side of the dining hall look vaguely familiar. Relief washes through me.

None of the Swallows of Ivy Bound are sitting with their Falconers. This must be a part of the hazing. Open rejection.

Lovely.

"Why did she do it, Ash? Do you know? You were the closest to her."

This from Dominique Rodrigue, a sophomore who lives at the end of our hall, right by the kitchen. We haven't spoken more than ten words all term.

"I really wasn't. And I don't, Dom. I don't know anything."

The whispering chatter at the adjacent table begins anew, drawing me back. What does Rumi have to do with Camille? I've seen nothing, nothing, to indicate they even knew each other. Hell, Camille warned me away, said he was dangerous. A pedophile.

I can hardly believe that was yesterday. Yesterday, Camille was alive and warning me away from Rumi. Yesterday, Becca and I were friends. Yesterday, I was still protected. Safe.

I can't do this. I can't sit and eat and pretend it's all okay. Can't gossip and can't laugh. But to get up and leave now will draw every eye in the place.

Camille did this to herself. So why do I feel so very responsible?

53

THE AFTERMATH

Some of the girls see the counselors, others sit in circles crying in jags, bemoaning the loss of a friend, but most just congregate in the sewing circle to tell lies about Camille and her suicide. Word of the abortion has spread, and speculation runs rampant. There are no secrets in a school as small as Goode, and with Camille gone, it seems all intimacies she shared are now fair game.

Vanessa and Piper act shell-shocked enough, keeping to themselves in their room, but how else did word of Camille's indiscretions get out? I didn't say anything. Maybe Becca, she was there. But I can't help but think it was Vanessa and Piper who leaked the news. It makes them seem important, ties them to the tragedy. It helps the school make sense of why Camille died.

Alone, I finally get in a nap, then pop in my earbuds, select my most hard-core London '80s punk scene playlist, and try to read a book by a programmer named Peter Seibel, a collection of interviews with famous coders. Dr. Medea handed it to me last week and suggested it might be a fun read, offered extra credit for a report. In normal circumstances, I'd agree and already be outlining the paper. But today, the text is dry as dust, the interviews boring and repetitive. I'm not in the mood.

The room feels so empty. My thoughts stray to Camille, looking for any signs that she either was depressed or truly hated me enough to sabotage my life at Goode, and finding none that stand out in my memories, I turn them, inevitably, to Becca.

Even though none of the Swallows had been with their Falconers this morning, I can't help but wonder...was the banishment this morning because I missed my appointment, or was it because I didn't jump right into Becca's bed last night?

Hell hath no fury like a woman scorned.

My mum said that to me once, a very long time ago.

I try out some adjectives ahead of the noun: hell hath no fury like a privileged, spoiled, imperious, conceited, false girl scorned.

Had I scorned her, though? No, not really. I was honest in my surprise and confusion. Surely Becca won't hold this against me.

I've never had a serious boyfriend—or a girlfriend—before. Becca wasn't my first kiss, far from it, but I'm still a virgin in all the ways that count. That I'd shy away from an encounter isn't an indictment of Becca, it's simply my own inexperience with these things. *Sex. The word is* sex, *Ash.*

I have no real objections to having sex with Becca. But I'd also like to have sex with Rumi, and that's what's confusing. Maybe I just need to try it with both of them and see which one works the best for me.

But now is not the time. Sex equates to intimacy, closeness, secrets. And I'm not willing to give my body in place of my safety.

I open my laptop and check my intranet Goode email. Assignments. More assignments. An invitation to Dr. Asolo's house for a supper party and discussion of Virginia Woolf four evenings hence. I look at the other addresses on the email; it's been sent to everyone in the class. All eight of us. And the dean.

I RSVP yes, then scroll through the Goode-approved websites online for a while, which are excruciatingly boring—how many turns around National Geographic is a girl supposed to take? I finally activate my VPN and override the system. I haven't looked to the outside world in weeks. I check my external email, the one I had before moving to America. Junk. Junk. Junk. I delete everything.

There is a draft email in the folder. What's this? I think back to the nasty surprise from Vanessa last night, that Camille was spying on me. I don't remember writing and saving any emails. Did Camille manage to get into my email, too?

I click on the draft but the second I do, I hear the onomatopoeic triggering *whoosh* that means the email has been sent. As Pavlovian as it gets, these notifications. I should talk to Dr. Medea about this. What a great study it would be. Can we shift perceptions with sounds, recode the world? AOL did it. Apple followed. Perhaps Ash Carlisle can, too.

I click on Sent emails, but the program crashes.

"Oh, bugger me." I reboot, which means I have to go through all of the steps again, activate the VPN, override the system, log in to my email, but the Sent folder shows nothing recent. Weird. There must have been an old email stuck in the outbox from the last time I logged out. Its date would correlate to when I originally sent the message. Who knows what it was?

Still, I delete this email account entirely. No reason to have it anymore, this last vestige of my old life. It's not like I've received anything except ads for new trainers and knickers in weeks. Nothing of worth. Nothing personal.

I have another account for that, like any good hacker. But there's no way anyone can access it, nor can it be tied to me in any way. It's totally encrypted, completely anonymous.

Just this small action makes me feel more in control. Good thing I haven't done too many illicit online activities from my laptop, or I could have really gotten myself in trouble. Even

though I've already wiped the computer, I double-check everything. Yes, it's all gone. Besides, Camille couldn't have found
out much. Her knowledge came from outside the school. Her
parents, undoubtedly. The prosecutor and the ambassador.

I give them both a cursory search online. Nothing leaps out.
There is a small piece in the *Washington Post* about Camille's
death, but it's more an announcement than a story.

I move on to the *Marchburg Free Press* archives and plug in the
name Rumi Reynolds.

Nothing.

Not a surprise. He was a juvenile when his father committed
the murder. I doubt even the American papers are so callous as
to name an innocent child in a report.

I try again. Murder at Goode School.

The hits are immediate and extensive. I'm still amazed I didn't
come across the stories when I looked at the history of the school
in the first place, over the summer, when the idea of attending
Goode had been presented to me. I never thought to look to see
if any of the students had died. Who does that?

*It's beautiful and old, and you'll get a fine education. Be able to write
your ticket to any college you want.*

"Go away," I say to my ghosts, and begin to read.

The afternoon bells have long finished tolling when I stop and
stretch. I don't know much more about the murder than what
the rumor mill and Rumi himself told me, outside of learning an
eyewitness at the scene helped prove the guilt of Rick Reynolds.
That, and a detailed listing of the body parts found on his living
room mantel. It wasn't just the eyes. He took her breasts, too.

Fucking freaky shit.

Reynolds is serving a life sentence in maximum security at
Red Onion down in Wise County. I look at the map I carry in
my bag—it is in the far southwest of Virginia, on the border of
Kentucky. He is very far away. I wonder if Rumi ever goes to

visit? I never asked how he feels having a murderer for a father. I should. See if it compares to my experience at all.

I haven't thought much about the rest of the country, but looking at the map, I see the vast spread of the United States, pushing westward away from my spot in tiny rural Virginia. What would it be like to get in a car and drive? I'd like to see the mountains of Colorado, the ocean along the California coast. One day, I will.

These thoughts are getting me nowhere, so I pull on my trainers and slip down the stairs to the back door. Yellow crime scene tape blocks the courtyard behind Main, and the shadow in the middle of the concrete slab must be the leftovers of Camille's blood, permanently scarring the gray circle. The thought makes me feel queer, slightly dizzy and nauseated.

I backtrack and head down one more flight to the basement door, which opens out on the plaza leading to the gym. I take a deep breath to clear my lungs of the rotting air of the dorm, suddenly cloying and unwelcoming, and jog off toward the arboretum. I have no idea what the rules are today, but getting some fresh air and exercise seems like the proper thing.

But even deep in the woods, halfway to town, alone except for the squirrels and birds, I feel like I'm being watched.

54

THE SCHISM

I'm in luck. Rumi is at the coffee shop.

I mean, I was hoping to run into him, but I don't realize how much until I see him, and my heart does a quick little dance in my chest. He is wearing a Goode baseball cap, looks as tired and wrung out as the rest of us, but he gives me a weak smile when I hurry in.

"If it isn't our little Brit. Want some tea?"

"Espresso. Or…something stronger? If you have it."

"Not sure that's such a great idea today, Ash. The town is crawling with sheriff's deputies and cops. Plus, the dean's mother is back and on the warpath."

"Oh. Right. Then, just the espresso."

He makes me a cup, sets it on the counter. The china clinks on contact.

"Are you okay? It was your roommate who died, yes?"

"Yes. Yes, I'm okay. She and I weren't close. Did you know her?"

Is it my imagination, or do his eyes shutter when I ask what seems like an innocent question? *Camille wouldn't fuck a townie.*

His answer comes quick and vehement. "I don't *know* any of the students at Goode."

"You know me."

"You're different. You're new. An outsider."

"An outsider. Goodness, thanks ever so much."

"Ash, sorry. That didn't come out right. I meant it as a compliment. You seem, I don't know…above all of this. These girls, they're so wrapped up in their money and their prestige, stacking the blocks of their lives against the *redbrick wall* so they can climb over and escape. And escape to what? More privilege? More wonderful experiences and perfect families and insane wealth? None of them are real. You aren't like them."

"I'm more like them than you think, Rumi. Your view of my classmates is pretty harsh."

"Wait until they cast you out, Ash. They will."

Again, I'm struck by the bitterness in his tone, and the strange sense there is more here than meets the eye. And recall the sinking feeling I had this morning when Becca dismissed me like I was a piece of shit from her shoe. Back home in Oxford… *No, Rumi. You're wrong. I do know what it's like to be cast out.*

The door chimes and I look over my shoulder to see Becca and the twins saunter in. My heart skips a beat, whether from fear or longing, I don't know. I am very confused. I like Rumi, I know I do. I came here hoping to run into him, to see if we can continue where we left off.

But there is something about Becca… She is a magnet, and I feel my body turn in the chair toward her in a gravitational pull. I don't understand my visceral reaction to Becca Curtis. Is it that I want to see myself in this gorgeous, gregarious, troubled girl, like calling to like, shadows calling to shadows? Do I want something more, a physical and emotional connection?

Or do I see a way out?

I might never know for sure. I do feel a bit like the walls are closing in, though. And I know what happens when I get claustrophobic. I don't make the best choices.

The light dies in my mother's eyes. Her heart thuds to a permanent stop. Is she gone?

Get out, get out, get out.

I smile hopefully, but Becca rewards me with a sneer.

"What are you doing here?"

"Having a coffee," I reply smoothly.

"Come outside, right now."

I cast a glance at Rumi, who is watching this little play with undisguised curiosity, then stand and step out onto the sidewalk.

Though we are the same height, it feels like Becca is looming over me. The twins join her, standing on either side, a triumvirate of young goddesses.

"Did I say you could leave campus, Swallow?" Becca hisses.

"No."

"No, what?"

"No, Mistress."

"Then what are you doing here?"

"Having coffee."

"Sniffing after that townie is more like it," Twin One says. "Just like that stupid roommate of hers. I told you I saw them together the other day, Becca."

"Well, why are you here?" I ask. I'm trying hard to be reasonable. There's something in Becca's eyes that is scaring me. Is she high? She doesn't look like herself. She looks possessed.

Becca laughs, a harsh caw. "You don't get to ask questions, Swallow. You obey orders. And I order you to go back to the dorms and wait for my summons."

"I thought you kicked me out this morning. When you wouldn't let me sit with you."

"Awww. Have you been crying, little Ash? Crying on the psycho townie's shoulder about how unfair your life is? Your *woe is me* act is growing thin. Not only do you have dead parents, you have a dead roommate now, too. Go home and think about why all the people around you kill themselves, Swallow."

The hateful jab burns through me like molten glass, shimmering and shattering in turns. I actually gasp.

"Becca. That is completely unfair."

"Tell it to someone who cares, Swallow. I will see you back in the dorms. Go. Now!"

She whirls away, back into the coffee shop, with her minions on her heels.

I stand for a moment, slack jawed and hurt, then slowly start to walk back to Goode, the fury building in my gut.

How dare she?

How *dare* she?

55

THE TRUTH

Kate sees Camille Shannon's family seated in the medical examiner's waiting room, white-faced and tight-lipped, so she does an about-face and walks out the door, around the building to the back entrance, where discreet OCME vans deliver their cargo to the morgue.

She starts to badge the guard at the door, hand drifting to her waist until she remembers her creds are in her boss's drawer. She tries a smile instead.

"Kate Wood. Charlottesville Homicide."

The magic words work. The guard nods a greeting. "Heya. We aren't expecting you, are we, Detective?"

"I'm here for my uncle. Sheriff Wood, Marchburg. The body from The Goode School?"

"Oh, yeah. Go on in. Dr. Singh's got her. I'll let them know you're coming."

"Thanks, man."

The autopsy is wrapping up when Kate arrives. The ME is a young woman, they get younger and younger, it seems. The old-school, cigarette-smoking, tuna-fish-sandwich-eating, gray-haired men are becoming obsolete, making way for shiny new MEs fresh out of school with expertise in cutting-edge forensics and more. Kate wonders for a moment if Tony feels the creep of white-male-privilege obsolescence in his department, then decides no, he's too young and progressive. He has a high number of female staffers because he respects their abilities, not because he wants a nice view day in and day out.

Irrelevant, Kate. Focus.

"You want to ask the parents, or should I?" the dark-haired ME is asking a redheaded tech in a stained coat as Kate enters the autopsy suite.

"Ask them what?" Kate gives the ME a wave. "Kate Wood, Charlottesville Homicide. I was on scene last night. Dr. Singh?"

"Call me Jenn, please. This is my lead investigator, Ron." Ron gives her a peace sign. "And this is a sensitive case, so I'll need you to sign a nondisclosure if you want to get read in."

"Seriously?"

"Family's request. Unusual, but it happens. They're pretty high profile."

"All right."

"The forms are on the counter. Ron, can you get her squared away?"

"Sure."

It's a standard NDA, so Kate signs her life away.

"You're Tony Wood's niece?" Singh asks when she rejoins her.

"I am. I assume he'll need to sign one, too?"

"Already has, he faxed his an hour ago. So, I've just finished up. I see no defensive wounds, we scraped her nails and there's no tissue. There was a good set of fresh, developing bruises on her left biceps, one oval in the front, four in the back. Someone had a hand on her arm, holding her pretty tight. That could have happened anytime in the past forty-eight hours. Can't say one way or the other if she was manhandled over the edge, though. Some small fibers in her throat, too."

"Was she gagged?"

"Don't know. No sign of fibers anywhere but in her throat, no abrasions around her mouth. Could be something was shoved in her mouth to keep her quiet, could be she inhaled something hugging a friend. Without any other indications, there's no real way to know, but I took samples. My most surprising finding, though, was a fetus, approximately seven, eight weeks. That's what we need to ask the family about. Paternity DNA. Whether they want to know who got their daughter pregnant. I was told they don't know who might be responsible."

"Oh, wow. We found a prescription for Cytotec, the pills were missing. We assumed she'd taken them."

"She may have. It's possible the pills didn't work. Normally, they'll discover that on a follow-up and do a scrape. She might not have gone for the follow-up."

"Or she did and when she found out the pills didn't work, she changed her mind. Or didn't take the pills in the first place. Unless we find some more data, it will be hard to tell."

"Which is why paternity will help. Find the baby daddy, find out more of the story."

"I can't imagine they're going to say no. I'm hearing the mother is trying to make a case against the school already. If it's someone with ties to the school, that will help her lawsuit. Nothing else remarkable?"

"I'm afraid not. The trauma from the fall is pretty typical, she had a skull fracture, subarachnoid hemorrhage, cervical fractures, spine compression, and deep lacerations to the back of her head, all consistent with a fall from a height. The fall caused her death, for sure. We're running a standard toxicology. BAL was elevated, she'd had a couple of drinks. Can't say she was drunk, but there was alcohol on board. Without any other data, I'm going to withhold the ruling on suicide or homicide until we get the toxicology back."

"What's your gut?"

"Mmm. Not enough data to determine. I'll have the report typed up from dictation and sent to your uncle."

Cagey lady. Kate doesn't blame her, she wouldn't want to be the one making this determination. "I appreciate it." They shake, and Kate heads out the back again, trying to avoid the family. She doesn't want to face them, to see the emptiness, the grief she knows she will find.

She calls Tony from the car, fills him in. Debates whether to head straight home or drive another hour into town. She hasn't been to DC in a while. She could grab a hotel and a show. Chances are there's a band she'll like at one of the venues. Maybe a cute guy.

In the end, though, she heads back to Marchburg. She's curious enough about whatever Oliver has sent her that she wants a glass of wine and her laptop. See if there's anything else to be gleaned from this case, see if she can answer her instincts, explain to them that they aren't getting the whole picture.

It is late when she gets back. Tony is gone, off handling a car accident down the mountain. She finds an anemic red wine in the back of his pantry, puts it back, and pours herself three thick fingers from his bottle of Lagavulin.

Tony's place is comfortable, simple. A bachelor pad. He needs a girlfriend, the woman's touch to make it a bit homier.

She curls up on the sofa with her laptop and the scotch, opens the email from Oliver, laughs at the dirty limerick he's written—so sly, Oliver is—then clicks open the file.

It is on the third page that she finds the photo. It's part of the crime scene shots from the day of Damien Carr's death. It is a reproduction of a painting, a classic family portrait. The label says *Sylvia and Damien Carr with their daughter, Ashlyn.*

Goose bumps parade down her arm.

She looks closer.

Sits back and lets her mental imagery go to work, decides she's going mad. Looks again. No, it's there. The shoulders aren't as wide. The nose is a little longer. The chin is a different shape.

The Ash Carlisle she met could be this girl's sister. Her cousin. But she'll bet good money that it's not the same girl.

56

THE EMAIL

Ford's morning is a blur of meetings, phone calls, consultations, advice, all of which have gone surprisingly well, considering.

The board assures her they will stand behind her and the school should a wrongful death lawsuit appear, and help fight against any moves by the alumni association to accept the endowment gift and force the school to go coed. She fields plenty of phone calls from concerned parents, but none of them seem to blame her.

A fresh press release is drafted by the lawyers, the school's wrongful death policy revisited.

The students see the counselors, and Ford walks among them, visiting the dormitories and chatting with anyone who wishes to talk.

Ford has to wait until after lunch to speak with Vanessa and Piper. She decides to go to them. It might make them more comfortable to have this interview in their rooms.

Standing at the entrance to their suite, Ford has to admit the renovation, while lovely, has taken a good deal of the character away from the dorms. She liked the dingy rooms she'd lived in, the dark wood walls and multipaned windows. As bright and airy as things are now, she can't help but wonder if the girls feel the improvements have ruined the school's personality.

Vanessa and Piper are on their couch, conversing in low tones. They jump to their feet when they see Ford in the door.

"Sit, sit. I only came to check on you."

"We're okay, Dean," Vanessa says, though the swollen eyes belie her statement.

"I know you're not, so you don't have to pretend for me. Camille was your very good friend."

"We don't know why she did it," Piper says, curling herself back onto the sofa. "I mean, she was pissed off about the whole thing with Ash using a fake name, but when Becca said it wasn't an Honor Code violation—"

"Camille took Ash to Honor Court?" This is news.

"Only a conference with Becca. She shot it down."

"I need to ask you something important. Do either of you know who Camille was seeing? Who might have been the father of the baby?"

A quick glance between them tells Ford all she needs to know. They do, and they're going to lie to her.

"May I remind you, ladies, that we have an Honor Code here."

The threat lands. "We don't know. That's the thing, we were just trying to figure it out. She didn't tell us."

"Camille didn't strike me as the type of girl who would keep something of this magnitude to herself."

"Her sister might know," Piper said. "Emily took her to the clinic outside of Charlottesville for the pills. But Camille didn't tell us who got her pregnant. On my honor, Dean."

"All right. If you two need anything, don't hesitate. I will reach out to Emily and see if she has any information to share. Take good care, girls."

She doesn't know if she believes them. Who are they protecting, and why?

Ford stops by Ash's room but it's empty. It has been straightened, the beds made, the clothes hung. Ford will have to clear out Camille's things, have them sent to Deirdre. Have the bunk bed removed. Ash gets a single for the rest of the year.

If only Camille had left a note. Something definitive. All they have to go on is the reactions of the people around her, teachers and students alike, all of whom say they didn't think Camille was anything but her normal, bubbly self, and the diary in which she spoke of death. She didn't say she wished for her own, though.

Ford knows full well that many suicides are shocks to the closest friends and family. That people who seem happy are sometimes the ones in the most danger of succumbing.

Ford wants to read the journal, at length, but it's been taken into evidence, and she doubts she'll be given another crack at it. She wants to talk to Ash again when she isn't under the influence of Becca, the sheriff, and whatever she'd been forced into drinking the night before.

But Ash is nowhere to be found. She's most likely with one of the counselors. Ford makes a mental note to send for her before dinner.

Down in her office, Melanie is at her desk, nose red and eyes swollen. "Anything new?" she asks.

"No. The girls are understandably rocked. Has the sheriff been in touch?"

"He left a message half an hour ago. He'll be along presently."

"All right. I'm going to check my email, have some coffee. Regroup before he gets here."

She plops down in her desk chair with a fresh cup of coffee. Sunlight spills in through her picture window, a shaft of light runs across the rug. It feels obscene that today is so gloriously sunny. It should be raining, the skies weeping the loss of a child; that's only fitting.

She opens her computer and clicks on her email. She receives a ridiculous amount, considering. She scans the headlines. Most are from parents, a few reporters asking for comment. She's had a lid on the situation and plans to keep it that way, so long as Camille's parents don't act first and start flinging the story to the press.

An invite from Asolo for her annual Virginia Woolf supper party Saturday evening—well, normalcy is best in these situations. She sends back a note: Good idea. I'll be there.

An email pops in while she's working. She doesn't recognize the sender, but it's come to her school address, so she deems it safe and clicks it open.

A photo is embedded in the email. Grainy. Black-and-white, clearly a shot taken at night.

It takes her a moment to realize she is looking at Camille Shannon.

And Rumi.

Locked in an embrace.

More photos fill the screen, loading one by one, telling the story of an interlude. A series of interludes.

A fight. A hug. A kiss. A farewell wave.

Ford shuts her eyes against what she already fears. The father of Camille's baby must have been Rumi.

More photos are loading. Her heart begins to pound.

This is her front door. Rumi is stepping in, and there's a flash of white she knows is her thigh.

The glint of glass.

A smile.

The door closing behind him.

Had he come from Camille's arms straight to Ford's bed?

She remembers the night perfectly. He'd shown up in silence, taken her against the wall. She'd assumed it was lust, but now she wonders if it was simply frustration that his younger paramour had turned him away.

Someone has seen them. She doesn't know what she's more frightened about, that her illicit affair will be revealed, or the much darker thought—Rumi knew Camille.

Rumi was having an affair with Camille.

It isn't a leap for her mind to ask, *Did Camille kill herself because Rumi rejected her for Ford?*

Worse is the next thought, even darker, more disturbing.

Did Rumi kill Camille to shut her up?

Every conceivable curse word she knows runs through her mind, followed by a single, edifying thought.

Who sent this?

Ford is not a computer genius but she isn't a Luddite, either. The email address is gibberish, but she clicks "More Information" in the header and a series of commands spill onto the page. This, though, is unintelligible. Letters and numbers that make no sense.

There is someone on campus who can decipher it for her. Can she trust him to keep his mouth shut?

She prints out the header, wonders what to do with the photos. Should she delete the email entirely? She can't let it sit in her school mailbox; Melanie could stumble upon it. But if she deletes it, is she hampering the investigation? And if she deletes it, what's to say it won't simply be resent? Or sent outside the school. To the parents. To the board. To the press.

Now she's in a real quandary. She's complicit regardless of the next steps she takes.

The crisis management lawyers she talked with this morning had been very clear. There are three ways to respond to a crisis. Yes, I did it, who cares? Yes, I did it, and I'm sorry. No, I didn't do it, prove it.

Prove it won't work—there's photographic evidence, which means the originals are out there. There's no way to pretend she didn't receive the email—somewhere, a server has registered she's opened it. There's no way to say *who cares*, either. Everyone will care.

Her mother's voice launches at full speed from the back of her mind. *How stupid could you be, having sex with a child?*

He's not a child. He's twenty. He's a man. He can vote. He can fight. He can pull a trigger.

Yes, Ford, but how long has this been going on?

That answer, if given honestly, is what will get her thrown out on her ear. Or perhaps put in jail.

Maybe there's a fourth crisis management response. Run like hell. But this isn't an option for her. Not really.

Her choices are quite limited.

Expose herself.

Expose Rumi.

Or wait for the anonymous emailer to expose everything.

A wild, terrible idea—*if I'm not here, I can't be hurt.*

She gives herself a mental shake. *Don't be a fool, Ford. You've made a mistake. That's all. Life will go on.*

"Ford?" Melanie calls from the antechamber. "Sheriff Wood is here."

Ford, startled from her dark thoughts, looks up to see the sheriff's car is sitting outside her window. She hadn't even noticed him drive up.

Without another thought, she deletes the email and exits the program. Yes, she is kicking the can down the road, but she needs time to think. To plan.

To talk to Rumi.

She pinches her cheeks and pastes on a smile.

"Send him in, Melanie."

57

THE BABY

Tony looks wrecked, dark circles under his eyes. He's wearing the same uniform as last night; she can smell spilled coffee and the acrid scent of his sweat.

She waits to see if his niece parades in after him, is relieved to see he is alone.

Though Melanie is floating around him like a hopeful lightning bug. "Sheriff? Coffee? Tea? I can send to the kitchens for some cookies if you need a boost."

"No thanks, Melanie. Appreciate it."

Melanie wilts, then pulls the door. If Ford wasn't freaking out, she would laugh. Yes, Tony is a catch. For someone.

He takes a seat across from Ford. Balances his hat on his knee. Yawns.

"You look as bad as I feel."

"You always were a charmer, Ford." But the recrimination is made without heat.

"I didn't mean to be rude. I'm sorry." She is. She needs him on her side, on Goode's side, now more than ever.

"No worries. I haven't slept. I wanted to drop by and fill you in. The official report will be filed tomorrow."

"Okay. Shoot."

"They found something on the post. Kid was still pregnant. Apparently, the pills didn't work, or she never took them. They took tissue samples for a DNA run. Since no one claims to know who she might have been sleeping with, we'll at least have something to go on. If you can tell me who she was seeing, we can get a match faster. Take a couple of weeks, minimum."

Two weeks. This is good news.

She has time to warn Rumi. They can make a plan.

"Oh, how terrible. I don't have any news on the relationship front, I'm afraid. What about her parents? Do they know?"

"No. The mom's a real piece of work, isn't she?"

"No comment."

"I hear she's making noises about a lawsuit? Care to comment on that?"

"Yes. She's a lawyer, and she's in pain. The two don't go well together. People always want someone to blame. Though I am to blame. It's my job to keep the students safe, and clearly I failed. I didn't even know Camille was suicidal. Though in my defense, no one else did, either."

"If you want to keep the family jewels intact, I'd refrain from saying that aloud again, publicly or privately."

"My mother agrees with you."

"Your mother is here?" Tony looks over his shoulder as if he expects Jude to be standing behind him, scowling as she always does when Tony Wood is in her presence.

"She showed up in town a couple of days ago. Almost as if she could smell the crisis brewing."

"Hmm."

"What do you mean, 'hmm'?"

"She have access to the keys?"

"Tony! My God. You're out of your mind."

"Timing's just weird, that's all. I didn't know y'all were getting along."

"We aren't, which is why the house on the square normally stands empty and she lives full time in New York. Don't worry. She's conniving, but she's not crazy. She'll be out of here soon enough."

"Why'd she show up now?"

"To push an endowment stipulation in my face. Someone in the alumni association thought they could get to me through her." At his blank look, she waves a hand. "It's irrelevant, they're setting up a play for Goode to go coed."

"Is that all?"

"It won't happen. And my mother does this. I don't talk to her for weeks and then she appears as if everything is normal and expects me to play along. She misses the school, I think. It was her life for so long."

"And it's not yours?"

"It is. But perhaps not in the same way."

"That's right. You're getting out."

"Would you please stop throwing that in my face?" She stands and goes to the window. She doesn't want to be too close to him right now. Doesn't need to have her barriers broken down. Because she could use a friend. She could use a man. Some real comfort. Some real love. Not being fucked against a wall by a handyman.

Well, that's over.

"Sorry, Ford. Sorry. Really. Gosh, you bring out the worst in me sometimes." He rubs a big hand over his face. "Guess I'm not as over you as I thought."

His eyes find hers, hopeful. She can't do this. If she opens this door again, she's going to end up stuck in this tiny town, married to a cop, nursemaid to a bunch of spoiled rich girls, sitting down for dinner every night to hear about the gruesome car accidents and deer slaughters and meth busts that make up 90 percent of a rural sheriff's work life. It doesn't matter that he's handsome and kind and crazy about her. No. No!

"Tony. You know I care about you, deeply. If I wanted to stay here, at Goode, things would be very different. But it's unfair of me to ask you to give up your life so I can pursue my dreams."

"I know. You've been clear. Hurt me a little now so you don't break me a lot later. Still, I miss you, girl."

She sits back down, puts her hand over his, squeezes the rough skin.

"It's okay, Tony. We're all stressed. We'll get through this."

"Right." When she doesn't leave any room for the conversation to continue in this vein, he tightens down again, back to business. "The shirt we took from the roommate? The fabric is a match."

Ford sucks in a breath.

"But. The piece we have tests out as standard 100 percent cotton, could be from anything of the same weight and color. I'm willing to bet there are a hundred shirts on campus that match the fabric. Not to mention, who knows how long it's been there? Without a perfect match and a hell of a lot of proof, it's not something that will hold up in court. Ash's shirt is torn, yes, but she says the shirt was a gift that she received the night of the incident. A decent defense attorney will have it struck from evidence in a heartbeat, saying the fabric was there prior to Camille going off the edge. No way to prove otherwise without more—fingerprints, DNA, something. If someone was up there with her at the same time, we need more. Right now, there's plenty of reasonable doubt."

"It might be circumstantial in a court of law, but she was wearing a shirt that matches with a tear in it. Is that enough for us to assume she was up there? That she's lying to us?"

"We need more to go on. She said the shirt was a gift. If she's telling the truth, then where did it come from? Who gave it to her? We need to run it down."

"She did seem quite frantic that we took it from her. It means something to her."

"I agree. Whether she was wearing it while killing her roommate, or it's just an innocent coincidence, she didn't want to give it up. I don't want to jump to conclusions, but it doesn't look good. Now, the key—how could she get access to your keys?"

"I've been thinking about that. I have to assume it's one of the secret societies, though, for all I know, Security could have been up there and left it unlocked. They deny it, but without cameras, we have no proof. It's a mystery we need to solve."

"Well, Ford, it's your school. That I leave to you."

"I appreciate that, Tony. I will look into it, from every angle. I promise. And the moment I know something, I'll reach out."

"Good. In the meantime, my office will continue running down what we have. Though I gotta say I'm not sure of the girl who was pushed off the ledge. I've read the journal. She really was a mess. If there was a note, I'd say we'd have a clear-cut case of suicide, and the ME didn't feel differently."

"I hate to say this, but I'd rather that be the case. The very idea someone on my campus could hurt one of my girls is too disturbing for words."

"Agreed. We'll keep an eye out, our ears to the ground. Step up the patrols, just in case." He stands, a knee cracking. "Oof. Getting old."

"Yes, you're just ancient, Tony."

He surprises her by laughing. She smiles along with him. The tension between them dissipates.

"I'm sorry for what I said last night, Tony. It was inappropriate. You were only doing your job."

"Yeah, well, I provoked you. And it's hard, I know, to lose a student. Bygones."

"Bygones. Let me walk you out."

She walks him to his car, tells him to take care and means it, then watches him drive away. He's a good man. A kind man. But he wants way more than she is willing to give. Not to mention all he said last night was true. She is getting out. Maybe not right now, but sometime.

The gates close behind him with a clang. She checks her watch. Almost time for the five o'clock bells.

She'll tell Ash about her shirt after dinner.

It hits her like a lightning bolt.

If the girl's half as good as Medea says she is, Ash can read that email header. Ash can tell her where the email came from. It's got to be safer to have her look at it than Medea.

Before she does anything else, though, she needs a private audience with Rumi. They need to make a plan.

She sends him a text.

My place. 10:00 p.m.

He writes back immediately.

Not a good idea.

No shit, Sherlock. She's well aware of the risks.

Mandatory.

Three little dots sparkle interminably as if the message is a long one. Finally, the return text appears.

No.

She is struck dumb by this. He has never refused her. Not once. He has always answered her affirmatively, whether it's personal or professional. He appreciates her. Her attention is only part of the relationship. She's given him a home. A job. A family.

And now he's going to defy her?

She sets down the phone. She must speak with him but maybe this is for the best. If someone's lurking around taking photos of her front door, the campus might not be the safest place. She can arrange to bump into him later today. He's working at the coffee shop, she knows. She knows his entire schedule. She drew it up, after all.

She straightens her desk, flicks away invisible lint from her jacket.

The door in the photo.

Ford thought it was hers because she's assuming guilt. But no one has made any demands or threats. All the cottages look the same from the front. It was dark. It was indistinct. Her face was never in it. Only a sliver of thigh.

Who else might Rumi be visiting?

Maybe whoever sent the message isn't trying to catch her out. Maybe they've given her exactly what she needs to escape this mess intact.

58

THE HAZING

Camille's suicide coincides with the start of Hell Week, as it's mockingly referred to among the Swallows. The tradition of Ivy Bound—and all the societies at Goode, it turns out—is to haze the living shit out of their Swallows for the first week after they've been tapped. It's meant to weed out the girls who aren't going to make it through.

That I am suddenly in a single and being given a sort of papal dispensation from the teachers makes it ten times worse. Becca wasn't kidding when she teased me the first day at Goode about a roommate dying. Not only do I get the room to myself, I'm given class credit that assures my GPA won't be taking a nosedive because of the effects the tragedy has on my ability to study.

The girls of Ivy Bound take full advantage. I am treated abominably. My first days as a Swallow are a blur of misery. A constant push and pull, so intense I fear I'll go mad with the humiliation and fevered pitch.

After her nasty showing at the coffee shop, Becca seems out to get me. With disdain dripping from every command, she runs me all over the school. The other Ivy Bound Falconers take a personal interest in me, as well, bossing and laughing, inflicting their own little tortures. One trips me as I scurry onto the seniors' hall to deliver hot tea to my Mistress; I lay sprawled on the floor, soaked in Earl Grey, while they laugh and laugh.

And they speculate. Openly.

I'm the one whose roommate jumped. What sort of asshole am I?

The Swallows are all covered in a terrible rash, the blisters clustered so tightly they ooze wet patches through our T-shirts. I eventually tape gauze to my stomach to try to stop the leakage, but this makes me itch even more. I'm not about to go to the nurse, so I self-medicate with double the recommended dosage of Benadryl three times a day, bathe in oatmeal, and cake on the calamine lotion. Combined with a severe lack of sleep, I move about in a daze, accepting both condolences and snide, knowing remarks with the same languorous attitude.

I can't focus on anything properly. I am exhausted. I am scared and sad and terrorized. My once regulated days have turned capricious and chaotic. I am reminded of the Bach fugue Grassley made me play; I am in a fugue state myself from morning to night.

The orders never cease.

Go get me a latte. Skim milk. Not that whole crap you brought me yesterday.

Yes, Mistress.

Fetch my sweatshirt, I'm chilly.

Yes, Mistress.

I need a book from the library.

Yes, Mistress.

My laundry needs folding.

Yes, Mistress.

I'm out of cigarettes, run into town and get me some.

Yes, Mistress.

Smoke this joint.

Yes, Mistress.

Drink this shot.

Yes, Mistress.

In ten minutes, you need to walk up to Dr. Medea and flash him your tits.

No, she can't do that, a Falconer interjects, *they'll kick her out.*

Good. She's a bitch.

Did you hear me?

Yes, Mistress.

Tell me.

I'm a bitch.

Yes, you are. Braid my hair.

Yes, Mistress.

I need five hundred words on the feminist impact of Elizabeth Tudor. By seven.

Yes, Mistress.

Go buy me a fresh notebook.

Yes, Mistress.

I'm in the mood for Jell-O. Red. Go to the kitchen and get me some.

Yes, Mistress.

I didn't say red. I said green. You are so fucking stupid, Swallow.

Yes, Mistress.

After three days of this nonsense, I'm pretty much ready to murder Becca Curtis. Gone are the tender moments, the kindnesses, the secret glances, the brushing of hands and lips. I didn't realize how often she touched me until it stopped.

In their place is an automaton blond monster, hell-bent on destroying everything I hold dear. My dignity. My sanity.

I itch and fetch and try to keep up with my studies, though the only real sleep I'm getting is on the cold, hard floor of the attics, and only a few hours at that. Becca has taken to forcing me to sleep on the floor outside her door, like a dog. A faithful dog. My book bag is stacked with my own dirty laundry, half-eaten snacks from the Rat, books, and papers I've been dragging from class to class. My fellow Swallows aren't in any better shape.

The teachers say not a word, so I know they're in on it. They can't ignore the thirteen girls dragging around Goode like itchy zombies.

I take every spare moment to sleep, relish the hour of chapel, and hurry happily to my detention in the dean's office to work off my JPs. The dean doesn't moderate our sessions, so I catch a few z's, set the alarm on my watch to alert me when my two hours are up and I'm due back on the seniors' hall for more Swallow duties. Today I am scrubbing the toilets in the attics…with my hair.

I don't know how much longer I can take this.

Finally, on day four, just as I'm about to break, quit, tell Becca she can take her industrial-size Pine-Sol bottle and shove it up her perfect little ass, I am rescued by the dean herself, who asks to see me in her attic room where we were taken the night of Camille's death.

Becca has no choice but to let me go, though it's done with a hiss and a promise to make things even worse for me when I return from my "pussy break."

Why I didn't walk away during Hell Week is something I will always wonder. Why I allowed her to treat me so poorly, so abominably, reflects on my upbringing. I allowed myself to become her victim, just like I allowed myself to become my father's victim, my mother's victim.

But why did I go along with them that night? Why did I not raise the red flag? Would it have made a difference? Would it all have happened differently?

Would they still be alive?

59

THE HORROR

The dean is waiting for me in her attic garret. She looks terrible. I've been so caught up in my own drama with the tap and Becca's advances and the aftermath of Camille's death that I haven't stopped to think about the adults. How they might be suffering. Camille's mother, who is threatening to sue the school—oh, yes, we've all heard about the threats—seems to be more litigious than heartbroken.

But what do I know of these things? If my child died suddenly without a decent explanation, perhaps I, too, would want to burn down the houses of all who knew her.

Though her eyes have dark circles beneath them and her skin is pale, Westhaven's hair is in a perfect chignon, and she's wearing pearls and a cashmere twinset the color of sunset. I've never seen her polished facade looking quite so mature before. She's always been elegant, but there's a fragility around her now that's becoming. It suits her, pain.

She greets me with a limpid smile. "Hello, Ash." Then a much more concerned, "Are you well?"

"I'm fine, Dean."

She doesn't believe me, but whatever. I'm too tired to care about keeping up appearances. I slump in the chair across from her little desk. "What's this room for?"

She glances around as if it's the first time she's ever been inside. A small, private smile crosses her face. "It's my thinking space. I practice speeches—I don't know if you've noticed, but I don't particularly care for public speaking."

Her confession surprises me. She looks so young at this moment. Young and tired and overwhelmed by the past few days of scrutiny on her and the school. It's very like a child to ignore the needs and desires of their parents—I've never stopped to consider what it must be like to be riding roughshod over two hundred unruly girls. One hundred ninety-nine now. I've been much too busy existing in my own strange bubble.

"I didn't. You always seem so self-assured."

"Ah, that's the practice. If you're ever afraid of something, Ash, you must face that fear head-on. Experience it, live it, breathe it, lean in to it. If you do, you'll conquer it. Let it run your life and you will always be its slave."

And if that fear is embodied in a sixteen-stone hulking mass who likes to hit? *Not feeling the "lean in" to that, Dean.*

"I also write here, sometimes."

This intrigues me. I've heard the dean is a frustrated writer. Giving up dreams to do the right thing; now, this is something I understand. I play it coy. "Letters?"

"I'm working on a novel, actually," she continues. "I thought I'd be living in New York, the toast of the literary circles by now. Instead—"

"You're stuck here, headmistress to a lot of ungrateful young women."

"I wouldn't put it quite like that. You're not ungrateful."

Oh, lady, if you only knew. "No, I'm very grateful. But you know what I mean."

"I do." She moves to the desk, rests three fingers on its battered surface. "Don't get me wrong, Ash. I love my job. I love this school. The students. All of you. But sometimes, it's very hard. I escape up here for a little quiet, someplace comfortable, and I work or think. Every woman should have her own place to escape to."

"'A room of one's own.' We've been studying Woolf with Dr. Asolo. I agree completely."

She smiles. "You must be wondering why I've asked you here."

"I assume it's something to do with Camille's death."

"Yes and no."

"Did the autopsy find something?"

"Not exactly. Well, yes. I can trust you, can't I, Ash?"

"Yes, of course." What the hell is this? Why is she trying to give me agency, now of all times?

"Camille was still pregnant. They're doing DNA to find out who the father is."

This strikes me as so sad. What a waste. "I'm sorry. Dean, Vanessa and Piper, did they come to you? Tell you?"

"What would they have to tell me?"

"I think they know who Camille was seeing."

The dean's demeanor changes. Her face shutters, that pained, scared look reappears in her eyes. "Oh. Oh. Thank you for telling me, Ash. I did speak with them, and they assured me they don't know."

Figures they were lying.

"Now, I have a little favor to ask. I received an email from a stranger, and I'd like to know if you can tell me where it came from."

"Dr. Medea—"

She hands me a piece of paper, a full header from the email

that she's printed out. "I'd like to keep this between us girls, if that's all right with you."

There's no subject. I can tell there were attachments, several of them, HEIF, the file type Apple uses. The images came from an iPhone.

I look closer, tracing the head. It's come from a throwaway account, totally anonymous. But the IP address, it's generated from Canada. Odd. The last time I set up my VPN, I hooked into a Canadian server farm.

Whoosh.

Oh, bloody hell. Was this email the one that was in my draft folder when I opened my program? The phantom Send?

I go back to the beginning of the head. Memorize the thread of numbers. My email should be untraceable.

I think.

I've backstopped everything, but I hadn't planned to send any anonymous emails to the dean of my fucking school.

And why has she come to me instead of Dr. Medea? What sort of trap is she laying? Is she handing me the tools of my own destruction? A way to get out of everything?

I can't see the details, but I can't help but wonder who is sending the dean images. And of what? I take a stab in the dark.

"What are the photographs of?" I ask.

Her face drains of color. Bingo. "You can see there are photos?"

"Yes, Dean. At least six attachments, all HEIF." At her blank look, I continue, "High Efficiency Image Files. Helps with compression and... Hey, are you okay?"

Her hand flutters to her throat. "Yes. Yes, I'm fine. Only... someone is playing a cruel joke, I'm afraid."

"There seems to be a lot of that going around."

"You can't decipher who sent it?"

"I'm afraid I can't. It's from an anonymous, throwaway account. It's probably already been deleted. It's an easy thing to do."

"Can you tell if it was sent from inside the school?"

Careful...

"That's trickier. Origins can be traced if given enough re-sources, but off the top of things, I'd say chances are it comes from outside. If it was inside the school, the intranet signature would be here, on this line." I point to the spot. "It's missing those designators. As a matter of fact..." I make a point of read-ing it again. "I believe this was sent from a mobile device, not a computer."

She blows out a breath, and I do, as well. She's not trying to trick me. Seems we both have something to hide here.

I don't have a phone. I'm safe.

"I appreciate your help, Ash. Yes, someone sent me some pho-tos, of one of our students, and I want to be sure we handle this carefully. It would be good if you didn't mention this to anyone."

"Will you show this to the sheriff?"

She shakes her head. "I don't think it has bearing on the case. Like I said, this seems to be someone playing a cruel joke. I think I'll delete it and we'll all move forward."

Good idea, Dean. Really good idea.

"Oh, one more thing...tell me, is there any indication this email was sent to anyone else? Or only to me?"

"I don't see any other addresses. Yours only."

The bells toll, the deep tenor clangs of the tongue against the brass especially loud in this space. Moments later, the dean's mo-bile rings. She glances at it. "Ah, this is Melanie. I need to go. And you're expected in English now, aren't you?" She smiles, benevolence incarnate. "Go straight to class, Ash. We don't want Becca finding you in the hallways, do we?"

See? I told you they are in on it.

60

THE SOLICITOR

I just make the last bell before Dr. Asolo shuts the door. I take my seat and she greets the class with the worst possible news.

"Pop quiz, ladies. If you've finished the reading, this should be a no-brainer. Put away your books and take out an exam book, please."

Groans leak throughout the room, and I join them. Is this really how we're welcomed back after the death of one of our own? How can she expect anyone to have done the reading?

I dig into my bag for the stack of exam books I keep there. One of the items I have learned a Goode girl mustn't ever be without is the pale blue, thin-paper exam book in which all tests and essay assignments, from pop quizzes to the dreaded midterms and finals, are taken. Centered on the cover are the words in bold *On my honor*, followed by two lines, one for printed name, one for a signature. By signing the cover of the exam book, the

Honor Code pledge is taken. No booklets are accepted without a signature.

I flip open to the first page and look to the whiteboard at the front of the room, where Dr. Asolo has written a single essay question under the essay title, *A Room of One's Own.*

What are the feminist ideals expressed in the text?

"Three hundred words, ladies. You have the hour. Go."

I start scratching away. This is an easy one. Low-hanging fruit. I loved the book, identify with the themes. Identify more than anyone at Goode can possibly realize, actually. A room of one's own... Even the title speaks to me. Though the way I've gotten to this point isn't the way I would have chosen. I doubt Woolf would have liked to achieve this status because her roommate died. Since I am now in dubious possession of this ideal, I think I'll include this thought in the essay.

I'm writing so furiously I barely notice when a note comes from the office. Dr. Asolo brings it to my desk.

"Ash, the dean needs to see you. You may finish your essay in your room this evening and turn it in tomorrow. You're dismissed."

I stop midword, staring at Asolo dumbly. Asolo nods in encouragement. "Go on, dear. Don't look so stricken. I'm sure it's nothing serious."

That's what you think.

This is not good. How many times am I going to end up chatting with the dean this week? What is it now? They discovered my lies and are throwing me out? Vanessa and Piper ratted me out? Becca reported me for some sort of violation because I didn't lick the toe of her shoe? Is it the email?

Is it all over? The jig is up?

Breathe. This is most likely an Honor Code thing—I contradicted Vanessa and Piper about their knowledge of Camille's affair. Though the dean brushed off what I said, she must have followed up, and they're insisting I face them as their accuser. I did nothing wrong being honest. We'll be able to clear this up quickly.

I cap my pen, stash the exam book in my bag, and hoist it to my shoulder. I'm going slow, dragging my feet. Asolo might not be worried, but I am.

The dean's official office is as familiar to me now as my own dorm room. I'm surprised to see a man inside. Not the sheriff, either, but a stranger. He's a ginger, wearing a double-breasted, blue, pin-striped suit that looks like it came straight from the back room at Gieves & Hawkes, his wingtips spit polished. His very being screams solicitor.

"Oh, Ash, there you are. Come and have a cuppa with Mr. Nickerson."

Her attempt at British colloquialism makes me cringe, but I step forward.

"Hullo, Ashlyn." Nickerson leaps out of his seat with a wide grin. He is young, probably in his early thirties, and as overly enthusiastic as a puppy. Tea sloshes out of the cup onto his pants leg, and he takes this good-naturedly, as if it is a daily occurrence, blotting it with his hand.

"Whoops. Quite a mess, so sorry, so sorry. Ashlyn, it's wonderful to finally meet you. I was a friend of your dad's. I'm so very sorry we lost him. He was a lovely man."

Oh, such a lovely man. You clearly didn't know him well. More important, why the hell are you here?

I take his proffered hand graciously. "I'm pleased to meet any friend of my father's. I go by Ash now."

"Yes, the dean here told me so. I'm sorry Charlie couldn't come himself, he's tied up, I'm afraid. Well, Ash. Let's sit. I have some news."

Charlie: Charles Worthington, my father's solicitor. The one who explained to me how things would work after they passed.

How the inquest would have to be settled before the estate could be bequeathed.

I can't fathom what this might be, am working hard to modulate my breathing so it's not too obvious I'm in a panic. I take the seat and accept a cup of tea. I would really prefer a cup of espresso, topped with a shot of vodka, spiked with a little "something-something" as Becca says, but I can hardly complain. At least the cup gives me something to do with my hands.

"You've come from Oxford?" I ask, after taking a dutiful sip.

"London, actually. We've had a rough go of it this autumn, I'm afraid. Snow, already."

"Ah. London. Snow, this early. How unusual. What's happening with the estate?"

Yes, what the ever-loving fuck happened with the estate? I thought it was being settled before I left.

"Well, of course, nothing has changed for you. Don't you worry, you're still completely taken care of. As you and your father agreed, you'll come into your inheritance on your twenty-fifth birthday, assuming all the stipulations are met."

"The stipulations? Whatever do you mean?"

"Oh, my. How embarrassing. I thought you knew. You have to have a college degree by your big twenty-fifth."

There it is, the crux of the matter. It's so shallow, so gauche, this desperate need for money. And the stipulations. I mean, it's not exactly a hardship, going to school. At least it wasn't until Grassley died. And I became a Swallow. And my roommate did a swan dive off the bell tower. And the dean started confiding in me.

"Right. That. Yes, I know about the degree stipulation. That's why I'm here, after all. Getting myself lined up to go to college." I shoot a glance at Westhaven, who is smiling at us absently. We pause, wait for her to chime in. This is a play, remember. Everything is timed to perfection; the way parts of the stage move in circles as the rest of the floor stays put. We maneuver around the truth, all of us do. Truth and lies, the moving circle and the sturdy planks, the very ground beneath our feet always unsteady.

It's the dean's turn for her soliloquy, and she delivers it masterfully. I couldn't have scripted this better.

"Ash has a very bright academic future. I'm sure there won't be any issue with her getting into the school of her choice. If I recall, you're interested in Harvard, isn't that right, dear? At Goode," she explains to Nickerson with maternal pride, "our girls get early acceptance to their school of choice. It won't be long before Ash gets to make her applications, and we'll have her set up nicely in no time. We could even go for an extra-early acceptance so she's in line next year instead of waiting until she's a senior if that helps with the estate? I'd be happy to make a few calls."

Nickerson lights up. "Ah, jolly good, jolly good. I'm sure that would be quite helpful to streamline everything. But I'm here with some other news, I'm afraid. Of a private nature. Normally, Ash, I'd ask to speak to you alone, but since you're a minor and his sole heir, my bosses asked me to have a witness signature on the papers, so I've asked the dean to stand in. Will that be all right?"

What the hell is this about?

"I have no secrets from Dean Westhaven." *On my honor.* When lightning doesn't strike immediately, I breathe a bit easier.

"Wonderful. Brilliant. Well, Ash, it seems your father had a codicil made a few months before he passed. Almost as if he… Well, never mind that. The codicil modifies his will. Now, don't you worry, there are plenty of assets to go round, but it seems he's left a good portion of his fortune to another… Ash, there's no good way to put this. You have a sister."

61

THE DECEPTION

The pain is so intense it numbs me. I can barely get out the word. Foreign. Wrong.

"Sister?"

"Yes. She's a few years older than you, and can you believe it, she's actually in Oxford. Or she was in Oxford. She decamped from the city a few months ago. We have her last knowns, but haven't been able to locate her. Your father both acknowledged her and added her to the will."

"A sister," I repeat. I am officially overwhelmed now. "Added to the will."

"Yes. I thought in light of your, well, you've been an only child since your brother's death, and having lost your parents... I thought you might be pleased to know you aren't quite so alone in the world. Even if she gets half the estate."

I nearly drop my teacup.

"Half?"

"Oh, yes. Half. I don't know all the details about how or why or when or who, but we're looking for her now. Because of the sensitive nature of this, we wanted to let you know right away. It's not above the press to get wind of these situations and we wanted to avoid a scandal or any impropriety. And we want to make sure there aren't any impostors, either. My firm has been asked to verify the identity of your sister, when we find her, by a DNA match with you."

"DNA."

Really, I've become a parrot. An utterly, completely numb parrot.

"Ash, drink your tea," Dean Westhaven encourages, forcibly lifting my hand to my mouth.

"I do think you're in a wee bit of shock. Well, it's big news, I'm sure. Too bad you're not a spot older, we could put a nip in that cuppa, eh, Dean?"

"Ash, are you well?" Westhaven asks, clearly concerned.

I've buried my face in the teacup, biting my lip so hard I taste blood.

"What is her name?" I ask finally. "My sister."

"Alexandria. Alexandria Pine. Mother's name is Gertrude. Little Alex is an orphan, too, poor love. Sadly, her mother died from a drug overdose a few months ago, so she is also alone in the world. According to her work records, Alexandria was employed by a tea and chip shop in Oxford less than two months ago. But she moved on, the café owner said she'd had a job offer in London. Better opportunities, better pay. Who knows, you might have been face-to-face with her and never known it."

Alexandria. "And this girl inherits half of my father's fortune? This…complete stranger?"

"That's the long and short of it, yes."

"Does *she* have to have a college degree?"

Now he looks distinctly uncomfortable, flushing from his neck to his hairline. Good. The shoe is on the other foot.

"Erm…well, no. She inherits immediately, I gather. Outside of a morality clause, there's nothing impeding Alexandria from taking her fortune as soon as we identify her. Forgive me, Ash, for sharing what the gossips are saying at the firm—your father only found out about her parentage recently. He wanted to make things right."

"How?"

"How?"

"How did he find out?"

"A letter came. From this Gertrude. Your mum found it, apparently. Held on to it for a while. But he got his hands on it, brought it to the firm when he asked us to start looking for the girl."

"And this woman, Gertrude. Who was she? You say she died from a drug overdose?"

"Yes. She was an addict. Heroin, I'm told."

I sit as straight as I can, the squashy chair making it difficult. "How, exactly, did Sir Damien Carr have a child with a heroin addict named Gertrude? That's simply ludicrous. My father had standards, at least." We both know what I'm talking about. "Damien Carr was ridiculously wealthy. From an excellent family. He was the fucking wealth manager for half of fucking Parliament—"

"Ash! Your language is inappropriate."

"Excuse me, Dean. I must be in shock. But for my father to dally with some sort of…addict, to get her pregnant, and to only now, after his death, be trying to acknowledge her? I'm rather curious, Mr. Nickerson. How many more 'sisters' will be coming out of the woodwork to claim their pound of flesh? This is an outrage. You should be ashamed, bringing me this nonsense. There is no legitimate codicil, my father would have told me."

Nickerson is still blushing. "I am sorry, Ash. I don't know any more than I've shared. I'm just the messenger." And with a flourish, he pulls out a kit from his briefcase and some paperwork. "We only need a cheek swab, no blood work, thankfully. And a few signatures. All very civilized."

My fury is burning hard and fast inside me. I want to run. I want to hide. I want to scream. Tears burst forth.

"Now, now. There's no need to cry. There's plenty of money to go round, and you're no longer alone in the world. Ash, think. You have a sister, someone you can build a relationship with."

I have to stop crying but I can't. The dean finally takes me by the hand and leads me to the bathroom off her office.

"Get it out, darling. You'll feel better. Splash some cold water on your face. We'll be here."

I sit on the toilet in this magnificent marble and chrome room and sob into my hands. For my lost mother. For my lost father. For my dead roommate, my lack of dignity, my ruined relationship with the one person who's shown me real kindness since I came to America. For the fucked-up mess my life has become.

Sister. Sister. Sister.

Inherits half. Half.

If I'd only waited. If I hadn't been so rash. The sorrow of it all is overwhelming.

It takes me twenty minutes to pull myself together. Nickerson and Westhaven are communing quietly when I finally return to the office. He turns with a hopeful look in his leprechaun eyes.

The very last thing in the world I want to do is swirl the tiny brush in my cheek, making the smooth skin raw with the force of its nasty, harsh bristles.

But I do.

What choice do I have?

We have to find my sister.

62

THE PRODIGAL

The fight was so intense, so incredibly off-the-charts intense, I can hardly believe I forgot it. It happened in April and resulted in a broken wrist for Sylvia. It was a knock-down, drag-out mess that spilled from their bedroom to the kitchens, out to the stables, where Sylvia shouted and screamed and threatened, then she came inside crying, saying she'd fallen on some loose straw, and had Cook drive her to hospital for a plaster cast.

Damien had stormed off on his horse, galloping away, dust rising in the distance, and came back well after dark. She'd locked the door and wouldn't let him in. Which wasn't good. Without Sylvia as a buffer, he directed his ire at me.

The black eye was visible for days.

This must have been when news of the sister arrived.

It all makes such perfect sense.

We spend our lives revisiting our very worst moments. Poking the sore tooth, the bruise, to see if it still hurts. Draining our current happiness because we don't deserve it, because feeling good, feeling happy, means we've done something wrong, stepped on someone else's shoulders, hurt or cheated or lied. We live to pick off the scab and taste the blood, fight and hate and fuck and love, and for what?

What is this life supposed to be?

I wanted happiness. I wanted freedom. I wanted to be free of them. The abuse. The hate. The pain. I know all of this, and more, now.

If I had any chance of escape, it meant getting my parents out of the way.

I thought on this long and hard as I wandered the fields attached to the estate. Murder is extreme. It is harsh. It is so very freeing.

Murdering Daddy is just so symbolic. So oedipal. And yes, a bit childish.

But he hurt me, over and over. Kept me hidden away so the world wouldn't see what he did to me. You've seen what he could do. If you had any real idea of how bad it got, you wouldn't be judging me so harshly right now.

And Sylvia, what a fucking waste. If she had ever stood up to him, maybe things would be different. If she had confronted him about his whore sooner, maybe none of this would have happened. We could have lived as one big, happy family.

I could have had a soul mate.

But this… It's his last laugh from the grave. One more arrow into my already shredded heart.

I never in a million years thought he'd have the balls to acknowledge an illegitimate child. To throw such a slight in the face of his long-suffering wife. To throw me, his flesh and blood, under the proverbial bus.

And *half*?

She gets half?

No. Absolutely not. This will not stand.

That is my money. My suffering. My horror. She doesn't get to waltz in and take half of my future without paying the ultimate price.

What a shock. Such a shock.

Poor dear. Poor duck.

This is a mess.

I think it's time for the two of us to have a conversation.

63

THE HEADLINE

I hurry out of the Dean's office and slink toward the library, fighting the urge to run and hide myself in a carrel and never come out.

Sister. Sister. Sister.

And then, *nightmare.*

Becca steps out of the trolley that attaches Main to Old East Hall and blocks my path. She is carrying a green file folder in two hands and oozing menace. What is she doing? Why is she following me? What sort of humiliation does she have waiting for me? The Mistress is cunning and sadistic. But now is not the time for games.

"What are you doing, Swallow?"

"Going to study, Mistress."

"In the middle of the day?"

"I'm getting behind on my work, Mistress."

Please, please let me go. I need to scream, I need to cry. I need to plan.

"Ash. Part of my duties to this school as head girl is to see to the well-being of our younger students. I've become worried about you."

Someone is watching. There's no way she'd talk to me like this, so stilted and foreign, so bloody affected, if we were actually alone. Must be an Honor Court thing. She wants witnesses. I do feel eyes on me, but I don't want to turn around.

"I appreciate your concern."

"I wanted to be here for you when you saw this. It's going to be difficult, Ash."

She actually sounds legitimately worried now. Worried, but also gleeful. She takes a piece of paper from the folder.

The headline is lurid, pulled from one of our most sensational rags, the one that finds alien babies in Buckingham Palace and exposes cross-dressing politicians.

Bombshell Report: Hidden Will Splits Carr Estate
With Unnamed Heir

Becca watches me, waiting to see how I will respond. If I hadn't just spent half an hour with the solicitor from my father's estate, I would have reacted, but now, I'm numb.

I crumple the paper into a ball and throw it on the ground. "I'm aware. I appreciate your concern, Becca, I do."

A flash of stormy green. "Mistress."

"I appreciate your concern. Mistress."

"That's better." She picks up the printout, smooths the wrinkles, puts it back in the folder. Smiles and hangs an arm around my shoulder. Whispers in my ear, fire in her hissing, fingers digging into my bones: "Don't think this changes anything, Swallow. Your little melodrama means nothing to me. Now go get my mail and have it back to my room within five minutes or you'll regret you were ever born and never get to meet the other Carr baby."

She saunters off. So silly of me to think she actually cares. Becca is cruelty personified. She is the paper's edge that slices open unsuspecting fingers, the pin buried in a shirt's collar, the tiny triangle of glass you step on crossing the kitchen floor.

Cruel. Bloodthirsty. But an annoyance.

I have bigger issues.

The mail room is actually a place I like. It's in the basement of Old East, and there's a small, private courtyard outside the glass doors with a bronze sundial in the middle of a circular garden. It's a pleasant spot. Many of the girls read their mail there, complain about the grades they've received. The teachers also put their graded papers and homework in the slots, folded lengthwise so they'll fit the narrow berths. They have no locks on the front—this school runs on the honor system, there's no reason to try to keep the mail under lock and key.

My box is always empty outside of schoolwork. The other girls get things all the time—care packages from their parents, boxes shipped with cookies and sweatshirts and new shoes. I only receive school-related material. I haven't received any mail from the outside since I arrived. I rarely check it, only when I'm expecting graded work.

But after I grab Becca's mail, something compels me to move to the other side of the room, to my own box.

The note is folded lengthwise, like a paper.

I pull it out, open it. There is only one sentence, in the middle of the page. The words are typed, all caps. I read it. Sweat breaks out on my forehead, and my vision goes spotty.

Six words. Six words and my entire world unravels.

SHE IS GOING TO EXPOSE YOU

64

THE INVESTIGATION

Kate and Tony are sharing a pizza and a couple of beers. Kate has been running him through everything she's managed to dig up, the photo, the case file from New Scotland Yard.

"Who do you think this girl is?" Tony asks.

"Everything about Ashlyn Carr, aka Ash Carlisle, feels odd to me. It could be my imagination. I'm going off a single photograph of a painting that's who knows how old. I can't find any other pictures of the whole family online, not of Ash herself. You always told me not to ignore my instincts. Well, they're on fire."

"She's a kid. Could a kid pull off a scam of this magnitude?"

"I don't know. I may be totally off base. But I think there is more to this story than we're seeing. A known teetotaler suddenly overdoses, and the wife, who has been publicly humiliated by the recent exposure of an affair, is so grief stricken upon finding him dead that she shoots herself? I'm not knocking the Met's investigation. The circumstances would raise red flags for me regardless. At the very least, it looks like a murder-suicide. At worst..."

"You think their daughter did it? Kate. Maybe this suspension is the vacation you didn't know you needed."

She laughs. "It's seriously screwed up, I know."

"No kidding. Okay. Let me play devil's advocate. Say you're right. Say the girl's an impostor. That she has a dark past. How could she fool all these people? And more important, if she's an impostor, what happened to the real Ashlyn Carlisle?"

"After Scotland Yard talked to her, and the funerals? That's one hell of a good question. Everything we have says she came to America, enrolled at The Goode School, and is living quietly in Marchburg under the watchful eye of Dean Westhaven."

"Except she's not living so quietly."

"Right. Her roommate is dead, and things are hinky with that. A teacher died, too. Westhaven hasn't brought it up, has she?"

Tony sets down his beer. "I knew a teacher died the first week of classes. Anaphylaxis. She had a tree nut allergy. How is that relevant?"

"She was supposed to be Ashlyn Carr's piano teacher. The girl is apparently a prodigy."

"All right, you have my attention," Tony says, and Kate tips her bottle his direction in a toast.

"Now what?"

She grins. "Now we talk to the dean. She's the one who interviewed Ash originally, correct? Let's see if she noticed any differences between the girl she talked to and the one in this photo. I'll have my guy in Scotland Yard start looking at passports and identification, plane tickets, credit cards, any activity we can find there. I've asked for the full files on the parents' deaths. Not sure if they'll let me see them, the coroner's inquest ruled them 'misadventure,' which essentially means they agree that the father died from an overdose and the mother shot herself in her grief. The case is closed."

"Convenient."

"Now you see where my head's at."

"Kate, I gotta ask…is Scotland Yard all good with you looking over their shoulder on this? The family is well-known, and from what you're telling me, private. The estate might not think kindly of you poking the bear."

"Oliver is totally on board with me doing some extraneous digging. I'm not concerned with the estate. There's no family left to piss off. The son and titular heir died young. The parents are dead. Ashlyn is the only one left."

"So, you think this girl we talked to is not only an impostor, she murdered this very respectable family to take the place of their daughter?"

"When you say it aloud… I know it sounds far-fetched, but I can't shake the feeling, Uncle Tony. Something is rotten in Marchburg. If it's not the same girl, someone in England will surely be able to confirm that for us."

He takes a long swig, a few bites of his pizza. "First, let's drop in on Ford, have a chat with her. She's the one who interviewed Ashlyn, she knows the girl's background. There will be official paperwork. We can figure this out pretty quick."

"Thank you for listening, for believing me."

He finishes the beer in one last huge gulp. "Oh, I believe you, Kate. I'm just preparing myself for the shit storm that's going to be unleashed if you're right."

65

THE DUPLICITY

The drive to campus is only ten minutes. Tony says nothing on the way, which is fine with Kate. She's lost in her own thoughts, too. But when they enter Marchburg's heart, he points to a well-kept Victorian house done up in grays and whites with a matching side garage.

"That's the old Westhaven place. You should see it inside. Chock-full of antiques, decorated to the hilt. There's a Bentley in the garage, too, a perfectly preserved 1934. Belonged to one of the earlier headmistresses. Ford doesn't live there, she stays on campus, but her mother stays when she comes to town. It's a shame, big gorgeous old house like that standing empty most of the time. Makes me sad. But that's what this town's like. It's all about the students. Most of the folks who grew up here have moved off to bigger towns and better lives."

"Yeah, they've crowded into Charlottesville and are busy wreaking havoc for me instead of you. Uncle Tony, this is none of my business, but is there something up with you and the dean?"

He glances over, though his eyes are obscured by sunglasses. "If you're asking if I'm compromised here, no. Ford and I saw each other for a while, off and on. Broke it off for good this summer."

"May I ask why?"

He is silent for a few moments, then sighs. "She's ambitious. Wants to get out of Marchburg, go to New York, be a big shot author. I'm almost twenty years her senior and not about to up-root my life. Timing's wrong."

"I'm sorry."

"Don't be. Wasn't in the cards."

The school looms on the horizon. Kate knows it's beautiful, but there is something about it that unnerves her. All those win-dows, perfectly in line, the dormers watching the quad, jealously guarding the girls inside. The expansive grounds, the cottages, the arboretum. The rumors of tunnels, the very real specter of murder. She wouldn't have enjoyed going here. The very air feels wrong, like a veil drifts between the school and the street, unseen and menacing.

They stop at the gates, which open inward with a deep, metal-lic shriek after Tony presses the intercom button and announces them. It's a bit like entering a prison, only here, the inmates are upstanding teens with daddy issues. She's shocked there aren't cameras on every corner. Is that to protect the privacy of the daughters of the rich and famous? You'd think someplace like Goode would be running the most expensive, elaborate security money can buy. But they don't. They use the gates, the redbrick wall, and a few security guards in golf carts to keep outsiders from ravaging their world.

What if they've let in someone who will ravage them from the inside?

Main Hall looks much like she's seen it before: multicolor banners declare Odds and Evens weekend is coming, students scurry about without a care outside of getting to their next class on time. That's another thing Kate would have hated, the uniforms, the robes. It's all so formal, so fussy. So entirely unnecessary.

She follows Tony to the dean's office. After a few small flirty greetings with the assistant stationed outside, he asks for her boss.

"She just finished up with a meeting. Hold on and I'll let her know you're here."

It takes five, but Ford finally comes to the door, color high, a little breathless. "Tony? Anything new on Camille?"

"Hi, Ford. We need to have a quick talk. Alone."

Is it Kate's imagination, or does the dean pale when she hears Tony's serious tone? What is this woman hiding? Kate hasn't been able to shake the feeling that the dean isn't sharing all she knows about the night Camille Shannon died.

Face it, Wood. You're looking for a disaster. Morbid much?

"Come on in. Can we get you some tea or coffee?"

"Not necessary," Tony says. When the door is shut and they're all arranged, he jumps in. "We've come across something of interest about one of your students. Ash Carlisle—Ashlyn Carr—specifically. Show her," he says to Kate, and she pulls up the photo of the painting on her phone.

"This is from the Carrs' estate. When the crime scene techs from Scotland Yard were combing the place, one took this shot. It's an official portrait of the family. Do you see anything odd?"

Ford takes Kate's phone and looks at the picture, squinting a bit. "That's Ash."

"Is it?"

"Well, it certainly looks like her. She's younger, obviously. Why?"

"I don't think it's her. The shape of her face is off, her chin, her nose. They could be sisters, but I—"

"Wait. Let me see it again." She stares at the photo.

"You interviewed Ash before she was admitted to the school, correct?"

"I did. But her admission was a foregone conclusion, which is not the usual. This was a bit of a unique situation. Her parents got in touch with my mother, who asked me to admit her as a personal favor. I was happy to do it—we had a transfer slot open, so the timing was good. And the Carrs were a very special family." To Kate, "You probably don't know this, but Goode has a waiting list. It's rather extensive."

"I assume that's an understatement."

"Well, yes. This situation… I'm bound by privacy here, Tony. She's a student, and I'm her guardian. Where are you going with this?"

"If Ash isn't who she says she is…"

"Then we'd have a much bigger issue. I hardly believe that's the case, though. Girls change dramatically in their teen years."

"Did you fly her here, or did you go there for the interview?" Tony asks.

"Neither. We talked on Skype. She came across as a very well-bred, articulate girl—for a sixteen-year-old. Half of their utterances are noncommittal grunts."

"Do you have a tape of this interview?"

"No, actually. I don't. There was no need, it was pro forma, more to make sure she understood the Honor Code than anything else. And soon after our conversation, her parents passed away. We worked with the estate and arranged for a scholarship because the money for her schooling was going to be tied up for a while. It's something we've never revealed, another little Goode secret."

"Why did her parents want to send her here? You said it was a favor?"

Ford taps a thumb on her desk. "Again, privacy. What happened before Ash arrived on our shores isn't something I can discuss."

"If you won't tell us, then we'll need to talk with Ash directly, let her tell us the story," Kate says.

"Not without representation. I'll call Alan and we can set up a time. But if you're questioning her, I won't let her do it without a lawyer. You understand, I'm sure."

Tony stands. "Call Alan. We'll be back tomorrow. Say, 10:00 a.m.?"

The dean looks startled that Tony has called her bluff. "I will make the arrangements."

"One last thing. You lost a teacher earlier in term?"

"Dr. Muriel Grassley. Poor thing. Her heart finally gave out. We had incidents with her allergies over and over again."

"This wasn't a one-time thing?" Kate asks.

"Oh, no. Not to lay blame, but if I had an allergy that could kill me, I'd be a bit more careful with my intake. She rarely checked ingredients. Yes," she says, looking out the window, "what a terrible term. Two deaths."

"And a new student whose family has just died, as well."

Westhaven shakes her head. "You're programmed to see the sinister in every situation. I have a very hard time believing that Ash is capable of any sort of deceit. You talked to her. She's a kid. A teenage girl. They're like wolves, untamed, unruly, and for the most part, unremarkable."

"But she's a Goode girl," Tony replies. "You always tell me Goode girls are special."

The smile is swift and fleeting. "You have to say something on the brochures."

66

THE IMPOSTOR

Ford buzzes Melanie the second she sees Tony's cruiser pull away.

"Get me Medea, right now."

Tony has Ford rattled, there's no denying it. Intimating Ash is some sort of impostor—impossible. The solicitor… No. Simply impossible.

Five minutes later, the handsome teacher appears, his forehead creased in worry. "What's the matter? Melanie said it was urgent."

"I need your computer services."

"On?"

"Can you bring up a Skype chat that I didn't record? I need to revisit an entrance interview."

He doesn't miss a beat, though she can see him visibly relax. "Depends on your settings. You might have recorded it without meaning to. Let me see."

She opens the program, lets him sit at her desk. Damn Tony and his niece's prying, now she's doubting herself, doubting Ash, doubting everything.

"Which interview do you need?"

She flips through her desk calendar looking for the exact date of her first meeting with Ash. "July 17."

He taps away, then sits back. "Sure, here it is. You want me to play it?"

"Wonderful. No, thank you, I'll do it. But let me ask, how was it taped?"

"You have auto-record on in your settings. Every Skype chat you've had is in the system. You have to dig a little to find them, but they're here."

"Oh, wow. I had no idea. I can delete them, right? There's an expectation of privacy, I had no idea I was recording everything."

God, Ford, could you sound any guiltier?

"Sure. Easy. But in this case, it sounds like you're lucky to have them all right at your fingertips. Want me to delete them? You just click up here, select All, then Delete."

"Good to know. I'll take care of it once I take a quick look at this old chat. Thanks so much, Dominic."

Her tone is meant to be dismissive but he doesn't leave. "While I'm here, a moment of your time?"

She doesn't have time, but she can't seem too anxious. "Sure, what is it?"

"I hate to bring this up, but considering the circumstances… A few of my students are falling behind. Jordan and Ash, specifically. Something's up with them. I think they're being bullied."

Oh, boy, are they.

Ford smiles and gestures to the chair, which he takes, looking anxious.

"It's tap season. They're being initiated by their secret societies. The tasks can be a little over the top, but no one's being hazed, I assure you. That's against the rules, and the societies always comply with the rules. They'll be back to normal soon."

"I see. Ford, far be it from me to comment on how you run things here—"

"But you're going to anyway?" She leans back in her chair, tapping a pencil on the desk.

He clears his throat. "Yes, I am. This term has been quite challenging, for me, for all the teachers. It feels like the students are running the show, instead of the other way around. I know you told me this elite program works differently than the usual private school curriculum, and I'm supposed to cut them some slack. But I fear I'm not as effective as I could be if the girls were, say, a bit more dedicated to their studies instead of partying."

"Partying? At Goode?" *Crap, Dominic. We're going to do this now? Really?*

"Ford, surely you've seen this. They reek of alcohol. They come to class stoned. And now we find out a student was pregnant and killed herself... Add in the bullying I've seen..." He holds up a hand. "Even if this is some sort of tap hazing, it's going too far. Ford, I fear you're going to have a major problem on your hands if you don't crack down immediately. If the parents get wind of this, or the board—"

She drops the pencil. "Are you threatening me?"

"No. No, of course not. But I'd like permission to discipline any of the girls who break the rules."

"You don't need my permission, Dominic. We do discipline here. Ash has been serving detention with me all week."

"Unsupervised detention isn't much of a deterrent. I heard her tell Jordan all she's done is sleep."

Ford has had enough of this. She has bigger problems than a puritanical teacher who isn't willing to get with the program. But she can hardly say that aloud.

"I'll be sure she doesn't get away with that from here on out. Melanie will stay with her. And give out all the JPs you want,

Dominic. I won't stand for the girls not showing the proper respect for their studies or their teachers. I appreciate you making me aware of this situation. The girls are given great leniency when it comes to the society taps, yes, but that doesn't include the use of alcohol or drugs. Confiscate any you find and let me know who is responsible. If we need to do a dorm search, we can. I've expelled girls for less."

Dominic seems satisfied by this show of force. "Will do. They haven't been careless enough to flaunt it, but I'm not so far removed from my school years that I can't see the signs." He stands, brushing his hands down his jeans. "I should let you get back to it. Thanks for hearing me out, Dean."

"Ford. Call me Ford."

He smiles shyly. Ah, she has read this correctly. If she wanted to, she could lead him by the hand to the couch for a holy hallelujah with Melanie listening fervently at the door, but she doesn't need any more complications right now.

Your mind exists in the gutter, Ford. Get it out of his pants.

When the door closes behind him, the smile drops immediately. Every fear she's had for the term has come to fruition. Drugs. Alcohol. Pregnancy. Death. And now, eclipsing them all, the idea that one of the students has lied about her identity to gain entry to Goode.

This cannot go on. The walls of this institution are strong, but even brick and steel can crumble under appropriate pressure.

She slaps the mouse to open the browser again. Her screen is filled with the image of a dark room and a young lady with blond hair that hangs in her eyes.

Ford clicks Play, watches, listens. Hears her own voice, sees her smiling, happy face in the small corner of the screen.

"Why do you want to attend The Goode School?"

The voice sounds right, the inflections the same, though tinny through the computer's speakers. "I have to admit, it was my parents' idea. I'm not too keen on being stuck at an all-girls boarding school. It feels like a punishment."

"It's an opportunity. But I'm not here to sell you on this, Ashlyn. Your parents have arranged for your admission, yes, and yes, most of the girls who attend Goode are desperate to be here. But they can't force you to come. I don't want you here if your heart and soul aren't going to be in it."

A glance down. Ash—or whoever she is—has that same mannerism. God, it's so damn dark. Why hadn't she noticed how dark the room was? Is this the same girl? She just can't tell.

She watches, oddly cheering past Ash on—*pull your hair back, I think I remember you pulling your hair back, do that and I'll be able to see your face clearly.*

There, yes, she pulls her hair back over her neck, then shakes it down to cover her face again.

Ford rewinds, then stops the video at the moment Ash's face is fully exposed.

There is no question.

The Ash at her school is not the girl from the interview.

They do have an impostor.

"Lies will flow from my lips, but there may perhaps be some truth mixed up with them; it is for you to decide whether any part of it is worth keeping."

—Virginia Woolf, *A Room of One's Own*

67

THE PHONE

Ford doesn't panic, not yet. She is logical. Cool in the face of adversity. Nothing rattles her. She closes the program, closes the browser, logs out of her computer. Tells Melanie she's going for a walk on the grounds, not unheard of this time of day, then heads directly upstairs to the sophomores' hall.

Has she been snookered by a sixteen-year-old? Is there something much more nefarious going on?

Ford has every right to search a student's room at any time. It's in the handbook, it's part of the Honor Code. She's never done it before. She's never had to. The girls police themselves and their classmates better than she ever can. An Honor Code builds trust, yes, but there's always the bit of rivalry that means some girls are looking for reasons to rat out their frenemies. Ford has always been good at sussing out what is real and what is animus and punishes accordingly.

But now she has no choice.

Ash Carlisle, whoever the hell she is, is hiding something, and Ford must find out what it is before the girl takes down the whole school.

She's a hacker; Medea says she has talent. She could very easily be the one who sent the email with the photos and she was simply lying about it.

That belies logic, though. Why, if she's an impostor, would she draw any attention to herself?

Ford needs to get to the bottom of this, and for that, she needs the originals. She has to inform Tony and his niece about what she's discovered, but she also can't have an investigation into a student reveal her own secrets.

Ash's room is monkish without Camille's things cluttering it up. Ford didn't give Ash's lack of accoutrement any thought when she arrived last month; now it strikes her as odd. What teenager doesn't have a thousand and one things around them? There isn't another room on the floor she could enter and see this level of minimalism.

Which makes searching it easy.

She finds the mobile phone taped to the inside wall above the door to Ash's closet. She gives herself a pat on the back for clear thinking. It's where she would have hidden it if she'd been trying to make sure no one found it.

She swipes it open. The battery is almost gone, and there's no passcode. How irresponsible, and how lucky.

The photos are easy to find, right there in the app.

That little bitch.

Ford is faced with a choice.

Take this phone into custody, drag Ash in, and find out why she has it, or delete all the photos and destroy the phone. It's not like Ash can come to her and ask for her phone back—she's in violation of the rules by having it. Ford should kick her out on her ear. She should kick her out regardless, though Tony might take care of that for her.

A Goode girl in handcuffs. Her mother will have her head. Something to be avoided at all cost. The girl knows too much. Push and pull. Push and pull.

Maybe the two of them need to have a heart-to-heart, get all this out in the open. Quid pro quo. *I don't expel your skinny ass, you don't reveal what you know. And who the hell are you, anyway?*

Ford is grasping at straws, and she knows it. Her mother wouldn't hesitate here, she'd have already thrown Ash to the wolves. Ford should do the same. She can't risk losing the school over a scandal, not on top of Camille's suicide.

Tony's worried face. He thinks Ash killed Camille, or that niece of his does and is planting that idea in his head. And now to intimate Ash had something to do with Muriel... Muriel... Ash quit piano.

She would have to, wouldn't she? If she wasn't the prodigy piano player, Muriel would have known quickly. *Out of practice, my ass.*

But had she eliminated Muriel because she was worried about being exposed as a fraud? That would be...diabolical.

"Ash? Do you have any—oh!"

Ford whirls around to see Piper standing in the doorway. She puts her hand behind her back immediately, praying the phone hasn't been seen.

"Dean Westhaven. Hello. I was just looking for Ash. I'm sorry to disturb you."

And she disappears before Ford can say a word.

Damn sneaky girls. What did she see?

Ford shoves the phone in her pocket and steps into the hall. "Miss Brennan. A word, if you please?"

Piper's tall frame stops dead. "Yes, Dean?"

"Why aren't you in class?"

The freckles go dark with a charming blush. "I got my period. I came up for tampons but I'm out, V doesn't have any. I was just seeing if Ash has some."

If she's lying, she's a smooth operator.

Why do you assume everyone is lying? Just because you're up to your neck in deceit doesn't mean everyone is.

"Are the bathrooms not stocked?"

"No, Dean."

Ford shakes her head. "I'll see to it. Off with you, continue your search."

Piper smiles gratefully and scoots off. The bathrooms aren't stocked, which means the support staff isn't on top of things. Students wandering campus, out of class, at all hours of the day. A possible impostor on the grounds. An affair with the handyman. Heavens, she's let Goode go. Let herself go, dropped her standards.

When are you going to wrap your head around the fact that you don't want to be here? You should find a replacement, someone who cares enough to make sure things are run properly. You obviously don't care enough about the school's management to be in charge.

Perhaps it *is* time for her to be thinking about naming a successor. But how would that look? Like she is running away the moment there's something negative going on. Like her mother. Jude fell on her sword without a second's thought. When asked, Jude said, "Goode is more important than any one person."

Ford almost understands.

Resigning in protest over a forced move to coed, though, that would be a legitimate out.

No. She needs to clean up her mess, but she's not going to run.

And she's not going to let anything ruin her. She is going to destroy this phone. Call Alan, set up the meeting with Ash and the sheriff.

And have a word with her wayward student. It's time she finds out exactly what Ashlyn Carr is up to. Answers must be given. By Ash, and by Rumi. He's avoiding her, she knows it, and she needs to get him alone and find out what his relationship was with Camille.

But to do it safely, she needs privacy.
Using her own phone, she texts Rumi.

Meet me at the house. Please?

She has to wait ten minutes for the reply, but finally, finally, three dots appear.

I can't get away until later. Is 9 okay?

Yes. Absolutely. Thank you.

Thank heavens. At the very least, she can find out what's going on with these photos of him and Camille.

She calls Alan next, who is happy to be of service. She asks him to reach out to Tony for more details. He suggests she wait to talk with Ash until he's present. She agrees, though she's lying. She has to talk to Ash first.

Then she stalks to her attic garret, stares out the window onto the quad.

How is she going to approach Ash?

68

THE REALIZATION

I retreat upstairs after the trip to the mail room, the damning note clutched in my hand. After the initial shock of the words, my head has cleared. It's strange how calm I am. The world is about to come crashing down at my feet, but my heartbeat is steady. My breath comes in regular sequence. My vision is hyper focused.

I sit on my couch in my quiet, empty room and set the note carefully on the coffee table.

This can mean only one thing. Someone knows.

But who? Who is the *she* in this warning? I'm surrounded by women, girls, variables of *she* from every corner.

Becca. Vanessa. Piper. Dean Westhaven. The cop.

Camille.

The number of *she*'s is astounding to think of. Any one of these girls could be about to wreck my life. *Think. Who has the most to gain from seeing you exposed?*

Piper isn't capable. She's a good girl.

Vanessa, though...

Which leads me to wonder, how long was the note in my box? While I've been down to the mail room several times since Becca tapped me, I haven't checked my own box in days. Camille has been dead for four days. Was the note placed before Camille died? Or after?

She.

Becca. Camille. The dean.

Sister.

Camille's sudden suicide.

She is going to expose you.

No. It can't be.

I'm jumping to conclusions, I know, but I can't help but think the absolute worst.

I heard my name that night. I've forgotten that small but eerie detail. I'd written it off as my imagination which was already in overdrive coupled with drugs and alcohol, but when I entered our dorm room, I thought I heard my name called.

Was it Camille, yelling for help?

Did Becca somehow find out Camille was going to share my secret and kill her to stop the rumors? Did she kill Camille to protect me?

The shirt she gave me had a tear in it. She gave it to me that night. We were apart for at least fifteen minutes. She had time to get up there. If Camille had been stashed away somewhere, it's entirely possible.

A chill runs through me.

Did Becca push Camille? Was Camille about to expose my past and Becca took care of it for me?

Is she capable of murder?

And then I remember. Becca's mail. I've forgotten to deliver Becca's mail.

I have to go face her.

I need to think. I need to figure this out.

I have to act like nothing is wrong.

I grab the mail and sprint up the stairs. Becca isn't in her room, and the relief is overwhelming. I set the mail on her desk and, before I am seen, slip into the stairwell and hurry back downstairs.

The notecard, folded in half, is pinned to my corkboard. It wasn't there when I left. There is a small bird wrapped in vines etched on the front. The Ivy Bound symbol. Becca was here, I've just missed her. Or maybe her minions, the twins, who knows?

I take the card with a shaking hand and move into my room to read it.

9:00 p.m. Commons. Mandatory for all.

Mandatory is underlined three times. Becca has called for a meeting of the Swallows. Why?

Oh, God. Who cares. If I'm in a group, I'll be safe. She wouldn't dare hurt me in front of witnesses.

"Ash?"

Piper sticks her head in.

I slide a book over both notes. "What are you doing up here?"

"Same as you, I suspect. Cutting."

O-ho, how wrong you are, little girl.

"Listen. I know things are really weird right now, but you should know the dean was in here ten minutes ago. I think she was searching your room."

"Searching my room? For what?"

"Your phone."

"I don't have a phone."

"She found one in your closet. I was watching. It had tape on it. She looked at it, swiped around some, then saw me and hid it behind her back. I had to spin a quick tale about needing a tampon."

"Why are you telling me this?"

"Because I'm your friend, asshole. At least I've been trying to be, though you don't make it easy."

I blow out a breath. "Okay, I'm sorry. I'm a little stressed out." *I'm holding a note that says my world is about to blow up. Know anything about it?*

"Maybe we could talk later?" she says, hopeful.

"About?"

"What's happening. Man, you are weird today."

"What do you mean?"

"Um, hello? The sheriff has been here several times, the dean just searched your room. They think you did something to Camille. And there's some rumor about you having a sister. And that you and Becca are on the outs. I just thought you might need a friendly ear, that's all. I know you wouldn't have hurt Camille. You're not that kind of person."

What kind of person am I, Piper? Do you really know me?

"Becca and I were never on the ins. Besides, there's nothing to talk about. I can't discuss a family matter. I appreciate you letting me know about the dean, Piper. But I need to lie down now, I'm not feeling well."

Disappointment crosses her face, but she nods. "No worries. I need to get back to class."

She disappears, and my mind dismisses her, but not entirely.

The dean in my room. Finding a phone?

Whose phone did she find? It's one rule I actually followed—I didn't bring a phone. I have other ways to communicate with the outside world, I hardly need a phone. They're too dangerous.

Then it hits me. The mobile signature on the email. She wanted me to decode where the email with the photos was sent from.

Shit. If the dean found a phone in my room, she's going to think it came from me, that I lied and said I didn't know who sent the email. It looks like me. It's going to be hard as hell to deny it without exposing myself.

Who is messing with me?

And why?

69

THE INITIATION

In case the dean comes looking for me again, I slip off into the arboretum, where I plan to cool my heels under my favorite hemlock until my appointment with the Swallows. While it's chilly out, the sun still shines, so I find a patch of warmth and close my eyes. When I wake, it's dark. Piper and Vanessa were right when they said I'd get used to the bells—they are easy to hear from all corners of campus, so I must have slept like the dead. The stress and the late nights with Becca finally shut me down. I feel better than I have in days. I can deal with whoever is trying to spook me. I've dealt with worse.

Since I'm relatively sure the dean has left Main Hall for the night, I head back to the dorm. I grab a tuna melt from the Rat and eat in my room, away from everyone, stoking the rumor mill even further.

After all the craziness that's gone on today, I didn't think I'd be relieved to go to an Ivy Bound meeting, but when the time comes, I am. I'm safe in this twisted little group.

At nine, I mount the stairs to the attics. The rest of the Swallows are in the Commons, waiting. Everyone is nervous, you can smell it coming out of their pores.

"What's happening?" I ask Jordan, who looks like death warmed over, but she shakes her head.

"No idea. No one knows. I'm scared to death. Amanda is a psycho, Miranda is, too. I think they switch places for fun. They've been torturing me with stupid tasks, taking all my study time. I failed a chem exam today. This is out of hand. If they take things much further, someone should complain to the dean. They're not allowed to haze us like this."

"I don't disagree."

"Swallows!"

Twin One and Twin Two, Miranda and Amanda, have appeared from the tunnel. They are dressed in cardinal red, like identical handmaidens, and stand by the door to the red staircase with manic grins on their faces.

"Follow," one of them intones and pulls up her hood. Oh, great. Now they're wearing spooky-ass hoods that scream ritual sacrifice. This is going to be a blast. Maybe I was better off alone in the woods.

The dirt tunnel path to the cabin has been trod often enough now that the cobwebs are gone. We dart through the tunnels in pairs for safety's sake, so no one falls down, trailing after the spooky sisters as they lead us deep into campus. Jordan grips my hand so hard the bruises Becca left the night of Camille's death flare up and I have to get her to switch sides.

We enter the cabin, which is dark except for candles lined up on the oak table and a fire in the fireplace, the first time I've seen one. It makes the damp space warm and cozy, and I'd relax if I weren't so scared.

"Oh! This is it," Jordan says, and the note of excitement in her voice steadies me a bit. "Whatever they have in store for us is going to happen tonight, early, because the police are roaming campus and they don't want to wait any longer to make us sisters. They must be about to get in trouble for the hazing."

"They're initiating us?"

A twin barks, "Shut up, Swallows, or we'll shut your mouths for you. Silence. Now."

The Falconers are dressed in red robes, covered head to foot. All that's missing is our leader. As I start looking for her, she detaches herself from the shadows behind us. Becca is resplendent in black, her hood covering her sunny hair. She is a crow. A raven.

Our Mistress.

We are placed in line, given a drink and a pill. This isn't a little one like the Ecstasy, and I'm immediately worried about what it might be. I can't lose control, not now. Not with so much at stake.

But when I try to refuse, my mouth is pried open and the pill pushed in, the bottle clanked against my teeth until I swallow it all down.

It doesn't take long to start working, I feel woozy almost immediately.

The bottle is passed again, and again.

They build up the fire in the grate. It is then that I notice the poker in Becca's hand. The tip glows red in the coals.

Murmurs begin. The acrid scent of sweat and panic fills the room.

Oh, no. No way. They're going to burn us?

The end of the poker has a curl on it. I realize it is the stylized wing of a bird in flight.

Not burn. Brand.

I don't want to do this. This is crazy. It's archaic. Inhumane.

Standing there with a red-hot poker in her hands, flanked by the red-robed Falconers, Becca intones about the meaning of Ivy Bound. About why we were chosen. About each girl's strengths, what she brings to the group.

She runs through all thirteen of us. Giving us the why.

The reasons vary. Humor. Kindness. Intelligence. Fortitude. When she gets to me, I find it hard to meet her eyes.

"Ash. You were fragile. Hurt. And yet you faced your fears with formidable internal strength. You are the heart of Ivy Bound. You are its soul. You will forevermore have sisters by your side to hold you up, who will sip at your power when they need their own. Your service to your sisters will go down in legend. You will never be alone again."

It's probably the pill and vodka, but I can't help myself from grinning. The smile in her eyes makes all of this worth it. What-ever else has happened, I have found someone special. She may be mercurial, but part of that is the situation into which I've been thrust, as a Swallow. Now that we're sisters—equals—we can begin our real friendship.

She finishes reciting the reasons for inclusion to the end of the line, then puts the brand in the fire again and beckons the first girl toward her.

There are screams. Faints. Stoicism. Tears. I stay in line, hands tucked under my arms to keep them from shaking, and shuffle my way forward. I am midway now. Four to go. Three. Two. And then, finally, it's my turn.

Despite the vodka, despite whatever pill I've taken, when I raise my shaking left arm and let Becca force the flaming hot metal into my rib cage to the left of my breast, equal latitude to my heart, I want to scream. It is agonizing. It is the most pain I've ever experienced, willingly or otherwise. But I grit my teeth. Tears pour down my face. I deserve this torture. It is cleansing, this pain. So intense, so severe. There's something about it I like.

And then it is over, though the sting remains. I am dipped in petroleum jelly and wrapped in some sort of plastic and sent to the end of the line, where Twin One is waiting with another dose of something to take away the pain, the cares, the worries. I down it gratefully.

When the last screams die out, Becca kicks dirt onto the fire, then faces us.

"Ivy Bound is based on integrity. You were chosen for your strength and your honor. You shine as an example of the best of Goode. The finest character, the strongest personalities, the kindest hearts. You have all been tested and found worthy. Welcome to the sisterhood."

There is cheering, hugs. Falconers and Swallows merge into a mass of sweaty, drunk, stoned girls.

Swallows and Falconers no longer. The Mistress no longer.

We are one now.

We are sisters.

We are Ivy Bound.

I've done it.

Becca seeks me out and pulls me to her breast. I collapse against her with relief, my arms snaking around her waist. She is warm and smells like jasmine, and it's just so nice to be held again by someone who loves me. She rubs a hand up and down my back, careful not to touch the brand, and it feels like a promise. I look up at her and she's smiling at me, tenderness in her eyes. I tuck a strand of hair behind her ear and touch my lips lightly to hers.

I am on the dirt floor before I can blink.

"What the hell, Ash?"

I have forgotten where I am. I am higher than high and in pain and drunk, and despite all of these things, I realize I've done something dreadfully wrong.

Becca is standing over me with a look of sheer panic on her face, and all around me, I hear whispers, louder and louder, some amused, some horrified.

"Did she actually kiss her?"

"Oh, my God, lesbo alert."

"I knew she had the hots for her."

"Wait, is Becca gay?"

But it is Becca herself who breaks me in two. Her voice is shaking and the rage monster I saw in her room is back. "Get out."

What have I done? Oh, my God, what have I done?

This isn't getting drunk at a party and hooking up, which is totally acceptable. Or even messing around behind closed doors. This was a kiss of love. I've just outed Goode's head girl in front of our entire secret society.

Apparently, there are still some taboos at Goode.

"Go!" she hisses at me.

"Where?"

"Back to the school. You are out."

70

THE DOOR

The door to the Commons swings closed behind me and I run, crying, down the stairs to my room. The pain in my side doesn't compare to the pain in my heart, seeing Becca look at me like that. Like I am some sort of freak. She started this. I didn't seek her out. She was the one who encouraged me.

Have I actually been kicked out of Ivy Bound? Is this even possible? She was talking about sisterhood and love and friendship and now I've been cast out, cast aside.

I didn't mean to do it.

How could she? How *could* she?

I am so dizzy. The room is spinning, and the air seems like it's wavering in and out. I don't feel the ground when I hit it. I don't feel anything at all.

I wake to chilled air sweeping around my body. I am on the floor in my room. I don't know how much time has passed. I am thirsty, and I crawl across the room to my water bottle. I gulp down the contents, but it's not enough, I need more.

I drag myself to my feet, and that's when I fully realize cold air is pouring into the room. Where is it coming from? My windows are closed, my door is closed. But cool, damp air is bleeding in.

Someone must have left the hallway window open to the fire escapes.

And someone has been in my room. In my bed. A gift has been left on my pillow.

The bird is small, soft in its mutilation. The nail is driven straight through its tiny heart, impaling both the body and the note, written in red ink—or the bird's blood, I don't know which—which says in big block letters: *WHORE.*

I stumble backward, away from the horror.

Fuck. Fuck. They're sick. Sick and twisted and wrong. How could I have ever wanted to be a part of this group?

I flee into the hall, retreating away from the mess, and see the door across the way is wide open. The draft is coming from a window on the far side of the darkened space. The sash is fully raised, letting in the cool air.

I trip almost immediately when I walk into the room, fall to my knees. I'm unsteady anyway, still feeling some of the effects of whatever drug they gave us, but someone has moved things around in here. Must be the janitors. And they left the window open. And something smells funny.

Cigarette smoke, I manage to put together. Someone was smoking out the window.

So much for the bright, shiny lock. If they leave the room open, what difference does it make?

I haul myself to my feet. I've skinned my knee, but I ignore the sensation of blood running down my shin. There is a shadow in the corner that has my full attention. My vision is adjusting to the darkness, the moon's glow gives enough light to make out the strange shapes and lumps through the room.

The planks of wood that used to lean against the wall are stacked up in front of the door, that's what I've tripped on. With them moved away from the wall, for the first time I see what they were hiding.

There is a door.

And it is open.

My first thought is to run. My second is more jumbled. Perhaps it was all a test. Perhaps I am not kicked out of Ivy Bound. Perhaps Becca is waiting for me. She complimented my strength. I need to be strong now.

Hope flickers in my chest. All is not lost after all.

I take a deep breath of the strange, dirty air and step through. There are stairs, winding down, gray concrete with black dots on them. It must be mold of some sort—the air here is overwhelmingly musty—but there is something lodged in the corner of the railing. It's a piece of cloth. I pull it from its spot. It is black and stiff. I notice a small piece of plastic flapping in the breeze, staked to the banister with a nail, rotted through. It is yellow, with black writing, but it's unreadable because of the holes and tears.

The black dots on the stairs… It's blood. And someone, or something, must have wiped their hands off on this piece of fabric and left it behind. And the yellow plastic—is this crime scene tape?

The blood on the cloth is old, dried. It flakes off onto my hands when I touch it like I've been doused in ashes from the fire. Gross. I wipe it off on my jeans.

Why do I have a feeling I've just discovered the real red staircase?

Something terrible happened here, of this there is no doubt. The pervasive dread creeping along my spine makes me want to turn around and launch myself out the window. I should turn back. Go to my room, lock the door.

But there is truth here, I can feel it. Though the truth about what, I don't know. Logic tells me this is the path to another variation of our secret society cabin, and I'm curious enough to follow the stairs down to see if I'm right. Especially if there is forgiveness on the other end.

The door above me closes softly. All the hair rises on my body. Someone has shut me in here.

I run back up the stairs but the door is locked. Locked from the outside. I swear I can hear breathing.

"Funny joke, ha ha. Open the bloody door, you arsewipes."

Nothing. No more sound. It's like I'm the only person in the world.

I slam my shoulder against the door, but it is closed tightly. I have no choice but to see where the passageway leads.

My natural claustrophobia combined with my emotional exhaustion at the past week's events make it feel like the walls are closing in. I drag in a ragged breath.

"Keep moving. It will be okay. They're playing a joke on you. The gits."

I call the girls a few more names—this has to be an Ivy Bound joke, it has Becca's sense of cruelty attached—and take the steps down. I don't know why I didn't think of it before. They've branded me, I am wearing the Ivy Bound insignia under my breast. They can't kick me out. They've shared their secrets. I caved when they needed me to be strong. They're giving me a second chance.

Relief is as sweet as water to my parched throat.

There is no light down here but my eyes have adjusted so I don't feel like I'm in total blackness. Still, I have to use the nasty dirt wall to keep myself upright. My hand keeps getting tangled in cobwebs, and it is totally freaking me out. What if I get lost down here in this tunnel?

What if it's not a tunnel at all?

Of course, it is. Don't be stupid. Piper warned you about them first day of term. You were in one for the tap. This isn't any different. It will open up into a cabin, and there will be a bunch of snotty bitches screaming and laughing because they've pulled one last prank on you. Just keep moving.

It feels like I've been walking forever before the air starts to clear and the path slants upward. I hurry now, desperate to get out of the close confines of the tunnel. The air changes, fresher, cleaner, then I hit a gate.

The lock on it is old and rusted. And open. Thank God. Someone has gone out this way and left it open.

Someone is waiting for me.

I step into the darkness, into the cool night air, heaving deep breaths to clear my lungs.

The moonlight spills over the ground and I see rocks, standing rocks. Then my brain does the math and I realize they are gravestones.

I am in a graveyard.

And I'm not alone.

"About time you got here, Swallow."

71

THE CONFRONTATION

I can't help it, I scream, but a hand clamps over my mouth so it comes out as a muffled *meep*.

"Shut up! Do you want everyone to hear you?"

Panic shoots through my body, and my heart starts to thud. I thought it would be Becca on the other side of the door, laughing, joking, jolly, and happy again.

But this is not Becca.

I know this voice. It isn't one I ever wanted to hear again. I look around wildly, how can I get away? How can I escape?

"I'm going to take my hand off your mouth. If you scream, if you call out…"

Something hard and sharp touches my neck. Christ, she has a knife. She's insane, this I've always known, but she has a bloody knife.

"I'm not insane, you cow, and you know it. How dare you say such a thing?"

Oh, my God, I said it aloud.

"I'm sorry. I didn't mean it. Please, don't hurt me."

The pressure on my neck subsides. She shoves me away. I stumble between the graves. My brain says *run* but my feet are planted as if the roots surrounding the graves have grown over my bones, as well. I can no sooner run than fly.

"What…what are you doing here?"

"What do you think? Cleaning up your messes. My God, you are a disaster. Every time I turn around, you are practically telling everyone our story."

"I haven't said a word. I swear it."

"You don't need to lie anymore. This little experiment is over. I need the money."

"What money?"

"Don't play dumb with me, *sister*."

She drops the word so casually, so caustically, that I close my eyes.

She knows. Oh, God, she knows.

"How did you find out?"

"The letter Gertrude sent to wreck our lives. The solicitors were sniffing around the flat in Oxford. Kevin said he was your boyfriend and they asked him to give you a letter. He gave it to me. It spelled everything out. Everything that matters, at least. Did you know we were sisters?"

How do I even answer this? I must have shock written all across my face because she smiles meanly and continues, thankfully, before I say anything.

"Well, we are. Damien was your father, too. Surprise!"

"I don't know what to say." This is the truth. I am at a loss for words. I am bruised and burning and the air around me coruscates. I have to fight down the nausea.

Yes, I know she is my sister. Of course, I do. And here I was worried about Becca. Becca is a gnat compared to Ashlyn.

She is responsible for all of this. I should have known. I should have seen this coming. I am so stupid.

"Half, Lex. You get *half.* And I don't think that's exactly fair."

"What are you talking about?"

"Stop playing dumb. I know they told you Daddy dearest left half the estate to you. I saw Nickerson here today."

She finally steps out from behind me, and I bite back my gasp of surprise.

Ashlyn looks like she's been living in the woods. Her hair is matted and dirty, her clothes covered in leaves and cobwebs. She throws a bag at me. I know what's in it. The vestiges of a life. An ID card, a passport. A bank card. The key to a flat.

"I need my life back, *Ash.*" This is said with such derision I cringe. Sod it all, this was her idea in the first place, for me to use the name Ash Carlisle.

Get it together, get it together.

"What are you saying? You want me to walk away and you're going to stroll into Goode and pretend to be me?" I ask, horrified.

"Oh, but who is pretending to be whom, darling sister? No, give me what I want and you can stay at this stupid little school. I'll even pay for it."

"You'll pay for it?"

She laughs, uproariously. There was a time when that laugh could set my heart alight, the joy in it, the freedom, the adventure. But now, I see it for what it is. A trap.

"A reward. You've done such a good job of being me. You'll claim your filthy prize, hand it over to me. I'll just say thank you and take the money."

"What money?"

"What is wrong with you? Are you high? Have you started down Mummy's path at last? The money you inherit from the estate, what else?"

"But there's no way. If I admit who I am now, they'll kick me out. The Honor Code—"

"Do you think I care about your stupid little school? This little world you're creating? I don't. You need to sign the paperwork and take possession of Daddy's cash, and I will relieve you of the funds and be off. No reason to wait until I'm twenty-five if we can do it now."

"You must be joking. I can't just walk away from this. That will blow up my life."

Her eyes are strangely lit as if there's a fire inside her. "Oh, are you settling in? Becoming one of them? Don't you realize you'll never be one of them? You'll always just be the daughter of a junkie, a chip shop worker. You have no future, you never did. I was willing to give you a chance to earn your own way, to get the education you were dreaming about. But since you managed to get yourself in Daddy's will, we might as well do this now. Sign the paperwork and hand over the cash."

"But if I sign the paperwork, they'll know who I really am."

"Sign it, or I'll walk into the school and tell them you've been keeping me captive so you could take my place and steal my money. Who do you think they'll believe? The impostor? Or the rightful student? Look at me. It will take nothing to convince them you've been keeping me hostage."

God, she is the most devious person I have ever known. Was this her plan for leverage all along? *Think. Think.*

I stand up straight. I'm taller than her, and I can look down, intimidate.

"I don't care for your threats, Ashlyn. Do you honestly believe I don't have proof you wanted me to do this? Do you think I didn't protect myself? You wouldn't dare blow me up. Yes, I might get kicked out of the school, but if you do that, I will make sure you get put in jail. No money will save you from a double murder charge. I know what you did. I know how you did it. You won't be able to blame their deaths on me. Fat lot of good Daddy's money will do you then, shriveled up behind bars, only allowed to see sunlight an hour a day. You'll go mad in there. Madder than you already are."

I've hit a nerve. Her face twists in anger, and she lands a stunning blow to my cheek before I have a chance to pull away. The punch knocks me to the ground. The pain is incredible, mushroom clouding until I feel it peak and begin to throb. It's almost as sore as the burn on my rib cage.

But my anger dissipates. This is what she's gone through her whole life. She was on the receiving end of our father's rages. How many black eyes did I minister to? How many times had she come to me with a bloodied nose or a missing tooth? He made her into this monster, just like he made me into a liar. We are a pair.

I roll over and get up on my knees. Her eyes are on fire now, the anger simmering, flames ready to leap.

"I'm sorry," I say, in the most placating tone I have. "You're right. I'll get you the money. You just have to give me a few days to figure out how to make this all work. I think I already have an idea. Wouldn't it be easier for you to just come forward as the illegitimate daughter? They've already taken my DNA swab. You go to the lawyers and do yours, I'll hack into the database and switch them. Easy. Then you'll receive the money, and I can stay here, at school. No one needs to know anything more."

She looks at me like I'm the insane one. "How could you *want* to stay here? They treat you terribly. That girl, Becca, she isn't your friend. She's going to hurt you, hurt you worse than you could ever imagine."

Oh, what little you know, sister. She's already torn me apart.

"No, she's not. It's a game. I've been tapped for a secret society, that's all. It's all in good fun."

"You can't possibly believe that."

Becca is the least of my worries.

But Ashlyn's sagging now—the beaten, cowed, unloved girl

is back. These sparks of fury that make her lose her mind are frightening, yes, but they're usually over as quickly as they start. It's like she's possessed. I've seen the worst her anger can do, lying on the floor of the parlor, pale, waxy, lifeless.

And on the headstone that sits atop a tiny coffin, buried on the estate.

And the blood on the parlor floor, leaking from Sylvia's body.

And in my flat, the guileless, endless sleep of my mum, Gertrude, the needle still dangling from the crook of her elbow. I'll never know if she did it on her own or if Ashlyn helped her along to make my part of the plan easier to stomach. I was too afraid to ask, too desperate to get out.

Ashlyn will do anything when her demon rises. I need to keep that part of her at bay for as long as possible until I figure out what to do.

She wasn't supposed to come here, ever. She was supposed to be in Tahiti, or Bora Bora, wherever she decided to go.

Though it sounds like she's been parked in Oxford, in my old flat, listening to the gossips and getting high with Kevin. Waiting for me to get the degrees in her name so she can inherit the estate and drown herself in whatever marsh she's picked. What a fucking idiot. I got her out. I handed her a new life, one she begged for. And I got hers in return, the one she hated.

It was a fair trade.

Daddy dearest wasn't supposed to name me an heir. When Nickerson told me about my phantom sister, so apologetic, so worried, I didn't know whether to laugh or cry. All of the plans, all of the machinations, the hacks, the identity theft, being an impostor—none of it was necessary. If I'd waited, had a little faith, I would have had enough money to pay for any education I could desire.

Mum always told me to watch out for a woman scorned. She said Sylvia would kill me if she ever found out.

Yes, Mum told me about their affair. It's why she ended up

taking pills, to forget the dynamic, exciting Damien Carr when he threw her over and married simpering Sylvia.

Damien killed my mother. No one else.

But little did she know it was Ashlyn who was the real danger, all along.

Think. Think!

None of the plans I've been working include the real Ashlyn ever showing up in Marchburg. Now that she's here and dancing on the edge, I have to reboot everything. Everything.

"You have to give me some time. I can work this, but it's going to be tricky."

The fever light gleams in her eyes. "You have twenty-four hours. I need to get out of this shit town. I don't know how you can stand it."

"You have to give me more than a day. I have to—"

She has a hand ripping my hair back and the knife at my throat so fast I don't even have time to blink.

"Listen to me, you stupid, hapless twat. Twenty-four hours, or I will blow up your entire world and dance on the ashes. You'll have the distraction you need."

She lets me go and disappears into the forest, leaving me alone with the graves and trembling hands. I sink to my knees, the past few months parading through my brain. I should have known better.

What am I going to do?

I'm going to run.

72

THE CONVINCING

I've convinced her. I can see it in her eyes. Even as she scurries away, back through the tunnel into the school, she is already plotting.

She's going to find a way, she always does. Alexandria is the brains of the family. She is going to find us a path out like she found us a path in, and I will have my fortunes restored. Once that happens, she can go on living whatever life she wants. I have no reason to kill her.

Well, none good enough. Not yet.

She is the one who most resembles Damien. She has his face and brains, yes, but she's been gifted with his ability to manipulate, too.

I make my way back to the abandoned cabin I've been sleeping in. It has a tunnel directly into the school, like most I've managed to sneak into, which makes it so easy to enter after dark, once everyone is asleep, and creep, creep, creep around.

Did you know the dean leaves her safe unlocked? What an idiot. Probably can't remember her combination.

I'm telling you, while the school itself is okay, Marchburg is a shit of a town. Who would want to live here? There's nothing to do. The only thing it has going for it is a view, but hell, you can get a view off a cliff in Italy. Why would you saddle yourself to a stupid little nothing town in the Blue Ridge Mountains?

Alex wanted this. She wanted it so badly I couldn't resist trying to make her dreams come true. But she's changed. She's no longer the sweet, adorable little Lexie who would do anything for me growing up. Now she's my sister, my flesh and blood. She's complicit. She knows the truth, all of it. And she has a power that I don't—the power of altering records. That changes everything.

Everything.

I had to come. I had to have her make this right.

But before I handle Alexandria, I need to deal with that bitch who's been hurting my sister.

73

THE EXIT

Ford hasn't been back in the Westhaven family house for a few months. Her mother's omnipresence is clear and literal, she's left dishes in the sink and newspapers on the table. Happily, Jude has retreated from the scene. Ford received a breezy text from her earlier:

Heading north to DC today for an emergency alumni meeting, sorry to miss you. I'll be back this weekend for the Odds and Evens celebrations, assuming I'm still welcome. Be in touch if you decide you need my help sooner.

Like that will happen. Jude's *help* is why she's in this mess with the school, and with Rumi.

Fretting about Jude will accomplish nothing. Ford needs a plan. But she wants Rumi's input first.

She cleans up after her mother, clearing away the mess in the kitchen, tidying and stacking and wiping, until everything looks show house ready, then hits the wine cellar. She needs a drink, and with Rumi coming, all she wants is a few moments alone with him to figure out what's happening. Perhaps a nice bottle of wine and some food will soften his stance.

He's been as much friend as lover these past few years. And she needs a friend right now.

She finds a good bottle of Bordeaux and leaves it to breathe on the counter. At 9:00 p.m. sharp, the doorbell rings. She hurries to the door, already annoyed. Why couldn't he come to the back door? He has the keys, he comes here to raid the library. What's he trying to do, advertise?

Come now, Ford. He simply wants to be treated like a man, instead of a perpetually disgraced welfare employee.

She forces a smile on her face and swings it open.

He's carrying a bottle of Jack and wearing her favorite green waffle shirt under a down vest, the one that shows off his glorious physique. Subtle.

She steps aside. "Come in."

He hands her the whiskey and enters. He seems bigger in this setting than in her cottage. Taller than when she saw him last. Thicker through the shoulders. Is that even possible? Or is she imagining things?

She closes the door behind him and locks it. Waits a beat— sometimes he turns with a wicked grin and jumps her immediately, but he makes no overtures, no moves at all, just stands there, broad-shouldered and grim-faced, so she gestures to the kitchen.

"I opened some wine."

"I don't want wine." He looks to be in a dark mood. He's not scowling, but he isn't being friendly, either.

She glances at the bottle—he's brought it to drink, not as a gift. Okay. She'll let him play this game. But she'll have to keep an eye on him. She can't let him get drunk, she needs him to help her plan things out. But a little lubricant might help.

"Bourbon instead?"

"Sure."

At least he's speaking.

"Let's sit in the kitchen. I'll make you an old-fashioned."

He catches her hand. His voice is gruff. "Ford. We can't keep pretending everything is okay. I only came to tell you this—whatever this is—is over."

She straightens, gently pulls her hand from his grip. "I understand. I'm not thrilled with your decision, though if that's truly what you want, I will respect your wishes. But, Rumi, we need to have a very serious conversation, about much more than just us. Let me make you a drink, and I'll get right to it."

He looks confused but doesn't resist anymore.

She mixes the old-fashioned too quickly, slopping the bitters into the glass, not getting the sugar totally mixed in, but she's angry and nervous. She needs him on her side. She needs him to cooperate.

She needs *him*.

Don't you dare, Ford. He's made a decision and you must let him go.

Finally, she hands him the drink, wipes off the counter, and sits at the table. He takes the chair across from her. She puts the phone facedown on the wood. It's been charging since she arrived and now has plenty of juice.

"I wanted to talk to you because someone sent me some rather incriminating photos—of us and of you. I am trying to decide how to handle things."

He sits stiffly like his back is hurt. "May I see them?"

"Of course."

God, they sound so stilted, so careful of each other. She imagines this is how a conversation about an impending divorce must happen, the gentle parlay as two lives break apart and begin their dissection.

He swipes through, face impassive.

And just like a wronged wife, she can't help herself, she throws the first aspersion. "Were you sleeping with Camille Shannon?"

He hands her the phone. "Yes. Not recently, though. I saw her a few times over the summer. But she ditched me for another guy."

"I see. Were you aware that she was pregnant when she died?"

"I was. At least, I knew she had been." The facade breaks. "It wasn't mine. She came to me when the pills didn't work. She had an appointment at a clinic in Charlottesville that she needed a ride to. I told her I'd take her. She threw herself off the bell tower that night. I don't know why. She was pretty determined to end the pregnancy and get on with term."

"Were you the father?"

He shakes his head. "No, I wasn't."

"Do you know who was?"

"Her stepbrother. She was head over heels for him, broke it off with me so she could spend all her time mooning around after him. She was very clear when she told me, explained the timing. We broke it off in July. She got pregnant in August. She was quite a little slut, but I didn't kill her."

"I didn't—"

"That's what you want to ask me, isn't it? You're sure I threw her off the fucking bell tower because I'm the only one who could have gotten access to your keys. And with these photos, all you have to do is tell your buddy Tony the sheriff and off I go to jail, truth be damned."

"Wait—"

"But that's not true. All of the secret societies have copies of your keys. Have for years. Everyone knows you never lock that safe. How do you think they move about the campus so easily? You are so naive."

"I'm not—" she says but he's up and storming out of the

kitchen so fast he knocks his chair backward and his drink topples to the floor.

She ignores the mess, runs after him. "Stop. Please. That is not why I asked you here. I couldn't possibly think you hurt Camille. You aren't your father."

He is in her face with a roar that makes her stumble backward in fear. "I'm not? How do you know? Maybe I'm just as bad as he is. Maybe I stalked her at school and stalked her at home. Maybe I raped her over the summer and got her pregnant. You don't know. You don't know! But I bet you've been giving good old Tony an earful. Yes, Ford, I know you're fucking him."

He's jealous. He does care.

She steps forward, grabs his arms. "Listen to me, right now. I asked you here tonight so we could discuss our relationship like adults. I am not seeing Tony anymore, that's been over for months. And I don't think you hurt Camille. I know that's not who you are. But I needed to know if the DNA test was going to show you as the father. Surely you can understand if that was the case, I couldn't let the school be blindsided. There are ways to handle these things, but being surprised isn't one of them."

A flash in his eyes. "DNA?"

"Yes. They are running DNA on the fetus. You'll be in the clear. We don't even need to mention you were seeing her. This can be kept between me, the sheriff, and the Shannon family."

"The lawsuit—"

"Trust me, Deirdre Shannon won't be suing Goode when she finds out the father of the baby was her own stepchild, Camille's brother, and it all happened under her own roof."

He blows out a whiskey-perfumed breath. "You sound happy."

"I'm not happy, I'm relieved. I think we should delete these photos. I've already taken care of it on my end. This is all that's left."

And she does, one after the other. They exist in the ether, yes. But she's deleted them off her computer, and now the phone that took and sent them. She's destroying evidence, but of what? An innocent relationship? Who is served by Rumi and the school being dragged through the mud?

Finally, she sets the phone on the counter. "There. We're covered."

"Do you have any idea whose phone that is?"

"I do. It's a separate issue, I think. I hope. I found it in Ash Carlisle's room. There are some issues being raised about her, and I searched her room."

"Ash?"

There is something in his tone. "Don't tell me you've been having an affair with yet another student."

"No, not at all. There's something about her, though. She's... I can't put my finger on it. Something's off. Plus, she's sad and lonely, and I think she has something going with Becca Curtis."

"Really? Interesting." That might explain why Becca was so determined to tap Ash; it would give them a lot of time to get to know each other better. Relationships between students are not an issue at Goode, so long as they are consensual. Respect for all sexualities is a hallmark of the school's charter—they had nondiscrimination policies decades before most other schools.

Rumi sags against the wall, rubbing his eyes hard like he hasn't slept in days. "I thought you'd be mad at me." He sounds like a little boy lost, and her heart constricts.

"I'm furious with you for having relations with a student, and I should fire you on the spot. But I've made some pretty massive mistakes myself, so why don't we call it even, have a drink, and talk this through."

He moves across the room so quickly she gasps. His kiss is soulful and sweet.

"Thank you. Thank you for believing me."

"I've always believed in you, Rumi."

"Forget the drinks," he says, low and urgent, and she laughs.

"Changed your mind? One last time?"

He tosses her that wicked smile she adores.

She leads him to her old room at the top of the stairs. It is surreal to see her things from childhood, the books, the trophies, the stuffed animals, the posters. A happier time. An easier time.

Her mother never changed the decor. Jude hasn't given up on Ford moving back into the house. The bed is large, the sheets sweet and clean.

Rumi doesn't notice the girlish details; he has eyes only for Ford.

She and Rumi, they are good together. Right together. When he kisses her, undresses her, properly, gently, as if this is their first time together, she realizes she doesn't want to break it off with him. Doesn't want this to be the last time. She's grown to care about him. Maybe she always has.

She lies in the crook of his arm afterward, sated and glowing, a leg thrown over his strong thighs, runs a finger down his chest.

"I have to tell you something," Rumi says.

"Mmm?" she says languorously, with a stroke of his flesh, because she knows what he is going to say. And she's going to say it back and mean it.

But he surprises her.

"It's about your mother… I heard her on a call when she stopped in for a coffee before she left. She was talking about you to someone named Ellen."

Ford feels the anger begin to rise. "Ellen Curtis? The senator?"

"Maybe, I don't know. She said you'd understand about the reinstatement."

All the coins drop for Ford. "Oh, my God. That bitch!" She's so angry she actually starts to laugh.

Rumi is looking at her quizzically. "You okay?"

"She sold me out. She's done a deal with the alumni association. Goode goes coed and Jude Westhaven, savior to the masses, will shepherd the new deal through if they make her headmistress again. Of all the conniving, horrible…" She rolls onto her back, staring at the ceiling of her childhood home. "Rumi, what do you think about New York?"

"Big city. And your mother lives there."

"What if she didn't? Or you didn't ever have to see her? If I went, would you be interested in going with me?"

"On a trip?"

"I was thinking something more permanent."

He sits up, drags her with him. The sheets fall to the floor.

"Wait a minute. Are you asking me to move to New York with you? Leave Goode?"

"Yes. That's what I'm asking."

The look on his face is sheer joy. "Yes, Ford. I'd love to move to New York with you. I can't wait to get out of this town."

"You and me both," she says, kissing his neck, realizing she feels free for the first time in ages. To hell with this school. To hell with her mother. To hell with the Westhaven legacy, the spoiled girls, the constant politicking with the board and the alumni association and the town. It is time for Ford to make her own way in the world.

Ford doesn't plan on falling asleep but when her phone rings, she realizes it's almost dawn. Rumi lies next to her, curled on his side, a hand on her hip. They've never spent the night together. She quite likes waking up with him in her bed.

She rolls over and answers the phone. It's Melanie, and her voice is shrill with panic.

"Ford? Ford? You have to come, right away. There's another dead girl."

74

THE TRAIL

Kate hasn't slept. She and Tony have been combing through the files as Oliver sends them from Scotland Yard.

Money is always the trail to follow. Kate isn't an expert, but she has done a few classes in forensic accounting. Between her and Oliver, they've uncovered at least fifty thousand skimmed out of the Carrs' accounts with no traceable landing spot.

There are payments made to The Goode School, too, though those stop as soon as the family dies.

They break for a snack. Oliver is on speakerphone.

"I have a theory," Kate says. "The impostor was close to them, no doubt. Someone who worked for the family, most likely. She saw a chance to inherit a massive fortune. She killed the Carr family, took Ashlyn Carr's place, and bolted to America to await the estate. All she has to do is go to this fancy-schmancy school for a few years, then get through college, and she inherits everything."

"It's hardly the first time something like this has happened. But where is Ashlyn Carr's body?"

"Drag the lake on their estate. I bet you find it there. This is a sick, twisted person we're dealing with."

"Hold on." Oliver is back a few minutes later. "All right. We're reopening the investigation into the deaths, effective immediately."

"Good. There might not be evidence in the house, but I bet somewhere on the grounds."

"Have you arrested this child at the school yet?"

"No, not yet. Trust me when I say she has no way out. Marchburg is tiny, she tries to run and we'll hear about it. How did y'all miss the money siphoning the first time around?"

"Easy. Accounting did a cursory pass through the financials, but they were looking for impropriety on behalf of Damien Carr, illegal payments and the like. Finding nothing that stood out, and no evidence to the contrary, they called the files clean. The estate was to be left to the daughter, but she didn't stand to inherit without a degree, and she had to be twenty-five. It's inviolable. No one thought she killed them. Why would she? It was easy to accept the double suicide theory. The daughter walked in and found them, called 999. The records are very clear.

"And the headlines were lurid. You have to remember, this was a man who had been above reproach for his entire life, and terribly private, too. Someone sent a compromising story, with photographs of Carr and his lover, to the press. The scandal cost him a very important position in government. He was, by all accounts, devastated."

"Enough to kill himself? It feels so odd, Oliver. That he would kill himself...and his wife would be so upset that she shoots herself?"

"Yes, but I know that timeline was investigated because you'd think he would kill her, then himself, right? But her fingerprints were on the gun, and his on the pill vial. And the pièce de résistance… He'd been dead at least an hour before she shot herself. The coroner's court kindly ruled it death by misadventure so the estate wouldn't be damaged."

"Are there no other relatives?"

"The son, but he, too, died. There's been some scuttlebutt in the rags about an illegitimate daughter, but no one's confirmed that. I do think it was someone close to the family. Someone who knew they could all be annihilated and get away with it."

"So, this girl manages to disappear the daughter's body, steps into the scene, calls for help, poses as the grieving daughter all the way through the funerals and conversations with the lawyers, then jets off to America to live a life of privilege here in Marchburg. And no one's been the wiser since. Amazing. Simply amazing."

"Quite."

"What about the IDs? Passports and the like?"

"She has a visa from the American government to study in Virginia. No credit cards, she's been operating on a cash basis. But we have her coming into the country under the Ashlyn Carr passport on August 25."

"Term started the day after. Okay. Timeline fits. Hey, did they have staff? They're supposed to be this super rich family, right?"

She can hear him rustling his papers. "I believe… Yes, they did. A small staff, the only live-in was a cook, Dorsey Throckmorton. There's an address in Yorkshire."

"Can you capture the photo of the Ash who came through customs and show it to her? See if it's the girl she knows?"

"I can. Good idea, Kate."

"Send it to me, too, just in case."

"I love it when you boss me around."

"Oh, hush, Oliver. Tell me this. How did she skim the money from their accounts?"

"Excellent question. We'll have to ask her how she got into the accounts. Maybe she stole the passwords. Again, everything points to someone who was close to the family. Why don't you take her into custody and we'll ask her directly?"

"Oh, we will. She has a track record of eliminating the people who get in her way. Tony wants to lay all the groundwork before we pick her up. The dean lawyered her up, so we have to wait until the dude comes up from Charlottesville to interview her again."

"Let me know what happens. We'll continue working here."

"Thanks, Oliver. You're the best."

I've got you now, you sick little girl.

75

THE NOTE

Becca, annoyed as hell, furious, embarrassed, hurt—oh, God, the look in Ash's eyes when she pushed her away was horrifying, the pain, the confusion, the realization, the rejection—storms back to her room in the attics. Initiation night is supposed to be a huge party and now it's ruined, everything is ruined. Her life is ruined.

She had no choice. She had to rebuff Ash's advance. What was she supposed to do, allow herself to be outed in front of the Ivy Bound sisters? It would be all over the school in a heartbeat and fed back to her mother by the dean, and her mother would pull her ass out of school and call her an aberration, the sanctimonious, hypocritical bitch.

Becca tried to feel her mother out last summer, after the video incident, when things had calmed down and Ellen wasn't quite so angry. Becca mentioned a friend of hers who'd come out as gay, and Ellen Curtis had practically vomited her pinot gris over the edge of the balcony of their Watergate West apartment.

That made it abundantly clear, there was no way in hell Becca could admit that she, too, didn't see herself married with two point three kids and a dog—at least, not to a man. It broke her heart that she couldn't be honest with her mother, that she hid the truth from the one person who used to matter so much to her.

She'd acted out instead. Ellen dragged her to a shrink, and Becca was wise enough to keep her mouth shut there, too. Instead, she told stories from her childhood, things she'd done, ways she'd lost her temper, and the doctor compliantly gave her drugs and a few different diagnoses that fit the symptoms she described to a tee.

Becca is fine. She has no mental deficiencies. She is simply a girl in love, and now...

She thought Ash was different. The way she watched, the way her eyes lit up. The way she'd kissed her tonight, freely, happily. And Becca attacked her. She miscalculated and ruined everything.

How could Ash ever forgive her? How can she ever face her again after this? She'd panicked. Would Ash forgive her for that, at least?

She turns up the stereo, throws herself on her bed, and starts to cry. The sobs come from deep inside her soul. She thought things would be different this year. That she wouldn't feel so alone. That she could finally be herself. It's not like the girls here would hold it against her, not really. But she is head girl. She feels some sort of responsibility to be everything that's expected of her.

She would have thrown it all away for Ash. She'd hardly hazed her, had protected her every step of the way. She warned her when the school started talking about her parents, and again today when the headlines started to blare Ash's own terrible news.

And when faced with the opportunity tonight to show everyone her strength, her leadership, how good she really is, Becca had squandered it, and ruined everything to boot.

Drained, Becca finally flips over and feels something crinkling beneath her. There is a package on her bed, wrapped in tissue paper. She unfolds it to find a bloodred scarf. It's lovely, thick silk. She winds it around her neck, withdraws the piece of paper, reads it, and bursts into fresh tears.

B—
Can we talk? All of this craziness with the Swallows and Camille
and the news from home, I just need a friend. And some privacy.
Meet me in front of the gates tonight. Midnight. I have something
I want to show you.
Love,
A

This was clearly left behind before the initiation. A gift. A promise.

Oh, yes, my little Ash. I knew I had you. And now I've lost you.

Would she still come? Why would she? Becca has just humiliated her in front of Ivy Bound, cast her down, kicked her out. Ash would be well within her rights to tell her to drop dead.

It is almost midnight now. She shuts off her light, goes to the window.

Is it her imagination, or is there a shadow out by the gates?

Is Ash there, waiting for her, after all?

She sees the flick of hair and the glowing tip of a cigarette. Someone is out there, wearing a gown that blends in with the night perfectly.

Her heart soars. After everything, Ash is still willing to talk to her.

Becca has to go, go now. She has to beg forgiveness. She has to make Ash understand why she rejected her so cruelly. She has to make her understand what is at stake.

She has to make this right.

She has to win her back.

She rushes down the stairs, then turns right, toward the dining hall. There is a tunnel connected to the last trolley, a hidden door into the darkness. She slips through it, traverses the quad, and emerges on the main street, out into the night. The air feels heavy with impending rain, the clouds dark and roiling above, blotting out the moon.

She jogs up the sidewalk to the main gates, the red scarf flowing behind her, to the shadow that waits for her.

Toward her heart. Toward her future.

"Ash? I'm so sorry."

76

THE MURDER

How do you kill a narcissist?

I mean, how do you attract one in the first place? Do you put off some sort of pheromone that says, *Hey, sexy lady, I'm easily manipulated, come check out my wares*?

I attract them. They find me. They seek me out—for whatever perceived vulnerability I give off, the pathos, the acceptance. They see me as a tool to their ascent, a shoulder to be stepped upon, a foil, a testing ground.

If I, sweet, biddable I, can be fooled into loving them, the whole world will, too.

Only I am not sweet. I am not biddable. I may send signals that I want to belong, that I want to be loved, but this is a false trail. I have been humoring you. I am curious to see what your plan is, what you intend to do. How you think you will rule over me.

I will extricate myself from your grip and wave you away.

You, the one who thinks the world owes you, may think you've made this choice.

But I am the spider. I am waiting at the center of the web for the blundering fly.

I am the real monster.

When faced with killing a narcissist, I find it easier than I always thought it would be. There is nothing I can do but give in to the urge to punish the wrongdoer. To unmask the manipulator. To show the world who you really are.

Thank you for wearing my scarf. You look so pretty in red.

Let's start with your eyes.

Oh, don't whimper. This won't hurt a bit.

77

THE GATES

The scene before Ford is a nightmare.

There are girls milling in the street, girls outside of the gates, girls inside the gates. They're all staring at something… She sees a flutter of black fabric, and she knows.

Rumi brakes hard, tires squealing, throwing her forward into the leather and wood of the front seat. She jumped in the back out of habit, ignoring his scowl of disapproval.

"Just drive. Hurry." And he had, peeling out of the garage.

She leaps from the car and races up the street, panting in panicked little breaths.

And sees why Melanie was so frantic.

One of her girls dangles backward from the tall, iron gates guarding the school's entrance. There is a red tie around her neck, forcing her head to an almost comical angle. Her face is obscured, her hair is damp, making it hard to decipher color.

She is wearing Goode School robes with a graduation stole around her shoulders.

Ford's first thought: *Another suicide. Oh, God.*

Her second: *Who is it?*

You know exactly who it is. Stop deluding yourself. And you know what this means. If you'd acted when you had the chance instead of frolicking with Rumi, she'd still be alive.

She drags in a breath and starts to gather the girls together. "Come here, ladies, come here. Stop looking."

Though she is looking, looking, looking. She already knows who is hanging on the gate, has that sense in her gut, but she has to be sure. She has to see for herself.

The eerie wail of a siren pierces the morning air—it's so damp, did it rain last night?—and then the siren is deafening, shrieking at her, screaming its impotent fury.

The squawk to silence is broken by Tony slamming the door of his cruiser and running into the scene. He stops when he sees the gates, his face white, then gestures, waving her off, and Ford understands immediately.

He has to look up close, I have to get them out of here. He doesn't want them to see her face, her beautiful face.

Rumi is by Ford's side now, too, giving orders to the girls to move away. His arms are stretched wide and he herds them back, back, until they are almost all standing on the sidewalk across the street.

"Come away, over here, that's right."

It's hardly far enough, but it gives the cops room to work.

Tony nods to the deputy who's ridden with him, and he starts putting up a cordon between the students and the crime scene.

Another approaches the body and, to Ford's absolute horror, begins taking photographs of the scene.

"Is this necessary?" she says to Tony, who nods, his eyes severe and dark. She hasn't seen him like this before, and it chills her to the bone.

His voice is remote, commanding. "Unfortunately, yes. Ford. Have you touched the body?"

"No. Melanie found her when she came in this morning, she called me, then you. Or you, then me, I don't know."

"Do you know who it is?"

"I don't."

But she does. Of course, she does. It's just too fitting, with everything that's happened, everything she's learned. What an ending to her story.

"Keep the girls away. You don't want them to see this," Tony says.

Rumi makes a cutting motion, which she reads as *I've got this*.

"We're working on it. I'm staying with you."

"Okay." Tony takes a few shots with his own iPhone, then gently, gently, reaches for the foot of the dead girl and slowly turns her around. She spins easily on the tie around her neck, bumping against the gate. Gasps and cries fill the air, and Ford cries out along with the rest of them.

Her face is ruined, holes where her eyes should be. Her skin is gray. Her hair runs in wet ropes down her face and shoulders, and a red silk noose is wrapped around her neck and tied to the bars of the gate. Her hands are covered in gore.

While moments ago, Ford was dealing with a suicide, now there is no question that this is something more, something deeper, and she feels faint. It is the most horrific sight she has ever beheld and she starts to sag, but Tony grabs her elbow and squeezes hard, holding her upright. "Don't. Stay with me. They need you. Be strong."

The eerie morning silence is broken by a sudden babble from the crowd behind them. Ford can hear Ash's name being bandied about, the girls whispering furiously behind their hands.

"Who is it, Ford?" Tony asks.

"Her name…her name is Becca Curtis. She's head girl."

"Oh, hell. I remember. I met her the other night, the night

Camille Shannon died. So why are the girls talking about Ash Carlisle?"

"We all thought it was Ash hanging there, Tony. They look so alike. Oh, God. Poor Becca."

Rumi approaches them, speaking low. "They're saying Becca and Ash had a huge falling-out last night. They think she's responsible. First her roommate, now her best friend," he says. "Her best friend, her girlfriend, it's all confused. I'm hearing both."

Ford turns to the group of horrified students. Somehow, she finds the strength to face them. Her voice rings clear through the misty air like a bell tolled.

"Where is Ash Carlisle? Does anyone know where Ash is?"

There is a pause, murmurs, then a voice from the back of the group. "I'm here, Dean."

Everyone gasps as Ash Carlisle steps forward. Her face is streaked with tears. She is dressed, unlike most of the other students, in jeans and white sneakers and a jacket. Her hair is wet, but not from a shower, it's damp and curling. She's been outside, that much is clear.

Ford also takes note that Ash is outside the gates.

"You need to come with me," she says, tone so severe Ash blinks.

"But Becca—" Ash's voice is strangled, torn, cracking with tears and something else, and her face grows even whiter when she looks at Becca's lifeless body, her ruined face. It's her first good view. Ash reaches out a hand as if she's going to move forward and touch Becca, and the sheriff grabs her, stops her. But he doesn't stop her words.

"Oh, God. Oh, my God. Dean Westhaven, I think I know who did this to her."

78

THE DECISION

Becca is dead. Dead.

Her hands are curled into claws, fingers red and black. One hand rests on her chest, two fingers tangled up in the red silk noose around her neck. Where she fought. Tried to get free. Her face is ruined, the gaping black holes where her eyes once were a testament to the insanity of a girl who wants to leave a mark on the world.

And make it look at first glance like this girl was driven crazy by some sort of demon and hurt herself, gouged out her own eyes and strangled herself on the gate.

But there is no doubt in my mind, this is murder.

Ashlyn killed Camille. Ashlyn killed Becca.

Her parents. My mother.

Ashlyn will kill me, too, as soon as I help her recover her money.

The tears are flowing freely down my face, I don't bother to check or hide them.

Ashlyn has done this.

Ashlyn has done all of this.

Ashlyn, Ashlyn, Ashlyn.

Get it together. Hold it together.

I can't think about myself anymore. She is insane. She has to be stopped.

Just look what she's capable of. Look what she's done. Nothing I've done comes close. Lies. Just lies. She is a murderer. I have to throw her to the wolves.

You get half, the nasty little voice in the back of my mind says. *No matter what, you can go anywhere, do anything, with half of Damien Carr's estate. You have nothing to lose, not anymore.*

The dean is staring at me as if I'm speaking in tongues.

I straighten to my full height, which puts me a full head above her. Even this simple motion makes me feel more in control. I've been slouching around for months now, trying to look smaller, wider. More like her.

"I know who did this. We aren't safe. We need to get everyone inside and block off the tunnels to the school."

"What are you talking about?" Westhaven asks, her voice edging toward hysteria. "Who did this?"

"Trust me. Please."

The dean doesn't move, and the sheriff is standing next to her like an avenging angel. Rumi is at her side, too.

"Rumi—" I say, and the sheriff explodes. Everything happens at once.

"Are you saying Rumi is responsible? You are blaming him?" he says, loudly enough that the remaining girls hear, and the whisper campaign starts again in earnest, a few squeals and "catch him" filling the street between us and them.

Rumi goes white. "I didn't have anything to do with this."

The dean puts a hand on the sheriff's arm. "He was with me, Tony. He didn't do this. Becca was troubled. I have letters from her mother, emails, records from her psychiatrist. The senator was worried about her daughter, worried enough that she sent me the doctor's notes."

They barely notice me pleading, "No, no, she didn't kill herself, there's no way. Please, we can't stay out here, can we have some privacy?"

But the damage is done. The girls of Goode need a logical explanation for this atrocity, and Rumi Reynolds, the son of the notorious campus murderer, is the perfect target. Whether he killed her or she killed herself because of him, the buzz is flowing hard, the angry hive looking for blood.

The sheriff has a hand on his cuffs.

Rumi is shaking his head, shock on his features.

I have to fix this. I speak loudly, so everyone can hear.

"No, Sheriff, you're wrong. Rumi didn't do this. Please, can we go inside?" I say again, and finally, he seems to hear me.

"You're saying it wasn't Rumi."

"That's right. But I think I know what happened, and it's a convoluted story. We need to get everyone safe, first."

The dark-eyed female cop has arrived, and the teachers are on the scene now, too. I see Asolo and Medea, pale and teary, standing together with their hands covering their mouths, and the dean goes to them, gives them instructions. She turns back and marches toward me. Gone is the kind, friendly woman who has been sheltering me since I arrived in America. She is a glittering Valkyrie now, furious and intent.

"Come with me," and she grabs my arm and drags me toward her car. "We'll go in the back." Yes, we can hardly drive through the gates. *God, Becca.*

"Rumi?" she says, calling her dog to heel.

Something flickers in his eyes and he cocks his head ironically as if to say, *Yes, Dean, anything for you, Dean,* then tosses her the keys. "Drive yourself," he says flatly. "I'm going to search the grounds with the sheriff's deputies for anything amiss."

"Look at the tunnel coming from the graveyard," I call to him. "She's been using it to get in and out."

"She?" the dean, the sheriff, and the detective say simultaneously.

It doesn't matter anymore. I can't hide any longer. It's time to come clean.

"My sister," I reply. "The real Ashlyn Carr."

79

THE SISTER

"But you're Ashlyn Carr," the dean says, brows drawn together in confusion, but there's something alight in her eyes. Is she pretending? Does she know?

"No. Her name is Alexandria Pine," Kate Wood says. "The rumors were right. She is Ashlyn Carr's half sister."

The dean looks stunned, but the sheriff simply nods at me.

"Kate's been talking with Scotland Yard. We'd like to hear it from you, though."

I have no choice, not anymore. "Yes, I am Alexandria Pine. You have to listen to me. Ashlyn is incredibly dangerous. She's the threat. Please, Dean. Can we go to your office? I'll explain everything inside. I… I can't look at Becca like this anymore."

The dean throws a look to the sheriff. "Go on. I'm right behind you," he says.

I climb into the Bentley, the smell of old leather and gasoline welcome, safe. So much better than the blood and effluvia and fear outside.

The dean slams her door and we're alone, watching the surreal scene from the comfort of our luxurious little bubble. She doesn't look at me, is staring straight ahead.

"Where were you last night?"

I gesture to the small bag on my shoulder. "In the woods. I ran away. I couldn't do this anymore. Becca—"

My breath hitches. *Be brave, little Swallow,* she says to me from somewhere beyond ourselves, and I clear my throat and start again. "Should we wait for the sheriff and the detective? The story is quite detailed."

"Fine."

The dean turns over the engine and shifts through the gears, drives us to the back of the school. The symbolism of the two crime scenes is not lost on me. The roommate dead out back, the lover dead out front.

Ashlyn is making sure I know I'm surrounded.

The dean parks in a slot right by the back door of Main, at the security office, and we filter inside, one after the other. The tension in her shoulders is palpable. I realize her hair is down; she's not wearing makeup. She's in jeans and a sweater and sneakers. She could be a student if it weren't for the paper-thin lines above her mouth and the incipient creases around those wide-set gray eyes.

She's not her usual Chanel-suited self. She's been pulled from her bed.

He was with me.

She spent the night with Rumi.

Holy mother. The dean and Rumi. I would have never guessed.

My first instinct is *wait until Becca finds out* and the arrow of sorrow that pierces my heart makes me gasp aloud. I've killed her. I've killed Camille. I've killed them all. It is my fault. If I had only been brave, if I had only said no. They would still be alive.

Inside the dean's office, I expect her to sit me down and force out the truth, but instead, she excuses herself, moves to her bathroom. I can hear the faint sounds of screaming, recognizable because I used to do the same thing when frustrated, fold a washcloth in half, bite it, and scream myself hoarse in fury at the injustices of the world. Then the toilet flushes and she emerges looking a little more clear-eyed.

"Tea," she says. "Then you can tell me everything. But before anyone else gets here...why did you send the photographs? Were you planning to blackmail me?"

"I didn't. Piper told me you found a phone in my room. It wasn't mine. It had to be Ashlyn's. She's behind all of this."

"How do you know?"

"Because technically, the email you showed me came from one of my accounts. We have a couple set up for emergencies. She must have logged into it from the phone, had the message sitting in the draft folder. When I opened the email to check it, something sent. I couldn't see what it was, and that made me nervous, so I destructed the email address."

"The message with the photos, it's not retrieveable?"

"No. It's completely gone."

The dean blows out a breath and goes about making tea.

I see what she's thinking.

"I won't mention it," I say and she nods, not meeting my eyes.

My soul hurts, so badly I want to bend in half and hold on for dear life. But I can't. We have to catch Ashlyn. We have to stop her. She has to be punished.

This momentary reprieve allows me to gather my thoughts, decide where to start the story.

The sheriff comes in, blustery and furious, his niece fast on his heels.

"What the hell is going on?"

"We're making a cup of tea," the dean says, sounding almost calm. But when she turns to hand me the cup, she looks terrified, and the sheriff is staring at me like I have an ax in my hand.

"Talk," he says.

I talk.

JULY

Oxford, England

80

THE PLOT

From the front window of the shop, I see Ashlyn coming down the street, swinging her bag, her Dr. Martens covered in mud. She's hiked across their fields to town again.

Oxford is busy today, packed with tourists come to see the colleges, to wander in the footsteps of C.S. Lewis, walk in the spots featured in the Harry Potter movies and the *Discovery of Witches* show, and otherwise soak up the cultural and architectural goodness the city has to offer. And they all want a proper British tea; the shop's been hopping since breakfast.

Ashlyn looks haunted today, hollowed out, as if she's been getting high and forgetting to eat again. I recognize the look: my mum, Gertie, spends all her downtime on the couch in our flat above the shop, smoking, snorting, popping, and otherwise ingesting any escape from the drudgery of our life she can steal or trick. The two of them probably have the same dealer—a right arsehole named Kevin, red hair sprouting from his chin but bald as an egg otherwise, who hangs around the tea shop passing out glassine packs to the area addicts.

I can't help the sigh. Ashlyn has been more and more erratic lately, bursting with grandiose plans and hidden conspiracies. Does her father pound on her a bit, absolutely. Do I feel sorry for her? Maybe, sometimes. Mum's drug-addled but loves me, though I don't know what it would be like to live in anything but perpetual squalor.

Ashlyn has everything, the whole world at her feet. Money. Beauty. Intelligence—when she's not high, that is. Parents who stay out of her way. If she would just shut up and put up with it, go to school, stop getting in her father's face all the time, provoking him, she could have the world. Twenty-five is the magical age for Ashlyn. She'll come into her substantial inheritance and can bugger off and never look back. Why she doesn't keep her head down is beyond me. If I were in her place, I'd do everything they asked. I'd love to go to school, to get a real education, not be stuck in this fucking chip shop with an addict mother and absent father.

Instead, Ashlyn sticks it to Damien every chance she gets. Which is why she needs me.

It's a good thing I have a knack for computers. The money's all right, I've been able to hide some from Mum and start thinking about what I want to do in the inevitable time to come—as much as I hate to admit it, Mum will overdo it one day, no doubt. I'll be stuck with the flat, scraping to make the rent with my shifts in the shop and wallowing in the irony that I stand outside the walls of the colleges, watching the students term in and term out, and I will never have a chance to attend. Oxford is bloody expensive, too expensive for my blood.

But without the money Ashlyn gives me to make Damien Carr's life a living hell, and a real influx of cash, I'm stuck. Forever stuck.

Ashlyn takes the table by the window. I bring her a pot of tea and a scone, clotted cream and jam on the side. Ashlyn smiles charmingly, showing the empty spot on the back left where she lost a molar a couple of weeks back, courtesy of her father's incredible temper.

"Sit down. Take a load off."

"I don't have time today, Ash. Mum's not feeling well, I'm running the shift alone."

"Don't worry, I don't want you to do anything. I need to talk to you."

Her eyes are wild, bloodshot, but happy. There's such an edge of insanity in this girl. I've seen it in her from the start, from the first day I was aware of her. Little Johnny's funeral will always be imprinted on my mind; it was the day my mother told me the whole story, the truth about our lives.

You can't ever speak a word of this. But if something ever happens to me, Alexandria, you go to them. Tell them to test your blood. They will take care of you.

I hadn't fully understood, not then. Not until I was much older, and my mother had lost herself in drugs and memories of the life she could have had if only she'd been born to the right sort of people.

The resemblance between us is remarkable, considering. How Ashlyn's never seen it as more than a fluke of nature, I will never know. But why would she? I am the daughter of a junkie. I work in a tea and chip shop. She is the daughter of wealth and privilege.

Never the twain shall meet, unless the former is serving the latter.

I remember, at the funeral, watching Ashlyn edging around the somber people, staring at the grave, laughing at the wrong times, putting her little hand into open pockets, working the crowd. Even then, inappropriate actions were her mandate.

Now, after extensive research, I know Ashlyn probably has a serious untreated borderline personality disorder. But unpredictable as she is, Ashlyn is the closest thing to a friend I have. And when she's being pleasant, watch out. She can charm the larks from the sky.

"Where's your mum?"

"In bed. I think." Or out for a score, but I don't add this. She's been high more often than not these past few months.

"When's the shift end?"

"Sully is coming in at five."

"Then I'll meet you at five. Don't look so scared, hen. Trust me. I'm about to give you the answer to your dreams. Now scoot. Customers are waiting."

The answer to my dreams. Oh, God, what has Ashlyn cooked up now?

81

THE SWITCH

"They're forcing me to go to this school in America, and I don't want to. You keep saying you want an education. It's perfect. You become me, I become you. We both get what we want most."

I shake my head, eyes wide. "No. No way. I couldn't."

"You most certainly could. You look enough like me to pull it off. You're brilliant, you sent that photo to Downing Street and no one was the wiser. You can alter whatever you need to in the databases. Our mothers won't care—I hate to point it out but Gertie is beyond help.

"I have all the money I've been saving, you can have half of it to keep you afloat until I get my inheritance. He's made this provision about the degree just to piss me off, I know he has. He hates me. Making me get a college degree before I can have the inheritance, it's completely unfair. But it's been done, too late to undo it. Though who knows. He might leave you something. He seems to have a soft spot for your mother."

This is said with an accusatory, inquiring glance—maybe she's been ferreting out the truth at last. As much as I hate him, I still feel a tiny squirm of pleasure at the thought but I push it aside. I want nothing from Damien Carr that he can give. All I want is what he can't possibly manage. Acknowledgment is the least of it. Love. The love of a man who punishes my sister because I am not her.

"I can't, Ashlyn. It's wrong. I could never pull it off."

"You can. Think of me as your fairy godmother. You'll get everything you've been dreaming about. An education. A life away from this hellhole. You are Cinderella now."

I look around the flat. Ashlyn isn't wrong, it is a dump. I have no prospects. Aside from finding myself a rich husband, I will be stuck in this life. And I don't want a rich husband. I want to learn things. Create things. I want to go to school so badly it makes my teeth hurt.

And now Ashlyn is offering me my dream.

I have to say, I don't trust her.

"But to take your identity… What does this do for you, Ashlyn?"

She spins in a ridiculous Mary Poppins–like circle. "Freedom. All the freedom I could ever want. I become Alexandria Pine, anonymous café worker, able to go wherever I please. No more bullshit schooling, no more bullshit attacks from Damien. You become Ashlyn Carr, beloved daughter of a scion, going away to school in America."

"There's no way we can pull this off."

"Yes, we can. My photo hasn't been in the press since Johnny died. No one will have any idea what I grew up to look like. Mother has done her damnedest to keep me hidden away. Around here, maybe, though he lost it and fired Dorsey, did I tell you? Thought she was stealing from him, though it was me who nicked the silver. But no one in America will have any idea you're not me."

My heart is bumping so hard against my ribs I have to put a

hand against my chest to calm myself. "Let's think about this logically, Ashlyn. Physical differences aside, age differences aside, *you* were the one who did the admission interview. The dean saw you. Heard you."

"You were there the day I did my interview. You know exactly what I said, I know you remember, with that freaky recall you have."

I had been there. One of the rare times I agreed to ferry a "package" to Ash, who was stuck on the estate for some sort of vital meeting and couldn't come to Kevin herself. I was getting off shift, Kevin was there, begged me to run it to her and bring back the money. I never liked visiting Ash in her palace, and I refused to be their drug mule, but Kevin offered me a hundred quid to run the errand for him, and I'd had a bad day in tips. For some bizarre, fated reason, I'd agreed.

Ash had grabbed the package, broke it open, took a bump, then made me wait for Kevin's money while she was on the computer talking to the dean of the school she was going to attend. I *had* heard the whole conversation.

"But we don't sound enough alike, or look enough alike..."

"Yes, we do." Ash pulls me to the bathroom, the cracked and spotted mirror. "Look. Really look. We could be sisters. The shape of our noses. The same eyes. Your lips are fuller, you cow, and your face is a little thinner. But we're close enough."

I have the urge to blurt out the truth—we are sisters, Damien Carr is my father, too. Something holds me back. I can't believe I'm even giving this ridiculous idea credence.

"I'm taller. And no offense, I'm thinner, too."

"You're taller and a beanpole, yes, but no one's going to be able to tell. I was sitting down. Seriously, thanks to Daddy's disdain for media, there are very few official pictures of me out in the world. You know everything there is to know about me, Lex, you've been around the family since we were children."

"And the piano? That woman talked about the theater director, who will be teaching you."

"You took lessons. You know how to play."

"But not like you. You're...magical." I feel ridiculous saying it, but she is really quite good. I can't even begin to pull off that sort of impersonation. There's no way. This is mad.

She softens a bit. "Thank you. I'll teach you everything you need to make it seem like you're just really out of practice."

"But we'll need paperwork...proof. I mean, I'm nineteen, and I look every day of it. How am I supposed to pretend I'm sixteen?"

"No one will know how old you really are. We'll make fresh IDs, a fresh passport. I know you know how."

"I said I knew a guy who dabbles, from the café. I don't know how to do it myself."

"See? Perfect."

"And how long am I expected to maintain this charade, Ashlyn?"

My sister, something I can never let her know about, smiles. "Forever. This is your chance, Lex. We switch places. You get out. You have the life you always wanted."

"And my mother? What about her? You truly think she'll go along with this?"

Ashlyn whirls away, stomps in those thick-soled boots to the center of the living room. I try not to count, but it takes her a whole five steps.

"Your mother is an addict. Mine is, as well, though her drug of choice is cold hard quid, not heroin. How long do you think your mother is going to be with us, Alex? No, don't get those tears in your eyes, you have to think clearly. She's not going to get off the needle anytime soon, and she'll be dead before anyone even thinks about this. It's the perfect plan. We're going to switch places. You'll have everything you ever wanted, and I, I will disappear."

She makes it sound so easy. So doable.

"All right. Say I agree. There's another rather insurmountable issue. How are we going to get around your parents?"

Ashlyn smiles and I feel goose bumps rise on my forearm. My neck prickles with unease.

"You let me take care of that. Leave me alone in this flat for ten minutes and I'll have everything I need."

82

THE EXECUTION

Death smells. I have to fight back the surge from my stomach. I can't lose it now.

Oh, Ashlyn. What have you done?

Damien—my father, our father—is dead, there's no question. He is devoid of color, past pale, waxy like a creamy candle, a string of vomit dripping down his chin. He has soiled himself; this is part of the stench. The rest is blood. But it's not his.

Sylvia is propped up against a chair. Her eyes are glazed over with pain. The gunshot must have nicked an artery, the bodice of her silk dress is thick with blood. It drips drips drips onto the parquet floor.

She sees me and raises a hand for help. She mouths the words weakly, but no sound emerges from her pale lips. Her eyes roll back in her head and she slumps forward.

I realize Ashlyn is standing by the curtains, a small smile on her face, pulling off gloves.

"You shot your mother?" My voice comes out in a squeak.

"Didn't have a choice. She was being difficult. Wouldn't take the pills I crushed up in the scotch. Damien did, though. Look at him!"

I don't want to look at him again, the image of his face is seared forever in the vault of my memory.

"There's too much evidence, Ashlyn. You're going to be caught."

"If *we're* caught, you mean—and it is *we*, my dear Lexie, not just me, you've been in on this little plan from the beginning, don't forget—but we won't. The tableau is just what you think it is. Damien was killed by Sylvia, she's poisoned him and, distraught, shot herself. Don't worry, the powder residue will be on her hands. Check her pulse for me, would you? Shan't be long now."

Ashlyn is insane. I've known this somewhere in my heart for months, years, really.

"I'm not touching her. You never said anything about killing them. I'm calling the police."

The shotgun is in my face before I can take a second breath. She backs me up against the wall.

"If you call the police before I tell you to, I will explain to them you created this scenario, that you were obsessed with me, with my family, because you had to live in squalor while we got served off gold plates and lived in this fabulous mansion. Who do you think they'll believe? You? You and your ratty, heroin-addicted mother, or me, the upstanding daughter of a peer?"

I see how neatly Ashlyn has boxed me in. If I weren't so terrified, I might have admired her ingenuity.

The shotgun drops. "You're free now, Alex. And so am I. Play your part and nothing bad will happen. Now, get ready. We have a few things to do, then you'll have to take my place. You'll have to be the one who comes in from the gardens and finds them like this, after you heard the gunshot."

OCTOBER

Marchburg, Virginia

83

THE CONFESSION

"I took her place from that moment on. It wasn't hard to pretend to be devastated, I was. And I told the police Damien had been distraught, that I thought he killed himself. I didn't think it was fair to brand Sylvia a murderer when her daughter was the psychotic one.

"I managed to sneak back home a couple of days later and found my mum dead on the couch. The needle was still in her arm. No way to know if Ashlyn was responsible or it was just her time, but either way, everyone was gone. Everything was done. I had no real alternatives after that but to follow through on Ashlyn's grand plan.

"You, Dean, made it so easy on me. I appreciate that. You showed such compassion."

Ford Julianne Westhaven has never wanted to run away from Goode so much as she does at this moment. But she has no choice, she must stay. She must find out why Becca Curtis is dangling on the gates, her photo being shot from every angle before she is carefully, gently, moved to a horizontal plane.

She must learn why Ash Carlisle is standing in her office, staring out the window, telling a story as insane and twisted as any she's ever heard.

No, this girl is not Ash. She is the impostor they've been worried about. Alexandria Pine. Damien Carr's illegitimate daughter.

Ford has to decide if she believes the tale she's being told. Is this girl the real monster? Or is there another, far worse, lurking somewhere on the grounds? The Grendel in their forest?

"It all started over the summer. Ashlyn decided she didn't want to do all the work it would entail to get a degree. She just wanted the money. She knew I craved an education desperately, more than anything in my life. And she knew I would never, ever, have the opportunities she did. This is what happens when you're illegitimate. Your agency is ripped away and you're stuck with the scraps thrown from the real family's table.

"I had no idea the lengths she would go to, but when I realized how crazy she really is, I knew the best thing for me to do was play along and get as far away from her as I possibly could. If I hadn't agreed to impersonate her, I have no doubt she would have killed me, too. As she did our brother, our father, and her mother. Possibly my mother, as well. I'll never know unless she tells me, but even then..." She turns from the window, resolve etched on her face.

"She killed Camille. And Becca, too. Anyone who gets in her way, who she can't manipulate, she simply eliminates. We're all in danger."

Tony isn't buying it; incredulity is written across his strong features. "You're telling me a sixteen-year-old girl masterminded an identity scam and killed six people?"

"Six people so far," Kate says, calmly. "That we know of. Are there more?"

"I don't know. And I don't think we can say Ashlyn did all the masterminding. It was her idea from the start for us to switch places, yes, but I'm the one who did all the legwork. The paperwork. But that's all I've done. I swear to you, I had nothing to do with the murders. Ashlyn kept telling me she was going to handle things, but I never in a million years guessed murder was her solution. And don't forget, she practically had a gun to my head the whole time. She made it quite clear I had no choice in the matter."

"Why didn't you go to the police?" Ford asks.

When Alex smiles, Ford is reminded of the flatness of a snake's eyes. "What would they have done? She's a master manipulator. She would have told them I cooked up the whole thing, that I murdered her parents, that I held her hostage. That's what she told me last night, at least. That she was going to tell you I held her hostage if I didn't go along with her."

"What does she want from you?" Kate asks.

Alexandria Pine takes a seat and lifts the teacup to her lips, contemplative. Gone is the hesitant, meek Ash. Alex is tall, straight, calm, focused. How had Ford missed this phoenix, hidden in the ashes?

"The money. It's always been about the money. She found out about the codicil to the will Damien created and came here to get me to transfer my portion of the estate immediately."

"Why didn't you?" Ford asks, almost curious now.

"I tried. The DNA test the solicitor did will show who I really am. I told Ashlyn the simplest thing for us to do was Freaky Friday this whole deal in reverse. I offered to let her pretend to be me to the solicitors, and I'd just switch the DNA results in the computers. It would make the switch official, and no one had to get hurt. She doesn't want to share the estate. But she isn't thinking clearly. She's been doing a lot of drugs. It's addled her mind. And her mind was twisted to start with."

Ford still can't even believe what she's hearing. "Why would she hurt Becca?"

"Because Becca hurt me." Alex raises her shirt and Ford sees the bandage on her rib cage. A small part of her whispers in silent agony. She, too, was branded, something the Ivy Bound society is expressly forbidden to do anymore. What was Becca Curtis thinking? She's brought back every hazing ritual outlawed by Ford when she came on board a decade ago.

Rumi told Ford she was naive. Maybe they've been doing this all along and she's simply not been paying attention. Or maybe Becca Curtis thought she could get away with it because of who she was.

"It's not only the brand," Alex says. "Or the hazing. Becca broke my heart, too. Ashlyn was furious yesterday and looking for someone to take it out on. She couldn't torture and kill me, not until I made things right, so she went after the one thing, the one person, I give a damn about. Becca."

She turns to Kate. "How did you figure it out?"

"A photograph from the crime scene, of a family portrait. After that, it was only a matter of finding someone from the household still alive to look at the photo from your customs entry. The cook confirmed for us who you really were."

"Dorsey," Alex says, smiling. "She was always so kind to me. Never sent me home hungry. I always wondered if she knew I was Damien's, or if she was just a soft touch. He treated her abominably. Another innocent caught in Ashlyn's crossfire."

"This is all very heartwarming, but where is Ashlyn now?" Tony asks.

"I don't know. I saw her in the graveyard last night—did you know there's a tunnel out from the sophomores' hall? It's down the stairs from the storage room across from mine. So convenient, these tunnels. She's been moving about freely for days, nicking food, lurking, snooping, stealing. She realized Camille was trying to spy on my computer, and though there wasn't much to see, Ashlyn couldn't risk it. She had to find out what she knew."

"So you're saying she killed Camille."

"Yes. It's the only logical explanation."

"Did she admit this to you?" Tony asks.

"She didn't have to. I don't know exactly what happened that night, I was being tapped for Ivy Bound. The shirt is the key, though. Becca gave it to me, I found it on my bed after I took a shower. I assumed it was put there in that fifteen-minute window, but then I realized, it could have been there the whole tap. Which means Ashlyn, who was moving in and out of the buildings at will, would have had access to the shirt and my room for a few hours. I assume she wrote the summons and got Camille upstairs, questioned her, pushed her off the ledge, then hurried back and put the shirt on the bed.

"It was a good plan, to make it look like either Becca or I were responsible. Unless she confesses, though, we may never know what really happened."

"This is quite a tale, Alex," Ford says. An impossible, ridiculous tale.

"It is. But it's the truth. I have no reason to lie anymore."

Ford wants to believe her. But there's something so strange about her story, something missing.

The convenient specter of a psychotic missing sister.

Something niggles at the back of her brain.

"The piano. You gave up the piano. Muriel told me you were just having an off day."

Alex smiles, delighted with this tiny bit of proof. "Not an off day. I never had proper lessons, only school lessons. Ashlyn taught me how to get through the meeting with Muriel. She is an amazing pianist, total natural. Do you know how hard I had to work to at least make it seem like I had the tiniest spark of talent? I learned enough to make it seem like I was just out of practice. It was a right pain in the arse, I'll tell you that. But

Muriel, she wasn't fooled. Not really. She knew something was wrong that went deeper. She saw it within the first few minutes, when I set my fingers on the wrong keys to start and had to shift over an octave. God, what a stupid mistake. I might have even stuck with it, pretended until she taught me more, but after that, I knew she'd be watching too closely. I had to quit."

The story is a good one. It might very possibly be true. Except...

"And then she died," Tony says, the words Ford is thinking. "Is this Ashlyn's doing, too?"

Alex's face falls. "I don't think so. I think that was just a terrible, horrible coincidence."

Is this girl capable of the lies, the deceit, it would take to pull off a stunt of this magnitude? Is Ford staring into the eyes of a killer?

Or is she some sort of split personality, and moments from now, the other part of her will claw its way to the surface and laugh at their pain?

And what is that smell?

84

THE SURPRISE

Oh, come on. Are you really buying into all of this crap?

We're just kids. Stupid, ignorant children. Too smart for our own good, too certain we know better than everyone around us. Too jaded by our backgrounds, even.

Alex was prey, a deer for the wolves. If you thought she was bad…wait until you get a load of me.

I envision the scene of the crime. Alex finding her lover's body, dropping to her knees. Oh, the wailing. Oh, the gnashing. The beating of breasts.

I can see them milling around out there. I'm too far away to see faces, but I can read their demeanor, they are in shock. A car pulls away. That's the dean's Bentley.

It disappears, and I move from Alex's room to the dark space across the hall. My lair. My ingress and egress. The window looks out onto the back of Main and I see the car pull in. The dean is driving, not her little boy toy, and Alex steps from the passenger seat.

Is she going to tell them everything? Or is she going to cover up my existence?

I light a cigarette, blow out the smoke.

Hmm. There's blood on my hand. The little bitch clawed me as I strung her up, flailing around like a grouse trapped in a raptor's claws.

I move back to my beloved sissy's bedroom.

I will admit, I was too hasty in killing Becca Curtis. I don't regret her death, not at all. But my immense anger at her treatment of Alex got the better of me, I'm afraid. Things might come to a head now, but honestly, who cares? I will be free of them all. I can let Alex go. She was so happy to go to America, to leave me behind, that she never even looked back. Only forward. Ever forward.

Will she come to sleep in this bed tonight? Will she run her hands along her body, dream of that girl who she thinks loved her?

We always hurt the ones we love, right?

Bull. Shit.

"Hey! Who the hell are you?"

No, who the hell are you, little darling? She is tall, like Alex, but with red hair and freckles. Oh, that's right, it's the suitemate. She is wearing a Goode sweatshirt long enough to cover her ass, yoga pants, and a pink baseball cap. I like the hat. I like the whole outfit, actually. It looks comfortable. Broken in. I bet I would look adorable in it.

Me, Ashlyn, the sweet little Goode girl.

"Piper, right? I'm the sister."

"The sister?"

"Ash. You've heard the rumors."

She looks confused. Maybe they aren't aware. "I don't think you should be in here."

"Why not? She's my sister, I have every right to be here."

"Um, no, you don't. You're not a student, and you need to leave. We're dealing with a tragedy and it's not right for you to be here."

"Oh, you're dealing with a tragedy?" I start toward her, and clever girl doesn't even hesitate, she backs away. She scrambles out the door, into the hall. I'm moving fast now, a train barreling toward her, and she backpedals right into the open door of the storeroom.

I know she's going to trip before she does; I see the ladders in the way. She goes down hard, her head hitting the floor with a terrible thwack.

"Oopsie-daisy. Did that hurt?"

It must have, she's out cold.

I relieve her of the adorable pink hat. Might as well take the sweatshirt, too, while I'm at it.

I set my cigarette—almost gone now—on the edge of the ladder and reach for her arms. She is as lifeless as a full-size doll, lolling about here and there, her arms swinging loosely. Dead weight.

I finally get her out of the sweatshirt and pull it on. It's warm, and smells good; whatever perfume she's wearing is vanilla based. I reach for the end of my smoke but realize it's fallen to the floor.

Oh well. I have more. Too bad it's not laced with a little something, just to make the time go by faster. I wonder how long it will be until Alex comes for a lie-down. We need to talk. I need to make sure she understands that the clock is ticking.

There is a *whoosh* behind me. A crackle. Then heat, searing heat.

It happens so quickly I barely have time to take a breath before the room is ablaze. The smoke billows, chasing me into the hall.

Uh-oh.

85

THE BURNING

The alarms go off with a clamor unlike anything I've heard before—sirens and screams, flashing white lights. The detective shoots us a glance and bolts out the door. The dean follows in her wake.

The sheriff puts a hand on my shoulder so I won't run.

"You stick with me, and I won't cuff you just yet. Understand?"

"It's probably not occurred to you, Sheriff, but I have nowhere to go. Goode is my home now."

His cell phone rings, and with another warning glance, he answers it. "Yeah, Kate. Yes. We can smell the smoke. Second floor? Got it."

The dean comes back into her office. "The security panel says there's a fire on the sophomores' hall. The fire suppression system should have kicked in by now. I don't know why it's not. It's new this year, they tested it, our art is—"

"Ford, we need to get everyone out."

The dean turns on me, face ferocious. "Did you do this?"

"Me? No, Dean. I swear it."

"The alarms started across from your room."

"It's her," I breathe. "You know it is. She ruins everything. She's trying to cover her tracks."

"Come on, we can do this later." The sheriff hurries me out of the dean's office with a hand clamped on my shoulder. There is pandemonium in the hall.

The detective runs up, breathless. "We have to get the gates open, Tony. The fire trucks need to park in front of Main."

"That's a crime scene. Damn it all, Ford, why don't you have cameras so we can see what the hell is happening?"

"You can berate me later. Damn, Tony, there's real smoke here."

She isn't wrong. There is a fire burning, and burning hard. If it started across from my room, it's Ashlyn, doing something to draw the attention away.

Has she done this for me? To give me a chance to escape the sheriff's custody?

Possibly. But there's nowhere for me to go. I refuse to run anymore.

Dr. Viridian, the chemistry teacher, is waving toward the dean. "The fourth floor is clear, so is the third. The fire is moving quickly. What happened to the suppression system?"

"It's not working, Phyllis."

Melanie, loyal assistant to the end, hurries forward, a handkerchief over her mouth.

"Dean, we have to get out. Now. The students are all outside. We're doing a headcount. A few are missing."

"Who?"

"We don't know. We don't know! But there are only 195 girls outside."

I hear the fire now. It chuckles to life behind me, the ceilings are starting to blister.

"Open the fucking gates, Tony!" the dean screams.

The sheriff is done playing around, he speaks into his shoulder mic, then herds us toward the front doors and out into the quad. The smoke is heavy, pouring out after us. I cough and cough the bitterness out of my lungs.

The gate is open—what have they done with Becca?—and the fire trucks come barreling through. They swarm the grounds, forcing us back, back, until the sheriff is pulled away and it's just me and the dean, standing in the center of the quad, watching.

They are too late. The delay getting Becca's body off the gate and opening it wide gives the fire enough time to sink its teeth into Goode. The winds following the overnight storms have started, the cold front howling through the trees, the forest bending, furious at this scary intrusion. The sparks fly from one end of the school to the other. The conflagration is intense, and it feels like time is standing still, though I know it's at least an hour that we stand, horrified, as the school burns.

Shouts, calls, water being sprayed. Nothing seems to work. We watch the flames grow higher and higher, the brick veneer blacken and crumble.

The firefighters put up a heroic effort. But when the roof collapses with a rending groan, the dean puts up a weary hand and says the words that doom The Goode School forever.

"Let it burn. It's cursed anyway."

86

THE ENDING

After the winds, the trees are nearly bare, leaves dried and fallen, the ancient branches revealing the nests of the birds who've roosted for the spring and summer. Soon enough, the nests will disappear, as well, their foundations rocked by wind and snow, the birds retreating to the evergreens for shelter.

Shelter from the storm.

This is what we are supposed to be given by our family. Care. Feeding. Love. Shelter.

But some families are different. They give only pain and fear and a frantic sense of need.

Every time I think about my father, I am reminded of the moment my mother told me how lucky we were. We had escaped him. We were free of him. We would never have to be subject to his temper, his rages, his hollow apologies. We were safe.

Only no one can escape the rule of a tyrant, not while the tyrant lives.

We were dragged back into the undertow of his world time and again until she was gone, and he was gone, and I was left alone to clean up the mess.

Do not mistake me. Damien Carr was a narcissist of the highest order. He fed off the power he accumulated, running the finances for the most powerful families in the country. He controlled my mother, he cheated on his wife, he abused his daughter. He walked delicately on the draglines as he built his web. But like an orb weaver, his sight was poor. He didn't see what he'd created, right under his nose.

Me.

When I went away to America, I thought I'd left all of this chaos behind. I had escaped, like my mother always wanted for me.

But there is no escape when you're caught in the monster's nexus. Only something bigger to fear, a stronger predator to be devoured by. I was plucked from the broken strands and thrust into a larger web, one less visible, less clear, but controlled by a force I couldn't begin to understand.

The dean puts a hand on my shoulder. It is meant to comfort, but there is no comfort to be had. It will all end now.

As the flames rise, licking the edges of the building, I swear I see Ash inside the windows. She is staring out at me, a hand raised in a farewell salute, a smile on her beautiful lips.

We are forever bound, she and I, through the blood that flows in our veins, and the blood we spilled together.

A whoosh. A cry.

Main Hall collapses.

And she is gone.

87

THE SENATOR

Senator Ellen Curtis's guests are in the middle of the third course—a gorgeous duck à l'orange, perfectly cooked—nibbling and laughing as she holds court over her dining room table like the doyenne she is when the chimes of the doorbell cause them all to stop.

Ellen ignores the ringing bell. Renata will get it, there is no reason to worry. It's probably the caterer, locked out of the back door.

"As I was saying, when the judge came into the room, every head turned—"

"Madame?"

Renata's quiet voice rings through the room. Ellen, fighting back a furious shout, looks at her housekeeper with a brow raised. "Yes, Renata?"

"There is a man to see you."

Ellen waves a hand. "Tell him I will be happy to speak with him tomorrow. We're having brunch."

"He is a policeman."

"Oh–ho, Ellie. Those parking tickets finally caught up to you," Jude Westhaven chortles, tipping back the rest of her glass of Veuve. "Renata, darling—" *Renaaaahta, daaaahling* "—could you get me a teensy refill?"

"Madame," Renata says again, not breaking eye contact with Ellen. "He says it's urgent."

Ellen rises, gives a reassuring smile to her guests, waves a per-fectly manicured hand. "I'll be back in a mo, have some more champagne, don't let the duck get cold."

Her heels click on the parquet floor, *snick, snick, snick, snick,* as she follows Renata, plodding along in her soft-soled shoes, out to the foyer. Ellen should institute a No Shoe policy, make everyone slip into lovely Chinese slippers like her agent friend, but she is so short, so tiny, the heels barely get her to eye level with the shortest of her male guests. She needs the boost. She hates staring up people's noses.

Despite the mincing poodle noise she makes as she crosses the hallway, she is grateful she is wearing the stilts when she steps into the foyer. The cop—and this isn't just a cop, but a detective, in plain clothes—is well over six feet tall. Handsome, too, dark hair slightly too long, soulful brown eyes, sharp jaw. When he sees her, he snaps to attention. All hail Queen Ellen. She is half-disappointed when he doesn't bow or salute. He nods instead.

"Senator Curtis?"

"Yes? What is it? Something's happened on the Hill? Not an-other bomb threat."

"No, ma'am. I'm sorry to bother you, but I need to ask you a few questions."

"What is this regarding, Officer?"

"Detective," he says tightly, and she smiles.

"So sorry. Detective…?"

"Robson. Detective Harris Robson."

"Detective Robson. What can I answer for you?"

"Can we sit down?"

"I don't mean to be rude, Detective, but I'm having a brunch for my alumni and several donors. Can you just tell me what you need?"

"It's regarding your daughter, ma'am."

"Becca?" Finally, a sliver of dread starts to build. But Becca is at school. The safest of all possible places for her, tucked away in the Blue Ridge, riding roughshod over her teachers and friends alike. They are so similar, Ellen and Becca. Never willing to step away from a fight. "What's wrong with Becca? Why are you here?"

That's when she notices the small, quiet woman standing to the right of the detective. Wearing a collar. A minister, or chaplain, of some sort.

The woman steps forward. "Ma'am, we're so sorry to have to tell you this, but your daughter has died. At school. Dean Westhaven will be calling shortly, but—"

The idea of blood draining from your face is such a cliché until you are faced with a shock, and then it fits. Ellen feels her blood pressure bottom out, puts out a hand, which the detective catches. He propels her to the foyer's sofa, sits down next to her, two cushions away.

Ellen has come to her senses. "How? How did my daughter die? Was there some sort of accident? This is preposterous."

Shock. She is in shock. She should be crying, she should be wailing. She is numb, light-headed. Can't think. Can't process the words. Becca, dead? Her Becca? Glorious, gorgeous, brilliant Becca? No, there is no way.

A moment of clarity: *the press is going to have a field day with this.*

The thought is tinged with regret and hate for the way her mind works, for the position she is in, that even when faced with the ultimate horror of the loss of her only daughter, her thought process would move immediately to the impact it will have on her career. But she has no choice. She is a senator, the midterms are coming, there's an upstart out of Reston who is pushing her way into the race, and the polls are tighter than she'd like. A death in the family will tip them in her favor.

"I must call my chief of staff, we need to prepare a statement."

"We have time," the detective says. "The school isn't going to make any announcements."

"No, I simply do not believe this," Ellen whispers. "How?"

"I don't—"

"How?" The command is unmistakable this time.

"She was found hanging from the school gates."

Dear God, Becca. What sort of message were you trying to send?

"Suicide? Impossible. I would have known if she was unhappy, if there was a problem. I spoke to her—" Ellen stops. When *did* she speak to Becca last? "Sunday. We talked Sunday and she was chipper and thrilled with the positive feedback she'd received on her thesis proof. She was happy."

"A thesis? In high school?"

"Goode isn't just any school, Detective."

The chaplain starts to speak again, but Ellen shakes her head and holds up a hand. "I don't need comforting, not right now. I need answers. There is simply no way my daughter committed suicide."

"We agree. The sheriff in Marchburg agrees. The death is being investigated as a possible homicide."

The race is hers.

"Someone killed her? Oh, my God."

The chaplain jumps in again. "I understand this comes as a shock, ma'am. Especially with a child so far away from home."

The judgment is clear. Senator Ellen Curtis has abandoned her child to a faraway school because she isn't mother enough to handle her senatorial duties as well as raise a willful teenager. She's seen enough of it from the press, she isn't about to take it from some random chaplain the detective dragged along, no matter how soft and kind her features. Screw that.

"Stop. Seriously, just stop. You don't know me, you don't know my daughter, and you certainly don't know the situation. For your information, Becca begged to go to Goode. Begged. I didn't send her there. Detective, I want answers. I want to speak with the dean immediately."

Harris nods again, gravely. "We don't have all the information yet, ma'am. The investigation is ongoing. Dean Westhaven wants to speak with you, too, as soon as we can determine Becca's last knowns before she disappeared and was found. There is an investigation underway. But there's been a complication."

"What?"

"A number of things. The last few days leading up to her death, for starters. There was some trouble, some infighting among the girls at the school. Dean Westhaven mentioned a secret society prank that went wrong…"

He goes quiet again, but she isn't falling for it. She knows all too well how few people like a silence, how quickly they jump in with words to fill the pause. She is not normally one of those people. But now, she can't help herself.

"When was she found?"

"Four hours ago."

"Four hours! Why wasn't I notified immediately? They kept a student's death quiet for four hours? My daughter's death? Me, of all people?"

"The locals needed to positively identify the body. Fingerprints took longer than we thought. We needed to be sure."

"My God, if you had to fingerprint her…"

The detective takes a breath. "Her face was mutilated. Whoever killed her put out her eyes."

If they think she is going to cry, they're wrong. She is filled with fury, and it is all directed at Ford Westhaven and her egregious handling of the school. Ellen shouldn't have been subtle about her bid to make the school coed. She made that endowment happen, she knows what the expansion will do for the school. She should have marched right into that shit hole of a town and told Westhaven that she owns the school now.

No more. She isn't going to let Ford fucking Westhaven ruin any more girls' lives. Or Jude, either, for that matter.

She stands, righteous fury on her face. "I am going to tear that school to the ground."

The detective and the chaplain share a look.

"I'm afraid it's too late for that."

Jude steps into the foyer, her eyes wild. "Ellen? I've just received a text. The school is burning."

EPILOGUE

New York City

Eleven Years Later

88

THE FLIGHT

She doesn't recognize me.

This is a good thing, though I am momentarily outraged. After what she did to me, it's insulting to see her eyes pass over me as if I'm just another person getting ready to step on the plane. She should be looking at me with horror, with shame and regret. With love. With happiness.

I am her sister, after all.

But her eyes light upon me and slide away, a small, polite, *I've already forgotten you exist* smile playing on her lips. All she sees is another privileged woman, sipping champagne in the first-class lounge before the doors to the flight open. If she had any idea what I've been through, she wouldn't act so smug.

She makes this flight from New York to London regularly. She has business to attend to all over Europe, the UK, the Americas. She's chosen an odd branch of maritime law that governs shipping and import/export issues, works for a company that distributes wine throughout the world.

After what she did, I can't believe they let her into law school, much less Harvard, but she convinced them she was the victim, that she'd been terrorized, that she was only doing what I forced her to so she wouldn't die herself. She didn't serve time. She was allowed to keep her visa. She inherited the bloody money, bought her way into Harvard, and has, by all accounts, lived a blameless life since.

God, she is such a superb actress. She always was a tremendous liar.

I haven't spoken to her in person since that fateful day. She surrounded herself with people so it would be impossible to get her alone. Of course, she assumed I was dead. They all assumed I was dead. But I knew the tunnels better than they. I scuttled out while the fire raged, down the mountain, away, away, away.

She's older. I mean, we all are, but I've aged a bit more than she. Granted, I've spent more time in the sun and she has a monthly appointment at the La Mer spa, dropping thousands at a time on treatments, but eleven years isn't much time.

Still, she looks good. Fit. Healthy. A few barely perceptible lines on her forehead, the blond hair carefully highlighted now instead of natural. Still tall and elegantly proportioned.

Today is her thirtieth birthday.

She didn't use her special day as an excuse to get out of the scheduled trip—she's too responsible for that. She doesn't mind spending the day alone. Though her wife protested, she wants the time to herself. To think. To reflect. A nice overnight flight to London, pampered by the flight attendants on British Airways. Life could be worse.

Life can always be worse.

This plane is set up with four seats across—one by each window, two in the center. She prefers to sit in the center seat, 2C, so I've chosen the one next to her as if we're traveling together. The seats become beds, our legs angling away at a 30-degree angle, leaving our heads only a foot apart. It is fitting, really, when you think about how much time we spent plotting and planning.

I listen to her every word. I know her every move. She thinks she's protected, but she's not. She never was.

The pills were meant for me. I mean, this is no way to live, skulking about, lurking, spying on my lost sister, watching her lead the life I should have had. Some call it stalking, but when it's information gathering, I think spying suffices.

I collected them assiduously the entire time I was watching over Piper as she lay dying, poor girl, before they realized the meds weren't working and switched her to the Fentanyl that robbed her of the last bits of her sanity, then the slow drip of morphine that eventually killed her. Took her a few years to finally give it up.

A pill for you, a pill for me. Though I've never taken one, never indulged. It would have been so much easier if I had. They are strong, so strong they made Piper see dancing uni-corns and butterflies—a better thing to see, I suppose, than the dark edges of a cloak and the reflection of your own wasted face in the scythe.

The police moved in and out of her room in the rehab facility for weeks, the crow-eyed woman and the bear of a man, think-ing she would remember how the fire started, what she saw that day, but her memory was seared away like the last of her flesh. They thought they could solve three mysteries at once if they understood her garbled words—Becca, Camille, the fire. They assumed I turned to ash like the rest of the school.

They were wrong.

I should have just killed the poor girl, put her out of her pain. But I wanted to keep my sister close, somehow, so I became Piper's titular caretaker. The BFF from school who wouldn't leave her side. Where was her real BFF? After a single, brief visit at the begin-ning, Vanessa never came again. Which made it easy to pose as her.

Was I doing penance? Perhaps.

The nurses loved me. No one doubted my sincerity. No one

thought twice about my devotion to my friend. Lucky for me, I suppose.

No, I never gobbled down her pills, as much as I wanted to, as much as I knew they'd make my pain go away. I've been saving them for the proper time. For a while, I thought I might take them all at once, standing on a stone bridge, watching the snow kiss the Seine. Perhaps I would change my mind at the last minute and throw them into the gray water. Perhaps I would keep them taped to the back of the bathroom mirror in the flat I would rent, let the delicious temptation of them sing to me day after day.

And then I saw her, quite by chance the first time—the first time—in the street, those red-soled heels clicking as she navigated desiccated dog shit on the grate in front of her Upper East Side brownstone, and I knew exactly what to do with the pills.

Takeoff is smooth. Dinner is served. The meal is tasteless, cardboard; drenching it in salt doesn't help a bit. I sip the wine, a meager cabernet—really, I expected better, almost a shame to even call it so—drink a cup of the freshly overbrewed tea, then wait for the bathroom lines to clear before taking my bag and stepping into the tiny space.

Eight pills? Nine? How many will it take to kill a woman of her size? I have forty. Forty pilfered OxyContin. One for you, sweet sister, one for me. I was afraid the security agent was going to ask to see the prescription bottle, so I used one of my old antibiotic bottles, excavated from the shoebox under my sink, the label so faded the date and name are indiscernible.

I twist open the top and shake one into my hand. Large, cylindrical, chalk white. Lick the edge, savoring the divinity in the acrid taste on my tongue.

Mmm. Death tastes so good.

It takes me a full five minutes to grind them into a fine powder with the heel of my shoe—not red-soled, I'll have you know—and return to my seat.

She sees me then, though she still has no idea who I am. I am gracious, as expected.

"Good flight?"

"Is that a question?"

Rude.

I want to launch into the speech I've rehearsed, the conversation to make it seem like I've only just recognized her, a hand on her arm, lightly, gently, my mouth in a tiny O of recognition.

Wait, aren't you the woman who went to the private school that burned down? I know I saw you in the papers recently, with the former dean, what's her name?

Westhaven.

That's right. She's a big-name author now. Wrote a novel about the school. Married to some young buck she was seeing, oh, wasn't that the scandal?

True love.

And wasn't there some incident with an impostor, sisters? All those girls, dead. What a shame. Amazing that they rebuilt. Of course, coed, but it's such a good school. Such a good reputation.

But she's already turned away, wedged in her earbuds, pulled up a movie. A delightful rom-com, a woman who needs a wedding date, by the looks of it.

Maybe we'll talk later.

Said the spider to the fly.

I wait.

I wait.

Finally, finally, the flight attendants do their dessert pass, and she takes a refill. Such a creature of habit, our little wine connoisseur.

Excellent. It's easier to obscure this powder in wine than water.

And here's the second moment I've been waiting for.

She unfolds from the seat—I always forget how tall she is— and heads to the loo.

I dump the powder in my wine and stir it with my finger.

And then I lean over, my hand snaking out of my pod into hers, and with a quick glance to make sure no one is watching— these seats afford so much privacy—I switch the glasses.

Easy.

Done.

She comes back and settles in again. Goes through her whole flight-nap routine, dabbing on ChapStick, spreading the pash-mina across her lean legs, pulling out the sleep mask, putting in the earbuds.

I play along, yawning and primping, as well, showing off a gold crown I had placed when I scraped together enough cash. That big open spot always bothered me.

The helpful flight attendant comes by one last time with her *it's sleepy time* bottle raised high. We chat for a few moments. I'd love a chocolate, thank you, no, no more wine for me.

There is a small kerfuffle to my left—oh, God, is it happen-ing already?—but I see she's only dropped her ChapStick. The flight attendant retrieves it, offers the bottle.

To my unerring delight, she swallows half the glass, takes a top-off of wine, stretches and sighs heavily, kittenish, and speaks.

"Ah. So tired. Wake me when we're landing, won't you?"

She smiles. Looks me right in the eyes and slides on her sleep mask.

When she disappears behind the black faux fur, I take a cel-ebratory gulp of my wine, then another.

"Cheers."

Cheers, I say to her quiet figure.

Cheers, I say to my old life.

Cheers, I say to the future. It's time for me to take back my life.

And something starts to claw at the back of my throat.

Spots. I'm seeing spots.

My breath slows, hitching in my chest.

Oh, God. Oh, God. What's happen—

89

THE LAST

She looks so sweet, asleep like this, with her mouth slightly open, her head turned to the side. I remember when she used to look like this, innocent in repose.

With a last smile to the flight attendant, I slip on my red-soled heels, my black sunglasses, and don my coat. I gather my carry-on from the overhead, stuff my pashmina in my tote, and she doesn't move. Still asleep. Precious princess.

Just another woman on a plane. Though forever asleep.

I leave the plane, walk up the Jetway, breath coming in tiny little sips. A hand moves to the small brand under my left breast, riding high on my rib cage, and I remember a girl with forest-green eyes and soft, silky lips. *This was for you.*

No one stops me. No calls. No screams.

I exit the terminal, hand my carry-on to the driver, slide into the back of my town car, and am off to the May Fair Hotel.

I don't look back.

Yes, I knew it was her. Yes, I suspected what she had planned. She's been stalking me for months. Listening. Watching.

Yes, I saw what she did when I went to the loo.

Yes, I swapped the wineglasses back when they were looking for my ChapStick.

She ruined my entire life. I refuse to let her take it, too. I had to protect myself.

And really, she did this to herself.

What? You disapprove? Do you actually blame me?

No, you don't. You'd do the same if you had to.

Happy birthday to me. I am finally, finally free.

★ ★ ★ ★ ★

AUTHOR'S NOTE

The Goode School, and the town of Marchburg, are complete figments of my imagination, an amalgamation of several private colleges and high schools in central Virginia.

That said... I have always wanted to write a boarding school mystery, and I come to the story honestly. I had the great privilege of attending Randolph-Macon Woman's College in Lynchburg, Virginia (class of '91), and I have woven pieces of the school's legends and tragedies into this story, all put through my own creative lens. Alumni will easily recognize Main Hall, the Skeller (I still dream of those tuna melts), Odds and Evens, Chilhowies, the trolleys, the sewing circle, and other unique-to-Macon details like Goode's version of the Honor Code. The rest are fabricated for this story.

A few ghost stories have also been molded to fit this particular tale, the red staircase chief among them. The Commons is named after a real attic room in Main Hall, colloquially called the Bean Bag Room, one that I lived below the spring semester of my sophomore year. Many a night, my roommate and

I were kept awake by footsteps, furniture dragging, and other unexplainable sounds overhead. The problem was, after several of these events, we would creep up the stairs to see who was there—and find the room empty. It did have a stunning view of the Blue Ridge Mountains during the daytime, though.

The haunted arboretum path is based in part on a real and terrible event, the on-campus murder of coed Cynthia Louise Hellman in 1973. The subsequent ghost story of the girl in purple clogs made it very hard for me to walk behind Martin Hall during my tenure.

Allegedly, the Underground Railroad did move through Lynchburg. Non-allegedly, there are tunnels under the campus, though they are not as accessible as they are at Goode.

Secret societies flourished during my tenure; I had the great honor to be tapped for more than one. Stomps, in particular, were great fun. That is where the similarities end, though. Yes, there was hazing, but Ivy Bound takes it to the extreme.

Goode's provenance as an all-girls high school begins one hundred years prior to R-MWC, which was started by William Waugh-Smith, one of the great champions of female education in his day. I daresay he and Sister Julianne would be fast friends.

I was quite dismayed to see R-MWC's board vote to go coed in 2006, against the wishes of most of its alumni. No knock on the subsequently named Randolph College, but I still believe that single-sex education has innumerable advantages, especially for women.

And all hail Virginia Woolf. I studied her great essay *A Room of One's Own* at length at R-MWC, and I took it to heart as I moved into the world.

One last personal note. If you are feeling sad, depressed, or suicidal, please reach out. The National Suicide Prevention Lifeline is available twenty-four-seven at 1-800-273-8255. You are not alone.

ACKNOWLEDGMENTS

So much of this story was based on my own experiences that I didn't have to do a great deal of research for this book, but there were several people hugely instrumental in helping fill in the blanks. Lisa Patton and Virginia Kay helped bring me up to speed on the intricacies of current Southern girls' boarding prep schools. Erik Franey helped bring Ash's computer skills to life. Laura Benedict kept me honest when I started veering off course. Paige Crutcher and Ariel Lawhon provided much needed queso dates and were always there for idea bouncing. Jeff Abbott was always there for those all-is-lost moments, and Leigh Kramer hand-held, cheerled, and otherwise kept the trains running on time. On our private Facebook group, the ladies of Randolph-Macon Woman's College jumped in with their favorite remembrances and ghost stories, which helped me flesh out my memory.

My team: Scott Miller of Trident Media Group, Nicole Brebner of MIRA Books, and Holly Frederick of Curtis Brown are truly the best a girl can ask for. The amazing group of people at MIRA and Harper Canada who work so hard behind the scenes to get this book out, into your hands, are the very best in the business. Many thanks to Craig Swinwood; Loriana Sacilotto; Heather Foy; Amy Jones; Randy Chan; Margaret Marbury; Miranda Indrigo; Ashley MacDonald; Olivia Gissing; Elissa Smith, Margot Mallinson; Chris Wolfgang; Lisa Basnett; Marianna Ricciuto; Erin Craig, Sean Kapitain, Malle Vallik; Carol Dunsmore; Leo MacDonald; Cory Beatty; Kaitlyn Vincent; Irina Pintea; Karen Ma; Michael Millar; and my incredible publicist, Emer Flounders, who all need a nod of thanks and oodles of gratitude. And cake. Let them eat cake.

For my family, especially my parents, for giving me the opportunity to go to R-MWC and explore my gifts in that wonderful environment, thank you from the bottom of my heart. And my darling Randy, the keeper of my heart. You were the sounding board for this idea from the very beginning, on that fateful drive across Florida, and I will forever be grateful you pushed me to follow my heart and write this book. I love you so much!

On September 23, 1992, my friend from R-MWC, Dail Dinwiddie, went missing from Five Points in Columbia, South Carolina, after a U2 concert. It's hard to believe it's been twenty-seven years since she went missing (oddly enough, to the day, as I'm writing this on the anniversary of her disappearance.) Someone out there knows what happened to Dail. It is my fervent hope and prayer that we find answers. If you know anything, suspect anything, please contact the Columbia Police Department Crimestoppers at 888-CRIME-SC (888-274-6372); text to CRIMES (9274637); or log in to www.midlandscrimestoppers. com and click on the red "Submit a Tip" button. Together, we can finally discover what happened that night, and bring some peace to Dail's family and friends.

I am forever indebted to the amazing booksellers and librarians out there who work so hard to elevate literacy in their communities. And for you. Keep reading, friends. I appreciate you so very much.